Where I Belong

KAY BRATT

Where I Belong

Also by Kay Bratt

Silent Tears; A Journey of Hope in a Chinese Orphanage
Chasing China; A Daughter's Quest for Truth
Mei Li and the Wise Laoshi
Eyes Like Mine
The Bridge
A Thread Unbroken
Train to Nowhere

The Palest Ink
The Scavenger's Daughters
Tangled Vines
Bitter Winds
Red Skies

Where I Belong

LIFE OF WILLOW

Part One

LONELY DAYS

Willow

WILLOW FELT AN UNINVITED SMILE break through as she passed by a weather-beaten three-wheeled motorcycle and noticed the small child who sat astride it like a little road warrior, bundled in multiple layers of clothes for warmth as she waited obediently for someone to return. Only about three or four years old, her tiny, black pigtails framed chubby cheeks and her dark, somber eyes told of the simple yet contented life carved out for her in the big world. The little girl had no idea that although she was obviously poor, she was free. If Willow stopped and waited, she felt sure she'd see a father return—or even a mother—a common sight in the place she now dwelled. It never ceased to make her feel a bit of buried envy, the sight of those bonded by blood, loyal to each other through riches or poverty.

Family.

A gift that living her childhood in institutional care had robbed her of. But still, she appreciated getting to see another way of living.

Village life compared to Beijing city life was like the difference between living on earth or another planet. They couldn't compare.

She took the long way back, going out of her way to walk through the mountain-encircled village, admiring the sounds of the gurgling spring that ran parallel to the dusty main road. Everywhere she looked was an eyeful of beauty. Just knowing how much Kai would appreciate the ancient trees and tiled buildings of the historical Lingshui Village made her long for him even more. It felt like years since she'd seen him last, though she knew it was only a handful of weeks.

Looking down at the beads encircling her wrist, she glimpsed the delicately drawn characters. *Our Friendship Will Last Forever*—that was what it said, but obviously, that isn't what Kai had meant when he gave it to her because he hadn't answered any of her letters. But even though her heart was hurting, she didn't regret the last few months. They'd made their escape from the orphanage and helped Rosi get the care she needed. More than anything, Willow no longer felt like a ward of the state.

Now free from the institutional life, she could blend in with the rest of the world. Finally having shed the labels attached to her, she hoped to never have to carry that burden again. But if Willow thought she'd been lonesome before, she was wrong. Her long days now gave a whole new meaning to lonely. As she struggled to carry the basket of freshly folded clothes along the bumpy path, she wondered what Kai and Rosi were doing at that moment. She envisioned Rosi, recovered enough to at least be in the laundry room at the hotel, happily sorting, folding, and giving orders. Kai—she wasn't so sure. She wished she could see them, but wishes wouldn't make her shared banishment move any faster—only the forgiveness of an uncle to a niece would free Willow from her promise to share Luyan's exile.

As far as the setting for her to make good on her deal, after the first two weeks when Luyan had tried her patience day in and day out, Willow had realized village life wasn't half bad. Sure, it was a far cry from having any sort of the conveniences Beijing boasted, but being here had given her a lot of freedom. And the best part was Luyan's imposed respite meant Willow didn't have to deal with keeping the girl on the demanding schedule she had tried to follow in Beijing.

Willow moved along, knowing Luyan had probably woken from her nap and would be as grouchy as an old boar. As she looked around, she thought being in the village was like going back in time. While there were some modern-dressed women and a few young men—and more than a dozen cell phones in full view—most of the people looked different from any she'd ever seen in Beijing. And the atmosphere was more laid-back and relaxed—charming even.

She paused for a moment, watching an old man as he sat straddling a homemade seesaw bench, sharpening the edge of a meat cleaver against the stone affixed in front of him. He whistled while he slathered oil on the dull blade, then rubbed the knife back and forth on the stone, using the sweat of his brow to make a living. Willow doubted he made much money, but it was clear he was content—his face shone with perspiration but lacked the visible signs of stress so evident in most people she saw around the city. To watch him was mesmerizing, but she finally forced herself to move along. When she started again, the old man lifted a hand up and waved at her,

"*Nihao*," he said, acknowledging her presence before he went back to work. Willow returned his greeting, even though he was no longer looking.

One advantage to being in the village was when she could get Luyan settled and could sneak some time for herself, she enjoyed the crisp, clean air and pretty scenery. But it *was* lonely, and it was so confusing that Kai had not written her a single letter. He hadn't even answered the one she'd left behind for him, so that told her he was furious with her. And it made her sadder than she ever thought she could be.

She approached the small house, and then stepped through the door. Thankfully, Luyan's father, Yilin, was standing there waiting to take the heavy load from her.

"Did you have any trouble finding the laundromat?" he asked.

"*Bushi*, it was right where you said it was." Luyan's mother had offered to wash the clothes by hand in the spring-fed stream, like she did hers and Yilins, but Luyan had rebuffed her offer—telling her it

11

wasn't sanitary—then pouted until Willow promised to take them and wash them in a machine.

"Does she know these were dried in the sun?" Wu Min, Luyan's mother, asked softly.

Willow shook her head and put her finger to her lips, then nodded toward the ceiling. The empress was up there, too good to come downstairs and interact with mere humans.

"Willow," Luyan called from their small room on the second floor of the house, her voice low and impatient, as if she'd already called out several times.

When Luyan shrieked even louder, her father shrugged and smiled. He and Willow had become silent partners in the battle to tame Luyan, or at least pacify her enough to keep the household calm. Willow's mother, Wu Min, was so intimidated by her stubborn daughter that she was useless when it came to settling her down.

Willow wiped her hands on her jeans before climbing the rickety, wooden stairs to their bedroom in the loft. Luyan barely ever came down herself, saying it was too difficult for her. Willow knew Luyan was just pouting, still angry with her uncle and her parents for being jerked out of her comfortable life of a princess. Willow could see how it stung, though she didn't agree about whose fault it was. To say it had been a shock to be delivered to Luyan's hometown was an understatement—both she and Luyan had been speechless when her uncle's driver had informed them of their destination and handed them the bus tickets. Willow was embarrassed at the fit Luyan threw while they stood waiting at the station, but her uncle's mind was made up. He was sending her home and if she didn't like it, her only alternative was to take to the streets, or find herself a new benefactor.

All the way to the tiny village, Luyan had fumed about her circumstances. Willow had listened sympathetically, but she'd been thinking if Luyan had been more careful, they wouldn't be headed to her hometown. What Willow worried about was how Luyan's parents were going to receive them. But surprisingly, her parents had stood waiting to meet the bus, their arms outstretched when Luyan climbed out.

They were nothing like she'd expected, and Willow's mouth had almost gaped open with her reaction to them. While Luyan's mother was pretty in a quiet, simple kind of way, she possessed none of the fire her daughter did. Without saying one word, she came across as meek and gentle. And Luyan's father, Yilin, was a tall and strong-looking man—weathered and brown from working outdoors. To match Luyan with them as a family had been difficult. Still yet, Willow had blushed scarlet when Luyan had put her nose in the air and strode past both her mother and father, even going as far as dropping her bag on the ground in front of them, as though they were mere servants stationed there to do her bidding. Willow held her breath, expecting a scene, but her father had quietly picked up the bag and followed his daughter, while her mother hung her head and trailed behind. Willow followed too, and then ran to catch up with Luyan when she bellowed for her to hurry up.

Around them as they had walked, young mothers toted babies on their hips and a few stray dogs ran in and out, dodging around them as they chased one another playfully. Willow had been captivated by the village and wondered at how Luyan could ignore the beauty of her hometown. More importantly, she'd wondered how Luyan could be so blind to the obvious fact that her parents loved her and were glad she was home, even if only for a short time. Lu Yan's attitude was baffling to Willow, yet here she was, climbing the stairs to be at her beck and call once again, spoiling her even more.

"It's about time, Willow. What took you so long?" Luyan said as Willow came through the door and sat on the trunk under the window. Her feet were killing her.

"Luyan, seriously? I've washed and hung your clothes today, mopped your bedroom floor, and in the last few weeks, have made about a twenty trips to the spring for water to supply you a hot bath. Don't even try to act like I've been lazy while you've barely left the bed today."

"I do appreciate your help, but it's not my fault these people here are so backward they don't even have a bathtub with running water."

"*These people* are your family, Luyan," Willow said, rolling her eyes toward the ceiling. Luyan had already stayed up late the night before whispering to her about how, from what she could see, her parents had not wisely used the money she'd sent to them. She'd fumed about the house still being the ramshackle, whitewashed brick hovel it had always been, the clothes her parents wore still plain, old-fashioned, and embarrassing. She'd even ranted they didn't own a car and their television played nothing but local news and screaming Chinese operas.

Willow was tired of her relentless complaining. "What do you want? Did you just call me up here to yell at me?"

Luyan's expression went from irritated to pouty. She ran her fingers along the tattered but soft bedspread. They were sharing the small, iron bed, while Luyan's parents slept on bamboo mats on the first floor. The couple had given up their room so their daughter could have her privacy. Still, it hadn't occurred to Luyan to be grateful.

"I'm bored," she said.

"You're always bored here," Willow answered. "Try to remember when you were a kid. What did you do for fun?"

Luyan studied a nail for a moment before she looked up. "We swam in the river. But if you haven't noticed, it's February and too cold now. Even if it weren't, I wouldn't go back into that water. Do you know some people actually still use the bathroom in a bucket and dump it in there?"

"Well, they did back then too. Probably even more so than today. But what did you do during the cold months?"

Luyan shrugged. "I don't know. I feel too lazy to think."

"What do you want me to do about it? You spend every minute

in this room. Why don't you get out and walk around? See some people? Or the sites? Your father said Lingshui has been here for over a thousand years."

Luyan answered her with a roll of the eyes.

"I could take you to see the Temple of the Goddess," Willow offered.

The word goddess perked Luyan up. "That sounds familiar. What is it?"

"According to your father, a five-toed dragon was carved into the temple wall when normally only four-toed dragons were allowed at the time. The artist had the permission of the emperor, and the carving has withstood all these years."

"Oh. I was hoping you were going to tell me this town had opened a spa." Luyan turned her head away at the impromptu history lesson. "What about shops? Is there anything new that wasn't here the last time I came?"

Willow sighed. "I don't know what was here the last time you were home, but there are plenty of small town shops. Probably nothing you'd be interested in— I can guarantee that. But it makes me sad you can't see the charm your hometown has to offer because you can't get the Beijing stars out of your eyes."

Luyan whipped her head around and glared at Willow, suddenly coming to life. "I hate this place! My parents shipped me off to Beijing with my uncle. Why should I have any affection for them or this shoddy village they call home? This isn't my home, Willow. It hasn't been for a long time."

Willow stood up and looked down at Luyan. She didn't feel angry—it just made her sad the girl had everything at her fingertips but couldn't see it. She sighed, then turned and walked toward the door.

"Look, I'm here because I made a promise. You know I didn't want to leave Kai and Rosi, but I'm going to act mature and make the best

15

of it. Right now, I'm going out to take a walk in the fresh, clean air of your village, Luyan. If you want to go with me, be outside in five minutes." She knew her words were wasted—Luyan wouldn't leave the house, for she thought there was nothing to be gained from it.

Kai

KAI CARRIED THE TALL TRIPOD under one arm and the bag of Johnny's gear with the other. His own bag hung by a strap around his neck. He shivered at the chill that hit his ears and hoped it wouldn't prohibit the client's ability to look natural at the shoot. The wind had picked up, another worry in the pursuit of making beautiful pictures for satisfied clients. Having clients in early spring was lucky—as most felt it too cold to be traipsing around Beijing to get their photos done. So Kai didn't have to be told how important it was to do a good job for them. As the warmer weather came in, so would the clients.

"Set up under that tree," Johnny called out behind him. Today was a family shoot—the kind that messed with Kai's head. A young mother, father, and their chubby-cheeked son stood waiting nearby. It would be an hour of torture for Kai, observing the family he never had and never would.

Following Johnny around wasn't something Kai had aspired to do, but at least he had a job. That meant he could contribute something for rent—even if his temporary bed was only the floor of Mama Su's neighbor's house.

From across the street, the old man Lao Qu had watched him come and go for a week, checking on Rosi and then leaving to shuffle down the street at dark, before one night, he'd come out and offered him a roof over his head. How he knew his status was officially homeless, Kai wasn't sure. But it could've been because he was forced to carry his bag around with him, and his hair had gotten greasy from days of not washing it. His clothes were looking shabby, as he only had a few different outfits to choose from and no money to have them laundered. He'd been sleeping in doorways and surviving off scraps left behind local restaurants. Snatch-and-runs, he called them, but so small and random they couldn't appease his hunger. He'd lost weight and suddenly looked like a stray alley cat, and had jumped at Lao Qu's offer.

Bottom line was the agreement couldn't have come at a better time, and since then, he'd been gratefully fattened up by Mama Su inviting him for dinner almost every night. They joked he'd grown at least a head taller since he'd been eating well, and judging by the sudden distance between the hem of his jeans and his shoes, they were right. Mama Su had helped him out by taking the cuffs down, which added a few inches to his pants, so at least now he didn't look like a clown.

Rosi was doing great, and each time he walked through the door, she insisted on showing him her pink-infused bedroom, as well as every little get-well gift she'd received from her many friends at the laundry room. She was excited about the littlest things, even down to a string of paper-cut hummingbirds strung across her ceiling that she claimed sung to wake her up each day. Kai still couldn't believe the girl's fate had taken her from the depths of despair in the orphanage, to being loved and living happily in a real home. Every kid he'd ever known in the orphanage dreamed of what Rosi was now living—though no one had ever thought someone like her could attain it. But then, most of them didn't look past the outside and realize what an amazing person she was. Kai was ashamed that, for years, he'd done the same, overlooking her because of her disability. He suppressed a smile when he thought how his small part in her life had helped get her to where she was. As for himself, fate hadn't been so kind, but he was still trying.

After he'd been kicked out of living at the hotel, he'd hit the streets every morning looking for a job before he found himself standing in front of the display window of a wedding shop. The bride and groom, posed in their fairy-tale clothes, reminded him he loved photography and that he was good at it. It took him only two days of asking around before he'd gotten Johnny's number, and luckily, he'd needed an assistant right away. When Kai told him the pittance he'd work for, he got the job on the spot.

Now he dropped the gear under the tree and began the process of making everything look perfect. The young woman chattered behind him, picking at the clothes of her husband and child as they waited.

Kai thought of Willow again and felt his teeth grind together. She'd disappeared like a thief in the night. Not even a note—nothing but an empty room when he'd returned from the hospital. He hadn't even had time to absorb the shock before a hotel employee had arrived and told him Luyan had asked he be escorted out of the premises. He'd barely had time to grab his things before he'd been shuffled out on the street like some kind of beggar. The humiliation of it all still made his gut roll. The suspicion that Willow knew about it and was a part of it broke his heart. But still, a small voice in his head refused to believe she'd ever purposely hurt him. Since that day, he'd staggered the line between being angry with her, and missing her. His emotions were all over the place, and they had been since he'd found her gone.

Behind him, he heard Johnny explaining to the small family about all the shots he'd take, if the child remained cooperative. The perfectness of it all made Kai cringe. They'd be shocked to know the young man assisting their photographer had spent a week sleeping on the street only a short time ago.

"Move everything to the other side of this tree. By the time they get that kid ready, the sun will have moved too far," Johnny said, coming up behind him.

Kai sighed, but he did as he was told. He looked over at the family, noticing the young mother had laid a blanket down and was changing the boy's clothes. The father looked down on them, his face red with embarrassment.

Did he not think kids had accidents?

Johnny helped him move the light and soft box, then rearranged the ladder so he could take a few overhead shots.

"So where has Luyan been keeping herself?" Johnny asked.

Kai shrugged.

"Don't want to say, eh?" Johnny said.

"I don't know." What did Johnny expect him to say? He *didn't know* where the empress was. If he did, he'd most likely know where Willow was. They'd both disappeared at the same time, so it told him they had to be together. And that also told him he'd had every right to distrust Luyan as much as he had.

"It's just eerie, you know, that first Luyan's uncle makes his wife disappear, and now his niece. Hopefully, she'll reappear soon, but she hasn't answered any of my calls or messages."

"His wife?" Kai pretended to be nonchalant, but Johnny's words did make him nervous.

"*Dui*. His wife disappeared years ago. The rumor is she displeased him—not sure how—but I guess that's all it takes for him to pluck you from his life and send you packing. No one knows where she is."

Kai didn't have any words, but thoughts swirled in his head.

"Maybe he just married Luyan off, and she's on a honeymoon somewhere," Johnny laughed and poked at Kai's ribs with his elbow.

That wasn't likely either. Luyan wasn't the type to elope or marry quietly. She was one to have the full dream wedding most couldn't afford—a match that would take at least a year of negotiations between families. Kai didn't know where they were, but he was sure it wasn't as simple as Johnny tried to suggest.

Finally, everything was in place. Johnny waved the couple over. The father carried the little boy and set him down under the tree.

Johnny spent a few minutes working with them for the right pose, then returned and settled behind his camera.

Before he could start, a sudden gust picked up, blowing the mother's long hair around her face. "Damn it! I can't take a photo with her hair like that," Johnny said. "And take that scarf off. It's going to get in the way too."

The mother frowned. Kai could tell she was beginning to tire of Johnny's attitude. "I love this scarf. I picked it out especially for today. It matches my husband's shirt."

Johnny stood up, putting his hands on his hips. "Do you want to do this or do you want to hire another photographer?"

The woman's husband started to scowl, and Kai stepped forward. "I think I can help."

Johnny turned to him, but Kai ignored him. He rummaged in his bag, then pulled out a few things and headed over to the woman. Bending low, he used a clothespin to secure the scarf invisibly to her shirt. Then he handed her a bobby pin.

"Use this to pin this side of your hair down, where the wind won't catch it."

"*Xie xie*," she said, taking the bobby pin from him.

He retreated, returning to his designated spot behind Johnny and the camera.

"Good thinking," Johnny hissed at him.

Kai shrugged. It wasn't a big deal—just a few things from the collection of items he'd picked up when Johnny had promised him a job as his assistant. Things he thought would make a photo shoot easier. He also had tape and even an old pair of women's stockings. He'd not expected to really need the things, but something had told him to bring them anyway. Now he knew why.

The young woman finished pinning the stray hairs, then looked up and smiled at Kai.

"I might just keep you around," Johnny muttered, and then

prepared to begin. Again. "Now if that kid will just keep his mouth shut, we can finish and get out of here. I have a date tonight—and one worth keeping."

Kai smiled. Johnny's patience was nonexistent. He felt a flash of sympathy for Johnny's date for the night. While he might be a great photographer, he definitely needed to work on his people skills.

Willow

WILLOW GRABBED HER BAG, SLAMMED her way out of the house, and went around to the back. If she didn't get away from Luyan, she was going to find her hands around the girl's neck… and it would take an army of gods from the afterworld to pry them loose. Luyan's mother had worked in the kitchen all day, cutting out dough for noodles and roasting a piglet, only to have Luyan refuse to come down for dinner. She was so selfish. She didn't even care that the cost was a huge burden to her parents, probably costing them several times the usual amount they'd pay for meal supplies. Didn't she realize her mother was trying so hard to win her over? They'd been there over a month, and Luyan hadn't given her parents a break yet. Every day, the atmosphere was tense, suppressed emotions bubbling and threatening to overflow. It made Willow steaming mad to witness such blatant heartlessness, and she didn't want to be any part of it.

She shivered. She was in such a hurry to get out of there that she hadn't grabbed her coat, and the morning was a crisp one. She'd only thought of her bag, of releasing her feelings into the journal it held. Pausing for a second, she considered going back, but then continued walking. If she went back, Luyan might beg her to stay, and Willow couldn't bear to listen to her complaints for another minute.

As she walked, she considered the conversation she'd had with

Luyan only hours before. Obviously, her uncle didn't think she'd rehabilitated herself enough because he was extending her vacation. Luyan was sure the reason was because her boyfriend had prolonged his stay in Beijing. Either way, she still wasn't allowed to return, which meant Willow was still chained to her side—at her mercy until her uncle called her back.

Within minutes, she found herself on the secret path she'd found the week before, and with each step, her stress melted away. The tall trees around her protected her from the howling winds and she breathed deeply, inhaling the crisp air into her lungs as her legs strained against the steep incline. When she reached the fork in the path, she decided to try the untamed side. It didn't appear to have been used in a long time, so at least she wouldn't meet anyone and have to pretend to be polite.

When she misjudged a wayward branch and swiped at it, sending it back to slap her face, she reached up and felt her forehead. *Aiya,* it was bleeding. Not bad, but enough that she pushed her palm firmly against it, willing it to stop.

She trampled through the tall trees, searching for a good place to sit, and feeling further from Luyan with each step. The challenge of the hike got her blood moving—made her warmer and caused her heart to pump louder, easing the pounding in her ears and settling the anger into something closer to irritation. Why did she even care about Luyan and her parents? She should just leave—go back to Beijing. But what about Rosi? And now that Kai wasn't responding to her letters, would he even want to share their room at the hotel? It would be awkward, but where else could she go?

When she was near enough to see better, she leaned against a tall pine tree, sliding down it to sit at the base of the trunk. She pulled her knees up and wrapped her arms around herself. Taking a deep breath, she dug her notebook out of her bag. She found a pencil, and after touching her forehead once more to be sure the bleeding had dried, she let herself write the words that swam in her head.

Dear Kai, the last time I wrote you, I told you about how I thought Luyan might be improving her attitude. We'd had one good day of a few smiles and a couple of kind words to her parents. I'm writing to tell you now that I was wrong—she's still the empress.

Willow paused, putting the pencil to her lip. She noticed her mother's ring was turned around backward on her finger. Reaching up, she turned it back to where both butterflies showed coming up the sides. She must've lost weight because now the ring slid easily on her finger. She wasn't surprised. Her appetite was close to non-existent since she'd left Beijing. She was worried about Rosi. And though Luyan assured her the letters were being delivered to the hotel, Willow was sick of agonizing over Kai and his strange lack of communication. She wondered if she should just mention it, instead of dancing around it in every letter. So far, her pride had stood in the way. But his silence was beginning to hurt more each day. She bent back over the paper.

I have to ask you something. I've sent you at least a dozen letters, and you've yet to reply to a single one. If you are still mad I left, just tell me that. Your silence is tearing my heart out.

Willow wrote the last character so hard she tore a hole in the paper. She sighed with frustration, catching a glimpse of something pink moving in between the trees about fifty feet ahead of her. Willow leaned a little to the left, taking care to stay behind the cover of the tree as she looked.

She froze. Could it be a wild hog? Would it smell her bleeding? She looked left to right, searching for a place to hide—just in case it was a feral animal. Then it moved again and Willow squinted, trying to make out what it was.

It wasn't a hog. Instead, it appeared to be a woman.

The woman had moved onto her knees and was using a small tool to rake leaves aside. Willow wondered what she was doing. Burying something? She couldn't be planting—it didn't look like any kind of garden Willow had ever seen.

Then something white caught her eye.

It was a cat. She looked closer. No—it was three cats! They looked well taken care of, their coats clean and full, rippling like an ocean of water as they moved about the woman like ghosts, competing for her attention. Willow could hear her speaking to them—softly, almost melodiously. She couldn't understand the words but enjoyed listening all the same.

Above the woman, Willow noticed something peculiar about ten feet up in a tree. It looked like a tiny doghouse that had been built to straddle two thick branches. Looking harder, Willow could see yet another pink-nosed white cat poking his head out of the door. Inside, Willow could see traces of material, probably laid there as bedding for the cats.

Even in the cold temperatures, she sat mesmerized. Who was this woman, and why was she all alone out in the woods? The miniature tree house was fascinating, yet just the presence of the cats at all was a captivating detail. White cats in China were thought to be a symbol of good luck or fortune, and hard to come by. Willow had never even seen a real white cat—the ones she'd seen in her lifetime were painted or embroidered, displayed in stores to be sold to customers pinning their hopes on superstitions to bring them a better life. To see a white cat in real life was really something. She wanted to know more about this quiet woman and her cats.

She appeared to be middle-aged—her body slim, boasting either long hours of manual labor or a lack of nutrition. Yet even though Willow could only see a glimpse of her profile, her face looked rounded and rosy. She watched and felt a moment of envy at the woman's ultimate solitude. There were so many times Willow had wished for something similar, some way to flee from the responsibilities thrust on her at the orphanage, the endless chores, the rows of beds, and being the big sister to so many frightened young girls. Yet, she'd had Kai, and he'd helped her through it. Did their friendship not mean as much to him as it did to her? She couldn't get her head around his refusal to communicate. Thoughts of his rejection made her think seclusion such as she was witnessing now would be a blessing. No voices, no prying eyes—and no responsibilities to anyone.

As she watched, the woman picked up something and tossed it into the basket tied to her back, then raked some more. She reached up and pushed a strand of hair out of her eyes, one that must have come loose out of the long single braid she wore. The lining of the jacket that had drawn Willow's attention to begin with looked homemade, quilted with several shades of pink. Her trousers were a faded blue, tattered at the bottoms as if they'd seen too many winters. Willow looked around, searching for the woman's house. She saw no structures of any kind that could give shelter.

She thought back to a conversation she'd had with Luyan's parents her first week there. They'd told her about the village, pointing out which ways she could walk and explore. Yet, she'd been warned not to go into the woods behind their house. Willow had thought their advice was because of animals or vagrants, but now she wondered if they knew of the woman.

Willow shifted. The twig her foot rested on made a slight crack, breaking in two. She cringed and looked up to see the woman pause, frozen in motion as she gripped another root from the ground.

Willow ducked back behind the cover of the tree in front of her, then didn't move or breathe. Finally, the woman went back to raking and pulling. Yet, it was obvious by the way the cats were suddenly on alert that Willow's presence hadn't gone unnoticed. They'd stopped moving around the woman and now stood looking into the trees, staring holes through Willow. Even from a distance, Willow could see their hair standing on end, giving away the fact a stranger was among them.

She held her breath a moment longer, then quietly eased up, grabbed her things to her chest, and crouched as she crept away. When she was finally out of sight, she put her things back in her bag, picked up the pace, and headed back to Luyan's home, lost in her thoughts of the woman and her cats. A secret—that was what she felt she'd found. And she'd keep it to herself until she could figure it all out.

Kai

KAI LAUGHED AT ROSI AS she loudly slurped her noodles. Her hair almost dangled in the broth. It had finally grown to her shoulders—a length the ayis at the orphanage would have never allowed, but it looked good on Rosi. She peered at him over the rim, her eyes twinkling from under the fringe of new bangs that made her look older than the last time he'd seen her.

"Kai, do it like this," she said.

He lifted his bowl and did the same, their slurping rising together so loudly Rosi had to stop and giggle. He wiggled his eyebrows at her, challenging her to continue. It was incredible how fast she'd gotten back her strength and her playful spunk. He could tell she was still taking things slower than before, but she'd made huge progress in getting back to herself.

Mama Su had invited him and Lao Qu over again for dinner. It was a simple meal of noodles in a brown broth, seasoned with scallions and mushrooms, but it hit the spot. His long day with Johnny, and the buildup of frustration and stress, melted away as he observed how happy Rosi was with a mother to call her own—living in a real home.

When he set the bowl down, Lao Qu waved at him to join him outside. The old man was still old-fashioned, leaving the clean up to the women as he scooted out to smoke. Kai stood, ready to join him.

Rosi reached out and put her hand on his arm. Her face was now serious. "Kai, why hasn't Willow come to see me since I came home?"

He felt like he'd been sucker punched. He was tired of lying for Willow. But still, he couldn't make himself tell Rosi the truth—that she'd skipped out on them for a better gig. All he could do was continue to state what he hoped was close to the reality.

"She's working with Luyan out of town, Rosi. As soon as they finish, she'll be to see you. Don't worry." It took all he had to keep his voice tame and confident.

Rosi still looked skeptical. "Why aren't you staying at the hotel now? When Willow comes back, she won't know where to find you."

"You can tell her because she'll come to the laundry area to see you first anyway."

At that, Rosi smiled. Kai crossed the room to join Lao Qu outside. He pushed through the door, letting it close softly behind him. The old man sat on the only chair on the small porch, so Kai sat down on the steps. He knew he was being ridiculous, but he still felt a sense of loneliness deeper than any he'd ever felt in his life, even being with Rosi and the others. It was an effort to keep up the cheerful act, and he'd be glad to go to bed and close his eyes to shut out the world.

"I heard what Rosi asked in there," Lao Qu said, taking a deep drag on his pipe before slowly blowing it out. "And I know what you told her isn't quite what happened."

Kai shrugged his shoulders. He should've known Mama Su would bring home rumors from around the hotel. People talked—and Luyan was a favorite topic among her uncle's curious employees. The sudden departure she'd made had to have caused a stir.

Lao Qu rocked the chair, the creaking of old wood filling the night air. When he stopped suddenly, Kai knew he had something important to say.

"I've been watching you, Kai. Your soul is restless."

"Maybe a little," Kai admitted. If he were being honest, he'd say a lot. But that would be sharing too much of himself, and he didn't want the old man to know how unhappy he really was.

"You remind me of a naked branch, tumbling in the wind with nothing to anchor you," Lao Qu said and resumed the rocking.

Kai let out a long sigh. He looked up at the moon, searching for the familiar markings that made up a face. Lao Qu was right—he *was* a tumbling branch. While most others had a tree to cling to and the roots of a family to anchor them, Kai had nothing—nobody. He'd carried the knowledge for years, but because he'd had Willow, it hadn't felt so lonely. Now, the truth hit him square in the face. He was completely alone in the world.

"Kai, do you want to talk about it?" Lao Qu probed.

He shook his head. "*Bushi.* But I do want to tell you again how much I appreciate you opening your home to me, giving me a safe place to lay my head."

Lao Qu nodded. "You are a proud young man—and a noble one. When you speak, you look me straight in the eye and that tells me you are trustworthy. Kai, my home is your home, as long as you need it."

Kai stood. "*Xie xie*, Lao Qu. I'm going to head back across the street and get some sleep. I have to be up at the crack of dawn for another shoot." Most of that was true, but what he didn't say to the old man was how much being around Rosi made him miss Willow. He stretched, said goodbye, and then made his way across the small lane.

Willow

"GET UP," WILLOW SAID BRAVELY as she used her foot to nudge Luyan. It was past noon and the girl still slept, her arm positioned over her face to block out the sun that came flooding in through the narrow window. Willow barely contained her temper. She was fed up with Luyan and her spoiled ways. It was time to make some changes.

"Leave me alone," Luyan moaned as she turned over.

Willow reached down, took hold of the heavy quilt with both hands, and yanked it from the bed, letting it pool at her feet.

Luyan popped up like a jack in the box. She pushed the hem of her sleeping gown down over her legs as she hissed through her teeth, "Willow. What. Do. You. Want?"

"I want you to get up and help me. We're giving your parents their room back today. Your days of having them at your beck and call are over."

Luyan blinked several times before shaking her head. "You're crazy."

"No, I'm not. They've slept on the floor for two months now. Your poor mother can barely walk this morning. And your father—he won't say it, but he's hurting too. This is ridiculous, Luyan. We are young—they are old. Simple. They're getting their bed back. And their privacy."

"What if I say no?" Luyan said.

Willow shrugged. "Then I'll just go back to Beijing."

Just as Willow knew it would, her declaration woke up the sleeping dragon. Luyan's eyes flashed, and she looked ready to blow smoke from her nose. "What about Rosi? And how will you get back? You don't have any money."

Willow smiled. "I can figure it all out if I have to, Luyan. I survived without you or your uncle's money for many years. I can do it again. I'm resourceful—isn't that what you said the day you met me?"

She was bluffing, but she wouldn't let Luyan know it. She *was* resourceful—but she wasn't stupid. She wouldn't jeopardize Rosi's medical needs or her adoption status. Until she knew all the paperwork had gone through, and Rosi was fully recovered, she had to play Luyan's games. And since she'd heard nothing from Kai, she was stuck. But it was time to begin to put some of her own games into play.

Starting with teaching Luyan to be respectful.

"But I need my privacy." Luyan changed tactics, whining now.

"I've figured it out. Your mother showed me the storage room off the kitchen area. It's full of clutter right now, but if you help me clean it up, your father said we could fit a small bed in there."

"The storage room? What about mice? Or roaches?" Luyan looked horrified.

"I've already checked it out. Your mother keeps a clean house and that includes every corner. There isn't anything scurrying around in there that isn't up here. So get up, Luyan. Today, you are actually going to accomplish something. And it'll make you feel better."

Luyan grabbed her pillow and threw it at Willow, making her duck. "I'm starting to wonder why I even want you with me."

Willow laughed. "You like me around because looking at me and knowing how much my life sucks makes you look like a superstar. So wonder all you want while you get your pampered butt out of bed and get dressed. Meet me downstairs in ten minutes, or I'm going to come up here and drag you down."

Luyan glared up at her. Willow almost laughed at the way her hair stuck up all over the place, but she knew that might be the last straw. She tilted her head and smiled sweetly.

"Don't think this attitude and bossiness is going to continue, Willow. I'm still in charge," Luyan said.

Willow left the room, silently laughing. She'd won. That was all that counted. And it would take all her patience to get Luyan to actually follow through with the project, but at least she'd caved a little.

Four hours later, Willow pulled another carton from the corner and opened the flaps. So far, she and Luyan had combined at least a dozen boxes of clutter into half as much, sorting and tossing as they went. And she hadn't completely lied—only stretched the truth. The storage room wasn't *dirty*, but it was clear the small space held years of overlooked items as well as dust and cobwebs.

They'd made great progress, clearing one side of the room enough for Luyan's father to bring in a borrowed bed big enough for two. It was only a frame and one small, stuffed mattress, but it would be much better than sleeping on the cold floor. He'd set it up, and then he'd disappeared, hiding from Luyan's wrath, Willow supposed. She was impressed. Luyan had even gotten into the spirit a little, using her need for perfection to work through years of grime to show a gleaming, glass window that instantly brightened up the room.

Despite the intermittent grumbling and small quarrels, they continued to work through the afternoon. Willow still wanted to clear out the other side as much as possible—or at least enough to make it look more like a bedroom than a storage room. She felt if she could make it cozy enough, maybe it would minimize the onslaught of complaints from the empress.

"I can't believe you want to sleep in here," Luyan said. She squatted in front of a box, pulling out a photo album.

"We don't have to stay in here. I'm fine with sleeping in the living room on the mats as your parents have been doing. You're the one who insists on privacy. We should have done this the first day we got here."

"Yeah—but if we sleep in the living room, we'll have to get up at the crack of dawn because they'll be crawling all over us on their way out the door."

"They do have to work, Luyan." Willow was losing her patience.

"They wouldn't if they'd invested wisely. Who knows where all the money my uncle sent them went to? Money *their own daughter* worked hard for." She flipped through the pages of photos.

Willow wouldn't bet Luyan had truly worked hard—but she'd keep her mouth shut on that one. She crossed the room and looked over her shoulder at the book Luyan held.

"Is that you?" The page boasted many pictures, but one in particular stood out. It was a little girl in pigtails being held high in the air by a man. Her frilly, pink dress contrasted against the wrinkled, gray work clothes the man wore, looking out of place. Yet, you could tell they belonged to each other by the look in their eyes.

Luyan nodded, keeping her attention trained on the photo.

"You looked so happy. And your father—*aiya,* he's totally captivated by you. What a proud smile." In neat lettering beside the photo, Willow read the caption of characters that together meant, *My Little Quilted Jacket.* She felt a rush of longing. The phrase was a common but age-old term families used to describe their precious daughters. She wondered which parent had written the sentimental words.

Luyan slammed the book shut. "Well, that was then and this is now. I'm no longer that little girl, and I'm surely no one's jacket." She stood, pulled a plastic bag from the corner, and started to toss the book in.

Willow moved fast. "Oh no, you don't. Your mother would kill you if you threw that away." Willow took the book from her and sat on the floor. "And you might not be that little girl anymore, but you're still lucky to have a family."

She ignored Luyan's snort as she studied the first set of photos, captivated by the progression of the small family from page to page. While boys were usually more coveted, especially in the small towns and villages of China, Luyan's parents looked enamored by their infant daughter in every early picture. There was even a scene of Wu Min holding both Luyan's tiny hands in what looked like her first steps. The joy she saw on their faces made their current strained relationship seem even sadder to Willow.

Finally, when she'd looked at every page, she set the book on the bed. "I'll take that to your mother when we're done in here."

"Fine. I'm going to the bathroom. Don't miss me too much," Luyan said as she left the room.

"We need to get some covers on this bed or the empress is going to be cold tonight," Willow called out to Luyan's departing figure, going to the old trunk that stood at the end of the room. She'd already asked Luyan to give her the blankets, but if she wanted it done, she guessed she'd have to do it herself.

The trunk was stacked high with boxes. She carefully set each one on the floor before opening the lid. The strong scent of lavender wafted up, making her eyes water. The trunk didn't hold blankets, but instead was another container full of what looked like more of Luyan's forgotten family mementos.

Just the kind of stuff Willow loved to look through.

She picked up a pair of embroidered silk slippers, studying them. They were no longer than her hand, and even with her amateur eye, she could tell the stitches were perfect, so close together you couldn't make out where one started or ended. The design on the slippers was cute—comical even. Made up with a colorful orange for the primary color, each one boasted the head of what appeared to be a tiger with short, yellow whiskers and even finely detailed eyes and ears. Willow could just imagine how much fun they'd been for Luyan when she was an infant, laying on her back and playing with her feet.

She put the tiny shoes aside and pulled out a long gown. It was traditional in style, but it appeared to be very old.

"What are you doing?" Wu Min startled her from the doorway, her voice quiet but disapproving.

Willow dropped the gown. "I'm so sorry. I was looking for bedding. I thought it'd be in the trunk."

Wu Min crossed the room, picking up the slippers and the gown. She dropped them into the trunk and softly closed the lid. "Please don't dig in there," she said. "The trunk contains things that are private."

"Of course," Willow answered, feeling her face redden. She didn't know what the big deal was, but it was the first time Luyan's mother had showed any sort of disappointment in her. It made her feel awful.

"We can just push this to the end of the bed, and you two can use it to sit on." Wu Min softened her tone, making Willow's embarrassment a little easier to bear.

"Great idea." Willow got one side and Wu Min got the other, then they lifted the trunk and moved it in front of the bed.

"I'm sorry if I startled you," Wu Min said. "Luyan told me you needed some blankets, so I came to tell you I was washing them up. That trunk carries a lot of old memories—some too painful to bring out."

Willow solemnly nodded. "I understand, and I'm sorry for being nosy." She pointed to the book on the bed. "There's one of your family albums, but I didn't get that out. Luyan did."

Wu Min picked it up and held it to her chest. "*Xie xie.* I was looking for this just the other day when we got the news Luyan was coming home for an extended visit. Yilin couldn't remember where he'd put it."

Willow sat down on the bed, and Wu Min sat beside her. "So you were both happy to have her come home?" Willow asked.

It took a moment before Wu Min answered. She picked at an invisible thread on the mattress first. "I know she doesn't want to be here, and even if she is unhappy, I'm content to have her for as long as she'll stay. And you too, Willow. You've proven to be a good friend." She raised her eyebrows. "I know it's not easy."

They shared a knowing smile, and Willow laughed. Not easy was putting it mildly. And Wu Min didn't know she was basically being blackmailed to be Luyan's friend. But if she were being honest with herself, she also had to admit she felt something for the girl—pity maybe, or even a strong desire to get her to wake up and appreciate her life—but something that made her want to stay long enough to help.

"It's okay. Village life is a nice change from the city." She heard a smacking noise and looked up.

"What's going on in here? Mama, you haven't even made my bed yet? Willow—move those boxes. If you hurry and get this room straightened up, I might just take a walk through the village with you," Luyan said from the doorway. She leaned against the wooden frame, sucking on a lychee from the pile she held in the other hand.

Willow looked at Wu Min, and they shared a laugh.

"I'll go see if the linens are ready to be hung out to dry," Wu Min said and skirted out the door. Even though she made a quick exit, she looked happier to Willow than she had in days. It was amazing. The more Luyan loosened up, the more her parents seemed to come alive. Willow wished she'd notice that herself.

Luyan moved into the room and sat down on the bed beside Willow. "What were you and my mother talking about?" she asked suspiciously.

"She was telling me how happy she and your baba were when they heard you were coming home for a while."

Luyan rolled her eyes. "They're also happy when I go back because that means more money for them."

Willow looked down at her hands, unwilling to let Luyan goad her into another argument about her parent's intentions. She studied her nails, dirty from the day's work, and then it hit her. Her ring was gone.

She jumped up, holding onto the hand where the ring used to be. "My ring! It's gone," she said, whipping her head around to scan the bed and floor.

"What do you mean it's gone? Where did you put it?" Luyan said.

Willow was relieved that for once, she sounded concerned for something other than herself. She knew Willow didn't own much and the ring was special for some reason—she just didn't know why.

"I didn't put it anywhere. I haven't taken it off." She knelt down and scanned the floor, looking under the bed. When she didn't see anything, she got up and headed over to the wall of boxes. Pulling one down, she opened the flap and began digging through it.

"Why would it be in there, Willow, if you didn't take it off?" Luyan sounded concerned, but she didn't move to help.

"Get up and look with me, will you? It must have fallen off while I was working. It's been loose on my finger since we got here." She tried to keep the urgency out of her voice.

"Well, slow down a sec before we have to check every last box in this room. When was the last time you know you saw it on your finger?"

Willow stopped rummaging through the box and searched her memory, trying to think of when she'd last actually seen it. The ring had become such a part of her that she never noticed it anymore, unless she was deep in thought and then she usually fiddled with it, turning it around.

That was it! She'd last seen it when she was in those woods behind the house and was writing the letter to Kai. Right before she'd seen the woman.

"Uh, I can't really remember," she said, not wanting to admit to Luyan that she'd been rambling where she wasn't supposed to be. But suddenly, she knew the ring wouldn't be in the boxes. It had to have fallen off in her panic to get out of there before the woman saw her. And if it had, she knew just where to find it. At least, she hoped she could, because it was absolutely the only thing she had that was proof once upon a time, she had a mother who may have loved her.

40

Willow

WILLOW WATCHED LUYAN'S FACE AS they walked, wondering what she thought of her own hometown. Was it familiar? Strange? Did she really hate it as much as she claimed? She'd made a show of looking through a few more boxes for her ring, but finally, she'd talked Luyan into going out. If she could tire her out, maybe Luyan would sleep for hours. If so, Willow would be able to go look for the ring without worrying about hurrying back.

She was also glad they'd come out together, she had to admit. It was the first time Willow had been able to get Luyan out of the house, and she planned to find out all she could about the sights and small-town gossip. Even though Luyan had kept herself secluded in the house since they'd arrived, Willow had taken to walking around the village every day. Although no one knew her, she was starting to feel a sense of familiarity—and with that came curiosity.

"It's so quaint here, how can you not want to be here all the time?" Willow asked. A few couples on bicycles pedaled around them, the young girls on the back throwing their hands up in a wave. Willow waved back, but Luyan ignored the gestures of hospitality.

Luyan snorted. "I'm meant for bigger things."

Willow thought for a moment, and then couldn't keep her tongue any longer. "Well, it appears to me your rich life in Beijing wasn't making you happy either."

"So? I'd rather cry in the back of a shiny, black sports car than smile on the back of a bike."

"Are you saying your Taiwanese sweetheart wasn't all that sweet?" Willow asked.

Luyan shrugged.

Willow stopped and turned Luyan so she was facing her. "Luyan, did you get exiled for seeing someone you don't even care about? That you don't even love?"

The stare Luyan gave her made Willow wonder if the girl even knew what love was. She seemed so empty—so lacking of any emotion other than jealousy and resentment. But still, something told her Luyan was putting on a façade of being something she wasn't. Surely, underneath it all, there was a person in there capable of real feelings. She wouldn't give up on her, at least not while they were in the village. What else was there to work on, after all?

"So tell me, do you know any of these people?" Willow asked, joining her arm with Luyan's as they started walking again.

Luyan shrugged. "I guess so."

Willow thought it would be wonderful to have grown up in a small village where everyone knew each other. She stopped and pointed at an old man arranging strawberries in small containers, then lining them up along a plank set up outside his small store window. "What about him? Do you know who he is?"

"I can't remember his name, but he's my grandfather's friend. He used to give me a piece of fruit every day after school."

"Whoa, stop," Willow said, grabbing Luyan's arm and bringing her to a halt. "You have grandparents here?"

Luyan jerked her arm away. "Of course, this is my mother's hometown. Her parents still live here."

"They're still living and you haven't been to see them? Not even once since we've been here?"

Luyan shrugged. "So? They haven't been to see me either."

Willow took a step forward. "Do you know nothing of tradition or manners? I don't have family, but even I know they're probably waiting for you to make the first gesture. Let's go now, Luyan. Please. I want to meet them."

Luyan shook her head. "You said we were taking a walk, Willow. You didn't say I had to be social."

"Come on. If you'll go, I'll sleep on the floor tonight and let you have the bed to yourself."

Luyan hesitated. Willow knew she had her—she'd been begging for the entire bed for days, saying she was too crowded. Willow waited patiently to see if her selfishness won out. Just then, something whizzed past her ears and she jumped to the left. Luyan stayed where she was, but she jerked her head around.

"What the—"

Two boys stood on the side of the road, laughing at the expressions their wayward throw had caused. The ball—or what felt like a torpedo zooming by—dropped a few feet away from them. Willow looked from it to the boys and felt like going over and slapping them, but she pulled on Luyan.

"Come on, it's just two melon-heads trying to get our attention."

"Well, they got it." Luyan didn't budge. She kept her hands on her hips and glared at the two boys. "I'm about to give these country boys a piece of my city mind."

The boys made their way down the street to retrieve the ball. Willow watched them, knowing by the swagger of the one who led that he was a troublemaker. She'd only wanted to take a nice walk—enjoy the moment of getting Luyan out of the house—but now, they were the center of attention. People around them stared, some laughing and others watching their discomfort.

Just before the boys got close enough, Luyan picked up the ball and held it to her chest. "You can have the ball back when you apologize," she said.

"Luyan, give them the ball and let's go."

The biggest boy, a tall, ruddy-faced teen around their age, smiled at his comrade and then stood directly in front of her and Luyan. The comrade hesitated, as if he was going to say something nice, but then he remained silent, peering at them with dark, intense eyes behind a pair of round-framed glasses. With one look, Willow knew he was the kind of boy who followed along and did what he was told.

"Hey—I know who you are." Surprise registered across the bigger boy's face as he looked directly at Luyan.

She shrugged, and then tossed him the ball.

"You don't remember me?" he asked, his expression turning to one of hurt.

"Should I?" she said, scrutinizing him.

The boy shifted onto his other foot, then Willow was surprised to see a rush of crimson climbing his neck and spreading across his cheeks.

"Spring Festival two years ago? Does that sound familiar?"

Willow watched Luyan and could see the moment she remembered. Realization registered on her face, and then embarrassment. "Let's go, Willow."

"It's about time you came home and stopped chasing those pipe dreams," the boy said, his tone turning icy again. "You ain't no better than the rest of us."

Luyan nudged Willow to move along, and like that, they were on their way again.

"Who was that?" Willow asked, surprised the boy had gotten away with his remarks. She'd never seen Luyan just give in and not bite back. That in itself told her something was up with the situation.

"Just a boy."

"It's never just a boy, Luyan."

Luyan's head bobbed up and down. "It is here in this backward town. It's ridiculous—you let one sneak a kiss behind the watershed and they think they own you forever."

Willow laughed. "Fine. But we're still going to see your grandparents. So let's go."

The old woman shuffled around the small, makeshift kitchen in the tiny courtyard, fumbling to grab the screaming kettle from the old cookstove with a tattered dishcloth. Willow watched her, amused but careful to keep a serious face. Before she'd showed them out to the covered outdoor area, she'd pulled from her cupboard the oldest porcelain tea set Willow had ever seen. She carried it outside to the small, round table and set it upon a beautifully carved teakwood tray. Then she lit candles and placed them in the little drawer under the tray that served as a heating compartment to keep the tea warm.

Willow was thrilled, but she contained her excitement. She'd never before been invited into such a historical home. The way the house was small yet still built to surround a tiny courtyard for daily entertaining was interesting. The wall facing the street was made up of old carvings covered with yellowed newspapers. The iron cookstove the woman kept going to took up one corner of the old cobblestone ground covering, with a few cupboards and countertops surrounding it—an area clearly used to cook for many generations. Willow knew that in the old days, most kitchens were outside, but she'd never seen one.

Off in the corner, Willow saw a tall, plastic hot water thermos, pushed aside and traded for fancier items now that company had arrived. The old woman puttered around, barely looking where she was going, an instinct for knowing where every item was ingrained into her from years of familiarity. Now she overturned three tiny, handle-less cups and poured the sweet-smelling tea.

The strong aroma of flowers wafted up to Willow's nose, and she inhaled the steaming cloud of comfort. "*Xie xie*, Laoren," Willow said, wrapping her hand around the warm cup.

"Call me *Nainai*."

Willow didn't feel comfortable using the title of grandmother for a stranger, but the woman's attitude didn't leave room for arguing, so she simply nodded. Now, as Luyan sat across the table, studying her nails with her most bored expression, Willow watched the grandmother move about and wondered how the woman's back had gotten so bent. Had she worked in the rice paddies all her life? Carried heavy baskets of vegetables from out-of-town gardens? For some reason, she thought of Mama Joss and the different ways two women of the same generation chose to live their life. She didn't know which was more difficult, but something told her Luyan's grandmother deserved a break. They'd only arrived half an hour before. When the old woman had snatched open the door, she'd startled them so much that they'd both jumped backward. Then she'd waved them in, leading them through the small house.

"What is that?" Willow had asked when they'd passed a large piece of furniture that appeared to serve as part table, part bed. Made with stone slabs across the front, the top was covered neatly with quilts and embroidered pillows running alongside the wall.

"A kang," Luyan's grandmother said. "Haven't you ever seen a real Chinese bed?" She lifted the quilt as they walked by, showing the underneath was a hard surface laden with bricks.

Willow felt her cheeks burn with embarrassment. She'd learned about the warming beds in school, but she hadn't ever seen one. All she knew was they were made with pipes running from the house's heating system to beneath the bed to keep those sitting or sleeping on it toasty warm throughout the cold seasons.

"Nainai won't take that monstrosity out of here and get her a modern bed," Luyan said. Willow caught her rolling her eyes at her grandmother's back as she waved them along through the home.

"A modern bed won't keep these old bones warm, child," the woman called out behind her.

They'd passed through the room and into the brisk, cool courtyard and Luyan's grandmother hadn't sat down since. As the old woman bustled around, she chattered on about the weather, the price of rice, and the matchmaking of several family members that Luyan acted as if she'd never heard of.

As they waited for whatever came next on such a visit, Willow looked around, taking in everything. A flimsy piece of pink gauzy material hung as a curtain leading to the inside of the house. The wind moved it gently, sporadically covering the long rows of painted Chinese characters flanking the doorway. Willow watched closely. As each character was revealed, she read the family name on one side and a quote by Chairman Mao on the other.

'*Firstly, do not fear hardship, and secondly, do not fear death,*' it read. Willow assumed Luyan's family had seen their share of hardship, especially her grandparents, who had most likely lived through the years of chaos the Cultural Revolution had created. She thought of Kai and his infatuation with history. He would love to have been with them, if only to pick at the old woman for her stories. Yet they'd not touched on anything of too much significance, and Willow was surprised the woman hadn't even wondered much about her—a virtual stranger to the family but now Luyan's constant sidekick. It made her wonder how much the old woman knew about their situation. Finally, the woman settled down and took a deep breath, launching into a new subject.

"Luyan, I've been counting the days since you arrived, wondering how long it'd take for you to come to visit your nainai. You lasted longer than we'd guessed, you stubborn child." She brought out a square tin with pictures of Mao carved into the sides. Setting it on the table, she popped the lid off, and then upturned half a dozen small, dry cookies onto a plate. "Perhaps you were scared to get your ears boxed."

Willow watched for the response, and she wasn't let down. Luyan rolled her eyes and shook her head, as if asking the gods for patience. Willow was amused—by the grandmother as well as Luyan's impatience. She watched the bun fixed atop the woman's head, noting how it bobbled back and forth when she talked.

"Your grandfather is in town—I expect him back any time, so we need to hurry and talk about your personal issues before he returns." She sat down at the table and heaved a huge sigh, as if the effort of preparing the tea took her last ounce of strength. And at her age, Willow thought that maybe it had.

"I don't have any personal issues to talk about, Nainai."

Willow picked up a cookie and waited. She let her eyes linger to the windowsill over the outside sink, counting out the small cups and half a dozen toothbrushes all standing up like little soldiers, frayed and worn but still willing to do the job. Next to them stood a thick mug with a wooly brush and razor waiting for their turn. Willow wondered how anyone could stand in the freezing cold air each morning to perform their daily hygiene routine. Even her days in the orphanage bathroom seemed more favorable—at least they had been sheltered from the wind. *Village people had to be tough*, she thought to herself.

Luyan's grandmother slurped her tea, and then set it down with a bang. "I tried to teach both my daughters the ways of a woman, and it was your mother's job to pass along the wisdom as my mother did for me many years ago. Wu Min should've told you sex before marriage never leads to anything but a river of tears. If you wanted to be that kind of girl, you should've been swallowing tadpoles to keep from being fertile. Now we'll have to deal with this quietly and swiftly."

Luyan's hand froze with the cup of tea suspended midair only inches from her mouth. "What are you talking about?"

Willow sipped her tea, enjoying the unexpected drama the day had brought. To see Luyan on the hot seat was thrilling her more than it should, but she still found it entrancing. She was beginning to like the old woman more each moment that went by. She was a sassy one—and it was fun to watch.

The grandmother jabbed at the air in front of Luyan. "You! With child!"

Luyan spewed her tea all over the table, and her grandmother threw the dish towel her way. She grabbed at it and blotted first her mouth, then the table where the tea droplets had sprayed. Her cheeks burned with embarrassment. She looked stricken. "Me? I'm not pregnant, Nainai! Who told you that?"

"No one had to tell me anything, child. You come home with the whiff of disgrace trailing you, and then you barely leave the house. What else could be going on?"

"Nothing! Uncle is angry with me—that's what's going on. I'm not having a baby, Nainai. Is that what the entire village thinks?"

Willow ignored the flash of anger that sparked from Luyan, but almost smiled at the relief that spread across the old woman's face. It was clear she held a lot of affection for Luyan. If it wasn't in her voice, she'd seen it in the living area from the dozens of photos displayed in cheap frames across a long, wooden shelf bolted to the wall. It was like a montage of Luyan through the years, from infanthood to the gangly years, and even a few professional photos that had obviously been cut from magazines Luyan had modeled in.

Her grandmother ignored the question about what the village thought.

"*Aiya*, your uncle is a wicked man, Luyan. I've told your mother and begged her to bring you home—to get you away from him. Finally, my prayers were answered." She bent her head, and Willow wondered if she hid a tear.

A loud bang interrupted her suspicion. They all looked up as the door opened, and an old man entered the small courtyard. He lifted a hand and muttered a gruff greeting, then went and stood in front of the cookstove as he pulled off his jacket and knit hat. The lines in his face were deep, but Willow also saw kindness there.

"Ye Ye, I hope you are doing well," Luyan said quietly, her voice carrying an air of respect that Willow had never heard her use.

The old man didn't look up or answer.

"She's not with child," the grandmother said loudly. "She's only here for a visit."

Luyan looked mortified. This time, Willow barely stifled a laugh. It depended on what the old woman's definition of trouble was, and if they were like Luyan's uncle, she and her husband hated the Taiwanese. But Willow wasn't going to be the one to point out that their granddaughter had other issues.

"Nainai! Stop with the talk about babies or I'm leaving."

The old woman waved a hand in the air. "Enough said, but we had to clear the air so your grandfather could relax. You know how that subject has brought discord into this family over the years."

The old man came to the table, and Luyan's grandmother went into the house. After retrieving a pipe and a pouch from somewhere, she returned and set it down. Willow waited for Luyan and her grandfather to speak, or embrace, or something—but instead, they ignored each other.

"How was business today?" the old woman asked.

"Slow. I had some problems today, and the boy didn't show up. My back is killing me from standing behind the counter," he answered gruffly. He didn't say who the boy was or what he did to make money, but Willow assumed it must be his hired help that had left him in a bad position.

"No one respects relationships anymore," Luyan's grandmother said. "In the past, if you were from the same village, you pitched in to help each other. Now, people are only motivated by money."

The old man nodded. "It's a constant battle between those who are allowed shops closest to the main streets, and those who are higher up in the mountain, forced to put their stores on the hilltops. It's always an argument going on about who is able to make more money. Everyone wants as close to the foreign tourists as possible. They just don't understand there are only so many in-town business permits available."

"You could all move to the city," Luyan offered. "There's plenty of opportunity to make money in Beijing."

Her grandfather snorted in derision. "Humph—the city is full of crooks and criminals. I'd rather die here poor than live there as a slimy business owner making his fortune from scamming innocent people."

Willow wondered if his statement was a hidden message about Luyan's uncle, but before more could be said, Luyan stood.

"We've got to go home, Willow. I need a nap."

Kai

KAI PICKED UP THE BROWN egg and peeled it, then popped half of it in his mouth. The burst of flavor exploding on his tongue was a delicious reminder of his childhood. When he and his mother had finally managed to get their own home—between times they'd lived on the streets—she'd also boiled eggs in soy sauce and black tea while he played, waiting for the few hours she always claimed it took for the egg to be ready to eat.

His mother had been on his mind all day, and he realized he was finding reminders of her everywhere. It was his own fault. When Lao Qu had left for his morning walk, Kai had dug the photos out of his bag and looked through them. He almost wished he'd never found the extra funds to get them printed, but then again, seeing her face on something other than the viewfinder of his camera felt good. Still, the photos left him with a burning hole of bitterness in his gut, a reminder of what might have been had fate not took her from him. He missed her. Still, after all these years, he missed her so much.

"Have another egg, Kai," Mama Joss said, bringing him out of his somber memories as she set another can of cola in front of him.

With the rainbow scarf she wore tied around her hair, she reminded Kai of an old gypsy woman. After he swallowed the last bite, he rubbed his stomach. He was bone tired after a long day of carrying equipment for Johnny. The food lay heavy in his belly, adding to his weariness.

"I'm not sure I can, Mama Joss. You've filled me up. *Xie xie.*"

"No, thank you for bringing me such wonderful gifts. You're a good boy. I'm just relieved I had something made up for you to eat. Those were from the batch I'm taking to the orphanage tomorrow for Suxi's birthday. She's not on the adoption list, so she won't be sharing one of those fancy cakes. Now, in addition to the eggs, I'll make her a sugary treat from the flour and sugar you brought."

Kai nodded and hoped she didn't see his face turning red. He'd used almost half his weekly pay to buy a huge bag of rice, along with smaller ones of flour and sugar. Then he'd had to pay for a pedicab to carry it all across town. But he knew how hard it was for someone like Mama Joss to make ends meet. She'd taken care of them many times over the years. He was glad to pay it back when he could. Of course, he'd thought of Willow and how she would've approved too. Even though he was angry with her, something in him still strived to do what he thought she'd want him to do.

Mama Joss came to the table and sat down. "Guess what I heard about Bihua?"

Kai looked up. The last he'd heard was that his fellow roommate from the orphanage was being sent to training camp for the army. He'd needed to be separated from the younger children so they wouldn't be bullied by him any longer.

"One of the ayis said he ran away from the military and came back to town. When they found him, he was hiding in a department store bathroom and started crying—begging them not to take him back." Mama Joss shook her head, yet Kai couldn't tell if it was from disgust or pity. "Of course, the orphanage wouldn't take him, so now he's back with the officials and probably feeling the sting worse for being a deserter."

"At least he's getting a taste of his own medicine. He's bullied smaller kids for years, so I hope they show him no mercy." Kai kept his tone civil and his words clean, but what he really hoped was that someone taught the tyrant a lesson by kicking his lumpy ass as many times as he'd dared to lay hands on anyone else.

Mama Joss nodded. "And Rosi? She's still doing good?" she asked.

"She's doing great. She's back at work almost full time, even though Mama Su won't let her do any heavy lifting. Rosi thinks she manages the entire laundry area, and Mama Su and everyone else just let her. They love her."

Mama Joss smiled. "Fate was good to that girl."

"Yes, it was," Kai said, thinking he hadn't been so lucky. He was still alone and probably always would be. "So, you haven't heard anything from Willow?"

"I was wondering when you'd get around to asking me that, Kai. I could tell it's a question that's been dancing on the end of your tongue since you got here."

"Well, have you?" He traced a deep scar in the table with his finger, letting it circle round and round as he waited. He prayed Mama Joss had gotten a letter, a call—anything.

He felt her hand fall on his shoulder and give a comforting squeeze. "I haven't. I'm sorry, Kai. But I'm sure she's fine. We know she's with that Luyan girl—so that tells us she's being taken care of. It's not as if we have to worry about her being on the streets with no roof over her head. When she's ready, she'll contact us."

Kai didn't look up. He didn't want Mama Joss to see the deep disappointment that his one hope had been shattered. Even though Willow hadn't reached out to him, he'd felt sure she would at least find a way to talk to Mama Joss. To have cut them both off with no communication could only mean one thing.

Luyan had successfully turned her, and Willow was done with them forever.

He stood and picked up his bag. Because he couldn't afford to waste any more money, he'd have a long walk back to Lao Qu's house. He'd promised Rosi he'd stop by and listen to her sing the song she'd been practicing all week, so he needed to hurry along.

"I've gotta run," he said.

Mama Joss stood too, following him to the door.

"*Zaijian*, Mama Joss." He got as far as the gravel path between the rows of houses before Mama Joss called out to him. He turned around.

"Kai," she said, "Don't lose hope. Willow is special. If she is meant to be a part of your life, then the gods will return her to you. Fate has a way of leading people exactly where they should go."

He dropped his eyes to the ground before she could see the shimmer of tears gathering there. He was supposed to be a man—not a sniveling boy. He hoped she hadn't noticed. Lifting his hand, he waved at her as he turned back around and headed for the street. He'd continue his work with Johnny—stick around for a few more months. Then, if no news came from Willow, he'd decided he would move on to a warmer climate. If he was destined to always bounce from place to place, he wanted to be where the winters weren't so ruthless. Lao Qu was kind to him, but he couldn't continue to impose on the old man forever.

Willow

WILLOW LAUGHED AT THE DOUBTING look plastered on Luyan's face. She sat at the table across from her mother, her hands and fingers outstretched while Wu Min first wet, then carefully stuck pink plum blossom petals to her daughter's nails. The weeks had flown by and now they were already in March. Some of the first signs of spring were now off the trees and pasted to Luyan's fingers.

"And you mean to tell me you've never used fingernail polish?" Luyan asked, her eyes narrowed at her mother.

Wu Min smiled gently and shook her head. "Now why would we spend good money on nail polish when we can do the same thing with nature?" She finished with the flowers, then tore tiny pieces off a long roll of cellophane and wrapped them around Luyan's fingers.

"People can also wipe their backsides with leaves, but please tell me you don't do that when I'm not here."

Wu Min sighed with exasperation, making Willow laugh again. Watching the two of them together was amusing. The day they'd switched bedrooms and dug into so many memories had broken the ice. Now each day Luyan gave in a little, allowing small pieces of her long-held armor to fall away, bit by bit. She still kept everyone at arm's length, but Willow could tell she sometimes liked spending time with her mother, even if she didn't say it and tried hard not to show it. There was still a lot of anger there, but with Willow as a buffer, the last few months had seen a dramatic change—and the few chances they were alone, Wu Min had thanked her time and again, telling her she was an answer to prayers. Willow just wished they would sit down and have a serious talk with Luyan, maybe try to iron out all the unsaid transgressions to try to put it behind them. But what did she know? She'd never been a part of a family. That made her think of Rosi and Kai and she felt a pain through her chest. A real, flesh and blood pain. She stopped laughing, putting her hand over her heart.

"Yeah, you'd better stop laughing, Willow, because you're next," Luyan said, giving Willow a look filled with warning.

"That's okay; I'll pass," Willow said. She was feeling irritated that after several trips back into the woods to look for her ring, she still hadn't found it. Not that she thought it was in a place anyone else would stumble upon it, but she'd become so accustomed to it that her hand felt naked without it on her finger. When she thought too much about it, it made her so nervous she felt short of breath, like she was about to panic. She'd had to fight against herself mentally to keep from running out there every day. But she didn't want Luyan or her parents seeing her go, then have them follow her. Each excursion had to be carefully orchestrated so no one would miss her.

Luyan had woken up cranky and complaining about the village lacking any sort of facilities for pampering. She'd once again mourned the lack of a spa, so her mother had concocted a plan. Already, Luyan had been treated to a steaming hot bath with water carried up in buckets, then boiled, and a thorough head washing and massage. Her mother had even taken the time to brush out her hair, coat it with almond oil, and then wound it around a couple of dozen soft pink curlers. Luyan was being treated like a little princess, and Willow only hoped she'd show some appreciation when it was all over with.

"Now leave these on your nails for at least an hour and when we take them off, it'll leave a pale pink color that'll eventually fade, but never chip," Wu Min said. She got up and took the cellophane with her, then slipped out of the room.

Willow watched Luyan as she sat there wrapped in her mother's warm, fuzzy robe, her hair stuck to her head in the tiny pink curlers and holding her nails up as she examined them.

"You look hilarious," Willow said.

Luyan rolled her eyes, pretending indifference, but Willow thought she was enjoying all the attention from her mother.

Someone knocked at the door, startling them both. Willow jumped up and went to it.

"Wait! Don't open the door with me looking like this!" Luyan followed, headed for the loft stairs with her hands covering her hair.

Willow ignored her and snatched the door open. Luyan froze—caught in motion. Outside on the front stoop stood one of the boys they had seen a few weeks before, when Luyan was almost struck with the ball. But it wasn't the bigger boy, it was the one who wore the glasses—the timid one.

"I-I-" he stammered.

"You what?" Willow asked, impatient to shut the door.

Luyan stepped around her. "What do you want?"

"I-I-wanted to talk to you and tell you I'm sorry Yunkun threw the ball at you. He's a d-d-donkey's ass."

Luyan put her hands on her hips. "That was weeks ago. But what does that make you? A donkey's testicles? You were right up in there with him."

The boy turned red from the tips of his ears down to the end of his nose.

"Luyan!" Willow hissed at her. The boy was humiliated, that much was clear by the stuttering, even if you ignored the fact that he looked like he was about to explode from the heat his face created.

"What? Does he expect me to just say okay—it's fine your best buddy is a jerk who does stupid stuff to get the attention of any girl walking by?"

"N-no. It was my cousin, but I don't expect anything." He backed up, his hands in his pockets, and tripped, almost falling.

Luyan busted out laughing. Willow pushed her out of the way of the door, slipping out and then shutting it behind her. "Look, I'm so sorry. She's as bad as your friend. Ignore her. What's your name?"

He recovered his balance, and Willow could see his Adam's apple bobbing up and down in his throat as he swallowed. "Fang Shuyang, but my friends call me Shu."

Interestingly, he didn't stutter now that Luyan was out of the way. Willow reached out and extended her hand. "I'm Willow—Luyan's friend from the city. Thanks for coming by. Really—it's admirable that you tried to apologize for your cousin."

He nodded. "I know Luyan too. We went to primary school together. She doesn't remember me, I guess."

Willow felt sorry for him. "Oh, I'm sure she would if she saw some photos or something. You know how people change when they get older. I bet you look different too."

He hung his head. "I recognized her the second I saw her."

Then Willow saw it for what it was. He was obviously awestruck by Luyan—maybe always had been. And to think what courage it took for him to come and apologize... it made Willow want to help him.

"What are you doing later?"

He shrugged.

"Well, what do people our age do around here?" She honestly had no idea.

He kicked at a rock, and then looked up. "We meet down at the river sometimes, just to talk or have a drink if anyone has any beer."

"What time?" Willow wanted to hurry him up.

A light came into his eyes. "Time? You mean you and Luyan could come? Are you sure she'll do that?"

"No, I'm not sure. I can't promise anything. But I can try. If I can get her interested, we'll try to head out there after nine o'clock. If we aren't there by ten, we aren't coming."

He nodded. "*Hao le*. Thanks. I mean—see you later." He took off toward the street, almost skipping in his excitement.

"Shu?" Willow called out to him, and he stopped and turned to her. "Next time you see Luyan, don't act like a scared little mouse. That's a good way to get stung by her. Be tough, Shu. Be tough."

He laughed, and then waved goodbye.

Willow turned back to the door, took a deep breath, and got ready to face the dragon. It was time to get Luyan back in touch with her roots. Let her mingle with what she called *the common people* to bring her down a notch or two.

Willow could hear the sound of the river mixed with laughter and a few shouts as they got closer. It had taken her over an hour to convince Luyan to come out, but finally promises of showing her old friends how successful she'd become were bait enough to get her up and ready.

It was a cool night. Even bundled up, Willow felt the chill. She figured she had an hour at most before Luyan began to complain. She had to keep her positive, or she wouldn't even manage that much time.

"It'll be good for you to connect with your childhood."

In the dark, Willow couldn't see Luyan's expression, but she felt the resentment in the air, directed at her.

"There'd better be wine," Luyan finally answered. "It's freezing out here."

"Wine! Where do you think you are? Your uncle's hotel? You'll be lucky if there really is beer."

"If there isn't any beer or wine, I'm turning around and going straight back home," Luyan said, her voice becoming even sulkier.

Willow let the silence fall between them as they drew closer to the river. She pretended for Luyan's sake, but she wasn't even excited about coming out. She'd learned a long time ago that she didn't fit in with normal kids. People like her and Kai were different—maybe harder. She didn't know what it was, but she always felt decades older than anyone she met her own age. Still, getting Luyan to mingle with people from her own village just might make her remember her roots and discover the village had something to offer. Maybe even make her act a little more human on a consistent basis. For Luyan's parents, Willow was willing to try anything.

The group saw them first, made obvious by the sudden silence as they approached.

Four or five teens sat gathered on the bank of the river, their shadows dancing by the light of a small bonfire. Willow felt Luyan hesitate, so she put her hand on her arm, urging her forward.

Shu stood up first and waved. "Willow. Luyan. Over here."

"*Aiya*, that's obvious, you idiot," Luyan hissed.

Willow jabbed at her with her elbow, trying to hush her. The others watched them approach, and Willow saw Yunkun, Shu's cousin who threw the ball at them. He sat with his head down, hair covering his face as he sheepishly ignored them. Another boy and two girls were also there, eyes trained on them.

Shu met them halfway and escorted them to sit by the fire.

"I can't just sit on the damp ground," Luyan said, putting her hands on her hips and staring at the ground like it was a swamp instead of a fairly clean hillside.

Willow pretended not to see the way the others looked at each other and smiled when Shu pulled the end of his scarf until it came loose from his neck. He folded it in half, and then draped it over a small spot on the hill, beckoning Luyan to sit on it. When she did, Willow breathed a silent sigh of relief that she hadn't embarrassed him with a refusal.

Shu dragged a Styrofoam box closer and sat next to them. He

pulled out two cans of beer, handing them out. Willow took them and gave one to Luyan, then set the other at her feet. She wasn't drinking—but she didn't want to make a big deal of it.

With their arrival, an air of awkwardness filled the air, making Willow remember again why she felt so uncomfortable with teenagers, even though she was probably the youngest there. Couldn't they just act mature instead of like elementary-aged children? She suddenly wished she were anywhere but there. Of course, it fell on her to try to make conversation. Either that or Luyan was going to scold her all the way home.

"So," Willow started, fumbling for something—anything—to break the ice. "Do you all live around here?"

She looked around to find everyone staring at her as if she'd grown horns. Finally, Shu cleared his throat. "*Dui*, w-w-we're all from this village."

Luyan laughed but cut it off when Willow elbowed her in the side.

He continued, seeming to shudder as he pointed at a boy on the other side of the fire, then kept pointing as he made the circle. "Luyan, you probably remember my cousin, Yunkun. And that's Xiao Niu, th-then Shaylin. They were in our class too."

Luyan mumbled a short hello to them, and they smiled back at her. Willow wondered if they were starstruck. Not that Luyan was a star—but in their eyes, who knew? She was the girl who'd gone away to the big city and had been featured as a model in magazines.

Willow watched them as they studied Luyan.

Xiao Niu was interesting to look at. Willow noticed her hair was a stylish, short cut feathered around her shoulders. She wore a clean, black-and-white checkered coat with a red scarf draped artfully around her neck. While the others wore cotton or wool gloves, hers looked to be a soft leather. Willow also saw she had a small hoop pierced through the side of her nostril, a surprising accessory for someone from a small village. Her attitude was somewhat superior—*though not as much as*

Luyan's, Willow thought with a small smile she hid quickly. The girl examined every inch of Luyan, a suspicious look in her eyes.

A quick glance at the girl called Shaylin gave Willow a bit of a warmer feeling. So far, she was taking small peeks at Luyan, trying to be inconspicuous. She wasn't nearly as trendy as her friend was, though she was prettier in a simple, clean sort of way. She wore her hair long, and the rosiness in her cheeks almost made her look girlish. Willow could see she was at least sixteen or more, but could've passed for younger in another setting. Her coat and shoes looked much more worn than her friend's, and Willow wondered what brought the two together. Then she looked at Luyan and knew sometimes, fate just worked in strange ways.

Luyan took a short sip of the beer, and then wrinkled her nose. "Is this all you have?"

The girls laughed when Shu nodded, and then they all got quiet again.

Willow looked around and silently said all their names as she examined each face. She didn't want to embarrass herself by forgetting. *Stuttering Shu. The bully Yunkun. Nose ring Niu, and Shy Shaylin.*

That left only one person yet to be introduced. Sitting taller than the others, the last boy—or was he considered a man?—quietly glared out at them from under the bill of his Mao-style hat. Even in the dim light, Willow could see his dark eyes glitter ominously. He could've been handsome, maybe, if he hadn't looked so dangerous and sulky. Willow wondered why Shu didn't introduce him. Come to think of it—Shu had also neglected to tell his friends what her and Luyan's names were. Willow cut him some slack. She knew he was nervous.

"As you all know, this is Luyan." She waved her hand at Luyan. "And I'm Willow, her friend from Beijing."

Most of them all mumbled some sort of lame greeting and went back to swigging their beer.

Nose-ring girl leaned over and whispered something to the girl

63

called Shaylin, getting a nod in return. Then she looked at Willow. "So, are you a model too?"

Willow shook her head. "No way. I'm the furthest thing from a model you'll ever see." She didn't mention her one foray into modeling—the mall box she'd been on display inside of—an event she'd like to erase from her memory.

Luyan laughed. "Willow thinks I'm selling my soul because people pay to have my face or body advertise their products."

"I do not," Willow said. "I just don't want any part of it for myself. You can do whatever you want, if it makes you happy."

"Not everyone has *the look* and can do what I do," Luyan said, her voice dripping with sarcasm.

Willow shrugged. She wouldn't argue the point—she knew she wasn't pretty enough, even though Luyan must have forgotten she herself had claimed Willow was beautiful enough to model or be an escort for her uncle. But that was just talk—she knew she didn't have a face that would captivate anyone for any reason.

Niu watched them for a moment, a satisfied smirk on her face at their arguing, and then she looked at Luyan. "Remember that time you sang on stage at our sixth year graduation?"

Luyan returned her look but didn't answer right away. Willow sensed some sort of silent war between them.

"Yes, I remember," Luyan finally answered, her voice slow and holding a hint of a warning that Willow had heard before.

Niu cackled with mean laughter, and Willow turned to Luyan. "What? What happened?"

Luyan shrugged. "My knees locked and at the end of the song, I fainted."

Willow sighed. These kids didn't know who they were messing with. Luyan would chew them up and spit them out. She fumbled to think of the name of the last magazine Luyan was featured in, but she came up empty. She looked to Shu, hoping he'd say something to smooth it over. Instead, Shaylin spoke up.

"It's okay, Luyan. You sang it beautifully. That's all that counts," she said.

Crisis averted. Willow knew the main reason Luyan had agreed to come was to be able to brag about her success as a model and escort to the wealthy. Willow suddenly wanted to help her out, yet obviously, neither she nor Luyan had thought of a way to bring it into the conversation without sounding too arrogant.

Willow was grateful at least someone had sense enough to divert Luyan's mood. She looked at the girl and noticed Shaylin didn't have a beer. Instead, her hands were wrapped around a steaming cup. Judging from the color of it, it came from the top of the fluorescent yellow thermos at her feet. Willow wondered what it was and wished for anything warm to sip on. When she looked up, Shaylin was looking at her.

"I've got green tea," she said, holding out her cup as an offering.

Willow slid closer to her, taking the cup. She tipped it, letting the warm liquid roll down her throat. It was delicious, and she felt the heat all the way to her feet. Grateful didn't even begin to describe what she felt. "*Xie xie*," she said, giving Shaylin a smile when she handed the cup back to her.

"No problem. I don't like beer, either."

Niu snorted beside the girl. "Only lately, Shaylin. I remember not so many months ago when we spent an evening up here... and you were more than willing to share a few beers."

Shaylin dropped her head. Willow knew if the light were better, she'd see the girl blushing scarlet. She felt bad for her, though she didn't know what the big deal was.

"Leave her alone," the dark, dangerous boy said.

"I'm not doing anything, Daming, just stating a fact. And don't tell me what to do. You don't have power over me," Niu returned and laughed.

So that's his name. Dangerous Daming. And whoa—he can speak, Willow thought to herself as she watched the three of them bicker back and forth.

"And you all are friends?" Luyan asked, a sarcastic edge to her voice.

Niu laughed—a sound that came out mean and sarcastic. "Some of us are friends, but some of us are married."

"Married?" Willow said.

"So it's true," Luyan said, her voice triumphant. She turned to Shaylin. "I heard you got married. But I didn't know you married *him.*" She nodded toward Daming.

"I'm not married yet," Shaylin said.

"Might as well say you are—it's not like you have a choice," Niu said, snickering. "Her father walked them up to the magistrate's office himself to get the marriage permit. They caused quite a village ruckus—you know how they are, the elders don't expect anyone our age to pick our own boyfriends. They act as though we're still living in Old China and need a matchmaker for every marriage proposal. I'm surprised we don't have a bunch of mindless, foot-bound concubines hobbling around here."

Willow studied Shaylin's face and could've sworn that even in the dark, it turned a deep crimson. It was hard to believe such a young, quiet girl was to be married. And they didn't act engaged—though who was she to know how someone should act? But these two—they acted more like strangers than two people in love.

"How old are you?" she asked Shaylin.

"Nineteen," Shaylin said.

"At least you'll get a wedding," Shu said. "That's more than my aunt got last year when she was in your shoes."

"Shu, go over there with the boys. This is women's talk," Niu hissed at him.

He didn't move. If anything, he looked even more interested in their conversation before he blurted out more. "My brother's married now, too. When he figured out who he wanted to marry, they weren't even allowed to see each other or be alone until they were engaged. Only when the wedding plans were in place could he even take her to a movie or a walk around the village."

"What if once they started spending time together, they'd have decided they didn't like each other?" Willow asked. She hadn't been around a lot of family dynamics, but still it surprised her in this modern day that such traditional practices were still followed. Village life never ceased to amaze her.

"He could've broken off the engagement. It wouldn't have been good, but it's allowed in certain circumstances. They aren't so strict with me, since I'm the little brother. I can see who I want when I want, now that the precious future of *elder brother* is secured."

Willow thought he sounded bitter. If he were smart, he'd be thankful he wasn't pushed into conforming to the traditions his brother was. Shu had his freedom! His brother—maybe not so much. Not to mention the pressure the poor guy would be under to provide for his parents when they became too feeble to work.

"Old ways," Luyan muttered. "My grandmother had never even seen her husband until the day of their wedding. Back then, an unmarried girl wasn't even allowed to look at a man. How ridiculous is that?"

Willow could hear snippets of the boy's conversation on the other side of the fire. Yunkun was busy talking to Daming about a basketball game being held in Beijing, and the possibility of it being piped in through cable television to the village.

The girls all sat silent. Willow wondered if Shaylin would go to live in her mother-in-law's house, as tradition usually required. She

67

felt sorry for the girl, but she wasn't sure why. Something wasn't right, though. She could feel that much.

"So do you work?" Willow asked, the question going out to whoever wanted to answer.

"Daming drives a delivery truck back and forth between villages, and I'm a teacher's assistant," Shaylin said.

"Not a real one," Niu said.

"What does she mean—not real?" Willow asked, taking the opportunity to speak just to Shaylin as Luyan engaged Niu in a debate about the village school system and its worth.

"Well, I don't get paid. Not yet. Our village won't officially accept me because I don't have my certificate. But I don't care; I love working with the kids."

"Is it a real school?" Willow asked. She noticed Daming was listening to the conversation, and the deepened scowl on his face showed he wasn't pleased.

Shaylin laughed. "Yes, it's a real school. It's nothing fancy, but it is in a building. We have a chalkboard and even some books. For the last few years, we've had an anonymous benefactor who has donated everything we need to do our job—well, except my salary. But the important thing is the children still get an education."

Willow took in her words, but her mind was on her old school and the way she and Kai had never been accepted by the crowd, always branded as orphans. At least in the village school, it sounded like they were all treated equally.

"My wedding is in a few weeks, Luyan. Will you still be here?" Shaylin asked quietly when the conversation between the other two girls had faded to silence.

Willow felt Luyan shrug in the dark.

"What will that be like?" Willow asked, suddenly curious about a village wedding compared to the fancy ones put on in the city.

"You've never been to a wedding?" Shu asked, his voice incredulous.

"Not in a village. Well, not in the city either, but I've seen a few on television."

"So different," Niu said, her voice laced with sarcasm. "Around here, they make a bigger deal, but spend less money."

"Please, can we talk about something else? I don't want to get into the details," Shaylin said in a whisper, looking over at, and then quickly away from the boys who sat on the other side. "But Luyan and Willow, you're both invited as my guests if you're still around."

"Yeah, Willow, you should see at least one village wedding in your life. It's kind of cool," Shu said.

Shaylin shifted uncomfortably again.

"Now, let's change the subject and talk about something else," Willow said. She was rewarded with a grateful smile from Shaylin.

"Like what?" Niu countered. "It's getting too cold out here. I might just go on home. I thought we were coming to hear all about Luyan's glamorous life, and here we sit still talking about the same boring news we talk about every day."

"Fine with me if you want to go home," Luyan icily agreed. "I'm not your puppet, talking and dancing for your entertainment."

The tension between the two of them was palpable. Willow felt a sweat rise on the back of her neck, despite the cold temperatures. Things weren't going as she'd hoped. "We could tell ghost stories," she offered. The atmosphere was getting tense, but she hoped if they stayed long enough, the others would warm up to Luyan.

That got a rise out of them, and the boys snickered.

"What about the crazy lady who lives alone in the woods?" Niu said, and the light from her nose ring glittered against the backdrop of the fire.

"She's not a ghost, dummy. She's real, and she's a witch doctor," Shaylin said so quietly Willow almost didn't hear her.

Willow perked up. She wondered if they were talking about the woman she'd seen—the one with the cats. How many other women lived alone in the woods? It had to be her. Even though from afar, she hadn't looked like what Willow though a witch might look.

"Is she crazy? Why does she live in the woods?" she asked, hoping no one picked up on just how interested she was. Something told her not to tell them she'd possibly seen the woman with her own eyes.

Shu fidgeted about nervously as the others watched, looking at him to answer. Finally, he settled back with another beer. "No one really knows where she lives. We only know she walked out on her family one day and disappeared in the woods. The rest is just a tale that's been building over the last fifteen years."

Luyan stood suddenly. "I'm ready to go for real now, Willow."

Willow looked from her to the others, wondering what they were all not saying. Even Shaylin looked guilty—as if she held a secret. But Willow didn't care how much they scared her, she was going to go back out there and find her ring.

"Fine, let's go," she agreed, using her hands to wipe off the back of her jeans. She looked up just in time to see Daming staring at her before he dropped his gaze back to the ground.

She felt a prickle of unease crawl up her spine as she followed Luyan away from the others.

Kai

K AI WAITED OUTSIDE THE FANCY building. Johnny had told him he'd be right back, and then they'd head out for another family session. Johnny's schedule was packed these days and he wanted Kai at every shoot, depending on him to be the buffer between what he felt were irritating human beings and his own inflated self. Johnny didn't care for doing the family shoots, but they were easy and provided additional monthly income to supplement the widely spaced artistic gigs he preferred. He'd even mentioned that morning he had something big brewing and might let Kai take on some of the less important shoots without him. Kai had to admit, it made him nervous, but still—he'd love to finally be behind the camera. He hoped it wasn't empty promises.

He looked at his watch. Johnny had been up there for almost an hour and was going to make them late for the shoot, which would in turn make Kai late for dinner and reading with Rosi. He had to admit, she'd surprised him. She was really coming along in her reading and writing skills, and she didn't let anything get in the way of her scheduled lessons. And helping her was improving his own reading skills more than any amount of schooling had. Together, they made a good team, and Rosi would be upset if he arrived too late. He patted his pocket, making sure the socks were still there. He'd seen them hanging in the window and knew Rosi would be ecstatic over them, especially since they were pink with the Chinese Idol emblem stamped on them.

He watched another pack of bicyclers and electric scooters zoom by, wishing again for some transportation of his own. Everywhere he went, he had to walk—unless he wasted valuable coins on the bus, and that meant he needed more time to get around. But until he could make some real money, he was destined to keep walking.

He checked his watch again. *Damn it!* How Johnny conveyed time was beyond Kai—he always showed up much later than he promised. Kai knew he was probably more obsessed with being on time and organized than most, so he'd try to be more patient.

Kai watched the people walking up and down the sidewalks, all engrossed in their own little slices of life. Where were they all going? What were the burdens they bared? Did everyone—or anyone—feel as isolated and alone as he did?

But at least he still had Rosi and through her, the semblance of a few people who cared. When fifteen more minutes went by, he thought about how disappointed in him Mama Su and Lao Qu would be if he missed dinner. He finally lost patience and went to the mirrored double doors. He tested one and when it wasn't locked, he entered the building.

The first floor was an area set up as a fancy lobby. A few people walked by, but no one appeared to be in charge. *What was this building?* He looked down at his clothes, for once grateful of the makeover and black outfit Luyan had supplied him months before. It had been a lesson in humbleness the day she'd declared he needed a new look, but at least when he was working, he had something to wear that didn't make him look homeless. And he had to admit, he liked the way women looked at him when he was wearing what he considered his *photographer clothes*.

Remembering Johnny said he was going up, Kai headed for the

elevator. Maybe inside it would be a listing of what was on each floor—giving him a clue to where Johnny was.

He hit the up button, and the doors chimed and opened. Kai stepped in, and the doors closed behind him. On the list, for the seventh floor, was a listing for the Bliss Production Agency. Kai pushed the button beside it, sure now it was where he'd find Johnny. He'd heard of Bliss and knew they were the top agency that photographers tried to get into to push their work out to the world.

The elevator rose quickly—too quickly for Kai to think up a reason for following Johnny into the building. The man didn't like to be disobeyed, and since he considered Kai his subordinate, Kai couldn't help but feel nervous. Then he thought of Rosi and his confidence returned. More than anyone, he didn't want to let her down and keep her waiting. So if Johnny got mad, Kai would just have to tell him he was helping him with his time management.

The doors opened, and Kai stepped out to a hallway lined with enlarged photos. A door at the end had Bliss Agency written in Chinese characters over the top. *So this was where the best Beijing photographers brought their work,* he thought. The first photo he came to was a stark black and white, portraying an emaciated man in a diner, sleeping with his head resting on his tattoo-lined arms—an expression of utter peace on his face. The photo evoked sympathy but also a curiosity about the man and his story. Kai had to admit, it was good. *Really good.* He felt envy stirring, and a hope that one day, he'd be able to make something just as startling and worthy of a place on a wall such as the one before him.

Slowly, he walked the hall, stopping at several more photographs to study them, noting the way the lighting was used or the subject was posed—*or not posed* in some circumstances when it was obviously a moment caught in action. He stopped at one where the depth of field was used to create a sense that the model was floating, and he noted it for a future shoot.

Just before he arrived at the doors, a glass-enclosed display case caught his eye on the opposite side of the hall. Above it, the sign read, "*Let Us Carry Your Karma*". Below those words, the agency slogan said something about representing photographers and what they were about, not the other way around. *Good concept*, thought Kai, especially since he'd heard that many agencies focused on building their own notoriety first, to the detriment of the actual photographer supplying the art.

He approached the case, knowing somehow it was the place of honor for the agency's current best work. He couldn't wait to see what it held.

The photo was huge—enlarged at an epic proportion to capture the magic of the moment. A glimpse of a red scarf wrapped around the slender neck of a young woman was the first thing that registered before shock stopped him in his tracks.

The young woman depicted was Willow.

He felt his breath catch, and a wave of dizziness hit him. Not only was the photo definitely of Willow—the one person in the world he had felt the closest to and who he thought had felt the same—but it was the photo he'd taken himself the night months before when Willow had given him her first kiss. He looked closer, hoping he was wrong and perhaps Johnny had actually taken another photo of her that same night, with the same pose of her looking out over the wall. But no, it was Kai's photograph. In it, he had captured the hauntingly sad look when she had thought she was alone and was vulnerable enough to let down her guard. There was no denying it—it was the moment Kai had captured. Yet, the characters that made up Johnny's name were scrawled in the corner, giving him full credit for a photograph that wasn't even his to claim.

He suddenly felt sick to his stomach. Even if the photo *was* taken with Johnny's camera, Kai felt it was a low blow to steal it as his own. His nails digging into his palms made him realize how hard he was clenching his fists. Cold anger—dark and heavy—emanated from him like a dark cloud. He had to get out of there. He needed to think. To calm down.

Then another thought hit him. If he recognized the photo for the moment it was, Willow would too. And knowing her as he did, he was sure she would be hurt and embarrassed. Her privacy—something she'd always guarded closely—had been compromised. She would hate him if she found out. He turned around, relieved to see the hall still empty. He needed to get moving for if he didn't walk away, someone was going to get hurt.

As he backed up, about to turn to go back to the elevator, he saw the photo had been named. Centered in a tiny piece of red velvet background was the characters to make up the title given to the photo he had created—the photo Willow didn't even know existed—it read *Face of The Forgotten*.

Willow

WILLOW SMILED BEHIND HER CUP of tea as she watched Luyan wiggle in her seat uncomfortably. While Luyan had the ability to intimidate her own parents, she looked unable to manipulate her grandmother. Luyan had started the visit out with her usual icy tone, but her grandmother was having none of it. The old lady had a knack for putting her granddaughter in her place with just one raise of her bushy eyebrow.

"*Dui bu qi*," Luyan muttered an apology after her grandmother stopped her rant about the walk through the rain to make the ordered visit. They'd been summoned, was what Luyan was so irritated at, though Willow thought it sweet the woman made time to see her only granddaughter.

"Don't apologize; just keep a civil tongue in your head. Tell me, have you been treating your mother better?" She walked to the table, plucked a small piece of fruit from the platter, and popped it into her mouth.

"I treat her just fine," Luyan said, rolling her eyes.

Willow found Luyan's grandmother staring at her as if waiting on affirmation. "They have been better around each other, I've noticed," Willow said.

Luyan shot her a grateful look and bumped her knee under the table.

"You'd better be. You have no idea the sacrifice she's paid for you and keeps on paying. And was that your uncle's driver I saw coming through town a few days ago?" the old woman asked, turning back to Luyan as she settled herself in a chair on the other side of the table.

That perked Willow's attention. Had the driver come with a letter from Rosi or Kai? Or news? What would he have been doing there?

"Not that I know of," Luyan said, looking nervously at Willow.

Willow knew that look, and it meant Luyan was lying. She wondered when the driver came and realized it must have been during one of her hikes up the hill behind the house.

"Well, I'm here to tell, I know it was him. Who else comes driving a fancy car like that up into these muddy roads? It's a statement, that's what it is. Pure bragging meant for all of us to see," the grandmother said saucily.

Luyan stared down into her cup, but the old woman wasn't ready to let her off the hook yet. "So why are you trying to hide it? You going back to the city, girl?"

"Luyan, was it him? Is everything okay with Kai and Rosi? Did he bring mail?" Willow asked.

Luyan let out a long frustrated sigh. "*Hao le*, it was him and no, he wasn't coming to take me back to Beijing, and yes, everything is fine with Kai and Rosi. Now—can I just enjoy the tea?"

"No letters?" Willow asked, a sinking feeling coming over her.

"*Bushi.*"

Luyan didn't meet her eyes when she answered no. Willow was going to have a long talk with her on their walk back home, and she was also going to let her know what she felt about her not telling her of the driver's visit. If she'd have known, she could've sent another letter to Kai—or even to Rosi. She felt her temper rising, but now wasn't the time to get her to spill the truth. The old woman had sent word for

77

them to visit, and while Willow had been excited about coming, just for a break in routine, she couldn't wait to get out of there now.

"So since you have no plans to go back to the city in the next few weeks, I suppose you two will be taking part in the village festivities?" The old woman sucked on the fruit, making loud, smacking noises.

"If you mean Shaylin's wedding, then yes, we'll be here," Luyan said, her voice bored. "I'm sure it will be a thrilling event."

Willow could tell Luyan knew she'd been caught in lie. She wasn't even making eye contact across the table.

The old woman got up and went to the counter that served as a small kitchen area. She'd declared because of the rain, they'd stay in the house, giving Willow more time to look around. Nothing had changed, but it was still interesting to her to see how families lived—a cozy dwelling that was such a contrast to institutional living. Simple things she'd dreamed of for years.

"You know that girl's pregnant, don't you?" Luyan's grandmother declared, surprising Willow out of her deep thinking.

"Pregnant?" Willow said, echoing the old woman.

Luyan shrugged. "Yeah, I knew it. It's not a big deal, Nainai. Tell me, why do you obsess over who is pregnant and who isn't? Don't you have anything else to do?"

Willow thought that was rude and waited for the old woman to lash out at her granddaughter again for being sassy. Instead, she looked out toward the window, a faraway look in her eyes.

"I hope she filled out a birth permit. It has to be completed in the first four months and her mother better have her following the official steps or there'll be trouble," the old woman said in one long breath.

"You have to have a permit to be pregnant?" Willow asked.

The old woman jerked her head back to them. "Of course you do. What planet have you been living on? The permit will put her on the radar of the family planning officers for this province. They'll monitor her so she doesn't terminate her pregnancy if she finds out it's a girl."

Willow knew of that problem firsthand. Most of the healthy girls in the orphanage had only one plausible reason for being there, and that was their gender.

"She can still terminate, if she really wants to," Luyan said.

"You're right. Laws or not, corruption is rampant, even in the healthcare segment. Yet, I doubt if that girl or her soon-to-be husband has the kind of money they'd need for an illegal ultrasound or for any *invasive medical procedure*."

Willow listened to them talk so nonchalantly about ending a life—a human life, as if it was simply a discussion about the weather. They wouldn't even call it what it was—an abortion. *Aborting life.* Their indifference was surreal. Or maybe she was just too sensitive? She didn't know, but it made her sick at her stomach. Finally, she couldn't keep it in any longer.

"That's repulsive! And why can't these young parents see that with all these little girls dying before they have a chance to live, it's going to make a terrible time in our country? In twenty years or so," now she was quoting from something Kai had told her, "China's going to have a huge problem on their hands with abduction and trafficking because there won't be enough women to go around... because we are killing our women!"

Both Luyan and her grandmother had frozen, watching with mouths open as Willow ranted. Finally, the grandmother came around and patted her on the back.

"Calm yourself, child. I'm sure they'll have a boy child and everything will be fine."

Willow didn't answer her. If that was how the women of the village felt, then nothing could be fine.

Luyan snorted. "I'm sure it won't, Nainai. Nothing has changed. Even the couples who keep their girl babies still believe having a boy is considered a big happiness and having a girl is a small happiness."

The old woman went back to her chair and sat down. "Things *are* changing, girls. Little by little, it's getting better. Back when I was first married, it was a lot worse, believe me."

Willow finally trusted herself to speak without anger. "How so?"

"First of all, even though my own parents loved me, they thought of me as a wasted mouth under their roof. I was a girl—unable to do heavy work on their land and unable to support them in the future, so I was considered a commodity to be used for them to get one step ahead," Nainai said, and then pointed at Luyan. "When I was much younger than you, my father sold me off to your grandfather's family for less than the cost of a pig. I didn't accept my fate gracefully—that much I can admit now."

"What did you do?" Willow asked.

"I acted up. But it was hard to move in with my husband's family and call his parents Mama and Baba. I was grieving for my own parents, but when I said those vows, as custom goes, I became just a relative to them and no longer a daughter. It took a long time for me to adjust, especially considering I was the lowest member of the family. In all arguments or decisions, I had no say, until I became pregnant, at least."

"They treated you badly?" Willow asked. Across from her, Luyan looked bored.

The woman shrugged. "There's a saying among men that is still used in the countryside, even today. "*Marrying a woman is like buying a horse. I can ride you and beat you any time I like.*'"

"Ye Ye beat you?" Luyan asked, her eyes wide with disbelief.

"He liked to threaten he would, but no, he did not. It was your great-grandmother. My mother-in-law ruled that house. Back then, it was customary for the mother-in-law to maintain displeasure for her new daughter up until they became pregnant, and she was all about following customs. The way she managed that was with a strap across my back, always telling me to move faster, to do more. I worked from sunup to well past sundown, keeping house, cooking, and even working in the fields when needed. But it was never enough. When I first knew I was going to have a baby, I was more thrilled to tell her than my own husband."

"Then did the beatings stop?" Willow asked.

The old woman looked lost in thought again, and Willow could just imagine her as a young new bride, nervous and afraid, living among strangers who took her for granted and treated her as a slave. She didn't know how she'd have taken living a life like that. She was so glad to have been born in modern China.

"Things changed, right?" Luyan said.

Nainai shrugged. "They did during each pregnancy. But I never did present them an heir. My mother-in-law used to tell me my resistance to join their family sealed my fate, and I was being punished by being only able to produce daughters. Until their dying day, my new parents never forgave me and never let me forget it."

Luyan slapped her hand down on the table. "They made your life hell, didn't they?"

"Sometimes, yes. But it wasn't too bad. You see, my mother-in-law had deformed feet from having them bound when she was six years old. Back in her day, if you had big feet, you were not only ridiculed, but your chances at making a good marriage were next to nothing. Her feet were only four inches long! She hobbled around, always looking as if she was in a faint as she went from one doorway to another, or from chair to chair. The older she got, the more difficult it was for her to get around."

Willow winced.

The old woman reached up and pinched her own nose. "And oh, the smell. Once her silk shoes were untied, they literally had to be peeled off. Mind you—it was putrid. Years of flesh left to rot gave her feet a stench of death and when I joined the family, it was my job to wash and massage them."

Luyan wrinkled her nose. "I wouldn't have done it. They could've beaten me all they wanted; I wouldn't touch any twisted, old, putrid feet."

Her grandmother nodded. "That's what I thought for the first year, too, Luyan. But you know what? Despite the beatings and cross words that woman had for me, I began to have a fondness for her."

Willow listened, captivated by her words.

Nainai continued. "The fondness was surprisingly started by pity, for I learned she had led an even worse life than me when she'd been married off to a stranger. Your grandfather's baba wasn't a kind man, Luyan. He was a tyrant to his family, and they kept their mouths shut and took it. My mother-in-law simmered for decades, but all that bitterness over her abuse for so many years had to come out some time. It was just unlucky I was the one who married into the family and gave her a whipping post for her pent-up frustrations. I always had hope, though, that one day I'd produce a son. Then, everything would be different. For then, I would have had a voice."

"That's so sad," Willow said.

"And pathetic." Luyan shook her head, a look of disgust across her face.

"Luyan, be respectful. That was her life," Willow hissed.

"Oh, and I was lucky. If I had been around when those feet had first been bound, I'd have dealt with pus and sores. But when I came along, it was simply deformed flesh I had to touch, and by the time she died, I was able to do it with a gentleness and compassion I never knew I possessed."

They sat in silence for a few minutes, all of them lost in thought, or at a loss for words.

"Nainai, we've got to get going," Luyan said, her voice finally solemn and respectful.

Her grandmother slowly stood and walked to the door, opening it for them. Just as they walked through, she told them to wait. Willow stopped and turned, her arm on Luyan's to stop her too.

They watched a small smile play across the woman's lips before she looked at both of them and sighed. "I miss her now. When she was on her deathbed, she only wanted me to be near her. Do you understand what I'm saying? It wasn't her son she called for—it was *me*. That's when I knew I had earned something from her. If not her love, then at least her respect. And that, dear girls, is something hard for a woman of old China to accomplish. Her final gesture of acceptance made it all worthwhile in the end."

She closed the door softly in their faces, before they even had a chance to bid her goodbye.

Willow

I T WAS ANOTHER WEEK BEFORE Willow finally found a time to sneak back into the woods—a long week full of tedious catering to Luyan, all the while working hard to bridge the gap between the girl and her parents. She'd spent many nights talking for hours to Luyan about her childhood, forcing her to dredge up memories she'd forgotten, forcing her to recognize how she'd been treated well.

During the day, she encouraged interaction between them all as a family, organizing card games and mahjong, refusing to take no for an answer. It was exhausting, and they didn't always get along. Sometimes, Luyan exploded with irritation at the grievances she felt her parents had done against her, but that she wouldn't talk about. Instead, she ranted about village life, how she missed Beijing, and moaned about her uncle refusing to allow her to return.

Finally, after a particularly stressful evening, it got to Willow again, filling her with an unrestrainable urge to escape and find the only thing she had of her mother. She'd grabbed her bag and left the house with her mind only on the ring, but she had to admit her curiosity was piqued as she found herself taking the same overgrown path to where she'd first seen the woman and the cats.

Halfway there, she stopped to get her breath. She must've been out of it the first time she'd come, because she sure didn't remember it being so deep into the thick grove of trees. Exhausted, she squatted against the base of an old tree and thought about the conversation she'd overheard that morning. Luyan's parents were discussing their financial woes when their voices carried over and into the storage room where she slept. She still wasn't sure why—with all of Luyan's help she'd claimed to have given them—they didn't seem to have much, but every morning, they both left to help with the family store… so where was their money? They were good people, that much was clear, and she wished she could do something to help them.

So far, Luyan hadn't picked up on any troubles, or if she had, she didn't mention it. Willow didn't think she'd care even if she did know. Her mind was on one thing only—getting herself back to her own opulent lifestyle in Beijing. Willow was a bit anxious too, as she was feeling more and more worried about Rosi and Kai as the days went on with no response to her letters. But from the messages delivered by the uncle's driver, Luyan's uncle didn't feel she'd learned her lesson yet. He was still refusing to bring her back.

Willow stood and continued up the steep slope. Just as before, the trees and the privacy they provided made her relax, giving her a measure of peace she didn't feel in the house she'd left behind. Maybe the woman wasn't so crazy, after all. Just maybe she'd found the secret to living a stress-free life—just hide away from civilization. Willow thought it sounded enticing, even if only for a little while.

When she felt like she'd have to stop again, she spotted the small plot of land and the cat house in the tree over it. She didn't see the cats, or the owner, and felt a small burst of disappointment.

Determined not to waste a moment, she hurried over. If she found the ring in enough time, she'd decided to use the quiet spot to pen another letter to Kai. She hadn't sent the last one, in rebelliousness of his own silence, but she still found herself wanting to spill everything about her life to the one person she'd always confided in. Even if all

85

the letters did were collect dust in her bag, at least it felt good to write them.

She'd barely started looking in the brush and leaves at the base of the tree when she heard a twig break behind her. When she looked over her shoulder, she gasped to find the woman standing over her, only a foot away.

She scrambled upright, dropping her bag from her shoulder in her haste to put distance between herself and the woman who'd seemed to appear out of nowhere. "Wh-what are you doing here?" she barked out.

The woman smiled serenely at her. "No, what are *you* doing here? This is my home. You, child, are the trespasser."

Willow looked around, and then back at the woman. "What home? I don't see a house." She wasn't about to tell her about the ring. She backed up several paces, the thoughts of the other kids calling her crazy swirling in her mind. But ironically, up close, she didn't look crazy or even witchy—she just looked tired.

"You don't see air, either, but you believe it's there, right?" the woman answered calmly.

Willow stared at her, wondering what kind of riddle she wove. She had half expected to see some sort of hideous scar or other physical reason on the woman—something to explain her isolation. But she was rather pretty. The silver strands shining through the black tresses of her long braid contradicted the woman's age as Willow would have guessed it if she were judging by her smooth, unwrinkled skin. But still, she had to be at least in her forties, and what would someone that age be doing walking around alone in an area too far from help if needed?

"Who are you?" Willow asked.

The woman hesitated, and then took a seat beneath the gnarled old tree. She patted the ground beside her, where the imprint from where Willow had sat still remained intact. "Would you like some company?" she asked, ignoring Willow's question.

So she didn't want to give her name yet. Willow could understand that. She was just some girl who'd walked into the woods. She sat down, but kept some distance between them in case she needed to bolt.

"Are those your cats?" As they'd talked, two of the white cats had climbed out of the treehouse and were winding their way around the woman's legs. When she sat, they fought for space in her lap.

"*Dui*, this is *Xiao Miao* and this is *Bai Miao*," she said, pointing at first one, and then the other. "*Da Miao* is around here somewhere, but he's a bit anti-social."

Willow reached out to pet the one called *small cat*, and it arched its back, burrowing its head under Willow's hand. The one called *white cat* took advantage of the first one's inattention and moved in, taking up more of the woman's lap. As Willow stroked the cat, she eyed the ground around them, looking for a glint of anything to lead her to her ring.

"So you live out here…" Willow's eyes wandered to the trees that seemed to stand guard around the woman before looking back again. "Can I ask why?"

The woman laughed—a soft, musical sound that made her cats arch their backs even more. "Sure, you can ask. But I don't know if I have the answer for you. First, you tell me—why have you stayed away so long since returning to Lingshui?"

Willow was taken aback. "Returning?"

The woman nodded. "Yes, returning. Your mother has just about worried herself sick over you and has prayed you'd eventually want to come home to stay. I'm just surprised you found me out here."

Realization flooded over Willow. The woman thought she was Luyan. Easy mistake—they were the same size and even looked similar.

"Oh, I'm not Luyan."

The smile disappeared from the woman's face, and quickly she stood. She brushed her hands off on the back of her pants, nervously looking from left to right, and then behind her. "You aren't? Then who are you and why are you out here snooping around?"

Willow stood too. "I wasn't. I mean—I kind of am today. But I wasn't when I came the first time. I was just looking for a place to be alone. I'm Willow—Luyan's friend from Beijing."

The woman stared at her intently, as if peering into her soul to search for the truth. Willow's expression must have convinced her she was telling it because she finally relaxed.

"I saw you before, you know," she said. Willow saw her eyes examine her from head to toe, then come back again to her hands, which were cold and felt brittle.

"You did?" Willow reached down to pet the cats again. She was embarrassed.

"Yes, and I wondered why you left without speaking to me."

"I thought you looked like a private person," Willow said.

"Well, I thought you were my spoiled niece coming to pry. But since you aren't Luyan, I apologize. But you're right; I am a private person. Not many people know I'm up here. And I'd like it to stay that way."

Willow bent and picked up the bag she'd dropped. She heaved the strap over her shoulder. So the reputed witchy-crazy woman was Luyan's aunt. Now she just felt irritation at Luyan for not telling her. She was also embarrassed again to have intruded on the woman's privacy, even if it wasn't planned. It was obvious, from the stories of the years she'd been gone, that she truly didn't want to be around people. She scanned the ground around her one more time, praying under her breath that she'd see her ring so she wouldn't have to come back.

"I'm sorry. I should go."

The woman nodded, and then held a hand up. "*Zaijian*."

For a second, Willow had hoped the woman would stop her from leaving. Maybe even show her where she lived—possibly share some of her story. But though she stared at her so intently it was uncomfortable, she didn't respond with anything other than goodbye.

Willow turned and headed back down the path. She resisted the urge to turn around and look again. If the woman wanted privacy— she'd give it to her.

For now.

The clock in the living room struck midnight, but it was too quiet between them and Willow wasn't sleepy. For months, they'd lain awake together when they'd gone to bed, Luyan talking endlessly, complaining of life in the village and reminiscing about her boyfriend. Usually, Willow would sympathize in just the right amount, but today, she had too much on her mind. Too much for the mind-numbing complaints Luyan threw out. So she didn't respond. Instead, she stared at the dark shadows on the ceiling, one hand making the motion of twisting the ring that was no longer there. She wanted to be alone—left to think about Kai, Rosi, and even Mama Joss. She even thought of the letter from her mother, tucked into the bottom of her bag. At least she still had that, and she longed to hold it again. But all of what she wanted had to do with memories and thoughts she didn't want to share with Luyan.

The silence between them felt huge. From the moonlight shining in through the window, she could barely make out the girl's profile, but she knew Luyan was getting irritated.

"Why aren't you talking?" she asked, giving their quilt a yank.

Willow yanked it back. She was sick of being cold through the night and waking up with no coverings. The longer her time went on with Luyan, the less patience she had with her.

"I don't have anything to say. And you usually do all the talking."

"Well, I would, but you act mad at me for something. What is it?"

"I miss Rosi."

It was true; she'd been thinking about Rosi most of the day. She missed her unbridled joy, and she missed how Rosi lit up whenever Willow walked into a room. She missed being loved like that.

"What about Kai?" Luyan asked, a sarcastic edge to her voice.

Willow hesitated. She didn't want Luyan to know just how much she missed Kai. Her longing for him went past just a simple want for something familiar. He'd always been there for her—a confidant when it came to hashing out the hardships of the orphanage, a supporter when she doubted herself, a friend when she'd shut herself off and had no others. Having Kai jerked from her life was like having an appendage ripped from her body. It hurt.

She wouldn't talk to Luyan about her feelings for him, although she did have some questions. "Luyan, why did your driver come here?"

"To check up on me for my uncle, I suppose. He didn't say."

"And he didn't have any letters for me? No word from Kai? Or Mama Su about Rosi? Nothing?" Willow tried to keep the disbelief out of her voice. She didn't want Luyan to know how much the lack of communication hurt her. Once again, she thought of the possibility of borrowing Luyan's father's phone—of calling the hotel and asking for Rosi or Kai. She knew that fear of being outright rejected by either of them was the main obstacle, but she'd also promised Luyan she wouldn't, at least not until it was time to go back to Beijing. And Willow always kept her promises.

"Nothing official, but he did have some hotel gossip."

"What gossip?" Willow asked. She assumed it was probably nothing she'd be interested in. There was always something going on behind the scenes with the hotel staff—girls in housekeeping fussing with the kitchen crew, groundskeepers failing to show up, and doormen getting angry with hotel patrons. None of it interested Willow because she didn't know any of them anyway.

"Kai and one of the housekeeping girls went on a few dates," Luyan said.

Willow heard the triumph in Luyan's voice just as she felt her stomach drop. Kai was dating? Now she understood why he hadn't answered any of her letters. He didn't care about her anymore. He'd moved on to someone else. But this time, maybe it would be a real girlfriend. She was hurt. Really, really hurt. But she wouldn't let Luyan have the satisfaction of knowing it. She thought fast—trying to find a way to change the subject.

"Tell me more about your aunt, Luyan."

Luyan was quiet for a moment. Then she turned over to face Willow. "Why?"

"I just want to know. You talk and talk about this village, your parents, your uncle, and how you want to get back to Beijing. I just find it weird your aunt is this mysterious person who no one speaks of. I mean—what really happened to her?"

"There's not much to say."

Willow felt a break in her hesitation. "Then say what you know. Is she still married to your uncle?"

Luyan shrugged in the dark. "I guess officially she is, though I don't know for sure. All I know is they had a big falling out a long time ago, and she came back to the village. She's my mom's sister, so she moved back in with her parents for a while. Then my uncle paid her a settlement to stay away, and she disappeared. I don't know where she is now—or if she's even alive or dead."

Willow didn't reply, though she wanted to scream at the girl that her aunt was alive and well and only a half an hour walk up into the woods—all alone save for some spooky cats. But something held her back. She wasn't sure why, but she wanted to protect the woman's privacy from someone as judgmental as Luyan. It was curious she felt so strongly for a stranger, but the woman deserved to keep her secrets close to her, whatever they might be.

Willow

"WHERE DID YOU GO LAST night, Luyan?" Willow's heart beat in her ears. As she was drifting off to sleep the night before, she'd thought Luyan had gotten up to use the outhouse. When she woke that morning, the girl's side of the bed was empty, showing she hadn't returned. Willow had a sinking feeling talk of her aunt made her go snooping around.

"Don't worry about it." Luyan continued to pull the hairbrush through her long hair, a smug smile pasted across her face.

Willow turned away from her and pulled her sleeping gown over her head. She slid into a thermal shirt, and then her sweater. Sitting on the edge of the bed, she pulled her jeans on over her feet and to her knees, then stood to bring them the rest of the way up. She moved methodically, but she could feel her irritation building.

"You know, you aren't allowed to just do anything you want. Sometimes, you need to respect boundaries."

"I'm respectful," Luyan murmured.

"Really? Why don't you just admit it, Luyan? You don't care about anyone but yourself. And to be honest, I'm getting sick of it. I think it's getting time for me to get out of this town." Willow didn't know what had come over her, but she felt ready to explode.

"What exactly is your problem, Willow?" Luyan tossed the brush down on the bed and glared at her.

Willow ignored her question. She put on her shoes, then grabbed her bag and without another glance, left Luyan sitting up staring holes in her back. *Let her wonder*, Willow thought.

Outside their small room, Luyan's parents sat at the table in the kitchen. They both looked up when she appeared.

"Noodles?" Wu Min asked, nodding toward a pot steaming on top of the cookstove.

Willow took a deep breath and tried to erase the tension on her face. Wu Min didn't deserve her wrath. "*Bu xuyao.*" She shook her head, turning down the offer of breakfast. She just wanted out, as far away from Luyan as she could get. She needed to think.

"Is everything okay?" Yilin asked, his eyebrows arched together in a question.

"*Shi de*, it's fine. I'm just going out for the day." She grabbed her jacket from one of the pegs on the wall and burst out of the small house, letting the door slam behind her. She wiggled into the coat as she gasped for breath, struggling to free her lungs of the stale and distasteful feeling of bitterness Luyan had left in her mouth. Something was going on inside her, and she didn't know what. It felt like all of a sudden, living with Luyan and being her companion wasn't possibly worth it. Then she thought of Rosi, remembering the years of rumors that adoption processes took ages. What if Willow left the village, and then Rosi wasn't finalized as Mama Su's daughter somehow? Or what if Kai got kicked out of the hotel and was made homeless again? But why was it all on her? And why did Luyan feel so possessive of her? What was it that made her want Willow with her night and day? Willow walked through the village, her thoughts circling round and round, not making any rhyme or reason, but unable to stop. She was losing it. Luyan was literally driving her crazy. She wished for Kai so suddenly and so strongly that she could almost feel his presence. He'd always been the only one able to calm her, the only one who would let her storm and then bring her down with a soft word or two.

He'd say, *Breathe, Willow, breathe.* Then he'd tell her to think of something peaceful.

So she did. She breathed. Then she thought of her last birthday and how he'd shared his past with her. He'd opened up and told her all about his mother. He'd finally trusted her enough to give her that gift. She felt ashamed she'd up and left without even telling him goodbye. She could just imagine his face when he read her letter. She could even make out the deep furrow between his brows he got when he was upset.

She sighed. Thinking of Kai was making her feel worse now.

So instead, she thought of the woman in the woods. Despite losing her ring, finding her and the cats—and even that peaceful place—had been her one bright spot in months of aggravation. Now she felt herself being pulled that way again.

At the end of the village street, she turned off and backtracked toward Luyan's family house. Just before she approached it, she scooted around the back and headed up into the trees, following the hidden path, hoping she wasn't about to make herself look like an idiot.

She took the hike slower—taking extra moments to give herself time to study the ground beneath her, looking for the ring. And maybe even to give herself time to change her mind. Yet, the closer she got, the calmer she felt. Even if she didn't run into the woman, she was at least finding a way to bring her blood pressure back to normal. The pounding in her ears began to subside, returning to a low hum through her veins.

She ducked to avoid a low-hanging branch and when she reached up to block her face, she found her fingers wrapped in the silky threads of a spider web. Jerking her hand around, she tried to throw off any eight-legged passengers, and when she returned her eyes to the path, there stood the woman.

"Were you bitten?" she asked, her face drawn with worry.

Willow shook her head as she wiped her hands on her jeans. Could her humiliation be any more complete? Now the woman had witnessed her acting like a lunatic, afraid of a little spider web. "I'm fine. I didn't even see the spider."

The woman pointed over her head. When Willow looked up, she saw it dangling from an invisible thread as it floated ominously back and forth. It was rather large, golden brown, and the black stripes on it made it look like no spider Willow had ever seen in the orphanage. She stepped back, covering her mouth, unable to suppress her revulsion.

"Good thing it didn't get you. That's a Golden Earth Tiger spider, and it won't kill you, but it can definitely wreak havoc on a person's body."

Willow crossed her arms and fought through a shiver at the thought of the creature sinking its fangs into her skin. Assuming it had fangs—which she didn't know but didn't want to find out. She was done discussing the spider.

"Yes, good thing." She walked a short piece away from the tree that held the spider, only looking back over her shoulder once to make sure it didn't somehow follow. "Listen, I came up here to say I'm sorry."

The woman walked with her. "Sorry?"

"*Dui*, to apologize. I didn't plan to invade your privacy."

The woman shook her head. "Don't worry, no harm done. That I know about, your presence hasn't brought anyone else up here snooping around. I would know it if it had."

She smiled to soften the words, and Willow knew she wasn't saying it to be spiteful. She was the keeper of the trees—or so it seemed.

"You know, I never caught your name," Willow said.

The woman held her hand out, and Willow grasped it. It was soft, warm, and comforting. They shook.

"It's Hanai. And I'm glad you've stumbled upon my quiet little piece of the world. I wouldn't normally ask this, but would you like to come in for some tea? I could use some company this morning."

Willow still hadn't seen a house or anything resembling a home. She nodded in agreement, realizing it felt good to finally meet someone who might simply want a friend, with no strings attached.

Time seemed to stand still as Willow followed Hanai. They trekked higher into the trees. Around them, the sounds of nature made a comforting backdrop. Yet other than the crunching of dry leaves under their feet, it was quiet around them. Willow listened to the woman's soft voice as she narrated their walk. From the lightness her voice took on, she seemed happiest when she was pointing out different birds and tree species. It was the most interesting thing Willow had experienced from living in the village thus far. She thought of Luyan briefly, and a feeling of disappointment washed over her that the girl was too spoiled to even know what she was missing.

"Did I notice a limp when you walked in?" Hanai asked.

Willow felt herself stiffen. No one ever asked her about her limp. Why did a complete stranger think it was okay to ask such a personal question? One that the answer to might be the very reason her fate had turned on her. "Yes, you did," she answered in a curt tone.

"It's very light—almost not even noticeable," Hanai said softly, not turning around.

Willow was glad she didn't have to look her in the face. "It may not be noticeable to some, but it's always there. A reminder to me."

"For what?"

"To never give up."

They walked on for another moment until Hanai stopped. "Do you know what that tree is?" she asked, pointing to a tall, leafless tree with a wide canopy of branches.

Willow didn't and, actually, living in an institution didn't give her much experience to draw from to recognize one tree from another, but that wasn't something she wanted to share. She shook her head.

"It's a Shantung Maple," Hanai said. "In the summer, the leaves turn yellow, and then fire-dragon red. It's a tough but beautiful old tree—one of my favorites."

Willow didn't want to tell her she wouldn't be around to see it. She hoped to be able to return to Beijing long before summer came around again. Already they were moving in on April, and summer no longer seemed far away.

"I imagine the summer and fall here in the country is something to see," she said.

Hanai nodded. "Oh, it is. We're lucky to have these woods, and when I made a huge change in my life, I came back here and instantly knew I wanted to envelop myself in the peaceful solitude they provided."

"Why do you say you're lucky?"

Hanai glanced behind her quickly, giving Willow a curious look. "Not just me—we're all lucky to have any woods still standing. Most of the forests and trees in China were destroyed a long time ago by Japanese armies invading our lands. And then a huge chunk of what was left intact by them was later destroyed or damaged during the chaos of the Cultural Revolution. Despite the ongoing efforts by the government to replenish our trees, you won't find too many forests."

"That's really sad."

Hanai nodded. "It is. Especially when you've come to love the language of the trees."

"Language?"

Hanai stopped and held her arm out to block Willow from taking another step. "Shh. It's harder to hear when there are so many leaves are on the ground, but if you listen hard, you'll hear them talking."

Willow listened, yet she heard nothing except a few birds. She wondered if perhaps the woman hadn't gone a bit crazy after all. Maybe the solitude of her life had her hearing things that weren't truly there.

"The real language of trees can only be understood when one knows what each tree stands for. The Maple tree represents stability, promise, and practicality. Even though at times it can look fierce, its very presence brings balance to the forest."

She definitely knows a lot about trees, Willow thought as they continued, walking for another fifteen minutes. Finally, they climbed a hill and just on the other side, they came to a small clearing.

Hanai stopped again, looking at Willow expectantly. At first, she didn't see the house, as it was almost completely covered by ivy. She peered closer and there it was, its roof coming to a sharp peak over the small structure as if it had suddenly emerged. The house was encircled by a stone wall extending out on both sides like arms welcoming them in as long-lost friends.

"This is my home," Hanai said.

Willow was captivated. The house, complete with dark green wooden shutters, was what she would call quaint. Rosi would've said it was something out of a fairy tale.

It wasn't a big house—yet didn't look overly small. The house and yard looked cozy and well kept, yet it was obvious Hanai preferred a natural landscape to a pedicured one. The chest-high wall was homemade, built with large stones and mortar, and Willow studied it as Hanai led her around the side to a gate. A fairly large dog with a spotless, golden coat met them and gave a few gruff barks before it was shushed, and Willow was beckoned through.

"You have cats and a dog?" Willow thought that intriguing. She'd never met anyone with so many pets. As she thought further, she realized she'd never met anyone with any pets, period. When she'd been a little girl, she'd wanted a dog, but living where she did, she'd always known it was not an option.

Hanai crouched down and met the dog nose to nose, rubbing its golden ears until Willow could've sworn the happy creature smiled. It was a beautiful animal. Its coat gleamed, and Willow could see it was well taken care of.

"I have two dogs. This one is officially named Taiyang—but I call her Sunny. The other one is being quite lazy right now, I'm sure. He's black as the darkest night, and his name is Moon. I guess you could consider him my sidekick, though both of them are loyal. I've found it's good to have two dogs to take turns on their watch—one is alert as I sleep and the other all day as I work."

Their watch. Willow caught that and wondered what the dogs were watching for. But she supposed if Hanai lived alone, it was a necessary security.

Hanai moved toward the door but paused along the path of cobblestones. She pointed at a sweeping Willow tree that sat near the edge of the house. At least thirty feet tall, the tree was the main focal point of Hanai's place. Even without the beauty of what would be lush green branches in the summer, it still stood tall and proud.

"Out of all the trees in this forest, that one is my favorite," Hanai said.

"It's stunning. I also have a fondness for Willow trees—as you can probably tell by my name," Willow said, feeling awkward for pointing out the obvious.

Hanai looked at the tree, fondness in her eyes. "That is the only tree here I planted myself. I had it shipped in from a well-known nursery in Beijing, and it was only a seedling. In only ten years, she has sprouted to be the majestic lighthouse to my home."

"She?"

"Well, yes. Since I gave her a name when I brought her home—I had to pick a gender. But I can't tell you the name. It's a secret of my soul."

Willow knew the doubtful look she wore was inappropriate, but she was unable to hide her confusion.

Hanai picked up on it right away. "Don't you have any secrets of the soul?"

Willow looked down at her naked finger where the ring should've been and thought of the letter. Only three people knew of it. Herself,

Mama Joss, and her birth mother. She'd never thought of it that way, but yes, the existence of the letter could be considered a secret of her soul.

She nodded.

"The willow tree is symbolic to my life in more ways than one. Each time I see it, I remember that one must be willing to bend to keep from breaking."

Her words made Kai's face come immediately to Willow's mind.

"Here is another important fact to know about the language of trees; since ancient times, the Weeping Willow has represented mourning. In old paintings, you'll notice when it depicts sorrow of any type—in many circumstances, the piece will also feature a Willow tree." Hanai went to the door. She paused in front of a rusty pair of brown shears hung over a small, mounted mirror near the door. She turned and smiled at Willow. "There's so much more to learn about the language of trees. If you decide to stick around, I'll teach you."

Willow nodded, though she had no intention of staying any longer in Lingshui than she possibly had to. She stared at the shears. Hanai was obviously superstitious because the mirror was an old trick to deflect evil and the shears represented cutting off bad luck. Hanai didn't mention them. She pulled a key from her pocket, unlocked the door, and then turned to Willow.

"One more thing before we go in. If kept in too long, secrets of the soul can haunt you and break you down until you shrivel up inside. It's determining which secrets to share that is the complexity of life. But enough serious talk, let's go in for that tea I promised you."

Willow took another sip. She wondered for more than the fifteenth time what exactly Hanai had put in her tea. While she was usually careful who she talked to, for some reason, she felt unusually at ease talking to an almost stranger. Her sense of easiness could have been the comforting setting, as Hanai's house was just as simple and calming as she appeared to be. In the one room they'd come to—the living room—it was clear much care had been taken to bring a sense of peace to whomever dwelled there. Colorful, braided rugs littered the floor, and the humble couch and matching chair was decorated with finely embroidered pillows. A small, cast iron wood stove stood in the corner of the room, a tall pipe extending to the ceiling and out through a hole, and the heat coming from it warmed Willow all the way to her toes.

"So, you grew up in Beijing. Do you have family there?" Hanai asked. In front of her feet, a black dog stood before turning in a complete circle and resettling down to resume its nap. Moon—Hanai had called it when she introduced it to Willow and commanded the dog to allow her in. Willow had only had a moment of fear when the dog had appeared to pause and consider the command, then accepted it and went back to his nap.

"Beijing? Um…" She thought of Kai and Rosi, and then Mama Joss. "Sort of." A visual of Rosi holding out her pinky made her cheeks start to burn with shame. "I mean, yes—I do. I have family there."

Hanai nodded. A pained look crossed her face before it was hidden by the mug she held as she took a long drink before she spoke again. "When will you go back?"

"Good question. I'm just waiting for Luyan to be ready. It could be any day." What she really meant was they were waiting on her uncle to be ready, but she didn't want to give away the details of Luyan's banishment—even though as her aunt, she probably already knew all about it.

"Hmm. I wonder too, when she will be ready." She looked up at Willow. "What exactly does Luyan do in Beijing?"

Get paid to look pretty. That was the first thing that came to Willow's mind. If Luyan wasn't acting as an adornment on some man's arm, then she was gracing the picture windows of clothing stores, or her face was plastered on some random billboard. It was as if she were nothing but an icon of beauty, with a soul no one cared to know. It all seemed so pointless. And what about when her beauty faded? Then where would she be? Willow didn't want to be around when that happened, as she knew Luyan would be even more difficult to handle.

"She models mostly," Willow finally answered, trying to keep her disapproving tone hidden.

"And her uncle. Do you see much of him?" Hanai pulled her legs up into the chair, curling into herself.

Willow had wondered how long it would take for Luyan's uncle to come up. It was inevitable his own wife would be curious about the life he led so separate from her own. With the question hanging in the air between them, she felt her first inkling of awkwardness in Hanai's company.

She shook her head. "I've never seen him."

"Does Luyan have a fondness for him?"

Willow hesitated. The truth was, though she'd never said it, it felt to her like Luyan hated the man—but she liked the opulence of the lifestyle he provided for her. With many of the small stories Luyan had confided in her, her uncle had proven to be a narcissistic, ego-driven fool. Still, if he were really Hanai's husband, Willow didn't feel right speaking ill of him. She didn't know what the arrangement was between them or if they even still considered themselves a couple.

"I don't know."

"I tried to warn Wu Min about letting him take her daughter to the city. I begged her to say no—to let Luyan grow up here in a simpler but kinder way of life. But he promised my sister that with his influence, her daughter would have a better future than she could here in the village. From what I've heard of the way Luyan has changed, they should've heeded my warning. She didn't used to be as she is now—she used to be a happy girl. One day, she'll find all the money in the world won't make up for the emptiness she feels."

The silence fell between them again until Willow couldn't stand it any longer. "Tell me again about this tea," she said, hoping to get to a safer topic than the one that involved the complexity of Luyan and her uncle's relationship, or the girl's unhappiness. Luyan would kill her if she knew Willow had been talking about her. And until she knew Rosi was set, she couldn't afford to get on her bad side.

"It's sweetened ginseng tea. Such powerful stuff that it can't be given to children, or drank if pregnant. Haven't you ever had ginseng?"

Willow shook her head.

"Tea made from the powerful ginseng is said to bring long life, strength, and wisdom to those who drink it regularly," Hanai said.

"I've heard of ginseng, but I didn't know it could be made into a tea," Willow said.

"Oh, yes. It's available in many forms. It can be put into a tea, ground into powder, or made into pills. In some of the villages, you'll even see the older men chewing on raw ginseng roots because they think you get more benefits ingesting it that way."

"Does it taste good like that?"

"Not really—it's bitter. Some think it tastes like black licorice, but the flavor hasn't changed much throughout time or modern cultivation. Most people don't know ginseng was discovered over five thousand years ago in the Manchurian Mountains. Today, the root is even more valuable since it has been cultivated almost into extinction."

"Just a root? So valuable?"

"Wait just a minute," Hanai said and hurried from the room.

Willow heard her fumbling around in the back of the house—the kitchen she assumed—before she came back out cradling what looked like a root from the ground.

She held it out for Willow to take. It was gnarly, with a thick trunk as long as her fingers, and stringy shoots protruding from it.

"*Rénshēn*—or ginseng—is made up of the character that means man and another that means plant root." She used the palm of one hand to draw the two characters of 人 and 蔘 with her finger. Then she pointed at the root Willow held. "See how it is shaped like a body with legs?"

Willow inhaled the clean, earthy smell as she turned it over in her hand, and then saw Hanai was right. With the trunk and the shoots, it did look like the shape of a human.

"That's strange. But yet—amazing too," Willow said. "I never knew."

Hanai's smile disappeared. "Yes, and because of the way it looks, it's been idolized for centuries through legends and myths. Now to find ginseng in its natural form is so treasured, some people will do almost anything to get their hands on it."

"Where did you get it?"

"Oh, I've got my sources. Ginseng is a staple in my home, as I'm a firm believer in the powers it holds. I make sure to always have some on hand." Hanai leaned forward in her chair. "Legend has it Chairman Mao only smoked cigarettes of rolled ginseng. Some think it helped him to think in the epic proportions it took for him to rule the entire country."

Willow shrugged. She thought of Kai and his dislike of Mao's reign.

Hanai obviously noticed her indifference. "You have to admit, he did live a long life."

That he did, thought Willow. The man was in his eighties when he'd succumbed to a disease. She felt it ironic a man who'd wielded such a strong arm of control was ultimately robbed of most of the control of his own body. Ginseng might be good—but smoking it sure hadn't kept Mao from meeting the end of his reign on earth in a less-than-desired way. She'd always thought a leader should go out in a blaze of glory—not as a frail and dependent patient. Kai always said he got what was coming to him.

"Willow? Come back? What are you thinking of?" Hanai asked.

"Oh nothing, just getting sleepy." She wasn't ready to share anything about Kai with the woman. "I need to go. Luyan will be worried about me." She stood and set her cup on the small table in front of the couch.

Hanai joined her and led the way to the door. "I hope you'll come back before you return to Beijing."

"Maybe. I'm not sure how much longer we'll be here, though." Willow went to the door and opened it, then walked around Sunny to get off the front porch. The dog sniffed at her, but this time, he didn't growl. For some reason, that made her happy.

"Thank you for the tea," Willow said.

They walked to the gate, and Hanai opened it. "*Zaijian.*"

"Goodbye," she returned. Then she hurried down the hill and to the path. If she were lucky, Luyan would've napped longer than usual. If she weren't, there'd be hell to pay.

Kai

ONE MORE ROUND OF FILTHY pots and Kai would be done. He could go home for the night and stretch out on his pallet to ease the kinks out of his aching body. His back was cramping, his fingers wrinkled like prunes, and though he'd worked long and hard, he knew his pay would be laughable. But finally, Willow would be proud. She'd constantly nagged him about keeping at the restaurants until one hired him, and she was right—since he couldn't work for Johnny any longer after his betrayal, he'd gone job hunting again.

Eventually, after several rejections, he'd hit just the right one when it was short-handed. After a few questions peppered at him about his experience, he'd been shown into the kitchen and though he'd told the manager he could cook, the barrel-bellied bald man had led him straight to the sink and a pile of dirty pots a mountain high. He'd even begun dreaming about the endless dirty cookware again, just as he had before. It wasn't a job he liked, and he already missed working with photography, but a man had to do what a man had to do. After seeing that Johnny had stolen Willow's photo, he could never work for him again.

But he did have a few things to say to him.

He looked at the grimy kitchen, still cluttered from a busy day of serving the working class. It was overwhelming, but he could and would finish—he had rent money to hand over. Even though Lao Qu would probably understand if he didn't have it just once, Kai was too proud to not find a way to pay the amount he'd set himself when the old man had offered him a roof over his head. He had standards and wouldn't take anything for free. Taking charity was what had started the beginning of the end for him and Willow. Luyan's face came to mind, and he felt himself grind down on his back teeth.

"*Kuai dian!*"

Kai heard the manager call out to him to hurry just as he heaved a sigh and set another shining pot on the counter to dry. "I'm hurrying." He kept his head down and mumbled under his breath. He didn't want to get fired the first week for being disrespectful.

The boss stomped into the kitchen and stood looking around. Kai expected some words of gratitude, just something considering he'd cleaned the pots in record time. He was getting faster each night—a real feat considering he'd been there for twelve hours already. He'd come in for the lunch shift, and the boss had kept him working straight through dinner. The fatigue and frustration he felt reminded him of the orphanage and his many go-rounds with Chef Wu. The nasty old cook would love to see he'd ended right back where he'd started—washing pots.

"When you finish, I want you to mop the floors," the man said, then turned and left the kitchen.

So his efficiency just brought him more work. *Aiya*, he was tired. At least he had plenty of time to think while his hands did mindless work. His face remained calm, yet his mind circled round and round to the photo of Willow and the betrayal of Johnny in publishing it as his own. And *Face of the Forgotten*—what the hell was that supposed to mean? Kai hadn't forgotten her—that much was true. But what Johnny could mean by that simply confused him. For the last two weeks since he'd walked away from her face on the wall, he'd tried to figure it out, to no avail.

Suddenly, he froze, his hand in midair, holding the pot he was about to set aside.

Willow.

Forgotten.

Orphanage.

Children.

Forgotten by parents.

Or—*forgotten by society?*

He dropped the pot and stared at the murky water in the sink. Surely, Johnny wouldn't use confidential information he had on them for his own monetary gain? Because if he did, and the director caught wind of it, Rosi's adoption might be jeopardized. Could he be that callous?

Kai shook his head, anger building as he stared into the water, seeing Johnny's arrogant smirk. He slammed a fist on the counter and cursed. Of course, his timing was perfect—as usual.

"What's your problem, boy?"

Kai didn't turn. He didn't trust himself. Instead, he reached over and picked up the towel he'd been forced to use for twelve hours. A dingy, dirty rag that should have been tossed a dozen pots ago. He felt his anger simmering just below the breaking point. *Stay calm, stay calm*, he chanted silently.

The boss stepped up behind him, so close Kai could feel his breath on his neck. "I said—what's your problem? You've still got work to do."

Kai looked up and around, knowing his eyes were black with rage but unable to help it. His voice came out low and deadly, almost unrecognizable even to himself. "I'll tell you what I'm going to do, boss man. You haven't given me one stinking break since I walked in here an hour before the lunch crowd. I've stood at this sink for going on twelve hours, and not once have I heard a kind word or a felt a pat on the back for my hard work—"

"Now you shut your—"

"No! You shut yours. I'm leaving. If you can't hire more kitchen help, then you need to get your waitresses in here to finish these pots and mop the floors. And if you can find a better, more efficient worker than me, you go right ahead, old man. I need to take care of something tonight." Balling the towel up, he threw it down on the counter. He wanted to throw it at the man, but he did need the job.

"But it's almost midnight!" the man said, his voice turning whiny.

"I'll be back tomorrow, but let's get something straight. I'm not your slave, and I'm not your boy. You'll let me take at least a dinner break and you will get me some damn clean towels."

He didn't wait for an answer. He turned and took the door to the alley, letting it slam behind him as his anger pounded in his head, threatening to blow right through his eardrums. Walking through the darkness between the two rows of businesses, he breathed deeply to calm the raging in his blood.

First, Johnny had messed with Willow. Then, he'd done something that could hurt Rosi. He felt his chest heaving with rage. If the man had any luck on his side at all, he wouldn't be where Kai could find him tonight.

He kicked at a trash can lid in his path and sent it flying. The noise reverberated in the still night. A stray cat screeched and ran for cover, but Kai didn't care. He was on a full-fledged crash and this time, Willow wasn't around to calm the chaos that quaked inside of him.

Kai didn't expect to find Johnny so easy, but knowing how he loved to party, when he'd finished researching what he needed to know at the Internet café, it only took him a quick walk to bar street. He only had to step into four ratty dives that catered to foreigners before he found Johnny taking center court at a table near the window. The flashy red shirt he wore stood out like a beacon, making it easy for Kai to keep his eyes on him in the crowded room.

109

Of course, Johnny was always looking out for his career, and that meant mingling with anyone he thought could give him a boost. Obviously, he thought he'd find that magic association in bars where the foreign fools drank themselves into a stupor and along the way spouted empty promises of business to be had and money to be made.

The Den was also one of those clubs the local girls flocked to—all in their quest to have a *waiguoren* to hang on their arms like some sort of sparkly bracelet, hoping it led to something deeper—maybe even a way out of their impoverished lives. Maybe he was cynical, but it was just after midnight, and he was sickened by the music pounding and couples staggering past him out of the bar, their hands searching and laughter escalating with the excitement of a possible connection. Kai thought it was tacky and thoughts of Willow ever being in a place like it made him more nauseous and determined to find out whether Johnny had taken her there on their one date. Yeah, Johnny had a lot of talking to do, and Kai wished he'd part ways with his drinking buddies and come on out.

He leaned against the wall and for once, wished he were a smoker. He'd spent a lot of time and effort trying to help Willow quit, but in this occasion, it would've been nice to have something to do with his hands to make it look like he had a reason for being there, instead of just cowering like a street thug waiting on his next victim.

Finally, another group of patrons moved toward the door. Kai looked closer and Johnny was with them—along with a trio of girls who looked more ready for a long nap than an after party. Kai didn't understand why guys would want a girl they had to get intoxicated in order to gain their interest. It was pathetic.

They emerged and before Johnny could even take three steps away from the building, Kai reached out and jerked him out of the crowd by the scruff of his shirt. "Johnny, I need to talk to you."

After he got over his miniscule second of shock, Johnny pulled back. "Get your hands off me. And where the hell have you been? You left me hanging to do all the family gigs alone."

The guys and few girls waited for Johnny a few feet ahead, talking and laughing amongst themselves.

Kai glared at Johnny. "Wonder why I left you hanging? How about copyright infringement?"

Johnny had already started moving toward his friends but the words—as expected—stopped him in his tracks. Even without him turning around, Kai could see Johnny knew what he'd done. He turned, the guilt flashing across his face, but it was quickly replaced with arrogance. He pointed his finger at Kai.

"Copyright infringement? Are you crazy? That was *my* camera, *my* pictures. You just try to mess with me, and I'll have you arrested for handling my equipment without permission. You might get out of it, but you'll spend a few painful weeks in jail until it's sorted out. How are you going to prove you took that shot? Look at you—a street kid. Look at me—a soon-to-be-famous photographer. Who do you think they'll believe?"

They stood facing each other like two warriors, neither prepared to break down, both looking for a weakness in the other.

"You invaded her privacy, and you've put Rosi's future in jeopardy," Kai said through gritted teeth. He wanted to knock the sarcastic look off Johnny's face, but he knew while it might give him some temporary satisfaction, it wouldn't help his problem.

Johnny shrugged. "I don't even know that kid. But don't forget, it's me who negotiated her release from that orphanage you all came from. You owe me—actually, you all owe me." He pointed his finger at Kai's chest. "And that photo of Willow might just give me the big break I've been waiting for. Bliss Magazine is considering running it, but they want more of a story."

Kai felt his anger peaking again at his indifference to Rosi's circumstances, but his attention caught on the last few words he'd heard. "More of a story? Just what have you already told them, Johnny?"

Johnny's body language changed like a chameleon, and suddenly he was back to the smooth-talking salesman act. "Listen, Kai. I know you think I did something dirty and maybe I did, but what if I gave you half credit? Maybe named you as my assistant in the piece if it gets to that point? I'll even cut you a part of my royalty—what about that? I just want the notoriety, anyway. That photo—it's haunting. It's going to cause a sensation. With or without Willow's knowledge, she's going to be a star." He spread his arms wide and his creepy smile even wider.

"Hell no, Johnny! I want you to retract the photo. Willow didn't give you permission. She wouldn't do that—she's too private and she sure wouldn't want to be the *face of the forgotten*, as you call it. She wanted to leave those memories behind!"

"Just one magazine spread, Kai," Johnny said. His group had resumed walking without him. Johnny hollered out for them to wait, turning his back on Kai.

"No. She doesn't even know I took that picture, man. She's not interested in being a star. Use something of Luyan's—she's your attention whore."

Johnny threw one more retort over his shoulder as he walked away. "And anyway, Luyan is old news, boy. Even her uncle doesn't want her around here no more. Willow has the real star quality, and her aloofness is what will make her popular. You need to come to your senses, Kai."

Kai fought the urge to yank Johnny backward and pound him until he relented. But if Willow were there, she'd remind him violence never solved problems.

He considered for a second—knowing it wouldn't solve the problem but also knowing remodeling Johnny's face would feel oh so good. Then he let him go as he breathed slowly, until he gained control over his emotions again.

He'd have to come up with a new plan.

Part Two

REFUGE

Willow

WILLOW STOOD AT THE GATE and looked at the house, willing Hanai to come out. She hadn't planned on coming to see her again, but when Luyan fell asleep after the noon meal, Willow found herself jumpy and unable to concentrate. Only when she'd finally decided to go had she felt her nerves begin to settle. She'd slipped out of the house and up the path, passing the cats. In what felt like only moments, she was standing in front of Hanai's gate.

Now she was at an impasse.

She looked down at the dog on the other side of the gate. Sunny growled low in her throat, looking ready to take a bite out of her, but Willow remained calm and tried to muster a smile. She held her hands out in mock surrender, but not low enough to lose a finger. "Good dog, it's okay."

The dog continued to growl, a low rumble in its throat as she warned Willow not to step foot on her domain. There was no doubt the mutt was serious—the golden hair standing up along the back of her head and down her back proved that. It was clear the dog meant business when it came to protecting the premises.

"*Ni hao*, Sunny, remember me?"

The dog stopped growling, and its ears perked up. Willow felt a glimmer of hope. If she could just get the dog to allow her to step through, she might be able to make it to the house to knock on the door.

She stared down at Sunny, one hand on the gate and ready to try, when she heard sound coming from the other side of the house. Birds squawking blended with the sounds of a woman yelling.

It sounded like Hanai. Was she in trouble?

Willow turned and followed the stone gate around the side of the house. In the area behind the house, she saw what looked like a small shed of some sort, and next to that, a wire chicken coop attached to another small building. Inside the coop, the chickens were in an uproar about something and they were all fleeing up the ramp into their hen house. Behind them, Willow saw what looked like a head of cabbage swinging from a black metal hook.

Hanai stood looking at the coop, her hands on her hips.

"*Ni hao*," Willow called out.

Hanai turned to her, and then frantically waved. "The gate is unlocked, hurry—come over here!"

Willow reached over and jiggled the latch until it gave, then she opened the gate and jogged to cover the distance between them. "What's going on?"

"A Sparrowhawk. It got in and was stalking my hens. Now I need to get it out of there."

Willow looked closer and saw the bird—a creature with cold, mean eyes and a gash on its pointed beak. It strutted around in the corner, drawing Willow's attention to its long, sharp claws. "That bird looks dangerous," she said.

Hanai nodded. "It is dangerous. It usually feasts on frogs and lizards, but has been known to get small mammals too. I'm just lucky I was out here, or I'd be less a few chickens—maybe even all of them."

"What can I do to help?" Willow hadn't even seen how the hawk had gotten in, much less how to get it out.

116

"We need to peel back these layers of wire in this corner. Then one of us will have to scare him out of there."

Willow never changed her serious expression. "That will be you. I'm scared of creatures that kill."

Hanai gave her a funny look, and then went to the corner of the enclosure.

The pen was suddenly empty, other than the hawk that glared at them in defiance, as if to tell them he wouldn't be taken alive. Willow realized that chickens weren't as dumb as she'd always thought. They'd sure been smart enough to disappear, and right fast, too. For a second, she almost looked at the small holes in the side of the nesting room, expecting the hens to be lined up and watching the showdown of hawk against human.

Hanai got her attention again. "I have two layers on here. The first layer is just regular chicken wire, and then another screen of smaller wire is on top as added security."

"That's a lot of security." Willow didn't know chickens were so valuable, either. She'd actually never been around chickens, or really animals of any sort. She had to admit, it was exciting.

"Has to be. Before I added the extra layer, a few owls reached their claws in and plucked the heads right off my chickens. That's a gruesome thing to find on a sleepy morning, let me tell you."

Willow swallowed the revulsion the image brought to mind.

Hanai moved to another spot. "I see a tiny hole where he must have worked his way in, but now he can't get out. I've got to peel this back."

She tried to grab at an edge, but she was too short.

Willow went over and waved Hanai out of the way. With one eye on the hawk, she put her foot in one of the holes in the wire and climbed up a few inches, then reached for the screen. Her movement must have scared the hawk because it took flight in the pen and hit the wire roof, then fell back down.

117

"Careful! If he gets to you, he'll slice you to pieces," Hanai warned.

That didn't make her feel any braver. It made her want to turn and run. Still, Willow tried again. She hooked two fingers over a hole in the wire and pulled. The wire began to move.

"That's it—a little more," Hanai said.

Willow felt the wire cutting into her fingers, but it felt good to be needed, so she kept pulling. When she had it back enough to form a hole just a bit bigger than the bird, Hanai told her to stop.

"You got it. Now watch out in case he comes at you."

Willow stepped down and stood back. She and Hanai watched, waiting for the bird to find the opening and get out of the coop. When it continued to fly up and drop down without hitting the hole, Hanai turned to her.

"I'm going to have to go in there and try to shoo him out."

Shoo him out? Was Hanai crazy? Though it wasn't that big, the bird had eyes that made it seem like a cold-blooded killer, and she didn't think getting into an enclosed area with him was the smartest decision.

"Please don't, Hanai. This can't end well," she said. Visions of the bird using its razor-sharp claws to mold Hanai a new face came to mind, complete with blood and gore.

"I've got to. Those are my chickens in there, and that nasty vulture isn't going to feast on a single one of them. They aren't just birds to me—they're my girls and I've promised to protect them." Hanai went around to the door of the hen house and opened it, then quietly slipped in.

Willow watched her as she eased closer to the hawk, one slow step at a time.

"Watch out. If he comes out, he should go straight up in the air, but these creatures are unpredictable," Hanai said.

Willow stepped back, putting more distance between her and the chicken coop. She looked at the hawk's claws again and felt a shiver run up her back.

118

Hanai took another step toward the hawk. It flew up a few feet, and then landed on its feet again, flapping its wings a few times before settling.

"I think you're making him mad," Willow called out. If what she thought she saw was correct, the creature had settled down even closer to Hanai than it had been before. Now only about four feet separated the woman from the bird.

"Oh, he's not mad. He's feeling cornered. That's even worse than mad." Hanai took another step.

"Maybe you should come out of there," Willow said, feeling nothing good could come out of this standoff. She didn't want to be there to witness any bloodshed.

"Not until he does," Hanai answered, her voice low and quiet. "Wait—I mean not until *she* does. Now that I'm closer, I can see this is a female. They're much bigger."

Male or female, Willow didn't care. She just wanted it out of there. "I know what, I'll come at it from this angle and maybe with us forcing it from two sides, even with the wire between me and him, it'll go the right way."

Hanai nodded. Willow knew she didn't want to make much noise.

"Get. Out. Of. My. Hen. House. Hawk," Hanai demanded, making each syllable stand alone as she stepped closer. When she got within only a foot or so, she stopped and looked at Willow. She nodded.

"Now," Willow said.

They both stepped forward, Hanai toward the bird from the inside, and Willow from the outside. The bird swooped up again, this time finding the open hole and slipping through. It soared up into the sky, then swooped down and landed on the branch of a towering hardwood tree. Willow was amazed at its wingspan and the mellow gold colors that made up its chest feathers.

"*Aiya!*" Hanai hollered, making Willow smile at the few feathers she'd somehow accumulated on top of her dark hair. "We did it!"

119

"So we did," Willow said. She realized she'd been holding her breath. "Well, that's my first chicken-hawk-mediation session, I'll have to say."

A feather tumbled from Hanai's head, and she blew at it to keep it from hitting her face. The feather jumped up in the air, and then slowly floated to the ground.

Willow let out a giggle, and then covered her mouth. She hadn't meant to act like a child.

Hanai leaned against the inside of the coop and giggled too. Suddenly, both of them were laughing, from the pent-up fear or the rush of relief, Willow wasn't sure. She only knew she hadn't laughed since she'd been yanked out of Rosi's life. It hurt a little—as it made her miss Rosi—but she couldn't deny it still felt a little good, too.

Hanai had brought out a pot and two knives, and they sat on stools watching the chickens as they peeled sweet potatoes. Sunny lay at Willow's feet—actually halfway on her feet, to be exact—and had refused to leave her side since the moment Hanai gave her the down command. Willow looked at her watch and couldn't believe how time had flown. And of course, Hanai had insisted she stay for some *hóng shǔ zhōu*—sweet potato porridge—as a reward for her help with the hawk. Willow had declined, but told her she'd help to peel them anyway before she headed back home. Hanai accepted the offer. But now, she worried Luyan might not be pacified again with a made-up story of Willow meeting Shaylin in the street and stopping in to talk to her.

"What's that other small building?" Willow asked, her eyes setting on a shed of some sort, several meters away from the chicken coop.

"That's my work shed."

"What do you do in it?" Willow asked.

"I work," Hanai said evasively, reminding her of Luyan in one of her coy moments. "Does Luyan approve of you coming here?" Hanai asked.

Willow almost dropped her potato. It was as if the woman had read her mind. "She doesn't care one way or the other," she lied, and then immediately wondered why. She should've just told Hanai the truth—that Luyan didn't know. Now not only was she bringing Shaylin unknowingly into her secret voyages, but Hanai would be part of the web of untruths.

"Good," Hanai said.

Willow picked up another one of the biggest spuds. Just looking at it reminded her of Beijing and the many vendors in the winter who sold the steamed sweet potatoes at street side stands. Sometimes on the way to school, the ayi would walk them past cooking potatoes. Willow's belly would embarrass her by rumbling as the sweet smell made it to her nose and down to her stomach. Sometimes, the ayis would even stop and buy a potato for themselves, but never share with the children they supervised.

Willow always thought it selfish of the ayis. As she got older, she also thought it cruel to the smaller children whose bellies never felt full from the meager breakfast of congee. Back then, she used to wish for lots of money so she could put a warm potato in the hand of every cold child in the line.

Yes, the potatoes were a reminder of what she'd left behind. That acknowledgement made her think of Luyan, and she looked at her watch and cringed. Luyan was going to wake up and pitch a fit when she saw Willow was gone again. She needed to hurry even though, if she were being honest with herself, she wanted to stay. She wanted to be right where she was, peeling potatoes and making small talk as she watched a flock of crazy birds cavorting in a pen.

"Are you attending the wedding in the village this weekend?" Willow asked.

121

Hanai kept her eyes on the potato she peeled, but she shook her head. "No, I don't usually go into the village. Who is marrying?"

Willow realized she didn't even know their names. "I'm not sure of the family name, actually. I didn't see an invitation."

"Invitations aren't needed, Willow. This isn't the city—here the entire village takes part in the festivities. Except me, that is. But then, I'm not really considered a part of the village any longer."

She sounded sad. Willow didn't know what to say, so she said nothing.

"It must be the Dao family."

The squawking escalated and Hanai looked up and whistled, her signal calming the chickens back down to a normal decibel. Willow still couldn't get over how smart they were. Once the hawk was out of the pen and they'd pulled the wire screen back into place, Hanai had called out to them that the coast was clear. Within seconds, they'd all come out, strutting down the ramp single file, looking like a procession of chubby old ladies, all gabbing and peering from side to side to see what they'd missed.

"Why is the cabbage there?" Willow pointed at the cabbage hanging on a chain suspended from the top of the pen.

"Mostly entertainment, but it's nutritious too. If I'm not around to watch them closely, I don't let them out of the pen as often, and they get bored. It's also good exercise because they have to jump for it."

Entertainment is right, Willow thought. The birds jumped and pecked at the vegetable, using it like a tetherball as their jabs sent it careening back and forth, like kids in a schoolyard. One chicken jumped into the air, missing the ball of cabbage, and Willow could've sworn another gave her a scolding and a disgusted look. She couldn't stop watching them and let out more than a few laughs at their antics, especially when Hanai started telling her their names.

"Flora is the boss," Hanai said, pointing at the tallest chicken, one with a beautiful white coat. "She's at the top of the pecking order and when the others forget it, she'll use her muscle to get her way. Though sometimes the smallest hen—Nora, the brown, sneaky one—will worm in and take the biggest part of the food. Then she and Flora will be angry with each other for the rest of the day, going to great lengths to avoid walking near one another."

"Do all their names rhyme?" Willow asked, a sarcastic smile on her face.

Hanai shook her head. "No, only Flora, Nora, and Dora. The rest aren't named—only the triplets. Dora is the funny one. She plays tricks on the others, and they all laugh at her."

"Wait—did you say triplets?" Willow raised an eyebrow, though Hanai was still looking at the potato she cradled in her hand.

"Yes, those three were from the same mama hen. Even without knowing that, I'd have known they were sisters. They go at each other all day long, yet just let another chicken try to pick on one of them. They'll stand together and fight if they need to."

Willow laughed. She listened as Hanai told more about the chickens, describing their personalities and quirks. The woman was serious about her hens—talking about them as if they were children. Willow felt a little sorry for her, so remote from people that cats, dogs, and chickens were her only source of companionship.

"How long have you lived out here?" Willow asked. She had so many questions, but she wasn't sure which ones would be too invasive.

"Close to fifteen years."

"Can I ask why would you want to be so isolated? Why not live in the village? Don't you ever miss being near your family?"

Hanai looked down into her pot of peelings for a moment. When she raised her face, Willow could see sadness in her eyes.

"I'd like to smile and tell you everything is exactly as I want it, that my life is my own. But I'd be lying to you and myself if I pretended that is true. The real truth is I miss certain aspects of the life I left behind when I came here. I miss the feel of someone's heart against mine, the familiar scent one knows of another, even the bond of trust built between two souls."

Willow didn't know how to respond to that or to the sudden tear making a slow path down the woman's face. The emotion in her voice was so thick, so deep, that any words Willow would offer couldn't possibly console.

Hanai paused, and then continued. "I lost something dear to me, but I chose this path when I changed that of someone else's. I had hoped to lead them to a better destiny, but I'm learning now perhaps I was wrong. Being near my family in the village would only serve to make me see more clearly the life I could've lived but instead gave away. So no—I do not miss living near my family."

Willow let out a long sigh.

Hanai used the edge of her sweater to wipe her face. "Why the long sigh?"

"Oh, I don't know. Your words just make me remember a part of my own life that was difficult." Willow could've bit her own tongue. She didn't know what had come over her, but she didn't want to talk about the orphanage! She wouldn't say another word.

"Which part?"

Don't tell her; don't tell her, Willow thought.

"I used to live in an orphanage." Willow clamped her lips together, disgusted at herself for her inability to keep her mouth shut. She was shocked at her own sudden lack of willpower. She hoped Hanai didn't think she was some loser who constantly felt sorry for herself.

Hanai let out her own sigh. "Do you want to tell me about it?"

"Not really," Willow said, shaking her head. She kept her eyes trained on the potato in her hand.

"Remember what I told you when we came in? About secrets? Sometimes, the hurt eases if you share the pain," Hanai said, her voice soft and comforting.

Willow considered her words. She couldn't imagine the anguish of her childhood ever being erased, but maybe here—in the cover of these woods—with a woman she barely knew, it could be the place to let it go.

She took a deep breath. "Everyone I've ever loved has said goodbye."

Saying the words did make Willow feel better, but Hanai looked like she'd been shot. Her face took on a pale, pinched expression, and Willow could see her lower lip quivering. She wondered why her confession made the woman so emotional. When she spoke, her voice came out shaky.

"Fate can be a difficult thing to understand, Willow. Sometimes, you don't see the purpose or intent of things until years after it has happened."

Willow wondered if they were back to talking about Hanai now. That would be fine by her, as she didn't want to delve into any more of her childhood.

"Sometimes I wonder if I made the wrong decision by befriending Luyan and coming home with her. I'm not much use here," Willow said, anxious to move the subject away from the more painful one she'd raised.

Hanai held up a finger, turning to look Willow in the eye. "I don't know about that, but I do know this. Every step you've taken in life is meant to bring you that much closer to your destiny. Never doubt yourself, Willow. For in you I see an amazing spirit of resilience, and something tells me you are a protector of those less fortunate—a badge of honor only earned by and awarded to few."

Willow shrugged. She wasn't sure what that meant, but it sounded like a good prophecy to her. Her future was still a mess of unknowns, but somehow, Hanai had made her feel better about it. She looked down at the growing pile of peeled potatoes.

Hanai threw down her potato and picked up another. Her hands worked quickly around it—peeling much quicker than Willow could.

Hanai didn't look up when she spoke again. "It is said sweet potato porridge is also a known cure for the blues."

Willow watched her for a moment longer, wondering why the woman had allowed her in—was even treating her like a friend. Not just any sort of friend—but a real one who was there to give as well as take. With just a few words, Willow changed her earlier decision.

"I guess I can stay for just a bowl or two."

Hanai nodded, a small smile turning up the corners of her mouth as she peeled her potato.

Willow

WILLOW HAD THOUGHT THINGS WERE going great. Luyan had the idea to invite Shaylin for tea, so once her school hours were over, they'd met the girl at the local shop. Shaylin's wedding was only weeks away and though she didn't appear as excited as Willow thought a girl should be, the way she recounted the details of what was planned showed her acceptance. All was well until, as usual, Luyan was the first one to put her foot in her mouth and turn the mood sour.

Willow kicked her under the table, but it was too late, her words had Shaylin turning scarlet and stammering out an answer.

"So why'd you sleep with him if he's so bad?" Luyan had blurted out as though simply asking about the morning weather. They'd been talking of Shaylin's friend, Niu, and how she'd moved into the city for a job at a major supermarket. Willow was just getting interested in hearing about the logistics of the girl sharing an apartment with four others and how she was battling with one of them for her right to rule the roost. But then Luyan had to abruptly change subjects and put Shaylin on the spot.

"It was good in the beginning," Shaylin said, her eyes staring into the caramel swirl of tea in front of her. "He was so sweet to me."

Willow felt her own cheeks burn and couldn't think of a thing to say that wouldn't sound too intrusive. Unfortunately though, Luyan had no such reserves.

"It's always good in the beginning," Luyan said. "But from what my grandmother has told me, it's usually the middle of the relationship that dictates the end of a relationship."

She had a point there, and Willow watched Shaylin to see if she truly thought it was the end of her and Daming before they'd even had the wedding.

When Shaylin looked up, her eyes were filled with hurt. "He said he loved me. He promised me I wouldn't get pregnant if it was just once. I'd never been with a boy before, and he treated me with such tenderness. I thought it was real. I thought I'd found my *airen,* my true love. But after—after, you know—he started being cold and it was like I didn't even know him."

"I'm so sorry, Shaylin," Willow murmured. When they'd decided to meet at the small noodle shop on the main road, she had no idea it was going to turn into first an interrogation by Luyan and then confessions from the poor girl she'd set her crosshairs on. Willow thought they were just going to be friendly. Now she knew Luyan had planned her attack the entire morning, determined to get to the bottom of all the juicy rumors swirling around the village. Speaking of being cold-hearted—Luyan was the one who'd earned that title.

Luyan shrugged. "So what are you going to do? Go ahead and marry him?"

"I don't have a choice. My father found out, and he's so angry. If I don't go through with it, he'll disown me. I'll have nowhere to go."

"That's really sad," Willow offered. "He should be taking his anger out on Daming for taking advantage of you."

Luyan rolled her eyes. "I wouldn't care what my father said. I would never marry someone destined to live in the village forever. What's Daming going to do? Drive a truck for the rest of his life? Go back to being a pig farmer like his father? That means you'll be a pig farmer's wife. Is that what you wanted? You should say no, Shaylin. Don't go through with it."

Shaylin sighed, and Willow saw it. She loved Daming. Or at least she loved the Daming she thought she knew in the beginning. And maybe he was one and the same. It wasn't up to her to cast stones. She just wished he'd be kinder to his fiancée.

"I don't care what he does to support our family, I just want him to act like he did in the beginning," Shaylin said wistfully.

Luyan snorted in contempt.

"It's her life, Luyan. Stop telling her what to do," Willow said.

"Daming's under a lot of stress right now. His father is working him hard to cover the expenses of an early wedding. He's picking up delivery jobs as well as working the farm. But I think after it's all over, he'll be better. And I do want my baby to have a father," Shaylin said.

Luyan pushed her cup out and stood. "Then there's nothing more to say. You made your bed, now you can lay in it—as they say. On that note, it's time for an afternoon nap. You coming, Willow?"

Willow felt like slapping Luyan for being so cruel. Couldn't she see her old friend was looking for emotional support? She wouldn't leave the girl on that note of unkindness. "No, I'm not coming. I'm not done talking to Shaylin."

"You're wasting your time. If Shaylin wants to act like a backward village girl and let her man dictate her life, we can't help her." Luyan shrugged and waved goodbye, then threw a ten-renminbi note down on the table and skirted out the door. Willow shook her head, and then looked up at Shaylin.

"I'm sorry about that," she said. Why she felt responsible for Luyan's actions, she didn't know, but the guilt made her squirm.

Shaylin looked embarrassed too. "It's okay, really."

"Must have been a rough school life getting along with her," Willow said. She could only imagine the crowd Luyan led around.

Shaylin filled her cup again from the pot on the table. She held it over Willow's cup and raised her eyebrows.

"No, but thank you," Willow answered her silent question. "I've had too much already. I won't sleep at all tonight."

Shaylin seemed to relax with Luyan gone. Without any more reason to keep her guard up, she suddenly looked younger to Willow. If anything, she appeared to be even more naïve, too. Willow wondered what kind of guy Daming was, preying on someone so sweet and innocent like Shaylin. She wouldn't judge Shaylin for sleeping with someone before marriage. She'd been in the position of being pressured before from different boys in the orphanage, and some of the girls gave in just to make their lives easier, but Willow—with Kai's help—had always protected her innocence, so one day when she did decide to give it, the moment would mean something. Hopefully with someone she truly loved. She suddenly thought of Kai and wondered if he was dating.

"Willow?" Shaylin called her name.

"Oh, I'm sorry. I was just lost in thought. What did you say?"

"I was telling you about my student. Her milk name was Hao Bong, but since then, her grandmother changed it to Pride. She's only seven, but she's already able to do mathematics that only the bigger kids have done before. Everyone thought she would be a horrible student because of her home life, but she's starting to be my star pupil."

"Her home life?" Willow asked.

Shaylin looked sad for a moment. "She lives with her grandmother. Her parents already had a son, and the mother refused to give Pride away when she was born as a second child, so Pride's father left them and took the boy. Then the mother was killed in a bus crash. They say the girl is marked with bad luck, but the grandmother tries her best to care for her. They're poor—so much so that as little as she is, Pride does farmhand chores for her neighbors in exchange for eggs and other staples. They have it pretty rough."

"That's so sad," Willow said.

Shaylin slammed her hand on the table, making Willow jump. To see her show so much emotion and be so animated was shocking.

"It is sad—and because her parents didn't follow the official protocol, Pride has no hukou. She may be pretty, and smart too, but it's as though she doesn't exist. She'll never be able to get medical care or go to a university. She won't even be able to marry one day because on paper, she doesn't exist! The only reason she's able to attend our school is because we look the other way when it comes to authorizing some of the children."

"The teacher—is she sympathetic?" Willow asked, realizing the real teacher—the one recognized by the village counsel—hadn't been mentioned.

Shaylin nodded. "She is. But she's so old, Willow. She basically sleeps through most of the day. I don't mind, though, because that leaves the teaching to me. They only keep her around because she never asks for a pay raise. Our school used to be revered in this province, but none of the officials even care."

"And you—you really don't get paid?"

"Not yet. But listen, I have to talk to you about something important. Daming is insisting I go for an ultrasound. His parents are paying for it, and if I'm carrying a girl, they want me to do away with her," Shaylin whispered from across the table.

"Do away with her? As in—" Willow searched Shaylin's face, unbelieving what she was hearing. It was only a week or so ago that Luyan and her grandmother had brought the exact same words out about Shaylin and the possibility of an ultrasound and what it could lead to. But she never thought—

Shaylin nodded solemnly. "Yes, as in you know what."

The tears showing in her eyes told Willow that even she couldn't speak the words. While someone with a colder heart, or a harder outlook, might be able to be nonchalant about abortion, Shaylin looked ready to collapse just bringing it up.

Willow reached for her hand. "Oh Shaylin, no. These days, it's not so bad to have a girl. And if Daming is truly from a farming family, you'll be allowed to keep your first child as well as try again for a boy. You can have two children!"

Shaylin picked up a napkin and swiped at her eyes. "I know, but he won't even listen when I tell him that. His family is old school, and they don't want to waste money raising a girl."

"Yet, they have the money for an ultrasound and a risky procedure to take away the baby and possibly even harm you?"

Willow watched her take a deep breath to calm herself, and then let out a long sigh.

"They're borrowing it. Not only for that, but also for their part of the wedding expenses. And Daming is bitter at me for putting his family in dire financial straits. My parents are totally afraid of his parents, so much so that they'll make me do anything in order to make them happy. Daming had put it in their heads that his family is well respected in his village, but I think he's exaggerating a bit. Their house is no better than ours, but Daming acts like they live in a palace."

Willow couldn't believe her ears. "Wait. Back up, did you say he's mad at you? As if he didn't have a part in this? Shaylin, do you think this is the kind of man you want to spend the rest of your life with?"

"I don't have a choice. I just pray my baby is a boy. Not that I wouldn't want to have a girl; I just don't want her to suffer for trying to be born," she said as she rubbed her stomach. "And please don't tell Luyan about this. I feel I can trust you, but I'm not sure Luyan wouldn't let it slip around Daming that I mentioned it, then he'd have even more ammunition to be upset at me for."

Willow nodded. The poor girl didn't realize probably everyone in the village knew by now she'd be having an ultrasound. "You can trust me. And Shaylin, I know you're busy with school and wedding plans, but please come by the house whenever you want to talk and we can go for a walk. And I have a favor to ask of you."

"Anything," Shaylin answered.

Willow hated to lie to her, so she straddled the truth and just left out a few pieces. "Sometimes I like to take off without Luyan, just spend time with nature. I've been known to stay gone a few hours, so if you'd be all right with it, if I'm gone longer than expected, can I say I was with you? You know how Luyan is—she can be relentless until she finds out what she wants to know."

"You have a deal, as long as you promise to come by my school sometime and let me introduce you to my kids."

"Deal," Willow agreed. She honestly couldn't wait.

Shaylin nodded and gave her a small smile, a silent gesture that told Willow she'd made a friend—a real one. Now she'd pray the girl would not be forced to interrupt the new life growing inside of her, because something told Willow Shaylin wouldn't be able to handle the emotional aftermath that such a drastic act would bring.

Kai

KAI PICKED UP THE LAST of the rancid dish towels and threw them in the basket at the door. One of the waitresses would take them home and wash them to earn an extra few yuan. Kai hoped she used bleach because they were laden with grease and filth so badly that he hated even touching them. He walked past the mop and bucket, suppressing a smile. The old man didn't ask him to do the floors any longer. Finally, Kai had gained some respect, though he'd had to show he wouldn't take this job back any other way in order to get it.

"I'm out of here, boss man," Kai yelled out. "Can you come in here and give me my pay?" After his blow up with Johnny, he'd come back and worked two weeks of twelve straight hours a day, and he was whipped. Even the simple, hard floor of Lao Qu's living room sounded enticing to him. He was finally going to get a day off and just wanted to use it to sleep until he could sleep no more. He took off his apron and wadded it up, then threw it in the basket with the towels. Grabbing his jacket from the peg, he struggled into it, feeling the pull of fatigue his resisting arm muscles gave as he guided his hands through the sleeves.

The boss poked his head in through the door and gave a thumbs-up and a grin. He waddled in and pulled a few bills from his pocket, holding them out to Kai. The man was happy Kai had returned—so happy in fact, that he'd even let him do some of the cooking before the pots and pans had piled up. Kai hadn't wanted to return, but he needed the money. Simple as that. He couldn't just stay for free in old man Qu's house, and more importantly, he had to find a way to stop Johnny. That would take money. So he'd swallowed his pride and showed back up for work.

Kai took the cash and quickly counted it. He pulled his wallet from his jacket and opened it, then added the bills to the growing wad inside. It wasn't anything near what Johnny had been paying him, but it was something. He'd also insisted he get paid daily, since the bond of trust between him and his boss had been broken. Because the boss knew he wasn't even giving him a fair wage, he'd agreed to a cash payout at the end of every night just to keep Kai quiet.

"*Zaijian*," he said, then slammed out of the kitchen and into the dark and cold alley. It would be a long walk home, but he wasn't going to waste any money taking the bus. He patted the wallet again, making sure it was secure. It held every penny he had—money he'd worked hard for and that was now pledged toward more than just rent. The more he'd thought about what Johnny had done, the more incensed he got. He was going to try to hire a lawyer, on Willow's behalf. When she found out he'd taken that photo of her and Johnny had published it, she may never speak to him again, but at least if she knew he tried to fight it being published, she might give him a bit of mercy.

The alley was quiet as he walked. Most of the other small restaurants and bars had closed a few hours before. The worst thing about working at the most popular eating shop on the street was it also stayed open the longest. Breakfast, lunch, and dinner—then even late-night snacks— his boss wasn't going to miss a single hungry patron. That meant long hours and backbreaking work for all who was employed there.

Kai turned out of the alley and onto the main street, still seeing no one around. He liked the late part of the night. It was so quiet— almost surreal how only hours before, the streets were hopping with excitement and life, but now resembled a deserted ghost town, only showing an occasional remnant of human activity. Around him lay discarded beer cans, a stray and bony cat ate from a torn bag, and a few taxi drivers parked at the curb while they caught a quick nap.

He jumped, then felt silly when a trio of college-aged guys came barreling around the corner at him. They were drunk and supporting one another as they staggered, laughing at some random joke. The taxi driver next to where Kai walked spotted them first and blew his horn, then started his car. The guys waved at Kai, then approached the car, opened the door, and piled in. Their night of partying was over, and Kai watched them and wondered what it might have been like to be living their lives.

An education, nights out with the boys, games of cat and mouse with girls they took classes with—it all sounded like something out of a movie or book. Kai puzzled at what kind of deity made the decisions to put whom in what directions of fate. Why was *he* chosen, out of all the boys in China, to lose his mother and live a life of poverty and achingly depressing work just to get by? Why hadn't the Gods of fate chosen to put him into a traditional family, where he could've followed a path of education and success? For that matter, why did he have to have an emotional disability that made it so difficult to control his emotions? Why? What had he done in a previous life that deserved what he was living now? He'd only known loneliness, hard work, and a feeling of oppression. He wondered—was that all he'd ever know?

He kicked at a can on the sidewalk and reveled in the loud clanging it made as it rolled off into the street. When it stopped rolling, he heard something behind him. He turned, just in time to see something gray and fast coming straight at his face. He ducked, but it was too late. Surprisingly, he didn't even feel so much as he heard the crunch of his nose shattering.

The impact sent him to his knees. The sudden drops of crimson blood dripping onto the pavement below him jolted him out of his daze enough for him to jump up, his hands instantly moving to cradle his nose as he faced off his attacker.

Not any older than him, two boys—not just one—stood there glaring at him. Both carried some sort of metal rod, smooth at one end and jagged at the other. Kai felt frozen in place, teetering between relief that the jagged end hadn't connected with his eyes, and rage that the blunt end had met his nose. There they'd done some damage—he knew that by his sudden inability to breathe out of it and the onslaught of blood that made his hand warm and sticky.

He didn't speak, only glared and stood as tall as he could manage through the sudden dizziness surrounding his senses. He didn't need to demand an explanation—he'd been around long enough to know what they wanted. They'd expected to knock him out cold and then take what they could from him. He'd also been around enough to know their sudden surprise at his unwillingness to go down could result in far more violence than they'd expected.

"Empty your pockets," the taller one finally got the courage to say.

Both of the boys looked like they had it rougher than Kai. Most likely, they were a part of a gang that recruited street kids and forced them to earn their keep through mugging, since they were too old for begging. As late as it was, Kai was probably their last hope for a take for the day, meaning they'd stop at nothing for a few bucks.

"I don't have nothing you guys want. I'm serious," Kai said, his voice muffled through his hand and the blood running into his mouth.

"Prove it," the taller one said, showing he was the one in charge of the duo. "Show us your pockets. Jacket and pants."

The smaller guy moved until he was just behind Kai, blocking off a way to retreat and run. Kai looked back and forth at them, gauging them to see if he could handle them both. But they had weapons, and two on one when his head was already spinning would be suicide. Still—this wasn't his first time being mugged. A year before he'd been taken to the orphanage, he'd been accosted in a dark street, just like this one. He was just a little kid back then, and the memory of his helplessness that night came back to him. His anger started to mount, taking form into the uncontrollable mass he rarely allowed it to get to. He was going to crash.

He wouldn't let anyone else take what was his. He just wouldn't.

Pouncing forward, he used the thrust of his foot to knock the tall boy off balance, feeling a surge of energy when he hit the pavement hard. The impact jolted him and he let go of the rod, letting it roll. Kai lunged for it as the same time as the smaller boy swung his own weapon. The boy missed Kai's head by a mere finger's space as the timing of the lunge put him just out of reach.

Triumphant he wasn't down yet, he grabbed the fallen rod and jumped back up, holding it like a bat as he swung it back and forth, making the smaller boy retreat a few steps. The tall one scrambled back to his feet, mad as hell. Both of them stood ready to take him on, but this time, Kai was ready and no longer defenseless. He gave a wide swing to let them know he had no qualms about using the pole on them, just as they'd used it on him.

As they sized each other up, a taxi driver cruising for a patron laid on his horn, making the two boys jump. Still, they all maintained eye contact, Kai moving his head from side to side, keeping both of them in his sights. The car rolled on, unwilling or too cowardly to step in and help. Kai felt the warm blood from his nose drip into his mouth, spitting in the direction of the cowardly driver.

He tried to convince them it wasn't worth it. "I don't have anything worth losing your lives over, boys. But if you think you need to check for yourself, one of you is going down. And probably for good," Kai threatened, his voice low and deadly. He'd learned long ago never to show fear. It would give an attacker even more adrenaline.

The bigger boy reminded him of Bihua, thick and awkward, only his body weight going for him as he held both hands out like weapons. If Kai had to choose, he'd take that one, just as one more way to exorcise his long-held resentment of the boy at the orphanage who'd caused so many so much fear and pain.

"Just take off your jacket and toss it over," the boy said, stepping forward a little closer, keeping his rod in front of him as protection.

Kai looked behind and saw the other boy had also stepped in a little closer. They weren't going to give in. That meant there was going to be more bloodshed. He'd give them one more chance, and then he was going to have to take them on. He didn't see any other way out.

He hesitated for only a second, thinking of Willow and considering if he had time to work another few weeks to build up enough to see the lawyer before the photo was put out. His pause was only as long as the blink of an eye, but it was enough. While he watched the taller guy come in closer, the one behind him came in for the kill. This time, it wasn't his nose that took the brunt of the hit, but the back of his skull. As he went down and the night got blacker, he thought only of the endless piles of dirty pots and pans he'd overcome, just to fill the pockets of two streets scabs. Finally, as though in slow motion, his head hit the pavement and he thought he heard his name being called out. Then he felt hit after hit as each strike made contact with every tender point of his already-aching body. He tried to cover his head, but his arms refused to work. The boys took turns, pummeling him, metal on flesh until he could only partially see the deranged glints of their eyes.

His vision swam with the color red, and then, as he strained to see, everything went black.

Willow

WILLOW LET THE BACK DOOR slam behind her and took the few steps all at once. She'd promised Shaylin she'd come early, and she was relieved Luyan had finally agreed to go to work with her mother for the morning. Willow wasn't sure why it was such a secret before, but Luyan had finally told her that her family worked together to run an herbal shop. While Luyan's father spent most of his time working with suppliers and picking up stock, her grandparents and mother took turns working in the store to serve customers. As she turned the corner around the house, she was stopped in her tracks at what awaited her.

"Sunny?"

Hanai's dog sat on the ground, her ears up and alert, seemingly waiting on Willow to emerge from the house. She held a paw up, delighting Willow with her gesture.

"What are you doing here?" she said, then knelt and gave the paw a quick shake, checking the small tag on its collar. It showed the character for the sun, which told her it wasn't just a lookalike dog—it was really Sunny.

She stood and looked around. Was Hanai there somewhere? She turned each way, searching the yard, and then walked around to the front yard.

She didn't see Hanai anywhere.

Sighing, she stared down at Sunny, who had followed behind her every step. The dog wagged her tail, looking happy to finally get some attention. For a second, she wondered if she should put the dog in the house. But she quickly discarded that idea, knowing Luyan and her family wasn't the type to accept an animal indoors. They would also just wonder where it had come from. It'd cause too many questions. But if the dog would stay put just outside the view of the front door area, she could return it to Hanai after she returned.

"I don't have time to take you back home right now, Sunny. Will you wait here for me?"

The dog sat down on its hind end and turned her head to the side, searching Willow's face as if she didn't understand the question.

"Why am I talking to a dog?" Willow mumbled under her breath. "Sunny, stay." She pointed at the ground and spoke firmly, then turned and started walking. When she got at least fifty feet away, she turned to see if Sunny had stayed, but she didn't see the dog. She stopped, looked down, and there she was. The dog was keeping stride with her.

"Sunny, what am I going to do with you?"

The dog perked an ear up, as though she were thinking about the question.

"Well, you've lived in this village longer than I have. I guess you know your way home."

She took off and jogged the last few kilometers to the small road Shaylin had told her about. Turning left, she laughed at Sunny when the dog took the turn right along with her. So far, it was starting off to be a great morning. She was out of the house, and she'd gotten Luyan convinced it would be worth her while to see what working in the shop was like. Willow was glad to see her softening toward her mother—if only a little—and it would be a nice few hours without having to listen to the girl's bitterness. She slowed to a walk, and hoped she'd be done

141

helping Shaylin with enough time to sneak up through the woods and take Sunny home.

If she wasn't too tired—otherwise, Sunny might have to find her own way back. Willow had barely slept all night after having woken up from a nightmare about Kai. She couldn't quite remember it; she only knew she'd felt afraid and she'd been dreaming of him.

Just before they reached the building she thought to be the school, a loud honk startled her and she moved off the road, yelling for Sunny to get out of the way too. Sunny jumped to the side along with her, and Willow turned. She felt her mouth drop open when she saw what was coming at her.

Full of schoolchildren, but unlike the traditional mode of getting kids to school, the contraption coming at her was a motorized rickshaw. Basically, a huge, open steel cage balanced on the back of a three-wheeled motorcycle. As it neared, Willow started counting heads and when it passed, she was up to twenty-eight children waving and pointing at Sunny. How they'd crammed so many into it astonished her, but the driver—a gray-haired old man—pulled up to the door of the small building just as Willow arrived. She stood aside, watching as the kids climbed out two or three at a time, some from the gate the old man opened at the back, others scrambling right over the side of the metal rails. Though they weren't dressed in identical school uniforms as Willow was accustomed to seeing in Beijing, each one carried a backpack of some sort.

One child threw open the doors of the school and Shaylin emerged, smiling from ear to ear at them as they made their way over and surrounded her and Sunny.

"Is it a she or he?"

"What's her name?"

"Can I pet her?"

"She's so big!"

The children bombarded her with questions, all related to the dog.

It was obvious that, like Willow, most children in the village had never had an animal for a pet.

Shaylin shuffled them along toward the door. "Come on, let's get started."

Willow pointed her finger at Sunny. "Stay."

The dog let out a sad sigh and sank to the ground, lowering her snout to lay on her paws, making the children hoot with laughter.

"I'm glad you told it to stay out here, Willow. Laoshi would have a heart attack if she thought we had a dog in her classroom," she said, laughing as she followed her students inside. She shut the door behind them, then stood and watched while the kids quietly found their desks and arranged their bags underneath the seats before sitting down.

Willow noticed they were seated by what appeared to be age—the smaller children at the front and the eldest at the back. She judged they were from age six on up to at least thirteen. In Beijing, classes were separated by age, but she supposed in the village, it would be too difficult to try to segregate that way.

"*Ni hao*, Willow," Shaylin said when she finally made it through the onslaught of kids. "I'm so glad you chose today to come. Laoshi Lufei is absent today, so you and I don't have to worry about how long you stay."

"Oh? I hope she's well."

Shaylin nodded. "She's fine. She takes a lot of days off because she knows I'll keep everyone on schedule. The officials don't know it, but she and I work it out where she can spend a lot of time resting at home because of the pesky spider veins in her legs."

She waved Willow through the door and shut it behind her. The room was one big, cavernous space, and it was drafty, even for February. The children opted to keep their jackets on, but each child had unpacked his or her books and stowed their bags under their seats. They sat at attention, waiting for the first instruction of the day.

Willow felt dissected under the gaze of so many curious eyes pointed at her.

"They're so well-behaved," Willow whispered.

"Not always, believe me. They're just excited to have a guest—especially of the four-legged kind. You never told me you had a dog," Shaylin said.

"Well, I—"

Shaylin cut her off and gestured toward a chair next to the wall. Willow went to it and sat. Shaylin made her way to the front of the room and stood behind a large, wooden table that served as a desk. She flipped open a book, picking the pencil out from over her ear.

"Roll call," she said, and then named the children as one by one they raised their hands. Behind the desk, Willow saw a large world map pulled down from the board, the colorful continents shining bright against the dark backdrop of the blackboard.

Willow was impressed with the way Shaylin seemed to possess a sense of self-confidence she hadn't the other times they'd met. Shaylin was in her element, and her eyes lit up as she worked and exchanged various tidbits of news with her children. One small boy of about eight or so caught Willow's eye as he fidgeted with his hair. It was longer than it probably should be—and so obviously cut at home—but the shaggy look fit his soulful eyes. His clothes must have been hand-me-downs, judging by the fact they were a few sizes too big and a coarse rope held up the pants, but Willow thought he was no less than adorable. His name, Dao Dao, meant knife or sword, but it couldn't have been a further match from the boy's obvious gentle nature.

"Pride?" Shaylin called, breaking Willow out of her thoughts to look for the girl Shaylin had told her about.

A little girl in the front of the class raised her hand, and Willow could see that she was indeed pretty, but she looked much too tiny to be seven. Though dressed in faded clothes, she appeared clean and well kept, her hair shiny and braided tightly in two plaits. When she heard her name, she beamed at Shaylin, making Willow wonder if their deep affection wasn't mutual.

"I brought you something, Laoshi," the girl said before Shaylin could call another name.

She paused, looking up from her book. "You may come up, Pride."

As Willow thought about the title of teacher the students easily gave Shaylin, the little girl slid out of her seat and unzipped her yellow jacket. She quickly crossed the distance between her and Shaylin, and when she reached the desk, she put her little brown hand into her jacket and pulled out a small, aluminum soda can with one flower tucked into it. She set it on the desk.

"You brought me a flower?" Shaylin asked, picking it up and holding it to her nose. She inhaled, and then smiled down at the girl. Willow noticed Shaylin refrained from telling Pride the flower was barely more than a weed with a few straggly petals. Instead, she treated it as if it were a rare, exotic bloom deserving a place of honor.

Pride nodded her head. "I found it in the pasture this morning when I was doing my chores, and it was the only one left. The pigs stomped out the rest."

Her sweet voice rang out, and Willow felt a surge of memories hit her all at once. The girl reminded her of so many children in the orphanage. Little girls she'd known who'd attached themselves to her in their need for affection—for someone to love them, someone to call their own. Over the last few years, Willow had tried to keep them at arm's length, knowing if they were to be adopted, it would just be more painful for her to say goodbye. But looking at Pride and the warmth in her eyes, she knew even held at arm's length, many of those little girls had still found their way into her heart. She remembered each and every one of them.

Willow smiled as Pride beamed with joy that Shaylin set the can with the flower on the front of her desk.

She agreed with what Shaylin had told her about the girl. Pride was a keeper.

Suddenly, Willow couldn't think of anywhere she'd rather be. Luyan was missing a wonderful morning and once again, Willow wondered what it would take for her to realize how enchanting her own village was.

The hours with the children sped by and Willow was surprised when Shaylin eventually clapped her hands and announced it was lunchtime. She couldn't believe how mesmerized she'd been over the impromptu history lesson.

The children drew their own blossoms as Shaylin taught the children about the importance of flowers during the Ming and Qing dynasties. They all listened with rapt attention while she described how every imperial palace, prince's mansion, and official's residence were always overflowing with various varieties forced or cajoled by the top horticulturists to grow out of season. When she told how in the old days before smog and pollution became a problem, that Lotus ponds scented the air for miles around, Willow almost swore she could smell the sweet perfume. It was clear—Shaylin had a way of weaving a magical tale around facts that made up what might otherwise be considered boring historical information. It was also clear her students loved her. Now some of them sat at their desks eating, while others played around outside with Sunny, and a few even napped on their desks.

"So you can't be a real teacher?" Willow asked as she nibbled at the rice Shaylin had shared with her.

"I feel like I am a real teacher. I'm just not official. But I could be, if I had the money to go to school and get certified. I already know I can pass the exams."

"How do you know that?" Willow had always heard the teacher's exams were even harder than the national placement tests to secure a place in China's overcrowded universities. Shaylin would have to pass both to become a teacher.

"I took a practice test Laoshi Lufei gave me. She's been prepping me because she said you never know when fate can turn." Shaylin finished her rice and put the container in the bag on the floor behind the desk.

"And what does Daming think about your dream?"

Shaylin rolled her eyes. "He doesn't want to hear about it. He wants me to get a job in a shop or selling trinkets to tourists. He even said I could make a lot of money doing foot massages for the foreign tourists who come through town so much. But I don't want to do that—I want to teach. I've wanted to be a teacher ever since I can remember."

Willow felt a flash of sympathy for Shaylin. "Do you think he'll change his mind later, and perhaps you and he can start saving for tuition or the placement tests?"

"No. He's not the change-his-mind kind of man. As soon as I have this baby, he'll let me have a few months at home, and then I'll have to leave his son with Daming's mother and go get a job."

"His son?" Willow said, raising her eyebrows. "Did you go for the ultrasound?"

Shaylin looked down at the dirt floor. "Not yet. I keep stalling. But he refuses to allow me to acknowledge the baby in any other way than as his son. He says we'll convince the gods to cooperate by refusing to consider anything less than the honor of having a boy."

Willow didn't respond, but a sick feeling in her gut told her Shaylin wasn't going to have an easy marriage. Daming sounded as old-fashioned and pig-headed as anyone she'd ever known. She looked up at Shaylin and wondered why bad things had to happen to good people. And it was ironic but she felt sure Shaylin's childhood friend

Niu, the one with such a sarcastic outlook on life, would probably be the one to get everything she'd ever wanted.

Just like Luyan.

Talking about Shaylin's fiancé made her think of Kai and how different from Daming he was. Kai was understanding and supportive. He'd always encouraged Willow to dream, and no matter what she'd have decided she wanted to do, there wasn't a doubt in her mind he would have insisted she could do it.

The kids from outside straggled in to take their seats and the ones napping awoke and stretched. Willow stood. It was time for her to go, especially since Shaylin had told her that after lunch, they'd have to buckle down and get to the hard lessons. Willow wanted to leave on a good note while the kids were still happy, and she hoped to have time to trek up to Hanai's house.

"Class, open your mathematics books to where you stopped yesterday. I'll walk our new friend out and be right back," Shaylin said, moving toward Willow.

"Laoshi Shaylin, I did mine last night at home," Pride said.

Shaylin stopped at her desk on her way over and looked down at the page the girl pointed at. "You sure did. I appreciate you working ahead, Pride, but don't go too far or you'll leave your classmates behind! You can read while I'm outside."

Willow stepped out of the door and Shaylin joined her, pulling it closed behind her.

"Thank you for coming, Willow," she said.

"No, thank you for inviting me. This was one of my best days since I've arrived at this village. I can understand why you love teaching. It's an amazing feeling to be in there among children who are just appreciative to even get an education."

Shaylin nodded and leaned against the wall. She rubbed her stomach.

"Something wrong?" Willow asked.

"Oh no, he is just kicking. And my back is starting to hurt a little."

Willow looked around and didn't see the motorized rickshaw anywhere. "I meant to ask you, why aren't the kids brought here on a bus instead of that motorcycle?"

Shaylin sighed. "We have a bus, but whenever this province goes over budget and needs to cut costs, we get the cuts. There's no money for fuel, so the parents went together and bought the motorcycle, outfitted it with the cage, and take turns picking the kids up in the mornings and bringing them home in the afternoons. It got too dangerous having them walking in the road every day. The trucks going in and out of the village never look out for them."

"I can imagine," Willow said, and she could. Even in the quiet and more laid-back lifestyle of the village, the truck drivers were apt to drive too fast and reckless for small children to be in their paths. She looked at her watch. "Well, thanks again. I enjoyed it."

Shaylin waved one last time and then disappeared back into her classroom. As Willow walked away, with Sunny at her side, she said a silent prayer Daming would continue to let Shaylin live her dream, with or without pay.

"And you can use Cinnamon for respiratory infections or cramps because it warms the body, and it's also good for heart palpitations. The old people around here also use it for arthritis," Luyan said and scooped another ladle of rice from the bowl in the middle of the table. "I never knew all that stuff before, though I do remember when I was a little girl, I'd sit in the shop while Ye Ye weighed the herbs out for people."

"*Dui*, once you were allowed to go there, we could barely get you to go to school. You thought you had a real job waiting on customers," Wu Min said, laughing.

149

"But only after they decided having a granddaughter was better than no grandchild at all," Luyan said.

"What do you mean?" Willow asked.

"You think my Nainai is so great, but would you still think that if you knew she never laid eyes on me for my first seven years? She was determined she wanted a grandson and that if she didn't accept me, the gods would grant her desire."

Wu Min looked uncomfortable. "But she came around, Luyan. That's what's important."

Willow watched as mother and daughter stared at each other and was surprised when for once, Wu Min held her gaze and didn't back down. Finally, Luyan shrugged.

"Doesn't matter. They're from the old generation and all of them are like that."

"Not true," Yilin said. "You can't label every person from that generation with the same beliefs. And times are changing. Now every day, I see grandparents with their granddaughters, treating them to candies and walking them proudly up and down the main street. Anyway, you won them over once they saw how people reacted to your beauty."

Luyan couldn't hide it that his compliment made her happy. But even without that, Willow thought lately she looked like a different person. Finally, she was letting herself go natural and maybe even accept a simpler way of life. Without her makeup and fussed-up hair, and dressed in a pair of jeans and a non-descript sweater, Willow thought Luyan could've easily passed for any girl in the village. And she looked so much more comfortable and at ease. Better yet, she'd opened herself up to what her parent's life was about when she wasn't around, and was showing real interest. It was nothing less than a miracle, Willow thought.

"So you found some good memories and you learned something. I'm proud of you, Luyan," Willow said, trying to keep a smile of satisfaction from erupting. A peek at Wu Min proved to her what she already knew would happen—the woman was beaming after finally being able to interest her daughter in sharing her company for more than five minutes at a time. Willow was happy for them, though if she knew Luyan like she thought she did, her excitement would fade like the wind and she'd go back to being the difficult girl they all knew her to be.

Yilin clacked his chopsticks against the ceramic bowl he held and laughed. "You should've seen old Wang's face when he asked for ginseng and Luyan told him he was too old to improve his bedroom stamina," he said, making them all burst into laughter.

"I had to remind her ginseng is also known to combat high cholesterol and lower blood sugar levels. Every man who walks through our door is not looking to become a crouching tiger," Wu Min said.

Willow sat back in her chair, taking it all in. She didn't even think they realized it, but for the first time since her and Luyan's arrival, they looked and were acting like a real family. She wished she had a camera so she could capture the moment for them, then that made her think of Kai and her feeling of joy dissipated, leaving her empty again. It was ironic how every thought of family always came back to him.

"Well, I've heard stories about old Wang," Luyan said.

Wu Min held her hand up, stopping Luyan before she could spill any village gossip. "So what did you do today, Willow?"

Willow thought about Shaylin and her students, seeing once again the sparse but practical old schoolroom. She didn't yet want to share what she'd found there—it was such a rare feeling of peace. She wanted to hold it close and personal for a while longer. She also couldn't tell them about Sunny or her short hike back to Hanai's house. The woman hadn't been home, but Willow had opened the gate and pushed Sunny through before leaving. Willow had wondered all afternoon where Hanai could be, but then thought about the patches of ginseng she tended, hidden throughout the woods, and knew most likely that was where she'd been.

"I just took a walk, and then rested mostly," Willow said, lowering her eyes so no one would see the lie.

"Oh, and we even sell *Sheng Jiang* if you want to take some to Shaylin. The ginger helps with morning sickness," Luyan said, the bitter tone back in her voice.

Willow looked up quickly. Had Luyan spied on her? Why would she even bring up Shaylin?

"Why are you telling me that?" she asked.

Luyan shrugged, and Willow noticed both Wu Min and Yilin lowered their gaze. Not everyone was supposed to know about the girl's predicament, but it was obvious they did.

"You and she seemed awful cozy the other day," Luyan said, her eyes narrowing as she peered over her bowl. "Maybe she's your new best friend?"

Now Willow understood. Luyan was jealous and just grasping at her suspicions. She didn't know anything, Willow was sure of it. "I barely know her, Luyan. But if you'd like, the next time I see her, I'll tell her you're concerned about her health."

Luyan met her eyes with a steely gaze, and Willow held it. She wouldn't cower under her silent accusations of disloyalty. And Willow thought she might even need a reminder—Willow was supposed to be her assistant anyway. Not her best friend. Getting up, she took her bowl and chopsticks to the sink, then turned and made her way outside. She needed some fresh air to take the sudden unpleasant feeling from her mind. Luyan didn't know how good she had it, or how bad Shaylin's life really was. Yet Willow wouldn't break her confidence by airing her secrets out to Luyan's family. She just hoped everything worked out for Shaylin, that the ultrasound would show a boy to keep her from such a hard decision, and Daming would return to being the gentle boy he'd acted like when he stole Shaylin's innocence. After all, Willow hadn't met another person in the village more deserving then Shaylin to find her happily ever after.

Willow

"BUT WHY WOULD A GIRL marry someone she doesn't love?" Willow asked. She hadn't meant to let the question escape from inside her head, but Hanai had talked on for so long about relationships that when she paused, it had just slipped out. They'd even discussed things Willow had never talked about with anyone—like how when girls gave their body to someone, their hearts were usually involved, but with boys, some could be emotionally detached if they chose. It was unfair, because it sounded to her like that was exactly what had happened to Shaylin.

They sat in Hanai's cozy living room, protected from the heavy rain outdoors as they talked softly. Willow had been relieved when Luyan had gone again to work in her family's store, so she'd decided to brave the weather to check on Hanai. Lucky for her, Hanai had said she'd just been wishing for company since she couldn't get outside to take care of any gardening or chores. Now they sat warm and comfortable, with the dogs at their feet and a crackling fire that was making Willow somewhat sleepy.

"Well, are we talking about you now, or someone else?"

Willow felt her cheeks burn. She pulled her socked feet closer to her on the couch, drawing them in as though they were her private thoughts. "Definitely not me."

"Then you mean your new friend, Shaylin." Hanai picked up the ball of yarn, knotting one end, and then ran it around the fingers of both hands. Then she gently picked from one side to the other, knitting without needles as she talked. "Sometimes, as you well know, it is not a love match that brings two people together. It's an act of responsibility one feels toward their family."

"Not in this case. Shaylin told me Daming swept her off her feet. But then he changed, and he no longer acts like the boy she fell for." Willow thought it unfair, how a man could change like the seasons, going from warm like a Beijing summer to as cold as the South China Sea.

"He may have swept her off her feet in the beginning. But it's my suspicion when she discovered he wasn't who she thought he was, by then, it was too late for her to back out without causing her family shame. Losing face in our community is a serious thing. If Shaylin has grown up in a household that follows the old ways, she'll do what her family expects of her."

Willow didn't like that answer. Why didn't Shaylin's father want what was best for his daughter? Didn't he want her to be happy? Was the man really so heartless he'd rather his daughter be bullied and belittled, than for her to find someone who would treat her with respect? It wasn't fair. Willow decided then and there that she'd never marry someone out of a sense of responsibility. Not that she had a family to please, but if she did—she'd make sure her own choices were honored first. Marriage was supposed to last forever, and if that was true, it should be built on a foundation of love. Even she, someone who'd never been loved, could figure out that much.

"She was born to be a teacher. And Daming doesn't want her to do it because she can't get paid," Willow said. Her voice must have given away her distress because Sunny struggled up from where she lay curled in front of the stove and came over, putting her snout on Willow's legs. She whined, begging to be petted, and Willow granted the favor. She'd always wanted a puppy when she was growing up; even though that was a pipe dream, considering no orphanage she'd ever heard of had allowed pets. Still, a girl could dream and that she did. She lowered her face until her chin was touching the top of the dog's head, causing it to wag its tail furiously. Willow would've loved to full-on cuddle with the dog, but she resisted the urge to pat the seat beside her as Hanai cleared her throat and gave her an answer.

"Then perhaps the problem we should be discussing isn't how to get her out of a marriage she is feeling forced into, but rather how to get her into the job she loves. Sometimes finding satisfaction in life can be like salve on all other sores of dismay. If they can solve that issue, others may fall into place. Who knows, when some of the pressure is off him, the boy she fell for may emerge again."

"But how? She would have to attend the university and get a teacher's certificate before the officials in charge of education in this province would even consider her. Shaylin and Daming don't have that kind of money."

Hanai shook her head. "It's disturbing how families put themselves into debt to pay for extravagant weddings when their children could use those funds for something to launch their new lives. Wedding memories fade, and then couples are left with the reality that marriage is hard."

"And you? Did you have an elaborate wedding?" Once again, Willow wished her tongue would have some manners. She didn't know what it was about being in Hanai's house, but she always felt overly comfortable and forgot to watch what she said. She hoped she hadn't stepped over her boundaries.

Hanai's hands stopped moving, but she didn't look up. Finally, she nodded. "I guess you could say it was between modest and elaborate. My parents didn't have the funds for anything too fancy, but where they lacked, my husband's family made up the difference. It's not an event I like to remember, though."

155

"I'm sorry," Willow muttered. She was truly embarrassed.

Hanai looked up and met her eyes. "No, please don't feel that way, Willow. I want us to be the kind of friends that feel free to speak around each other."

Willow smiled at her, relieved for her kindness.

"Is there anything else you'd like to ask me about my own marriage—other than the wedding?" Hanai asked. "I'm sure the secrecy surrounding it has made you curious."

Willow didn't want to be too intruding, but if Hanai could just answer one question burning in Willow's mind. For her age, Hanai was a pretty woman, and she'd proven to be just as kind and compassionate as she was lovely. From everything Willow had seen, she was also a hard worker and resilient. So what was it about her that her husband didn't like? She supposed she'd have to ask if she really wanted to know. "I was sort of wondering, why are you and your husband not together any longer?"

Hanai pulled the yarn from her fingers and set it down in the basket at her feet. She looked away, staring out of the only window in the living room at the rain pattering against the glass.

"We were in love once, and we had a whirlwind romance and a modest wedding. Then, like I said, real life came calling and something caused a chasm between us. When things didn't go as planned, we both changed, turning into different people. When I thought I was about to lose him forever, I relented and did the one difficult thing he'd asked me to do, thinking it would be better for everyone in the long run, and that my gesture would build a bridge back to where we'd started."

"And it didn't?" Willow asked.

Hanai turned back to her, and Willow could see her eyes were brimming with unshed tears. "Oh no, only after it was all done and couldn't be changed did I realize he'd asked too much. I only wanted to give him my loyalty, but his demands cost me everything. He took too much—leaving nothing remaining in which to salvage our marriage."

Willow was silent. Hanai's words didn't make much sense to her, but then, she figured they probably weren't meant to. The woman obviously wrestled with something too hard to explain—or something too painful to share. Willow could sympathize. She also had things locked up deep inside that would be impossible to share with anyone else. She carried a lifetime of hurts, disappointments, and feelings of abandonment that unless someone had been through it with her, they could never understand. And realizing that, she knew there wasn't much she could say to console Hanai for whatever it was that grieved her and had caused her to hide from the world.

"I'm so sorry, Hanai," Willow said quietly. She gave Sunny a nudge and the dog obediently turned and went to Hanai, switching loyalties to give comfort where needed.

Kai

KAI STRUGGLED TO OPEN HIS eyes, but they were so heavy. He felt warmth flood his face, and then heard a soft buzzing in his ear. He tried to swat it away, but moving his arm caused such a streak of agony that his eyes popped open.

He shrank back from the huge face hovering over his, the features so close they were too distorted to be recognizable. He saw that the warmth he'd felt came from a ray of sun shining through the window, resting across the bed he lay in.

"Kai! You're awake," Rosi said, backing away enough for him to see the relieved smile spreading across her face.

"Where am I?" He looked around, trying to focus as bursts of pink assaulted him from every angle. Above his head, it looked like birds swayed gracefully in the sky.

"My room. You don't remember us bringing you here?"

Kai struggled to sit up. When his body refused to cooperate, he sank back down into the downy comfort of the bed, such a contrast from the pallet on the floor he'd been sleeping on for weeks.

Of course, he was in Rosi's room! All the fluff around him should have been his first clue. But how? Why? He tried to remember but got nothing.

Mama Su appeared at his side, and she laid a hand on his chest.

"Don't try to move, Kai. You've been through a lot. Your arm is casted and in a sling, so don't jostle it."

"What? Why?" Kai peered down at his arm, and then suddenly everything started coming back to him.

The taxi driver honking his horn.

The metal pole.

Masks of fury.

A kick in the ribs.

Then another.

He took a deep breath and winced when it sent streaks of agony through him. He was in bad shape—he could feel it even without anyone's confirmation. Still, he wondered exactly what they'd done to his body.

"Besides your nose, you have a broken arm and three cracked ribs," Rosi said matter-of-factly.

Kai felt his face burn with shame, embarrassed that he'd had his ass kicked by a couple of skinny street kids. But he'd been like them before, and he knew hunger and desperation could make you much stronger than imaginable. He should've just tried to give them some of his money. Made a deal.

His money!

He tried to sit again, this time getting Rosi's small hand to cut him off. "Where's my coat? Where's my wallet?"

Mama Su pulled up a metal chair, bringing it close to the side of the bed opposite where Rosi stood. "Kai, you were beaten pretty bad. The police found you unconscious in an alley wearing nothing but your jeans and shirt. They brought you to the hospital without even shoes on your cold feet. Whatever you had in your wallet is gone, son. I'm so sorry."

Along with the pain, Kai now felt sick at his stomach. All that work, eighteen hours a day, for nothing. Now he didn't have the money to see a lawyer. He wouldn't even have the money to pay his rent at Lao

Qu's. He couldn't stay there if he couldn't pay. He didn't care what the old man said; he just couldn't. He'd go back to living on the street first.

"I've got to get out of here. I need to get back to work," he mumbled, feeling dizzy with pain.

"You can go back to helping Johnny after you've recovered, Kai. You won't be going anywhere for a while," Mama Su said.

"Yeah, Kai. You're staying in my room, and I'm sleeping with Mama Su. You can't leave until you're better. But don't worry, I'll take care of you," Rosi said.

He looked at them both. They had no idea how important that money was. And they didn't even know he'd washed dishes to earn it. He'd been too embarrassed to tell them about quitting as Johnny's assistant. And that would've required telling them why, so he'd avoided it. Yet, he didn't want anyone to know he was back in a nasty kitchen, doing grunt work again.

He looked down at the thick, white cast encasing his arm in the sling and thought of something else. "But how did you pay for this? The cast? The hospital bill?"

Mama Su patted his good arm, and Kai felt something soft folded into the corner of it, resting against his elbow. He tried to look down his nose to see what it was, but his eyes blurred, then crossed, making him even dizzier. All he saw was the frayed edges of a bandage covering his nose.

"That's my monkey, Kai. I want you to hold it for now," Rosi said.

Kai made to move again, but the rush of agony stopped him.

Mama Su laughed. "Okay, Rosi. Let me clear some of Kai's cobwebs so he can feel better."

He looked up at her, grateful she could see how confused he was.

"Kai, when they got you to the hospital, you didn't have any identification, but you kept muttering on about the Lotus hotel. An officer took a photo of you on his phone, took it to the front desk of the hotel, and the girl there recognized you. She called me, and I called Johnny. He arranged for your care and has paid all the expenses, including the best pain medicine he could get the doctor to write a script for. He cares about you, Kai. You've got a good boss."

With those words, Kai closed his eyes, swallowing the lump of disgust that came up in his throat. Mama Su had no idea Johnny didn't care for anyone and would do nothing from the kindness of his cold heart—every move he made had a motive. And he knew just what Johnny's was. Bribery.

Willow

WILLOW STEPPED OUT INTO THE drizzling rain and balanced the laundry basket on one hip as she reached back and shut the door to the house. Even though Luyan was getting out and now working a few afternoons a week at the shop with her mother, she still expected someone to do her laundry for her. Luyan still acted like an empress, and she'd feigned disinterest when asked about what had changed her outlook on the town, but it was clear she reveled in the way people who had known her well as a child routinely stopped in and treated her like a celebrity, fawning over her beauty and success.

Really, Willow didn't mind doing the laundry all that much. Except for today, the weather lately was beautiful and the laundry gave her a reason to be out of the house. When she finished, she'd had more opportunities to go and visit Hanai, as well as another few afternoons assisting Shaylin at the school. And it wasn't as if she was doing any more than she'd always done at the orphanage. At least here, she had a lot of freedom, and the clean air she breathed had worked wonders on her skin and hair. She hadn't felt so light and healthy in a long time.

She took what she thought was the last step, since she couldn't see it, and before she could stop herself, she fell sprawling over what felt like a mountain of an obstacle. The basket hit the muddy ground, the clothes went flying all over the place, and Willow landed palms down with both hands in the mud.

"Sunny!"

The dog yelped, then jumped back and looked at her with an accusing expression.

Willow let out an exasperated sigh. It was no less than the fourth time in six days Sunny had found a way out of Hanai's yard and made a beeline for Luyan's house, then sat waiting for Willow to come out. *The only thing saving the dog from a tongue lashing now was that the clothes were already dirty*, Willow thought as she quickly picked them all up again and piled them back in the basket.

"Sunny, you've got to stop doing this. I have things to do, and I can't keep spending my time tripping over you or taking you back home." She stopped talking to look at Sunny and find her soulful eyes staring up at her, swimming with an apologetic look.

"*Aiya*, fine. Since you're going to give me that look, I'll admit I love having you with me," Willow conceded as she gave the dog a quick rub behind the ears.

Sunny's tail thumped with the rhythm of the rain.

Willow started walking, feeling more pep in her step since she didn't have to spend the afternoon alone. Sunny would need to sit outside the laundromat, but just having her along on the walk was like having a friend. And while the clothes were washing, Willow would find an eave to sit under with the dog. They could watch the people go by—now she knew she was losing it, and she thought how funny Rosi would think her for feeling so close to a dog. But then, wasn't life a little easier with a bit of comedic interruption once in a while? Looking down at the dog, she smiled. She might even enjoy pretending the dog was hers for a few hours. What would it hurt? She clicked her tongue, and Sunny took it as a command to heel.

Well trained, too. Yes, pretending would work out fine. "Hurry up, Sunny, we don't have all day."

After two long weeks of rain, Willow was relieved the morning of Shaylin's wedding was turning out to be a clear, beautiful day in the village. "Where's that music coming from?" Willow said, looking around. For a second, no one other than Sunny seemed to hear her question. The dog—once again having been waiting for her when she'd left the house—tilted her ear and searched Willow's face for more information as to what she was perplexed about.

They'd been waiting for more than an hour for everything to start, and the loud music that blasted from seemingly every direction was starting to grate on her nerves. Finally, Luyan's baba decided her question deserved an answer. Willow was grateful to realize she wasn't invisible after all.

"There's speakers placed around some of the shops. They play the village song each time there's a wedding or special event. Just like they used to during Mao's reign," Yilin said.

Along with most of the village, Willow, along with Luyan's entire family, had come to see Shaylin and Daming get married. Standing on the street side with Luyan, her parents, and grandparents, Willow felt like an outsider, but she wanted to support Shaylin so she'd stay.

Luyan's grandmother looked down at Sunny and clapped her hands. "Why does this dog keep showing up? Scram, dog, scram."

"It's Willow's dog," Luyan said in a bored voice.

Willow stepped between Sunny and the old woman, just in case she needed to defend against a random kick from one and a snarl from the other. "She's not my dog!"

All of them had been wondering why the dog kept showing up, but Luyan's parents had conceded when she'd argued the dog took nothing away from their family, so shouldn't be run off. Nothing they knew of, anyway, though after dinner, Willow did manage to sneak her a few scraps from her own bowl each night. And each time she'd taken Sunny back to her own home, it hadn't stuck. Hanai had laughed at her and told her the dog had a stubborn streak, and obviously felt a connection to Willow. So back and forth they went, each time for nothing as the next day, Sunny just reappeared on the front steps again like a little phantom canine.

"Look at the gold carpet they've laid at the door," Wu Min said, pointing at the building everyone watched as they waited on the wedding party to show.

"I can't believe they didn't have their wedding in the city so they could use my uncle's hotel," Luyan said, a whiff of superiority in her voice.

"Your uncle has never offered use of his hotel to anyone here, granddaughter," Luyan's grandmother said. "And nothing he could ever offer could replace what he took from me."

Silence followed that statement, leaving Willow to believe there was much unsaid. Each time Luyan's uncle was brought up, the air turned icy. Willow was glad she had managed to avoid him.

"It's common for many of the modest families to be married in the town hall. It's a place laden with deep history," Luyan's grandfather said.

"What sort of history?" Willow asked.

"Over one thousand years of history in this town, child," Luyan's grandfather huffed out, and then stepped away a few paces. He appeared to be tired of their chattering.

Luyan's grandmother perked up, finding her chance to talk about old times. "Lingshui is known for producing twenty-two scholars before the end of Imperial China. That very hall is where many of them were honored as they received their diplomas. It's also where during the Cultural Revolution, all the village farmhands would gather for meetings or to exalt Chairman Mao with quote recitations or songs."

"That's enough, Mama," Wu Min said. "You're going to bore Willow with all that old talk. And anyway, now they send all the scholarly types to Beijing for schooling."

165

Far from boring, Willow found it captivating and hoped the old woman would keep talking. But as more people gathered, filling up the sides of the main road, the waiting took on a more tense feeling and the conversation quieted, giving Willow more time to think back to the comment about Luyan's uncle.

She thought of Hanai and strained to look up and down both sides of the street. She'd hoped the woman would possibly venture into town for the festivities, but so far, she'd not seen her. No one mentioned her either, and since the family didn't know Willow and Hanai had become friends, she reluctantly refrained from asking about her.

Willow felt a nudge and looked beside her to find Shu.

"Willow, Luyan, s-s-so glad you made it," he said, his stutter showing his nervousness at approaching them.

"*Ni hao*, Shu," Willow said, giving him an encouraging smile.

Luyan greeted him briefly, and then looked out over the crowd, acting nonchalant. But something in her body language changed, alerting Willow she was glad Shu had joined them.

"Where's your pesky cousin?" Luyan asked.

Shu pointed to the other side of the street and a pack of boys laughing and making a ruckus. "He's over there with the other boys, getting ready to light the fireworks. It's going to be huge."

"This wedding will be much less opulent than some we've had here," Wu Min said. "I heard the girl's family wanted to see her married here in town because that'll make four generations of brides in their family who've said their vows on this street."

"Shaylin's father is a stickler for tradition," Shu said.

"Remember the last wedding? The family hired so many fancy cars to bring up the procession that they turned our street into a mud hole. I hope Daming's family has better sense than to do that," Yilin said, ignoring Shu's attempt to join in the conversation.

"What about the senior official who was sacked last year? He should've known better than to put on such a lavish wedding for his son.

Especially when President Xi Jinping recently warned anyone affiliated with the party to keep a low profile and stop their extravagant ways," Luyan's Ye Ye said. He was speaking to Yilin, but Willow strained to hear anyway.

"Extravagant ways that can't be supported by their supposedly meager salaries," Yilin said. "I heard he's called corruption a threat to the party's survival and has vowed to go after powerful tigers as well as lowly flies. I wonder which category the fired official fell into, and if the wedding was worth losing his job over?"

Just as the words left his mouth, Willow caught sight of the first car. A long, black stretch limousine with red roses taped all over it made its way slowly up the street toward them. Behind it, another dark, flower-covered sedan followed, then another.

"Only three cars," Luyan's Ye Ye said, and Willow couldn't tell if he approved or not.

As the cars neared, the noise of the crowd escalated in cheers and whistles. The limousine stopped and the driver hopped out, then ran back to open a door in the back.

First, Daming climbed out and waved at the crowd, a painful-looking smile plastered on his face. Dressed in a dark suit with a red tie, he didn't seem too thrilled. He turned and bent in toward the inside of the car, holding his hand out.

Willow gasped when Shaylin slowly climbed out. She'd told Willow she was renting a dress, but she hadn't said much about the details.

It was beautiful. Not surprisingly, Shaylin had decided to dress western style, as so many new brides throughout China were doing. She'd forgone the traditional red dress. Instead, she was dressed in layer upon layer of white satin accented with a deep red sash to match the bouquet of roses Shaylin clutched, making it by far the most gorgeous gown Willow had ever seen in real life.

"She looks scared," Luyan said and gave a little laugh.

If she only knew, Willow thought, but she agreed with Luyan.

Shaylin didn't fit the picture of what a happy bride should look like. With her hair done up in curls and flowers, pinned back with pearl-encrusted barrettes, she was lovely—yet her smile appeared frozen and she moved stiffly. Willow felt a burst of sympathy for her, knowing the event so far must not be all she'd hoped for. For Shaylin's sake, Willow felt nervous and bit at her nails, hoping the rest of it went well.

Shaylin and Daming waved at their friends and neighbors as they made their way into the building to sign their marriage contract. The family members from their car and the others followed them, smiling and giving their own waves to the cheers and whistles, until they were all inside.

"What happens after the ceremony?" Willow asked.

"They stay behind closed doors for nine days to get to know each other," Luyan said, giggling loudly. Shu laughed too, showing his support for Luyan.

Wu Min reached out and swatted Luyan's backside playfully. "No, they don't do that anymore. Willow, don't listen to her. There'll be a feast and most likely, the men will drink until they are drunk. The women will gather and gossip. Kids will play, and then it'll all break up when the sun goes down. That's the cue for the bride and groom to settle in to their new home, if they have one."

"But Shaylin's stuck living with Daming's family. I would never," Luyan said. "I wonder if he even paid a dowry, they're so poor."

"No, Luyan, you aren't right about that. Daming's family isn't rich, but they aren't poor either," Shu said. "They were one of the first in the village to have indoor plumbing. They've also got a refrigerator and a car. Shaylin is getting a pretty good deal, if Daming can just find a more dependable job. So I'm sure he paid a dowry."

Luyan didn't answer, and Willow thought it looked like she was pouting because of Shu speaking back against what she'd said.

Wu Min spoke. "In the old days, the groom's family would bring the dowry for the bride through town for all to see before delivering it to her parent's home."

"The old ways were far better," Luyan's grandmother said, a hint of derision in her voice. "Now the bride tells the groom what she wants, and the money for it is given to her in two payments. The first installment is given soon after the engagement, then the second a few days before the wedding. The bride buys all the things on her list, and on the wedding day, the groom's father pays the bride's family in cigarettes to carry it all to her new home."

"What if the groom is poor?" Willow asked.

Luyan's grandmother shrugged. "Even the poorest family can come up with some way to make sure their son marries as well as can be. They save from the time he is born, or they borrow from their family members. A son's marriage is everything."

Willow nodded she'd heard, then she noticed around her that families passed around thermos' of tea and packages of rice cakes or cookies. An early pack of fireworks went off, causing children to shriek and run. Willow saw Yunkun across the way, laughing gleefully at the noise he and his buddies had made. The atmosphere was the most festive Willow had seen in the village. She smiled, thinking it was good the people had a chance to relax and enjoy life once in a while.

Suddenly, the door of the town hall flew open and Daming came out first, carrying a broomstick with a paper bird swinging from it. Shaylin followed. Once out in the open, she jumped, trying to grab the bird. In her efforts, she fell against Daming and he supported her, then nudged her back to try again. When she caught it, the crowd erupted with a background of the rest of the fireworks blasting off behind them.

"That was for us. Now they'll not touch in public again, if they follow the old ways," Luyan's grandmother said.

Willow doubted that would be the case at their young age. In Beijing, it was common to see young people holding hands and even more. Though admittedly, she had noticed a lack of public affection in the village, but she supposed it just came down to how traditional Daming was raised to be.

As she watched, Shaylin and Daming stopped playing around and took on a more somber pose. An older man stepped forward and pulled a sheet of paper from his pocket, unfolding it. The crowd quieted, and he began to read.

"They're reading out a list of the groom's relatives," Luyan's grandmother whispered.

One by one, the man announced names and at each one, Shaylin and Daming kneeled together on a piece of red carpet thrown in front of them, their heads bowed, quiet for a few seconds before standing again. The ritual went on for more than twenty names, making Willow worry for Shaylin and the fatigue it must be causing her.

Finally, the reading of the names ended, and Daming and Shaylin ran to the car and climbed in.

"Now what?" Willow asked.

Shu turned to her and gave a wide smile of anticipation. "Now we eat."

Two hours after the sun went down, the village turned quiet and the air crisp. Willow walked between Shu and Luyan, headed back to the house. Sunny brought up the rear and Luyan's parents led the way, holding hands in a rare display of affection the festivities had brought out. Willow thought it a nice family moment for Luyan, other than the fact her grandparents had left hours earlier, anxious to get in before dark and their usual early bedtime.

Holding onto her full stomach, Willow sighed with satisfaction. Shaylin's reception feast had been wonderful, full of dishes like barbecued pig that was so crisp it melted in her mouth, steamed shrimp on egg white in rice liquor—a spiciness to it that burned her lips but was worth the sting—and even a velvety white custard she had never seen or tasted before.

Instead of a traditional wedding cake, Shaylin's mother had special, larger-than-palm-sized baked pineapple buns brought in from a caterer in Beijing—pastries so big that she, Luyan, and Shu had all shared just one. The delicacies were brought out centered on simple white plates with small slabs of butter on the sides, and they'd been quickly devoured by all. As they walked, Willow was sure she could still taste the crispy, greasy but sugary outside, and the fluffy bread inside surrounding the juicy pineapple cubes. It was the most delicious thing she'd ever tasted. Her thoughts were immediately drawn to Rosi and how much she knew the girl would've loved the treat.

The stack of gifts from families in the village had included clocks, embroidered art, and many sets of linens for the day Daming would have his own house to take his bride to.

Shu walked them as far as the house and then said goodbye, his eyes lingering on Luyan as she gave him a flippant wave and disappeared through the door behind her parents.

"*Zai jian*, Shu," Willow said gently. She could see how much he longed for Luyan's attention, but she wished he'd move on before the girl broke his heart. He was much too kind to tame a girl like Luyan—one with stars in her eyes and the drive to reach a level of fame he'd never understand or be able to support with his meager background. Shu needed a nice country girl—not an empress.

He waved as she shut the door behind her, still seeing his eyes gazing upward toward the bedroom window he knew Luyan was most likely behind.

Willow

THREE WEEKS LATER, WILLOW FOLLOWED in Hanai's footsteps, staying behind her in the narrow path as they went. She'd come knowing she didn't have but a few hours to spend before joining Shaylin at the school, but still, she'd felt an irresistible pull to the homestead as she'd come to know it. But instead of cozy time talking in the house, this time, Hanai said she felt like taking a walk. As they moved through the woods, Sunny quietly padded behind them. Hanai joked it was only because of Willow the dog deigned to skip her afternoon nap at all.

"She's smitten with you. I've never seen her act like this," Hanai said, laughing.

Willow tried to shrug it off, but she felt sure Hanai picked up how happy that made her, judging by the stupid grin she couldn't wipe off her face to know the dog liked her. "She's a good dog," Willow said, keeping her voice nonchalant.

"So how did you get away from babysitting Luyan today?"

Willow laughed. "She's working at the shop this morning. Then at noon, she promised a boy he could take her to lunch at the noodle shop."

"A boy?" Hanai raised her eyebrows.

"*Dui*, his name is Shu. Apparently, he grew up with Luyan. He's been following her around like a lost pup. I've tried to tell him she thrives on that kind of behavior and as long as he caters to her, she'll dangle him along."

"Yes, that sounds like my lovely niece," Hanai said. "She'll chew that boy up and spit him out if he's not careful."

"I guess Shu doesn't mind it." Willow stopped and bent down, seeing a bright flower randomly peeking out from a pile of leaves. She moved the leaves away from it, giving it room to grow, and then stood again.

Hanai must have approved of her gesture because she'd waited, and when Willow looked at her, she was smiling.

They moved on.

"I love nature, too," Hanai said as she pointed out a redheaded woodpecker above them, frantically pecking on a tall hardwood. "Look at the little worker go! He's amazing, isn't he?" Willow nodded and Hanai kept talking, showing as usual how animated she became when hiking through the trees. "It's called drumming, and when they aren't looking for insects, they're pecking as hard and loud as they can to attract a mate."

Willow gave a little laugh. Even birds didn't like to be lonely, so she wasn't alone in that, at least.

Hanai looked up at the sky and sighed. "When I lived in Beijing, this is what I missed. The clean air and the peace out here."

"I'm surprised at how much I've come to enjoy it, too," Willow said. That was an understatement. Though she longed to get back to Beijing and check on Rosi, and see exactly what was up with Kai, she also felt some sort of connection to her new surroundings. She couldn't exactly describe it—she just knew it was there, and she enjoyed the unfamiliar feeling of peace that being surrounded by nature brought to her.

"I want to show you the most important part of my work," Hanai said.

She soon led the way back to the place Willow had first seen her. When they stepped through and over the last part of the path, the tiny house of cats was directly ahead. Willow looked and saw one of the cats poke its head out of the tiny door, then scamper down the tree, headfirst as it grappled the trunk with its claws until it was close enough to jump down to the ground.

Behind her, she heard Sunny stop, and then whine. She wanted to play with the cats, chase them, or maybe even eat them. But obviously, she knew that wasn't going to be allowed because she didn't try to go after them.

"Why do the cats live out here and not with you?" Willow asked.

"I've made them a home out here because they're my security against rats and other small animals. They've never known the comfort of living close to a human, so as long as I keep them fed and dry, they are happiest here where they can use their natural instincts to hunt nighttime prey."

"Security? For what?"

Hanai ordered Sunny to stay put and when the dog obeyed by sitting, she went to the small patch of ground below the tree that held the cat house. She bent down and separated the vegetation until she found what she was looking for. "Stick! Come see, Willow."

Willow joined her and saw Hanai gently supporting what looked like a weed to her. "Why did you say *stick*?"

"Remember when I showed you the ginseng root?" Hanai asked.

Willow nodded. Who could forget a root that came out of the ground shaped like a human body?

"This is ginseng. There are rituals when it comes to finding it, developing it, and harvesting it. Legend has it that in ancient times, ginseng plants were really fairies and whoever was lucky enough to catch one and eat it would go to heaven and live forever—but only if the fairy was caught in the dark. Ginseng likes to hide to keep its freedom from hunters so we yell *stick* when we see it, then it freezes and can't run away."

Willow didn't think it looked anything like what Hanai had shown her that day, but she supposed the root under the ground was there and looking like a little human figure. "When do you pull it?"

Hanai laughed. "I don't pull it or pick it. I gently dig it up, but only when it's ready. The best ginseng is left in the ground for years to mature. You can identify each plant's maturity by the number of leaves and offshoots. A young ginseng only has three leaves. By year two, it has five leaves and creates the shape of a human hand."

"What about this one?" Willow asked.

"This one is three years old. It has two offshoots, and each one has five leaves. By five years, it'll produce five offshoots. If it can remain out here that long without being discovered, that is."

"Discovered?"

"Yes, there are lots of diggers trying to find my plants. If they found all my patches, I'd lose a lot of money from lost harvests. That's why I don't mark them. Some ginseng farmers will tie up a ginseng plant to keep it from escaping, as they believe it can. But if I do that, it's easier seen."

"Ginseng sounds like a magical being or something," Willow muttered.

"Yes, many believe it does have magical powers," she said as she moved some leaves to show Willow another plant. "See, this one is about three years old. But if you ever find one with six offshoots, it is extremely rare and precious. I've had a few, and they've sold for a lot of money in the market."

"These simple plants bring you a lot of money?" Willow was astonished. It didn't seem to be much to it.

Hanai stood. "Oh yes. What doesn't go to my family's store is sold at the markets in Beijing. Luyan's father gets a great price for my best batches—usually enough to support me, my parent's store, and the whole family if we all live within our means. But I've got my biggest crop coming in this year, and I plan to do much more with the profits, as well as support my family."

"You do all that for them? But—but—" Willow didn't know how to say it.

"What? You think they don't treat me as they should? That they leave me out here all alone?" Hanai smiled. "There was a time I thought that as well. It took me a few years to forgive the transgressions I felt they'd done against me. But I've come to know this, Willow. If you hold a grudge against someone, it hurts you much more to carry that pain than it does the person you were holding it against. It's cliché, but true—forgiveness will set you free."

"But your mother—and your sister—they don't include you in their lives," Willow said. Her words made her realize how much she'd been thinking of the way Luyan's family simply ignored Hanai's existence and how much it bothered her. She also wondered about the money that Luyan's uncle sent from Luyan's earnings. Where did all that go if Hanai was supporting Yilin and Wu Min?

"That's my choice. I asked to be left alone out here because it is what my restless soul needs. My first days and weeks out here, it was hard to put even one foot in front of the other. At first, the life I left behind made me long to dissolve into the earth and just stop breathing."

Willow could relate to that. Each time she'd showed up to her finding place, hoping to finally find her mother only to be devastated once again—abandoned again, over and over—she'd felt the need to just stop. Stop everything. But Kai had gotten her through it.

Hanai stood and looked at Willow. "Being here has given me the space and the time I've needed to heal. And my isolation makes me realize that only I am in control of my own fate. Each decision is made by me—so I need only blame myself if life doesn't go as planned."

Willow thought about that. Her life hadn't gone as planned, either.

But she didn't see how she had any control over it. Her destiny had been set for her long ago when Mama Joss found her alone in a pile of leaves.

Hanai reached out and put a hand on Willow's arm. "Time heals everything, Willow. And it wasn't always this way, but it's my choice for my family to stay away."

Family. Now that was something Hanai had that Willow could be envious of. Even though they didn't seem to be there for the woman, something told her when the time ever came that they *were* needed, Hanai believed they'd show. And that was something Willow would never have.

"I need to get going, Hanai. Shaylin is expecting me at the school to help out. The teacher is still out with some sort of leg problem."

Hanai nodded. "Let's go back to the house first, and let me give you a ginseng root. You've learned a lot today you can share with the children. If you like, I can tell you an old legend that goes along with the herb that will be sure to intrigue their imaginations."

"That would be great," Willow said, glad to move on to a safer subject that didn't involve the complication of family ties and betrayals.

"You said you'd tell us about the fairy," Pride said as she tugged on Willow's hand. In only an hour, Shaylin had already gotten them through their multiplication and division tables, and taught them at least fifteen new characters. It amazed Willow how fast the children learned and appeared hungry for more. Even the older kids at the back of the classroom sped along with their work, anxious to move on to the next subjects.

"And I will," Willow said to her as she led her back to her desk at the front of the room. Shaylin had called for a break to allow the children to go outside and use the outhouse—and give Sunny a pat on the head—but Pride had refused to leave their sight.

Shaylin sat down and crossed her leg over the other, reaching down to rub at her ankle. "My feet are killing me."

"They look swollen," Willow said, feeling sorry for her.

"Because she's getting fat," Pride said, causing both Willow and Shaylin to laugh. Now that Shaylin was married, she'd told her students about the baby. Willow wasn't sure it was wise, considering what might happen if it was a girl, but she'd kept her thoughts to herself.

"Run along outside, Pride," Shaylin said. "Give us some adult time before Willow tells you the story. You have ten minutes to get some fresh air."

Pride looked crestfallen but she obeyed, leaving Willow alone with Shaylin.

"You aren't fat, Shaylin," Willow said, trying to suppress a grin.

Shaylin waved her hand in the air. "Oh, I know. I'm barely even showing. But thanks for coming again, Willow. I love having the kids all to myself without Laoshi Lufei looking over my shoulder, but it can get tiring."

"Anytime. But you haven't told me yet how it's going living with Daming and his family. I've been worried about you, but Luyan said if it was too bad, you had enough sense to go back home."

Shaylin's eyes went to the floor. She reached up and grabbed a strand of hair, winding it around her finger. Finally, she looked up. "You saw the boy in the back row wearing the knit cap?" Shaylin asked.

"The quiet one?" Willow glanced at the boy. With his head bent and his face a mask of concentration, Willow recognized the boy who'd been called Dao Dao.

Shaylin nodded. "That's Daming's little brother. Since we're basically sleeping in the living room, we have to lie alongside Dao Dao, and Daming's still acting as if he's angry all the time. But Luyan's wrong about one thing, I can't ever go back home. My father is relieved I'm married and can have this baby without his losing face. Going home is not an option," Shaylin quietly finished.

"When do you think you two might be able to get your own place? Maybe it's the stress of living with his parents that has him on edge."

Shaylin shrugged. "Daming doesn't make that much money right now. He's the lowest on the seniority list of truck drivers and only gets a load when no one else wants it. It's not dependable income by any means. And his father doesn't pay him for work with the pigs. He feels it's Daming's responsibility to help with the family business. But if I can get a paying job, then maybe we can find a place to rent."

"But you love working with the kids, Shaylin. Isn't there something you can do to stay here?"

"Not that I know of," Shaylin said just as the kids all started coming back into the building. They quietly took their seats, all of them rosy-cheeked and looking revitalized from their time outside.

"If you want to give them the ginseng lesson, I'll take a break outside and get some fresh air," Shaylin said.

"Yes, please, Willow," Pride said, a determined look across her face. Willow had a feeling the girl never let anything get by her. She was not only adorable with her big, brown eyes, but she was also precocious for her age.

"*Hao le*, everyone look up here. How many of you know what this is?" Willow pulled the ginseng root from her pocket and held it up for all to see. While she had their attention, Shaylin grabbed her jacket and slipped out the door.

Dao Dao raised his hand at the back of the class. Now that Willow knew he was Daming's brother, she could see the resemblance in his face, though Dao Dao had kinder eyes and didn't possess the air of defiance his brother carried with him.

"Yes?" Willow pointed at him, alerting him he could answer.

"Ginseng. My father chews it," the boy said, and a few girls groaned in disgust.

"Very good. Now who knows the legend of how ginseng came to China?" Willow asked. The class was silent, waiting for her to continue.

When no one raised their hand, she backed up a few paces until she was leaning against the teacher's desk. "This is the story that was told to me, and I'll pass it down to you so you may tell your children one day."

"Hurry, Willow, tell us," Pride said, wiggling in her seat impatiently.

"Pride, you aren't supposed to talk without raising your hand," an older girl chastised from the last row.

Willow waved her hand to dismiss the rebuke. "It's okay. This is how it goes—one day, a rebellious ginseng fairy fled from her palace in the sky and landed in China to bathe in a mountaintop lake. When she returned to heaven, her father learned what she'd done. He was angry with her for coming to earth unaccompanied and unprotected from the danger of mortals. In his anger, she fled from him and went back to the mountaintop in China. There she met a man."

Pride's hand shot up into the air.

"Yes, Pride?" Willow called out.

"Was he an emperor?"

Willow shook her head. "I don't think so. From what I heard, he was a mere mortal of no importance, other than being the one who stole her heart. But when she pledged her love to him, there was such uproar in the heavens that she would lower herself to fall for a mortal, it caused an epidemic to wash over the human world."

"What's an epidemic?" one of the smaller boys asked.

"An epidemic is a sickness," Willow said. "And when the fairy realized what she'd caused, she tried to help by scattering ginseng seeds throughout the forest. The seeds grew into this magical plant that cured the infected population." Willow held up the ginseng root.

Pride raised her hand, and Willow nodded.

"Did she marry the man?"

"She did, but her father was so furious about it that he snatched her up and put her in a heavenly cave where she spent the rest of her life all alone. Her earthbound husband died with a broken heart, having never been able to see his beautiful fairy wife again."

"I don't like that story," Pride said, disapproval all over her face.

Willow laughed. "Not every story can have a happy ending. But at least the fairy died knowing her sacrifice saved the human race, right?"

Shaylin returned and looked around the class. Somber faces returned her gaze. Shaylin walked past them to the front of the classroom, leaning in to whisper to Willow. "Thanks for your help, Willow, but what in the world did you do to them?"

Willow laughed and held out the ginseng. "I just told them about this, but I promise next time, I'll be less depressing."

Shaylin wrinkled her nose, and a look of confusion crossed her face.

They shared a laugh, and then Willow waved goodbye to the kids. On her way out, Pride held up her arms, making Willow reach down to give her a quick hug and a promise to come back soon. Like Shaylin, she could see how the students were able to make a person long to return again and again.

Part Three

BELONGING

Willow

"WE HAVE TO HURRY," WILLOW said to Hanai as they walked briskly, following Sunny to the little schoolhouse. Without even noticing, the days became milder little by little until before they knew it, spring had completely slid in and summer was around the corner. Everything in and around the village was blooming with rich greens and flowers of many colors. Despite still missing Kai and Rosi, Willow had to admit being a part of Luyan's family life and finding her own place in the picturesque and relaxing village agreed with her. She wished she could bring them here, to see another way of life—something different from the Beijing bustle.

She picked up the pace. They couldn't be late! They were due at the school. This time, it would be Willow's first time standing in as a teacher. Shaylin's baby was coming soon and she'd had a rough night, so she'd sent Daming's little brother running to Luyan's house at the crack of dawn to ask her to stand in. Willow had agreed, but she'd left extra early and shown up at Hanai's house, then begged her to accompany and assist her at the school.

Hanai hadn't wanted to come but when Willow wouldn't let up, she'd finally shown her in and asked for a few moments to get ready. Even though she was going under duress, Willow thought it would be good for her, maybe even make her see what she was missing by being such a recluse.

"It's going to be so sunny and warm today, maybe we can take the students for a walk through the countryside—call it a field trip," Willow said.

Hanai didn't respond. Willow knew the closer they came to the main road where they might meet people, the more nervous she became.

"I just don't understand where the real teacher is?" Hanai asked as they passed the small fruit stand. An elderly man waved and Hanai turned her head, ignoring him.

"I only know she's been out a lot in the last few months, something about her legs. If you ask me, she's just getting too old. They need to let Shaylin sit for the exams and then hire her. I know she could pass if they'd give her a chance! She's a great teacher."

Hanai kept step with Willow, matching her stride for stride as they hurried along. "I haven't heard anything about Laoshi Lufei stepping down or retiring."

"That's just it. She has no reason to step down when Shaylin is doing all her work and she's getting the pay. Why would she retire?" Willow said, exasperation entering her voice.

They arrived at the school, and Willow went around the side. In the furthest window, she found the hidden key Dao Dao had told her about, and she came back around and unlocked the door. She felt the excitement building in her chest, mixed with a little anxiety, but she was grateful Hanai would be there to help her keep order.

Willow stood over Pride as she dipped the paintbrush in more paint, and then let it hover over the rectangle of paper on her desk. "Remember, Pride, bamboo stems rise from the ground and reach for the sky. So put your brush at the bottom of the page and pull it upward."

Pride touched the brush against the paper lightly and made a light upward stroke of just a few centimeters. "Like this, Willow?"

"Exactly like that—it looks perfect to me," Willow said. As she watched Pride work, she thought of Mama Joss and the prints of bamboo shoots on the wall of her cozy home. She missed her. "Now pick up the brush and leave a tiny space before you start the next segment of the bamboo stalk. Then you can start another one, and make it a different size. I'll move on and help someone else while you practice."

She and Hanai had worked together through the morning, helping the students with their hardest lessons, intent on getting those out of the way first in case they took longer than expected. Then they'd led them outside and taken them on a short nature hike behind the school, more of a quick romp through the woods than anything educational, but it had helped to alleviate some of their nervous energy and won some favor for the interruption in the usual schedule.

Now the kids had returned from their lunch break, and they were thrilled to practice art for the rest of the afternoon.

Willow wasn't sure who it came from, but she heard one student mumble he wished she'd teach his class every day. That made her smile, but she knew they loved Shaylin too.

She moved on to the little boy who sat next to Pride. "Oh, don't forget, you can use your brushes to make different widths, as well as make the stalks lighter or darker than the other," she called out to the class.

Hanai worked with the older students in the back. Willow had discovered out of the two of them, Hanai was the most artistically inclined, so she thought it fitting she work with the students who would take it more seriously. They'd already moved on from doing the bamboo stalks to painting the delicate leaves. Hanai was a bit shy, but every once in a while, Willow could hear her soft voice encouraging a student.

Willow strained for a moment, listening to Hanai's latest tip.

"Think of your brush like a ballerina and the very tip is her toes. When you start the leaf, your dancer should be balancing on her toes, and then as you paint, she'll come down flat on the soles of her feet, then steadily rise up again. This will make your leaves look more real by being thin at the top and bottom, but wide in the middle," Hanai said as she moved on to the last row of desks.

Willow listened intently. She'd never heard it taught that way, but it made sense. She wished her art teacher in Beijing could be there and listen to Hanai use kindness and analogies to make the children actually *want* to learn, instead of the demands and ruler rapping the old man employed for his own outdated techniques. She and Kai had shared many a laugh over Kai's imitations of the stiff, narrow-minded art teacher. But Hanai, she could teach him a thing or two.

"Willow, can you come over here for a moment?" Hanai called softly from the middle row of desks and students.

Willow made her way over to where Hanai stood, looking down at the work Dao Dao hovered over.

"Look at this," Hanai whispered.

The page was covered in bamboo stalks and leaves, the brushstrokes so fine they looked close to perfection.

"You did this, Dao Dao?" Willow asked.

He shrugged, pulling his cap down lower over his eyes. He'd seemed even more quiet than usual, barely answering Willow when she'd asked about Shaylin, but finally saying she was fine although exhausted.

"Have you had private lessons for drawing?" Hanai asked him.

He shook his head, confirming what Willow already knew. Shaylin had told her about Daming's family and their disapproval of Dao Dao staying in school. They thought since he was destined to fall into the family farming business, or possibly even work as a truck driver like his older brother, it was wasted time he could be spending working their land. As it was, Shaylin said they worked the poor boy half to death and barely left time for his homework. It showed in his homework too, she'd said, and either that, or just plain genetics led her and Willow to think perhaps the boy wasn't very intelligent. Now Willow felt guilty for her assumption. It was clear Dao Dao wasn't a scholar, but he was destined to be an artist. His gift was natural, not something that could be learned, that much she knew.

"That's extremely good work, Dao Dao." Picking up the paper, she took it to the front of the class. She used a clip to hang it on the board behind the teacher's desk. When she turned around, she saw a rare smile pasted across the boy's face.

"Today, the student-of-the-day award goes to Dao Dao," she said.

The class rose an octave in noise, many unbelieving that the boy would be singled out in a positive way, as he was usually the one who kept a low profile. As they started to get louder, Willow remembered she was the one in charge, and the one who'd better remind the students today wasn't just a day of fun.

"Remember, your teacher is going to quiz you on the history of bamboo, so I hope you all listened," she said, looking out over the rows of bent heads. She'd had to consult one of the class encyclopedias, but then had been interested to teach about the many uses of bamboo in early China. From firewood to paper, shoes, rafts, hats, and many more items that had evolved over the years, bamboo was an endless source of surprise. On the health side, she'd learned bamboo contained sugar, protein, fat, and vitamins. Today was not only a lesson for the students, but she'd learned a lot about bamboo and it's many uses in China.

She went to the blackboard and picked up the eraser, then began wiping the board clean. As she made wide strokes back and forth, she smiled to herself. She couldn't think of any day she'd had since coming to the village that had turned out more perfect.

Kai

K AI STEPPED OUTSIDE OF LAO Qu's house and breathed a sigh of relief. It was his first day free of the cumbersome cast and sling after weeks of feeling completely helpless. He'd spent the first six or so days at Mama Su's, unable to walk more than a few steps to free himself of the hurricane of female attention heaped on him, but as soon as he could, he'd moved back to Lao Qu's. At least there, he didn't feel suffocated by pretty, soft things.

Turned out his arm wasn't truly broken, just badly dislocated and strained. His ribs actually hurt more than the arm, but after a few days, it was bearable. Now, he only winced when he moved too fast. Physically, he was just about back to normal, but mentally, he was a wreck. His time being cooped up had given him too much time to think.

The more he'd thought about the last few months, the more he realized he was sick of life pushing him down. First, he and Willow had found a slice of happiness in their little world with Rosi. Then Rosi got sick. When they'd gotten through that catastrophe, Willow had mysteriously just disappeared with Luyan.

He'd decided to wait for her, and finally snagged a job doing something he loved, but then Johnny had to go and screw that up with using Willow's photo, and he was forced to go back to kitchen work. Then, just when he thought he was finally going to be able to do something—something important—for Willow, he'd been beaten and mugged. Now he was back to square one—alone and penniless.

He looked into the blue sky and held up a fist. "What? What have I done to deserve all this?" he yelled, and then let out a long breath of frustration. He just didn't get it.

When he looked back down, his eye caught the glint of something shiny and metallic around the hedges. He walked off the porch, curious to see what it was, and was surprised to see a brand-new electric scooter pushed back between two flowering bushes. Where had it come from?

Before he could consider the source, he heard a slapping of feet behind him and turned to find Rosi running across the street toward him.

"Kai, did you see your new bike? I want a ride!"

He gave her a puzzled look. "That's not mine, Rosi."

She crossed the final few feet and bent over, putting her hands on her knees as she struggled to get her breath.

"Rosi, you shouldn't be running. Come sit down." Kai took her arm and led her around to the steps, then guided her down until she was sitting. These days, whenever she become overexerted, he felt a rush of panic that her heart might not hold up, even though the doctor had assured him that since her surgery, she was fine. He'd never be able to forget the day she'd collapsed at her birthday party and been rushed to the hospital. The whole thing played in his mind over and over.

"Kai," Rosi said, breathing a little easier as she spoke. "Your boss, Johnny, he came by early this morning and left this for you. He said to be at the Haidian park at noon for another shoot."

"You saw Johnny?" Kai couldn't believe after everything he'd said to Johnny when he'd come to Mama Su's to check on him, the man still wouldn't give up. Johnny may have paid all the medical expenses for him, and Kai appreciated it, but the truth was, he wouldn't have even been on that street if it weren't for their falling out about Willow's photo. He didn't blame Johnny because he'd been attacked, but he also didn't feel bad about letting him hold the medical charges. That was the least he could do.

"Yes! That's what I'm trying to tell you." She dug in her pocket and came out with a set of keys on her finger, shaking them at Kai. "See, these are your keys now. And Johnny said you could take me for a ride—but only if you want to. You want to, right? *Dui*?"

She looked so eager that Kai didn't have the heart to tell her no. Even if he wouldn't accept the bike, what would it hurt to give it one little spin? Rosi had mentioned before how she'd love to be on the back of one of the many millions of electric bicycles fighting for space on Beijing's roads. Kai had catalogued that simple wish long ago as something she'd probably never see. He looked at the bike again, admiring the curved lines and the gleam of the new wheels. Hell—even he would like to feel like he had something of value for just a minute.

Or maybe two.

He hesitated as Rosi held the keys out. When he took them, Rosi rewarded him with a triumphant smile.

He'd give the bike back. He just needed to take one ride first.

A half hour later, Kai leaned down, close to the handlebars, as he and Rosi coasted under the Luxi Bridge. After he'd taken a short spin on the bike himself, to make sure he could control it and knew where to find the brakes, Rosi had flagged him down. As soon as he pulled up to a stop next to her, she hopped on behind him, flinging chubby arms around his middle, then proceeded to squeeze the breath out of him as she giggled with glee.

"*Tai kuai le*! Too fast, Kai." She stopped laughing long enough to shriek in his ear. "You're scaring me."

Smiling to himself, he shook his head. He wasn't even going fast at all. Judging by the other electric bikes and rickshaws that weaved around him, she should've been able to tell. Still, he did have to concentrate in order not to run over a random pedestrian as they tended to unexpectedly step off into the bike lane if the sidewalk was full, and the last thing he needed was to deal with the local *chengguan* to file an accident report. That'd be a sure route back to the orphanage and from there, who knew where.

They'd been riding for at least an hour and Kai had to admit, the feel of the machine under him and the purr of its smooth motor was going to make it hard to give back. He'd never owned anything like it—and it would sure make his life easier. There was nothing worse than squeezing on the crowded buses each time he needed to go across town.

At the large supermarket, he pulled into the parking lot and went to the end to make a wide turn. They'd gone far enough, and Mama Su would be worried if he didn't get Rosi home.

Before he could get turned around and out of there, a city bus pulled in and bullied him over to the side of the lane. Kai coasted to a stop, putting his feet down to balance the bike as they waited for the bus to move.

Rosi was quiet, watching all the people and even waving at a few who turned to stare at her. He had to give her a lot of credit—she knew she looked different and that it caused others to look, but she never got irritated. She just took the opportunity to flash another smile. She was a better person than he was, probably than he'd ever be, because the staring only made him want to punch them in the face.

"Kai, Kai, Kai…" Rosi chanted, bouncing up and down on the seat.

"Rosi, settle down," he said, struggling to keep them upright. Her sudden movement almost made him lose his balance as he straddled the bike. "The bus will move in a minute."

"No, Kai. Look!" Rosi pointed around his head at the side of the bus.

Kai strained to see what she was so interested in, looking around a pack of people lining up to board the bus.

When he saw what she did, he almost did drop the bike. He scrambled to keep it upright and Rosi dropped her feet to the ground, helping to straighten them out.

"It's Willow! Look, it's really her!"

And yes, it was, but his tongue suddenly became so awkward he couldn't speak to confirm Rosi's statement. Kai had spent the last few months looking for Willow on every street and through every window. But now, eerily, Willow was directly in front of them— splashed across the side of the bus on a life-sized portrait of her staring out into the blue. He shook his head, trying to clear his vision. But no, his eyes weren't playing tricks; it was the same portrait of Willow that Kai had taken and Johnny had sworn would only be in one magazine. Kai could feel his blood start to boil as he heard Rosi sounding out the characters, reading aloud the caption underneath the poster.

"*Face of the Forgotten; Beijing's Dirty Little Secret*. Kai, why is Willow's picture on the bus? What does that mean?" Rosi asked, her voice thick with confusion and a bit of awe.

"I don't know, Rosi."

The bus finally finished loading and pulled away from the curb, freeing them to leave. Kai needed to get Rosi back home, and then he knew exactly where his next stop would be. He was going to be late for the shoot at the park, but he hoped to catch Johnny before he took off for his next appointment.

They had some talking to do.

After taking Rosi back home, Kai got to see what the bike would do. He rode it at full speed, recklessly weaving in and around other bikes and people, not caring who he angered on his ride to the park where Johnny was supposed to be working. He ignored the pain in his arm, focusing on his anger instead—and the feel of the wind in his face, skimming past his ears, only intensified his resolve.

At the park, Kai coasted up between two other bikes at the metal posts. He turned off the ignition, climbed off, and lifted the seat, hoping Johnny had thought to put a lock inside the shallow storage compartment. He first saw a folded-up piece of paper, and then saw the glint of metal peeking out from underneath.

He picked up the paper and unfolded it. It was unfamiliar characters, but within a few, Kai knew it was a message from Johnny. He skimmed it quickly, anxious to hurry up the hill and look for him. It read, '*Kai, I know you've had a rough time of it and I hope the bike makes things easier. Come back to work, I need my assistant. Your friend, Johnny.*'

Friend. What a joke. Johnny was no more his friend than Chairman Mao was a literary genius. The now-dead leader thought spouting a few inane proverbs into the ears of those who'd put them in a book turned him into an intellectual, just like Johnny thought one shiny electric bike made him a friend.

Not even close. He crumpled the note up and shoved it back into the compartment, then pulled the lock and chain out. After securing the key into his pocket, he ran the chain through the tire spoke and entwined it around the metal bike stand, then snapped the lock on. He stood and scanned the park, looking for Johnny and his equipment.

In the sea of dark heads, all clamoring for their own little green piece of heaven, he didn't recognize anyone. Around him, families were gathered, some lying on blankets, others playing games of Frisbee or flying kites. He thought of the one thing that always came to mind when he was in places like these, that everyone has someone but him. He hated going into family parks alone, but he pulled his shoulders back and started walking.

Once past the open area congested with families, he passed a soccer field and hurried along to the music of players shouting out to each other. He looked for a tree-lined area, or somewhere that would make a good backdrop to a family photo session where Johnny would be near.

As he walked, he thought of Willow and their day in the park together. It was her birthday, and the day she'd hoped her mother would finally return to the last place she'd ever seen her daughter. When no such thing happened, Willow's dream of having a happily ever after with her mother continued to be out of reach, making her fall into a deep silence that cut him to the heart to witness.

He'd done all he could to help her out of it and that day, he'd felt as though they'd become even closer. She shared her pain of feeling abandoned yet again, and he'd finally shared his story about his own mother, of how, because of him, she'd died in the bitter cold night.

A little boy ran by, and Kai jolted to a stop to miss tripping over him. Watching the boy noisily chase a wayward Frisbee brought him back to the present.

Willow, if she were here, would appreciate that Kai cared enough for her to try to protect her privacy. So maybe they were forgotten—left to find their own paths in life with no guidance from their mothers—but that was their business and not to be preyed upon by the entire world. And if the director of the orphanage caught wind of what was going on and how it would make her establishment look less than favorable, who knew how it would affect Rosi's adoption status? Could they possibly revoke everything and take her from Mama Su?

Kai couldn't let that happen. Rosi was happy and no one was going to take that away. No one.

He followed the path around the right, toward a pack of trees. There, he saw Johnny, surrounded by equipment and several curious gawkers. The couple being photographed leaned stiffly toward each other, trying unsuccessfully to look natural.

Kai walked toward them, knowing immediately by the body language of all involved that it had turned tense. Johnny was a great photographer, of that there was no doubt, but sometimes, his ego turned what could be a memorable shoot into a stressful experience.

When he got close enough to see and hear what was going on, he lingered back, watching.

"Not like that! I said to look into her eyes, not her cleavage," Johnny yelled, throwing his hand into the air.

Kai shook his head. If he were the photographer, he'd calmly explain to the couple that the eyes were the most important part of the photo and could make or break the mood trying to be captured. Sometimes just explaining to people the thought process behind the magic could help everyone involved reach the goal.

He also noticed the feet weren't placed exactly how he'd do it. And their legs were stiff—from his school of thought, he figured if while posing that it could bend, then it should bend.

He didn't notice Johnny had stopped shooting and was looking at him until he heard his name.

"Kai—you're a little late, but I'm glad you made it," Johnny said, a fake smile plastered across his face as he covered the distance between them. "You look better than the last time I saw you, when you were laid up in the hospital. How'd you like the bike? It's a sharp little number, huh?"

Kai gave him a steely look. He didn't want to start a discussion in the middle of someone's shoot. That wouldn't be right. Johnny had left the couple hanging, just sitting there, frozen in the pose they thought he wanted. "Finish up what you're doing and then we need to talk."

Johnny leaned in close to Kai, whispering, "I've about had it with these two. They won't listen. What do you say, Kai, can you finish them? I'll take a walk."

He didn't wait for Kai to answer; he simply turned to the couple. "This is my partner, and he's going to finish the shoot. He's good— you'll love his photos. Everyone does."

He turned back to Kai and winked, then sauntered away.

Kai felt his blood pressure rising, and his blood pounding in his ears. Johnny had a lot of gall to think he could just order him about after what he'd done. And partner? So now, he'd been promoted from assistant to partner, but only in words. And he caught the sarcasm about everyone loving his photos—Johnny was referring to the one of Willow.

The couple stared at him expectantly. Kai took deep breaths as he made his way over to where Johnny's camera sat propped on a tripod. He'd take their photos because it wasn't their fault Johnny was an ego-driven idiot. They were simply caught in the middle. He looked at the camera, just sitting there waiting for him to handle, for him to use it to find the beauty in what anyone else would think was just one more clingy couple. And maybe a few shots would calm him down so he wouldn't go to jail for beating Johnny's face in later.

"Tell me again why you had them turn away from each other for that last pose?" Johnny asked, stretching his legs out on the grass in front of him.

Kai eyed him with barely concealed resentment. They hadn't broached the subject of the photo yet, as the couple had left just seconds before. Johnny had packed up his equipment, and then sat down against the tree, gesturing for Kai to join him.

"To create visual tension," Kai muttered. He didn't want to talk about photography—at least not anything recent. The memory of the bus and Rosi's astonishment at finding Willow's face on it wouldn't let him concentrate on anything other than getting an answer.

Johnny shook his head. "I thought you could only do family photos, but you're good at the romantic couple staging, man. I'd have never thought to put my couples forehead to forehead like that. The pose brought some genuine emotion into the shot. I think that's what I've been missing."

The silence fell between them, bringing in a new level of awkwardness and unspoken grievances. Kai felt Johnny was trying to butter him up, avoiding the conversation he had to know was about to happen.

"You never did say—did you like the bike?" Johnny broke first.

"Doesn't matter, I'm not keeping it," Kai said, raising his eyes to look straight at Johnny. "And you lied to me."

"Lied?" Johnny's brow creased with confusion.

"I saw the bus. Willow's face was splashed all over it." Just saying the words brought a new level of anger to Kai, and he felt his hands curl into fists at his sides, hovering in the grass. "You told me it would be in *one magazine*. One. Not shown all around Beijing."

Johnny stood up and wiped his hands on his jeans. When he finished, he held them up in a gesture of helplessness. "I didn't lie. I just didn't know. I found out like you did and went straight to the editor about it. She explained the possibility of it going out to a wider circulation was in the fine print of the photographer contract and release I signed. They have exclusive rights to use it to draw more readers to their magazine."

Kai simmered. Because Johnny was too stupid to read the fine print, now Willow's privacy was shattered. But he had to know the rest. "What's the article in the magazine say?"

Johnny shrugged. "I didn't read the copy after it was published. All I know is they asked me a bunch of questions about who Willow is, and I told them she was a runaway from the welfare institute, with no one to claim her. I said I didn't know her that well and sure didn't know where she was now. They wrote something about the travesty of Beijing's forgotten kids, I guess. I don't know."

"You don't know? You don't know? Well, did you ever think opening your fat mouth might get us in a lot of trouble? Might even screw up the life of one little girl who never wanted anything other than a mother to call her own?" He seethed, waiting for Johnny to answer—to even acknowledge what he might have done to Rosi. When he didn't, Kai felt like reaching over and punching him in the face. "That's just it, isn't it, Johnny? You don't care about anyone but yourself. You're a selfish prick."

Johnny's head jerked up and he pointed a finger in Kai's face. "Call me selfish? I wasn't going to tell you this, but I talked to Willow and she gave me permission. Said she didn't care—that she's done with Beijing."

That stopped Kai's train of thought. Willow had talked to Johnny? *No way.* If she'd been in the area, she would've come to find him and Rosi. He knew she would. He knew Willow better than anyone in the world knew her.

"You didn't talk to Willow. You don't even know where she is," Kai said, faking his confidence and careful to use just the right tone to bait Johnny into giving up anything he might know.

Johnny winked at him. "I did more than talk to her. I saw her—even took her out for a night on the town. If you know what I mean," he taunted, then picked up his two bags and moved along the path to leave.

"That's another lie, and you know it," Kai yelled at his back, following him.

Johnny turned around, a sly grin creeping onto his face. "If it's a lie, how do you think I know about her butterfly-shaped birthmark?"

Before Kai could even think through a response, his fist acted on its own and connected with the soft tissue of Johnny's nose. First, the bags hit the concrete pathway, and then Johnny's hands flew up to cover his face, but not in time to stop the waterfall of blood pouring from it.

Kai felt a crash coming on and feared what he'd do to Johnny if left to blaze out of control. Disgusted, disappointed, and unbelieving that Willow would—or could—get so close to such a disgusting creature as Johnny to disrobe in front of him enough for her hidden birthmark to be seen, Kai turned and walked away. All he could think as his blood pounded in his ears was he obviously didn't know Willow as he thought he did.

And in addition to his arm, that hurt like hell.

Willow

"Do you like him or not? That's the real question, Luyan." Willow released a long sigh of frustration. She and Luyan had once again come to visit her grandmother, and the old woman had opened the conversation up to ask her granddaughter about spending so much time with Shu. Of course, Luyan wanted to be evasive and had deflected every question thus far.

"Maybe," Luyan said, blowing the steam from her cup of tea, and then smiling slyly.

Willow suspected that *maybe* didn't quite explain it. Luyan and Shu had been seeing each other most every afternoon for the last few weeks. When Willow had finally asked her about her Taiwanese boyfriend, Luyan had brushed her off and said she didn't want to talk about it. It was nothing less than a miracle the empress was interested in a small-town boy with no connections, but the truth was in her actions, and she couldn't deny she'd been sneaking off to be with Shu much too often to just be friends. Willow just hoped when they returned to Beijing, Shu wouldn't be left with a broken heart.

"Isn't he a little young for you, girl?" the woman asked.

Luyan's mouth opened in outrage. "Nainai, I'm only a year older than he is. What does it matter?"

The old woman puttered around the room, pushing the same pile of dust around with her broom as she talked. "Back in my day, the girls were always married off to much older men, not the other way around. Except in very rare cases."

"Well, thank the gods we aren't back in your day anymore," Luyan grumbled, and Willow kicked her under the table.

"Don't be rude," she whispered. She wanted to be invited back, and Luyan's ability to rub everyone the wrong way might just prevent another invitation. Yet, as cross as the old woman pretended to be, Willow knew underneath it all, she wasn't a difficult person. She was just lonely. With Luyan taking on more responsibility in the store, now her grandmother was staying home most days, saying her gout was acting up too much to be standing around waiting on customers. Willow suspected that as she grew older, she was less inclined to want to spend time with other people, instead content to be surrounded by family. Luyan needed to appreciate that someone wanted and needed her in their life.

And anyway, the old woman told such amazing tales. The last time they'd come, she'd read them their fortunes from their tea leaves. Willow didn't believe any of it, but it was fun to hear. And she'd told Willow she was wise beyond her years. That wasn't a huge revelation as people had been telling her that forever, but the old woman had stared at the tea leaves for ages before her eyes had filled with tears. Reaching out, she'd given Willow a warm hug.

"Lao—" She started to address her with the customary title for an elder and was cut off.

"I've told you before, Willow, call me Nainai."

Luyan snickered into her tea.

"*Hao le*. Nainai, I was going to say, why don't you come sit down and get off your swollen legs? You can tell us a story."

The woman perked up, obviously thrilled someone wanted to hear a story from her. Willow noticed but tried to ignore Luyan rolling her eyes.

"What kind of story are you after?" Nainai said.

Willow shrugged. "Whatever you want to talk about. What's your favorite story?"

Nainai came to the small table and sat down. Cupping her chin in her hands, she stared into space for a moment. "Today might be a good one to tell you girls about the Ladder of Love. Have you heard it?"

"Nainai... we don't really have time—" Luyan started, but Willow interrupted.

"Yes, we do have time. Tell me about the Ladder of Love."

"*Hao le*, but first, let me get something." Nainai hopped up from the chair. Faster than she normally walked, she crossed the room and opened up the trunk that served as a side table in front of their kang bed.

"Now look what you did! We'll be here all afternoon," Luyan whispered.

"I heard that," Nainai said from across the room, laughing.

"We have plenty of time, Luyan. What else were you going to do today? You're supposed to be taking a day off." Willow knew her day off probably involved Shu, but seeing how it wouldn't be appropriate for her to visit Luyan's grandmother without Luyan—she was glad she'd talked her into coming.

"I'm planning a new display in the store window," Luyan said, her voice taking on a measure of pride Willow hadn't heard from her in a while. "I finally convinced Ye Ye he was wasting the opportunity to grab people's attention as they walked by. With some creativity, we'll get some shoppers in who didn't even know they wanted to come in an herb shop."

"Yes, he told me about that fancy line of tea you've ordered from Beijing, and those expensive teapots you're going to display. I hope you know what you're doing, girl. That's a big investment with no guarantee of recouping it," Nainai grumbled out from across the room.

"It will sell, Nainai. I promise," Luyan said, winking at Willow.

Nainai returned and laid a yellowed newspaper clipping across the table. She carefully unfolded it, making sure not to let the crisp creases split. Willow leaned over it and saw several photos, one of a young couple and several of an older one. Nainai pointed at the paper. "This is Liu Guojiang and his wife, Xu Chaoqing. They're the couple who were named China's greatest love story of 2006."

"What's so special about them?" Willow asked. She'd been hoping for an older story, but obviously, something about this one had captured the interest of the people. She had to know more. She examined the faces of the younger couple first, seeing a glimpse of attractiveness under their evident poverty. Then she looked at the photo of them in their older years, and noticed that the deep lines and many creases didn't camouflage their contented smiles.

"Well, first you have to know that China came to know the couple only after an expedition team discovered more than six thousand steps carved into the side of a mountain. They followed the steps and found a small family, headed up by Liu and Chaoqing."

"Six thousand?" Willow asked. Six thousand was a lot of steps. Just how many kilometers, she didn't know, but it had to be way up a mountain!

"Yes. Six thousand. The story goes that Liu was just a child living in a small village called Gaotan when he saw Chaoqing for the first time being carried in her wedding palanquin. As custom goes, if a bride touches the inside of a child's mouth, he'll have good luck."

"That's gross, Nainai," Luyan said.

Nainai continued. "Liu and his mother approached the bride and pulled back the curtain to the palanquin. When Chaoqing touched Liu's mouth, he was so scared he bit her."

Willow laughed. She could imagine a frightened little boy biting a stranger who dared to poke her finger in his mouth. She couldn't blame him.

"Years later, when Liu was almost two decades old, he met

Chaoqing again, though this time, she was a poor widow and mother of four children. Her husband, who at one time was the richest in the village, had died, and they'd lost everything. She and her children were penniless and surviving only on the wild mushrooms they collected from the side of the mountain. Liu felt sorry for her and began helping her. At first, he only carried water and chopped firewood to keep the children warm. Then later, he helped her plant and harvest gardens to keep them all fed. After a few years, he fell deeply in love with her and asked for her hand in marriage."

"Wait—he was a kid when she was getting married. So how old was she?" Willow asked.

"Ten years older than he—something like you and that Shu boy," Nainai said.

"Nainai, I told you, I'm only a year older than him. And I'm not marrying him anyway. He's a friend. That's it."

Nainai flashed Willow a sneaky smile and winked. She smiled back. She knew Luyan's grandmother was trying to tease her granddaughter.

"Anyway, Liu's family was completely against the marriage and threatened to disown him. The widow, Chaoqing, told Liu to find someone else to marry because she'd fallen in love with him too and didn't want him to lead a life of ridicule for being with an old woman."

"Thirty is an old woman?" Willow asked, her eyebrows rising in wonder.

"In those days, it was," Nainai said. "But Liu was adamant. He married Chaoqing, then they and the children moved high into the mountain to get away from all the gossip and petty meanness their union caused."

"They just randomly made camp on a mountain?" Luyan asked.

"Not randomly. They found a hut and made it their home, only coming down to the village occasionally for supplies. They were stubborn, even forced to protect themselves against wild monkeys and tigers. But over the years, Liu and Chaoqing worked to make their own hand-fired tiles and built a bigger and sturdier home, one that would last for many generations."

"How did they pay for supplies?" Willow asked.

"Among other small things, they wove shoes and raised honey. They sold their wares below in the market and to tourists hiking the mountain. They didn't need much. As the story was told, Chaoqing had at one time lived in the finest house and wore the best silk clothes, but she'd never known contentment until she married Liu and made do with what life brought her, never being envious for more."

"So what about the stairs?" Luyan asked, and Willow could tell she was finally getting into the story.

Nainai smiled. "Well, remember, Chaoqing already had three children before she met Liu. Then, after their union, he gave her four more. Several of their seven combined children went to school, and then later moved off the mountain to live in the village. Liu never fell out of love with his wife, and he cared deeply about keeping her safe. When she began to make more trips down to see her children and grandchildren, Liu started carving the stairs by hand. It took him over fifty years, and he went through almost four dozen chisels, but he was intent on making a safe way for his bride to go up and down the mountain. And that, my girls, is the story of the Ladder of Love."

"Oh, that is sweet," Willow said. "They gave up the comforts of village life and the acceptance of family and friends for love. Are they still living?"

Nainai looked sad for a moment, as if she'd known them. "No, they're buried together on that mountain. Theirs was a true love story, and they never spent a night apart." She held a finger up and pointed at them. "Maybe if you girls search hard enough, you'll find your own Liu Guojiang. A simple love—that's what's important."

Luyan snorted her disagreement, though Willow noticed she said nothing. For herself, the glow of the story faded a bit as she thought of Kai and how once, she'd have thought they could possibly have grown to be like the old couple, in love and on their own, dependent only on each other, and content living a simple life. Simple would've been easy for them as they'd never known anything more. Not like Luyan, who expected the world on a golden platter.

Luyan stood. "Great story, Nainai, but we've got to go."

Willow

THE TAXI DRIVER CAME TO an abrupt stop alongside the curb in front of an old, dilapidated building, and then turned to them. After some heavy negotiating by Shaylin's mother-in-law, he had driven them to a place on the outskirts of Beijing, a town bigger than the village but small compared to a city.

"One hundred ten renminbi," he said, holding his hand out over the seat.

Willow watched as Shaylin rummaged in her purse and brought out her wallet. Opening it, she pulled out the bills, handing them over. She asked him for a receipt and as they waited for it to print, Willow scrutinized the building.

"Are you sure this is it?" she asked Shaylin.

"That's the address Daming's mother gave me. She said she called ahead and they're expecting me."

Shaylin had asked Willow to accompany her to the procedure, claiming Daming had to work and she didn't want her mother-in-law to be a part of what could either be a joyful moment or a sad announcement. Basically, she needed a friend, and Willow was glad to fill that slot for her.

The street looked like a hubbub for clothing vendors, but the building the driver pointed out was nondescript. A few people could be seen sitting inside the front door, perched on cheap plastic chairs. The front window was wide, but newspapers taped across it kept the interior private.

They climbed out of the car. Willow followed Shaylin through the doors and to the front desk. A young woman sat there, staring at a small screen that played an old Chinese soap opera. Willow didn't see a computer anywhere, and she felt her first stirring of unease. It didn't look like what she'd imagined a doctor's office should look like. Instead, it could've been the dismal lobby to any starter business— anything other than a medical establishment.

Against the wall in the small room, the few girls she'd seen from the street sat in the row of plastic chairs, their faces impassive as they fiddled with their cell phones or other items. One held a small baby, swaying it back and forth on her knee as she hummed. She was a young mother, and she looked exhausted. Willow wondered if she were here for the same thing, and if she was from the city, how she'd let herself get pregnant after already having one child. That sounded like a sure road to heartache.

"I have an appointment," Shaylin told the girl behind the counter.

"Name?" the girl asked, her voice low and bored. After Shaylin told her, the girl picked up the handset of the phone, dialed a number, and held it to her ear. "Your four o'clock is here," she said into the receiver. She hung up the phone and looked back up at Shaylin. "They'll be in to take you back in a few minutes. First, you pay."

"How much?" Shaylin asked.

"Three hundred renminbi," the receptionist said.

Shaylin opened her purse and pulled out the money her mother-in-law had given her. She slowly laid it out on the countertop. The receptionist took it and tucked it into a drawer.

"You'd better get a receipt to give to Daming's mother," Willow said.

"No receipts," the receptionist said, looking up at Willow as if she'd lost her mind. Then she told them to take a seat.

Shaylin nodded and crossed the room to the chairs.

They both sat down, and Willow leaned in toward her. "This place is strange."

"Strange how?" Shaylin whispered back.

Willow shrugged. "I don't know. Too quiet, I guess. Just strange. And it smells weird."

Shaylin shrugged back at her, picking up a ragged magazine from the table beside her. Willow watched as she flipped through it, barely taking time to look at a photo, much less to read any of it, before she moved on to another page.

"Want to talk about it?" Willow asked.

Shaylin dropped the magazine back on the table, shaking her head. "Let's just wait and see what they have to say."

Willow stood and went to the table, looking for something to read. She picked up the same magazine Shaylin had discarded and took it to her seat.

A girl about their age came in, gave her name, and then sat down beside them. Willow ignored her, assuming if she'd come alone, she probably wasn't up for conversation.

She turned pages quickly, bored with the many fashion spreads and advertisements for perfume and makeup. The photo spreads made her think of Luyan, and she realized talk about returning to life in Beijing had been rare lately. Could Luyan finally be realizing that selling herself in front of the camera was a soul-sucking career that would leave her empty one day? She doubted it, but she could always hope Luyan would come to her senses.

In the middle of the magazine, someone had placed a brochure. Willow plucked it out. She was just about to set it aside when the title on the front of it caught her eye. *'The Model Abortion for a New Generation!'* it read. Willow felt a lump of horror in her stomach. She tucked it back into the magazine where Shaylin wouldn't see it, but she propped it where she could read the text under the headline.

'Painless. Strictly confidentiality. Guilt free.'

The pamphlet sounded like an advertisement for the latest miracle medicine, and the jovial tone of the wording made Willow cringe. Of course, she wasn't too ignorant to realize the best place for an abortion clinic to advertise would be a clinic that performed gender recognition ultrasounds. Still, it made her angry Shaylin could have easily seen the same brochure and been faced with that ugly word again. She felt sorry for her—the magic of carrying a new life was being sullied by the fear of her husband and his family that she wouldn't be able to produce an heir to their name. It was ridiculous.

She had another thought, remembering when she'd overhead the ayis at the orphanage talking about abortion. They'd said the government was starting to get serious about controlling it and had banned advertisements in public or in circulated newspapers. Yet, they were still slipping through. Willow didn't have any doubt the government didn't care how many abortions were performed, as long as it kept the population numbers down. It mattered nothing to them that so many girls and women were being forced into terminating the lives of their future children by the very people who they called their family.

A woman—or nurse, Willow supposed—holding a clipboard, showed up at a side door and called Shaylin's name. They got up, following her through the door and down a short hall. Before they got to the room she was leading them to, Willow peeked into another room and saw a line of women sitting in what appeared to be recliners, all hooked up to IV pumps as they either slept or stared vacantly ahead. Each had a flimsy, neon-green blanket folded over their lap—a lame attempt at giving them comfort.

"What's that room?" Willow asked.

"Recovery room," the nurse answered briskly as she showed them into a small, whitewashed room that smelled of alcohol. She opened a cupboard, pulled out a paper gown, and tossed it on the examining table. "Take off all your garments and put this gown on."

"Recovery for what?" Shaylin asked, but the nurse dropped her clipboard into the metal slot on the door, closing it behind her as she left.

Willow caught Shaylin's worried look as she went to the examining table. "Why do you have to take off all your clothes just for an ultrasound?" she asked. "Don't they just need access to your stomach?

Shaylin sighed. "I don't know, Willow. I've never done this before."

Willow turned to face the wall, giving Shaylin privacy to undress. In front of her, a poster displayed the inside of a woman's body. At nose level, Willow studied the uterus, the most interesting organ ever created. In school, she'd thought of it as a small cave, a safe haven for a child to feel protected as it grew and readied itself to face the world. She heard Shaylin rustling the paper gown behind her as her imagination again went to try to imagine what it was like in her own mother's uterus. Sure, she'd been warm and safe for the moment—but had her mother caressed her own growing stomach in anticipation, or had Willow's impending birth caused her as much stress and turmoil as Shaylin's baby was causing her?

"You can turn around."

Willow turned to find Shaylin perched on the table, hunched over as she held the paper gown together. Again, she felt sorry for her that her pregnancy was not a joyful one because of her family—or Daming's family's—superstitions.

"I hope the doctor hurries. I have some questions for him," Shaylin mumbled.

"Is everything okay?" Willow asked. She looked at the machine standing next to the table, a small monitor with a handset, obviously the ultrasound machine.

Shaylin shrugged. "I've had some cramping and a bit of spotting. But it might just be stress. I'll be glad to hear the heartbeat, though."

"I'm sure the baby's fine," Willow said. Shaylin was such a quiet person, keeping most of her worries to herself. The way she kept up such an optimistic outlook in the classroom with her students while she was shouldering such stress at home just amazed Willow.

The door opened and a nurse walked in, unsmiling like everyone else they'd seen in the building. Willow was starting to wonder what it was about the clinic that made everyone so sour.

The nurse went to the sink and washed her hands, then began rummaging through some drawers. "Lay back."

Shaylin did as she was told, and Willow went to her side. "Is the doctor coming?" Shaylin asked.

The nurse brought over a tube and pushed aside the paper gown, exposing Shaylin's brown stomach. She squirted some gel on, and then used the tool on the machine to rub it in. Willow thought she looked unwilling to actually touch Shaylin herself. Just as Willow was about to speak up and ask the same question about the doctor, the nurse finally answered.

"The doctor doesn't do this part, I do."

Shaylin nodded, but Willow was confused. What did she mean by *this part*? How many parts to the procedure were there?

The nurse flipped a switch on the machine, and a noise started. It sounded like being underwater, the pulse of what was happening in Shaylin's stomach loud and alive.

"You've got a lot going on in there," Willow said, smiling at Shaylin.

Shaylin let out one small giggle, and Willow could tell the thought of her baby in there made her happy. Finally, the nurse found the loudest part and stopped moving her wand. On the screen, the fuzz cleared up enough to show a faint outline. It was a baby. A real baby! Willow felt a burst of joy for Shaylin.

"Lookie there, Shaylin! That's your baby," she said, barely containing herself. Even though she'd known Shaylin was carrying a child, seeing the form of it on the screen made it so much more real.

"Listen," the nurse scolded. As they listened, they made out the faint thump of a heartbeat. The nurse moved the wand a bit more, and then the sound came through loud and clear.

A smile of relief spread on Shaylin's face, and Willow could tell she'd been more worried than she'd let on.

"The fetus has a strong heart," the nurse said, her face still impassive. "Now let's see what the sex is, in case we need to move you to the procedure room. The doctor has a full schedule today. You'll need at least three hours to recover, putting you here until closing time at least."

Willow wanted to correct the woman and tell her it was a baby—not just a fetus—but she held her tongue. This was Shaylin's business, not hers.

"What do you mean, in case we need to move to a procedure room?" Shaylin asked as she watched the screen.

The nurse moved the wand around, trying to get a clear picture of the sex organs. "Your file says if it's a female fetus, we are to immediately terminate."

Willow gasped, unable to contain her shock at the nurse's words. Nothing had been decided about that, and surely, Shaylin was too far along for that now.

Shaylin was obviously also shocked and sat straight up, making the nurse drop the wand in surprise.

"Now look what you did, I'll have to wash this and reapply the gel," the nurse scolded.

"Did you see the sex?" Shaylin asked her, her voice firmer than Willow had ever heard it.

"No—you didn't give me a chance to hone in on it. Now lay

back and let me rinse this off. You're making me hold up the doctor's schedule." She went to the sink, her back stiff and unyielding.

"Well, let me help you open his schedule up then," Shaylin said. Climbing down from the table, she went to the hook where her clothes hung. She grabbed them and held them against her. "I don't want to know if my baby is a boy or girl. I'm going to keep it no matter what, and I won't have you, your busy doctor, or my husband's family tell me what to do with my child."

Bravo. Willow wanted to stand and clap out loud. She was so proud of Shaylin that she could run over and hug her. But they needed to present a strong front and not appear to be two silly and naïve girls.

The nurse looked shocked into silence, making Willow think it was a rare thing for anyone to talk back to her. "No one is going to bully her into doing what they want," Willow said to the nurse, and then turned to Shaylin. "I just can't understand their thinking."

"Oh, I do. Daming and his parents don't want to waste our birth permit on a girl."

The nurse turned around and shrugged. The first hint of softness showed on her face. "If you are carrying a girl, you'll have a long road ahead of you without the support of your husband and family. Do you understand that? They might even disown you. Are you prepared for that?"

Willow watched Shaylin. For a moment, she looked unsure, but then she pulled her shoulders back and nodded. "Boy or girl, this baby is mine. It's not just a fetus, it's a living, breathing human being, and I love her—or him—already."

The nurse dried her hands, and then crossed the room to Shaylin. She patted her shoulder. When she spoke again, her voice was kind. "They won't refund your money."

"It wasn't mine anyway," Shaylin said. "And I thought I was only paying for an ultrasound. I would have never gone through with a termination. I know that now."

Willow couldn't believe how sneaky Shaylin's mother-in-law was, calling ahead as she'd done and arranging an abortion if needed. That should be Shaylin's choice—no one else's. Willow steamed with anger.

"Girl, you're so naïve. An ultrasound is a mere fifty renminbi, not three hundred. But I admire your strength. Many girls go through with the procedure only to live a lifetime of guilt and regret over what might have been." She lowered her voice to barely over a whisper. "Sometimes, the burden they carry for the rest of their lives is heavier than if they'd only followed through with having the child. I've seen it all, and there are many disillusioned should-have-been mothers out there. There's a reason China has the highest rate of suicide for women in the entire world."

And Willow bet the nurse had seen a lot—probably more than her share of heartache. In that moment, she felt a burst of compassion for her. Something told her the nurse didn't want to do her job. The evidence was in the lines of worry in her face and the heavy aura she carried.

"Come on, Shaylin. Get dressed and let's get out of here," she said.

Kai

K AI CARRIED THE TWO HEAVY suitcases and followed the man to the elevator, waiting quietly behind him. When the doors opened, the man stepped through and Kai followed, then set the bags down to catch his breath. He got one good look at the man's fine suit and his slicked-back dark hair before he jumped at the rebuke.

"Pick those up off this floor!" the man scolded. "That's real leather you're manhandling with no regard."

"*Dui bu qi,*" Kai apologized, grabbing the bags quickly to hold them up. He should've known better, but after the last six hours of carrying luggage up for at least three dozen new patrons in the hotel, his arms ached—especially the one that had recently recovered from the sprain.

The man huffed and brushed an imaginary piece of lint from his stylish black suit. Kai kept his eyes downcast but he knew what he'd see around him, watching the same scene unfold as he had each time in the elevator. While some of the hotel guests had been friendly, the majority of them had treated him as if he were a servant to be ordered around. And really—he was, and crazier than that thought, he was grateful for the job.

The elevator passed the first few floors, the bell dinging with each number as it rose. A few awkward seconds more and they'd be there, then he would follow the man out, carry his luggage to his room, and hope for a small tip. In the first few days, the other guys had schooled him on bellhop etiquette and the right way to pose as he waited, open for a tip but not overly anxious. So far, in the last few weeks since Mama Su had gotten him the job, he'd done fairly well with the amount he brought home. Still, he was hoping to save enough to get him to a new level in life. He'd not be a bellhop or a dishwasher for the rest of his life, but for now, as long as Luyan didn't come back and ruin it for him, he'd stay. The work was easy and he was putting up more money, saving for a time when he could get his own place and possibly buy his own photography equipment. Funny, Johnny hadn't thought to bribe him with a camera—or maybe that was on purpose—but Kai was determined to one day be better and bigger than he was. And he'd have more integrity than to steal other people's work, too.

The bell rung one last time and the doors opened. Kai stepped back, giving the signal to the customer for him to leave the elevator first. After his little lint show, the man had pulled his smartphone from his pocket and was completely engrossed in something he saw on it.

Just when Kai thought the doors might close again before they could get off, the man tucked his phone back in his pocket and strutted out. Kai followed, waiting as the man struggled with the key. Finally, he opened the door and entered with Kai behind him.

Kai set the two bags on the carpeted floor in front of the bed. He looked around, realizing the room was almost identical to the one that he, Willow, and Rosi had stayed in. He felt a streak of nostalgia, missing the short time they'd come together and pretended to be a family.

"Will there be anything else?" he asked. *Please give me a tip, please give me a tip*, he chanted silently in his head.

The man dismissed him with a hand in the air and Kai headed for the door, slowly in case there were second thoughts. But no, he made it out the door and closed it softly behind him. No one called out to him to turn back and receive a small bill that to the giver might not have been much, but to the receiver would mean he was that much closer to a better life. Kai sighed, hurrying to the elevator. The day was still young. Hopefully, it would provide a few more patrons who were a bit more generous to the lower classes of the world.

Kai sat across from Ning and watched her put the straw to her mouth, wrapping her pink-lined lips around it in a perfect bow as she slurped her pearl milk tea. Every few sips, she looked up at him and giggled, a sound he still hadn't gotten used to, despite it being their third date.

"Are you sure you don't want some, Kai?"

He shook his head for the fourth time. The pearl milk tea, or Bubble Tea as most called it, wasn't something he liked. For one, it left a bitter aftertaste—not to mention it was named after the Chinese word *bōbà*, which meant large breasts. He wouldn't admit it, but he felt ridiculous even ordering it, despite the fact that being seen drinking it was the latest fad raging through Beijing.

"I'll stick to green tea," he said and lifted his cup to his lips again.

She laughed again, soft and high, an unbelievable irritation to Kai's senses.

"Don't be such a country boy. You're missing out." She turned the cup toward him and tilted it. "See the black bubbles? They look like pearls, but they're chewy and delicious."

He knew what they were. The bubbles—pearls, or whatever she wanted to call them—were made of tapioca but tasted like compacted congee to him, a flavor that always brought to mind his memories of his years in the orphanage. He shook his head again, declining the offer. How many times did he have to tell her he didn't like the Taiwanese drink? He caught himself before letting out an impatient sigh.

Ning was a nice girl with a pretty face, but Kai still felt awkward with her.

After finally coming to terms with what Johnny had told him a few weeks before, he'd realized that Willow had obviously moved on, so he needed to do the same.   Dealing with Rosi was a different story, though. She'd been convinced Willow was going to come back now that she was a star—*as Rosi had put it*—and by sharing the good luck, they'd all be well off. Mama Su had told him Rosi had danced around the laundry room for days, ecstatic and telling everyone about Willow's face being on the city bus. He'd finally asked her to stop talking about it around him because each time it was brought up, it felt like a sucker punch to his gut.

Things had started looking up a few days after he'd begun working at the hotel, opening doors and carrying endless amounts of luggage, when he'd run into Ning on his way back down to the lobby. He'd remembered her instantly—she'd been the first girl to ever flirt with him when he'd seen her months before outside of the hotel room he, Willow, and Rosi had stayed. That day, they hadn't had a real conversation, unless you counted asking for toilet paper, but when he'd seen her again, he'd immediately thought to ask her out to get even with Willow for seeing Johnny.

Maybe it was an immature reaction, and a creep move, but he knew Ning would be an easy date with low expectations. Maybe even so low he could handle them.

"Do you want to see a movie?" she said, breaking him out of his thoughts. "The new *Planet of the Apes* is showing, I think something about the Dawn."

He shrugged. In addition to not wanting to spend the extra cash to see the American-imported movie, he didn't want to go anywhere else but back to Lao Qu's house and to bed. But he was forcing himself to act like a human and behave his own age instead of like an irritable old man.

"I guess we can, if that's what you want to do," he finally said, though sitting through two hours of apes running around wreaking havoc on humans wasn't something he cared about. Why couldn't she be interested in something about China—a movie that delved on their long history? But Ning wasn't that kind of girl, and she never would be.

Ning lit up, her smile showing she was thrilled their date night wouldn't be cut short.

"Finish your bubble tea," Kai said, feeling guilty he was using her to nurse his broken heart, but unable to help himself. He watched her and couldn't help but compare her to Willow. Her face was the first complete contradiction. Ning was from the Maoming area and her skin was darker. Her face was rounded and her cheeks rosy and girlish, while Willow's was more mature—like a woman's. And Ning was older than he was by a year or so but still short, barely coming to Kai's shoulders, making him feel like a giant as he walked next to her, completely different from the easy stride he and Willow kept because of their closely matched height.

His eyes moved down to study the flouncy dress Ning wore. She was all flowers, bows, and ruffles, a concoction Willow would've had to be forced into at gunpoint. It looked nice on Ning—he wasn't taking that away from her—it just felt weird to Kai to be with such a girly girl. He only knew it didn't take makeup, curls, or fancy clothes to make Willow beautiful. She was just naturally pretty.

Then he wished he could kick himself under the table.

Willow was gone. She hadn't cared enough about him to leave a note, make a call, or even stop by and talk to him when she'd come to town to see Johnny. It made him sick that she'd set her sights on someone with money—someone with no soul. The bottom line was he obviously didn't mean as much to her as she had to him. And that crushed him.

At least tonight was going better than the first evening out Ning and he spent together. After getting the courage to ask her out, he'd picked her up when her shift ended at the hotel, and they'd gone to eat a simple dinner of noodles and steamed buns. It was Kai's first real date, which was embarrassing enough, but conversation had been difficult because she'd asked too many questions about his childhood, family, and past. Questions he couldn't and didn't want to answer. He'd spent the two hours strategically redirecting everything back to her until she'd finally called him mysterious and stopped with the inquisition, but only after Kai had felt first one drop and then several others of perspiration making a line down his spine. But he'd made it through that first date and even another. He still couldn't say seeing someone else had cured him of obsessing about Willow, but he was determined.   He would eventually get over her.

Just like she had gotten over him.

Willow

W ILLOW HEARD THE POUNDING AT the door, but it didn't register that she wasn't dreaming until Luyan's father poked his head in their room and his low voice brought her awake.

"Willow? Get up."

She sat up, rubbing her eyes as she tried to shake the sleep from her head. What time was it? The moonlight shone in from the window, telling her it wasn't yet morning. She was exhausted. She and Shaylin hadn't returned from the clinic until well after dinnertime, and Willow hadn't gotten to bed until later than usual. Her thoughts were jumbled with fatigue.

"What?" she mumbled when Yilin called out to her again.

"Come out here. There's a boy on the porch. He says he's a student, and he wants to talk to you."

Beside her, Luyan growled at them to be quiet as she turned over to face the wall. She yanked the quilt, and Willow felt a rush of cool air on her legs. Flipping them over the side, she slipped her feet into Luyan's sleek silk slippers. She still didn't have any of her own, instead borrowing when she could to keep her feet from hitting the bare floor.

"A boy? What boy?"

Yilin leaned against the doorframe, fatigue showing in his face. "He said his name's Dao Dao."

That woke Willow out of her detached state and she stood, reaching for the extra robe of Luyan's she'd been borrowing. She struggled into it, her mind racing about Shaylin and what it meant for Dao Dao to be at her door. The baby must be coming early—that was all she could fathom. But why come to her? She wasn't a midwife. She had no idea what to do if someone was in labor.

"I'm coming. I'll be right there," Willow said.

Yilin turned and headed back toward the stairs. "He looks harmless. I'm going back to bed. But can you tell him the next time he has something to say to wait until the morning?"

Willow shuffled out of the room, crossed over the kitchen area, and went to the door. She pulled it open to find Dao Dao huddled against the side of the house, trying to stay out of the cool night wind. He didn't wear a jacket. Instead, he had a small blanket wrapped around his shoulders, gripping it with one hand under his neck. Sunny sat between him and the door, watching Dao Dao in case he tried to enter without an invitation.

Willow pulled at his arm, guiding him in through the front door and out of the wind. She beckoned Sunny in, too, and the dog padded in and sat in front of the stove. Willow hoped Yilin wouldn't get back up and catch the dog in the house. "Dao Dao, what are you doing? Is Shaylin okay?"

"No, she's not. Daming found out she backed out of the ultrasound. Mama has convinced him it's a girl baby and it's going to ruin the family. Now he's more determined than ever to be rid of it."

Willow led Dao Dao to the couch, and he sat down. She sat beside him, putting an arm around his shoulder. He was trying to sound tough, but his wide eyes told her he was frightened.

"Get rid of it? That's crazy—she's way too far along. Is he really that stupid? And she might be carrying the boy he wants so badly!"

"Shaylin told him no matter what it is, she's keeping it, and he went crazy. She got scared and took off, Willow. We don't know where she is, and I'm worried about her."

Willow looked into Dao Dao's eyes and searched to see if he was telling the truth. "Dao Dao, did Daming hurt her?"

He hung his head. "I don't know. I went outside when they started arguing. She ran out past me, and I went in to see what Daming was going to do."

"Did he send you here to find out where she is?"

He quickly shook his head. "No! He doesn't even know I left. He and my parents were in the kitchen talking, I heard them say she probably went to her mother's house, so I snuck out. I thought I'd catch up to Shaylin, but I couldn't find her."

"Okay, I'm going to get dressed. You wait here, then you and I can go look for her," Willow said, hurrying back to the bedroom.

She quickly dressed, slipping her feet into her shoes and grabbing a jacket as she left the room. Luyan never stirred, and Willow was thankful she didn't have to explain to her what was going on. If they could find Shaylin and help her work things out with Daming, maybe the village rumor mill wouldn't get involved.

When she came back to the main room, Dao Dao was sitting on the floor beside Sunny, stroking her back. The dog looked like she was in ecstasy with the serious petting job she was receiving.

"Let's go," Willow said, making both of them jump. "Dao Dao, you need to get back home before you get into trouble. Sunny and I will try to find Shaylin."

Dao Dao answered her statement with a stubborn pout.

"Do you want Daming to know you were on Shaylin's side?" Willow asked, knowing for as old-fashioned as his brother was, he'd expect complete family loyalty. And so far, none of them thought of Shaylin as family. At least, not that Willow could tell by the way they treated her.

"Shaylin is more than my sister-in-law. She's my favorite teacher.

225

And she's out there alone somewhere. I'm not going home until we find her."

Willow grabbed one of Yilin's jackets from the peg by the door. It would swallow Dao Dao with its size, but at least he'd be warm. At the door, Sunny whined and used her paw to scratch in an attempt to open it.

"Fine. But you'd better move fast. I think Sunny knows we're on a mission and with any luck, she'll help us find Shaylin." Willow suddenly remembered the nurse's words about China's women and the high rate of suicide. She said a prayer under her breath that Daming's words weren't so damaging that Shaylin would even think of a thing like that. But still, something in her gut told her to move fast. They had to find Shaylin before Daming did.

Willow moved quietly through the town with Dao Dao right on her heels. They'd been out over an hour. They'd already checked a few places when she suddenly knew where Shaylin must be.

"What if she's not there?" Dao Dao whispered.

"Then we keep looking."

Along the way, she had questioned Dao Dao about his family and if he thought they'd really harm Shaylin or the child she carried. He said he didn't know what his parents would do, but he felt sure Daming wouldn't be able to make good on his threats.

Willow wasn't so sure. After all, Shaylin probably knew Daming better than anyone did, and here she was, fleeing and hiding to keep her baby safe.

It was impressive how such a young boy could have his own morals and values, and for the next half hour of walking, Willow was glad to have Dao Dao with her to keep her company against the dark shadows of a sleeping town.

When they finally approached the small schoolhouse, she turned, holding her finger to her lips. "We have to go in really quietly. If she's here and hears us outside, she might think it's Daming and run."

She beckoned for him to wait while she went around the back and found the hidden key. When she returned, he was still there, hunched over with his hands in the pockets of Yilin's coat, shivering at the sudden wind that had come up.

Willow quietly put the key in the lock and turned the knob. Pushing the door open slowly, she put her head in first to look around.

The lights were off and nothing appeared to be out of order. She scanned the room, letting her eyes adjust to the moonlight, but no one was there.

"I don't see her," she said. Disappointment filled her, mingling with a helplessness that she knew of nowhere else to look for Shaylin.

"Can we go in and warm up?" Dao Dao asked, rubbing his hands together.

"Just for a minute."

Willow held the door, letting Dao Dao and Sunny pass through before shutting it behind them. They moved into the room, moving further from the howl of the wind outside.

"It's a cold night, and she shouldn't be out in it," Willow said. Sunny came to rub against her legs as if in agreement.

"What were you going to do if you found her?"

"I'm not sure," Willow said, pacing the floor to warm up.

Suddenly, she heard something.

It sounded like a whimper, and it came from behind the teacher's desk. Sunny heard it too and immediately went around to investigate. When she didn't growl, Willow knew it was safe to look.

She held her hand up for Dao Dao to be quiet, and then she approached the desk. When she walked behind it, she saw feet coming from beneath it.

"Shaylin? Is that you? Please come out," she said, trying to peer under it. With the desk facing the window, the shadows behind it

227

completely blocked her vision. All she could see was a person. But it had to be her.

And it was.

"Is he outside?" Shaylin asked.

"Who? Daming?" Willow said. "Of course not. It's just Dao Dao and me. He came to find me when you took off. He was worried."

Shaylin slowly crawled out of the small space, holding her belly.

"Are you hurt?" Dao Dao asked, alarmed when he came around and saw her.

"Only my pride," Shaylin said. "I've been cowering in there like a child, unable to stand up for myself."

Willow helped her to stand, keeping hold of her until she'd steadied herself. "There's nothing to be ashamed of, Shaylin. You are doing what any good mother would do—you're protecting your child."

Shaylin threw her arms around Willow, breaking into sobs. "What am I going to do? I have nowhere to go. This is the only place I even thought of where I feel safe. But he'll find me here eventually."

Willow patted her back, hushing her before she spoke. "I have an idea, but it will entail a bit more walking through the cold, if you think you can handle it."

Willow helped Shaylin along the path, clutching her arm to make sure she didn't stumble. In the dark, it was hard to see but after so many trips back and forth for the last few months, she knew it fairly well and could traverse it with just the dim glare of moonlight shining through the trees. Even if she couldn't see well, Sunny led them through. She just had to keep her eyes on the dog's light-colored coat.

"Are you sure she'll be okay with this?" Shaylin nervously asked.

"Yes. She'll be fine. Don't worry. And she's not a witch—that's just a bunch of rumors and lies. She's really nice."

"I hope Dao Dao got home safely," Shaylin said.

"He'll be fine. He's tougher than he looks. You should've seen him, Shaylin. He was determined to find you." They'd sent Dao Dao home after telling him to be careful of what he said. He'd pledged to never tell he'd found Shaylin, and Willow believed he'd stand by his word. He was a good kid.

Now she just hoped Hanai wasn't angry with her for bringing someone to her sanctuary. "It's Luyan's aunt, you know," Willow said, unsure about telling Hanai's business but wanting to ease Shaylin's mind that they weren't going to meet a total stranger.

"Well, that makes sense," Shaylin said, obviously out of breath. "I'd always wondered about her. There have been so many rumors over the years. Does she live alone?"

"Yeah, she lives alone. It's a small house but bigger than Luyan's, so she should have room for you, at least for a while until we figure out what to do." She noticed Shaylin holding her side.

"Let's rest for a minute. You can catch your breath." Willow led her to the base of the tree she'd stopped at the first time she'd found the trail. Shaylin carefully sat down, but Willow stayed standing to keep guard.

Sunny stopped where she was, a few feet ahead of them on the trail. She sat down, her expression ferocious as her ears perked to listen for danger.

"Does Luyan and her family know she lives out here?" Shaylin asked.

"I'm not completely sure, but I think they do and they just leave her be. She likes to be alone from what I can figure out."

"Then how are you and her friends? How did you even know about her if Luyan doesn't know you've been out there?"

"I stumbled into her," Willow said, describing the day she'd first seen Hanai—also now remembered by her as the day she'd lost her ring—and she told Shaylin of the friendship they'd forged when she'd returned to look for it.

"Did you ever find your ring?" Shaylin asked.

"No, I still look for it every time I come out here," Willow answered carefully, not ready to convey to anyone what the ring really meant to her. "Come on, Sunny. Let's keep going."

Willow stood and helped Shaylin up, and they continued behind the dog. When they climbed the small hill and rounded the corner, they could see a small light on in Hanai's window.

Sunny gave one loud bark, and then Willow heard Hanai's other dog, Moon, start up. He barked and howled, making Willow hesitant to go inside the gate as she normally would. Moon was inside the house, but if Hanai let him go, she wasn't completely sure the dog wouldn't charge them. Moon was the fiercer watchdog of the two and he'd accepted Willow, but she didn't want to test him in the middle of the night.

"Let's wait here," Willow said. "Hanai will probably come out to see what Moon is upset about."

Just in case, Willow kept Sunny on the outside of the gate with her. If anything, she felt sure the dog would protect her from Moon if need be. Within a minute or so, they saw another light come on at the far side of the house.

"Hanai! It's Willow," she called out when there was a lull in the barking.

The front door opened, and Hanai poked her head out. "Willow?" she called out.

"Yes, it's me. I have a friend with me," Willow answered.

Hanai squinted out into the dim morning. "Who?"

"It's Shaylin, the one who just got married. I told you about her," Willow said, getting impatient. Shaylin was exhausted, and they needed to get her off her feet. Even for just long enough to let the swelling ease up.

"Moon, down," Hanai called out just as the dog slipped around her legs and out the door. When he heard the command, he immediately stopped and sat, letting out a low but terrifying growl.

Willow reached over the gate for the release and tried to open it. It didn't move.

"I'll have to come unlock it," Hanai said. "Wait a minute. Moon, stay." She disappeared back into the house, the door slamming shut behind her.

Sunny ran off toward the back of the property. A few seconds later, she emerged on the other side of the gate. She trotted over to Moon and licked his muzzle.

"She's telling Moon we're friends, to chill out," Willow said.

"You think so?" Shaylin asked.

"Yes, look at his tail now." Willow pointed at Moon again. Where the dog's tail was erect and at alert, now it wagged back and forth, raking at the ground he sat on.

"Luyan's aunt doesn't look happy to see us," Shaylin said.

"Well, I'm sure we probably scared her, coming at this hour. Let's just see what she says."

Shaylin looked like she was about to cry, and Willow couldn't blame her. She'd first gone to her own parent's house, but they'd turned her away. Their own child! They'd told her to go back home and work it out with Daming. Then Shaylin had run to the school, knowing there was no working anything out with him. When Willow had found her, she was crying, exhausted, and her feet were swollen.

Hanai emerged, now bundled up in a long, quilted yellow bathrobe. She came to the gate carrying a key and unlocked a padlock Willow had never seen before.

"I didn't know you lock the gate," she said as they waited.

"Only at night," Hanai said. "I don't take to visitors much, especially ones that come in under the shade of dark."

Willow thought she heard disapproval in Hanai's tone. The woman opened the gate and waved them through. Then she stood there with her hands on her hips, examining them from head to toe as if she'd never seen Willow before. Finally, she spoke.

"I'm assuming since you're here at this time of the morning and you've brought a stranger to my home, this is some sort of emergency. Start talking, Willow, because you have some explaining to do. I thought you understood my need for privacy."

Willow was taken aback. She wasn't sure now if Hanai was going to let Shaylin stay or not. Maybe she'd misjudged the woman's well of kindness. But she had to give it a shot. For Shaylin—and her child. They couldn't go back.

"Okay, but can we go inside? Shaylin's ankles and feet are swollen. If she can just prop them for a little while, I'm sure she'll get some relief."

Shaylin didn't say anything, only stood there like a frightened deer.

Even in the dim light, Willow could see the scowl Hanai wore and her few seconds of hesitance felt like an eternity. Finally, she turned and led them toward the door.

"I'll make some tea. Get in here and put her feet up. Give her a blanket."

Willow heaved a sigh of relief as she gestured for Shaylin to go first. They were going in, and that meant a bit more of a chance to get Hanai on their side. If after tea, Hanai asked them to leave, their next stop would be to talk Luyan's parents into keeping Shaylin hidden under their roof. But she suspected because of the friendship that she and Shaylin had forged, Luyan's house would be the first place Daming would look for his young wife, so she hoped it didn't come to that.

Kai

"MAMA SU, HAVE YOU SEEN Ning?" Kai asked. He'd finished his shift half an hour before, and Ning was supposed to have met him at the corner across from the hotel. When she hadn't shown after fifteen minutes, he came back into the hotel. Instead of taking the chance of being reprimanded for wandering around the hotel when he was off shift, he'd decided to check with Mama Su. Even if it wasn't her department, the woman had an uncanny ability to know where everyone was at all times.

"She came to restock her cart with sheets about an hour ago, but I think she said she had one more room to do on the second floor. She's coming back down to drop off the last load of soiled bedding for the day, if you want to wait."

He went over to the folding table. Using his hands, he heaved himself onto it, letting his legs dangle over the side. A girl he didn't know grabbed a tall stack of pristine white towels, moving past him and out the door. He looked around, trying to see if Rosi was in and around the room somewhere amongst the several carts of soiled and clean laundry.

"She's in the kitchen," Mama Su said as she held a sheet high in the air, her fingers grasping two corners and bringing them together, just to do it again for a tighter square. "If you're looking for Rosi, I mean."

He nodded, then jumped down and grabbed a sheet. Why was he just sitting there staring when he could be helping the woman? She'd already done so much for him. He watched her movements, mimicking them as he tried to fold the sheet the same way she did.

"You'd better be glad she's up there or she'd be begging you for another ride," Mama Su said, smiling at him.

Kai laughed. He'd decided to keep the bike. He felt he'd earned it, after all he'd put up with. Johnny hadn't paid him what he was worth and had taken the credit for all his photos—especially the one of Willow. Not only that, but he'd made Kai work to keep his low-key clients happy while he pursued fame and fortune in the modeling world of magazines.

So the bike was well earned.

And Rosi enjoyed going for rides so much that most every evening ended with at least a short ride around the hutong.

He looked around, seeing they were alone now, but it appeared as though she still had plenty of work to finish before her shift ended. He'd wait for Ning in the laundry room, and maybe he'd see Rosi before his date. He should've known, though, if she wasn't doing laundry, that she was visiting or catching a snack in the hotel kitchen. Rosi had not only charmed everyone on Mama Su's crew, but she'd enamored the staff in the kitchen too. Always willing to help when needed, Rosi had stood in to do dishes and even chop produce on occasion.

Mama Su had regaled them at dinner with stories of how since her return to work, Rosi had won over just about everyone in the hotel, many times having them argue over her, coveting the aura of joy she brought to every room. Kai only wished he had that kind of power to make friends. It was no secret only a close circle of people really understood him, but he wasn't unfriendly, just a bit reserved. His entire world consisted of only two people who could pledge to know who Kai was—and he realized how sad that was.

Mama Su finished another sheet and added it to the growing stack on the table. Kai wondered if she ever showed fatigue.

"Kai, I've wanted to talk to you for a while now. Since Rosi isn't here, I think it's as good a time as any."

He waited. Like him, Mama Su wasn't big on just chatting, so a requested conversation had to mean something important. Immediately, his thoughts went to Rosi and the adoption process. Was Mama Su having second thoughts? Had the article about Beijing's forgotten children come around to cause problems? So many thoughts swirled in his imagination, though he only nodded. He put his clumsily folded sheet on the pile Mama Su started. His face reddened when he compared it against the nicely squared corners of the others in the stack.

Mama Su patted the tabletop, and Kai obliged. He was terrible at folding sheets anyway. He'd been so relieved when Mama Su had gotten him a job as a bellboy instead of working with rows of washing machines and dryers, though he would've taken that too.

After pulling up a metal chair, Mama Su crossed her arms over her chest.

"Have you heard from Willow?"

Kai shook his head, not trusting his voice to keep his anguish in at the mention of her name.

"Well, I don't know the details, but I've heard a bit about Luyan being in trouble with her uncle. I hope Willow isn't involved in it."

"What kind of trouble?"

Mama Su shrugged. "All I know is it's going around that the uncle is displeased with Luyan and gave the authority for her room to be rented to customers. But it isn't my place to gossip."

He couldn't give a reaction to that news. Why should he care she no longer had her own private hotel room? He fiddled with the stack of sheets next to him, waiting for Mama Su to go on.

"What do you think you're doing?" she said, her eyebrows as high as they could possibly go.

"What do you mean? I was helping you," Kai said.

"I mean with Ning. Please tell me you aren't serious about that girl."

Kai sighed. He had wondered if Mama Su would ever come out of her usual closemouthed stance and say what she thought about him moving on. With the outburst Rosi had given when she'd found out Kai was dating Ning, he'd thought he would've heard from Mama Su about it sooner rather than later, if she'd decided to confront him, that was.

"I wouldn't say I'm serious," Kai said, his voice trailing off. Then he looked her in the eye. "But like I told Rosi, it's time I move on. Willow did, as we can all see, and no one has cast any disappointment her way. Why do you want to pick on me for doing the same thing? And why can't Rosi understand it's not my fault?"

He knew he sounded like a child but the truth was, he respected Mama Su and didn't want to think she felt him anything less than loyal. And as for Rosi, she'd looked at him as if he'd kicked a puppy when she'd found him and Ning holding hands in the employee's section of the hotel courtyard. She'd almost caused a scene, declaring Kai belonged to Willow, before Ning had dropped his hand and ran back into the hotel. Since then, he'd tried to keep their public displays of affection to a minimum, but the truth was that Rosi was going to have to eventually come to terms with it. Even though Kai still didn't see Ning as someone he could be with forever, the girl did expect him to treat her like he was interested at least. And that meant sometimes holding hands.

"I'm just concerned," Mama Su said.

"She's from Maoming. She already told me that," Kai said. "Her brothers knew Luyan's uncle, and he agreed to give Ning a job. So they sent her here."

"Is that all she told you?"

"I don't know what you mean, but if you're thinking she comes from a questionable background, it can't be any more so than mine. I went from being a street kid to an orphanage and then back to the streets. It doesn't get any better than that in the questionable category."

Mama Su held her hand in the air, stopping him from saying more. "Don't talk like that, Kai. What happened to you, Willow, and Rosi isn't any fault of yours. You were all three victims of circumstance, and you didn't choose your paths."

Not choosing their paths was true, but really, Kai felt like he had nothing else to offer the world. Seventeen and washed up—that was what he was. At least Ning acted as if she wanted to be with him, and that was more than he could say for Willow. She had bailed given the first opportunity for something better.

"I see that look in your eyes, Kai," Mama Su pointed at him. "I've spent a lot—and I do mean a lot—of time listening to Rosi tell her stories of life in the orphanage. One thing that's stood out to me about you is you not only had the skills it took to supervise and run a kitchen, but you carried compassion with you that made all the other children respect you."

Kai had never thought of it that way. He hadn't tried to be compassionate; he just wasn't a monster like some of the others who used their weight and prestige to bully kids into doing what they wanted. Like Chef Wu.

Mama Su lowered her voice, almost to a whisper. "I've heard some things about Ning's family."

He felt his brow crease in confusion. What was she talking about? Despite coming from a poor family, Ning was as wholesome as they came.

"Like... what things? Can you be more specific?"

Mama Su looked at the door again, and then stood. "I don't want to pass on any rumors, but I care enough about you to give you a warning. That girl isn't as naïve as she leads everyone to believe. Just be careful, Kai."

237

Kai was still puzzled, but Mama Su turned from him and went back to folding her sheets. She was done talking. And Kai needed to think. He hopped off the folding table. Mama Su's words had reminded him of an afternoon when a beggar woman had approached him and Ning, asking for a coin. Kai had been embarrassed at the way Ning had brushed the woman off, causing the beggar to lose face. He'd dug in his pocket and given a few bills, mostly out of regret for the way Ning had treated her. He remembered thinking how Willow would've never been so callous.

"I'm going outside. If Ning comes down, please tell her to hurry up."

Mama Su turned just as he was almost through the door. "Kai?"

He stopped, looking back at her. Her face wore a pinched, concerned expression.

"Don't tell Ning about our conversation. I don't want to borrow trouble. And you don't either. You're a good boy, Kai. A good boy who's been dealt a tough hand in life. Don't let your past make you susceptible to falling into something you can't get out of—or even something that makes it impossible to hold your head high."

With that, she turned back around, having said more to him in one conversation than everything she'd said in all the months he'd known her put together.

Kai would think about her words, and he'd be on the lookout for trouble. But still, Ning might be immature and a bit selfish, but he couldn't believe she was sneaky or smart enough to be involved in anything too terrible. Mama Su was just being protective—she had to be. As for holding his head high, he wasn't much yet, but one day he'd be somebody.

And he kind of hoped Mama Su was around to see it.

Willow

WILLOW KNOCKED ONCE, AND WHEN she heard Hanai call out, she entered. The scene that greeted her was no longer one of awkward silence, as it had been the first few days of Hanai getting used to someone constantly being in her space. Now Shaylin reclined on the couch, looking relaxed, her legs up and feet propped on pillows. Across the room, Hanai sat in her chair, knitting and talking. On the floor in front of her, Moon slept, not bothering to even get up and do his job.

"He heard Sunny give a bark when you came up," Hanai said, nodding downward toward the dog. "He knew it was you two."

"What's going on?" Willow asked, closing the door behind her.

"Knitting. Shaylin's baby is going to need a new layette," Hanai said. "Shaylin is making socks."

Shaylin shot Willow a sad smile and held up a pair of tiny, yellow knitted socks. "Yellow. Can go either way."

"I wish I could knit. I'd help you," Willow said, taking a seat on the floor beside Moon. Sunny dropped down there too, nudging Willow's hand mid-stroke of petting the other dog, showing her jealousy and need for attention.

"Hanai can teach you," Shaylin said, sitting up and moving her feet to the floor. "After I learned to cast on, she taught me how to do these socks. She said a few more weeks of practice and I can possibly make a shirt."

"Uh, I don't think you have a few more weeks before the little one comes," Willow said, making Shaylin smile.

Once they'd explained the situation to Hanai about Daming wanting her to abort her child, it was amazing how fast Hanai had agreed to let her stay on until the baby was born. What to do after that, they hadn't figured things out, but the hope was that Shaylin would have a boy. Then everything would be fine so she could go home if that was what she decided she wanted to do. Shaylin still felt protective over Daming, saying his mother was the one pushing him to be so difficult, but Willow wasn't convinced. She hoped Shaylin never returned to her egotistical, bullying husband.

Hanai laughed. "*Dui le*, I can teach you both. It's not hard. Knitting is a task that just takes a lot of patience and no hurrying. And it's soothing, too. I taught myself. It's not that complicated, but you're right, Willow. I don't think we have weeks left. So I'll do the basic items first and get them out of the way. We don't want that baby feeling cold on his or her birthday."

Willow wished they didn't feel rushed to get some things made but since Shaylin's run for freedom, Dao Dao had been feeding her information about Daming, his family, and even Shaylin's mother. All of them were furious because they couldn't find Shaylin, and though her mother had already, according to custom, ordered the entire layette for the baby to come solely from her, she'd declared Shaylin would never see a piece of it, not even the traditional piece a month before birth to hasten the baby's delivery. It wasn't only Daming's mother who was being difficult; Shaylin's mother had definitely not stood by her daughter. Though Shaylin wouldn't talk negatively about her own parents, Willow could see the hurt in her eyes when her mother came up in conversation.

"Willow, has Luyan figured out where I am? Or has she gotten suspicious about you coming out here so much?" Shaylin asked, the fright showing on her face even though she tried to hide it.

"No, she thinks I'm working every day at the school until late afternoon, even when I'm not," Willow answered. "And I have stopped by there a few times, just in case Luyan asks the teacher if she's seen me."

"Do the kids miss me?" Shaylin asked.

"Yes. From what Laoshi Lufei says, Pride has been so sulky she won't even do her homework," Willow said. "And she came to school with her hair a mess and didn't even bring her lunch."

Shaylin sat up straight. "Willow, something must be going on at home. You need to make a visit—check on her grandmother."

"She lives with her grandmother?" Hanai asked.

"Yes, and the woman is old," Shaylin said. "Pride has to do a lot inside and outside to take care of them both—she does too much, actually."

"I feel like she's fine, Shaylin. She's just upset because she expects to see you every morning when she walks in."

Hanai put down her knitting. "Girls, now that Willow is here, I have something to talk to you about."

Willow turned to Hanai, noticing she sounded serious. *Here it comes*, she thought, *now she's going to say Shaylin can't stay any longer.* Already, in only seconds, Willow's mind jumped ahead, trying to think of other alternatives to keep her safe from Daming.

"Willow, I see those wheels turning. Just listen to me for a minute. I'm not putting Shaylin out."

Willow could feel the weight lift off her chest with Hanai's words. As for Shaylin, she still hadn't regained her color, but relief was still apparent.

"Yesterday, when I asked you girls to stay here and look out for each other, I took a trip to visit the Secretary of Education of this province."

Shaylin looked shocked. Willow got up from the floor and went to sit beside her.

"For what, Hanai?" Shaylin finally croaked out.

Willow could hardly believe Hanai had gone to the city. From what she'd come to know of the woman, nothing could get her to leave the sanctuary of her home in the woods.

"It's time someone went to bat for you, Shaylin. You've been working for this village for years, putting in long hours to help educate their children. It's time they recognize that."

"But they'll never hire her because she doesn't have her teaching certificate," Willow said. The fact Shaylin also hadn't gone to college was unspoken, but she wasn't going to embarrass her by stating it aloud.

"That's the point," Hanai said. "They've agreed if Shaylin can get a high enough score on the *gaokao*—the usual exam for college entry—they'll let her move on and take the teacher's exams without the standard mandatory requirement of a completed college degree."

Willow felt something amiss, but Shaylin looked nothing less than cautiously optimistic.

"The gaokao is notoriously difficult. What if I can't pass it? Or if I do, what if I don't pass the teacher's exam?" Shaylin said.

"Pfft," Willow snorted. "You can pass all of it with your eyes closed. That's not even a worry. I just can't believe they'd do something like that for a small-town girl with no connections."

"I have the connections," Hanai said, pointing at her own chest. "You both know I was married a long time ago. I've never done it before, but this time, I dangled my husband's name shamelessly. He still carries some clout and is known in and around Beijing."

That was an understatement, Willow thought. According to Luyan, her uncle was on par with a rich official or movie star.

"And they'll do it just based on his name?" Shaylin asked, her nose wrinkling with distrust.

"No, I'm not going to lie to you. It's going to take some money changing hands. But don't get me wrong—I'm not asking them to pass you. They won't do that. The bribe is simply to get them to agree that if you pass the tests on your own, you can be a certified teacher. You have to do all the work, Shaylin."

Shaylin looked speechless. But Willow wasn't.

"But neither Shaylin nor I have any money," she said. "And I just can't ask Luyan for more. She's already done so much to help me with another friend." Willow didn't mention Luyan had borrowed the money from her uncle. No sense giving more information than was needed, and anyway, Willow planned to pay it back one day.

"Don't you two worry about that," Hanai said. "I'll get the money. This is for your ears only, but my biggest crop of ginseng yet was harvested last spring and it's been drying out in the work shed. It's ready now, and I'm just waiting for Yilin to take it into the city. With what it will bring in, I'll have plenty enough to help with the family store as well as to pay what it takes for you to take the required exams."

"No, Hanai, I can't let you do that. Your crops are how you survive. You can't spend your money on me. Anyway, it's too much of a risk," Shaylin said, her voice low and quiet, her eyes downcast.

Willow knew Shaylin well enough that she could tell she was already doubting herself and her ability to pass any tests. For a girl who'd only gone to high school, obviously the thought of college exams as well as a teacher's test was terrifying. Though she didn't want Hanai to give up her own income to make it all happen, Willow felt grateful Shaylin would have a chance to have her dream job.

Hanai stood. "It's already decided, Shaylin. I'll share something else with you girls. I've already been keeping that school afloat for many years with anonymous donations. My support has been the catalyst to allow girls to continue getting the same education there that the boys do. So this isn't something out of the ordinary. If anything, it's a selfish gesture, as it's my wish that you will be the next teacher for

Lingshui Village. I can't think of a better gift for the children than to have their favorite laoshi back in the classroom—this time for good."

Shaylin looked up and slowly smiled. Willow could see the tears shimmering in her eyes. Likely tears of gratitude and maybe even hope—or tears that just possibly, even though she was poor and had never had any chances at furthering herself, meant this time her dream was within reach.

"I also brought back several study books. You can get started after dinner," Hanai said.

"You can do it, Shaylin. I know you can," Willow said as she reached over and squeezed her shoulders.

"But except for Laoshi who took it a million years ago, I don't even know anyone who's ever passed the gaokao," Shaylin said.

"Yes, you do," Hanai said quietly. "I did."

Willow

I N ADDITION TO A SMALL table and chairs, Hanai's cozy kitchen now included a large blackboard, tacked just a bit uneven on the wall where an embroidered calendar once hung. They'd done the best they could with it. For the last few weeks, in addition to her other studies, Shaylin was using the board to stare at and memorize characters, only to be tested at the end of the evening by either Hanai or Willow.

The bombshell that Hanai herself had passed the gaokao still hung in the air and made Willow curious, especially about the story she'd told about giving up her chance of an education in order to keep working and put her young husband through school. She'd told them even though many in the country were starting to protest against the gaokao, saying the process robbed China's children of their curiosity, creativity, and childhood, Hanai had been driven to pass it.

Willow felt maybe since Hanai was from a humble family, she'd had something to prove. Still, when she'd proven it, she'd then given up everything for her husband, and now he was the rich businessman while she lived a poor hermit's life in the woods. Willow didn't understand it, but something told her even though she didn't know the man, she'd bet Hanai was the more content of the two.

"This will never work. I'm wasting my time as well as yours, Hanai," Shaylin said, laying her head on her arms.

"It will work, and you *will* get a high enough score. Have faith in yourself," Hanai said.

Willow stroked Sunny's warm back as she watched them interact, noticing how they looked like a true teacher and student.

"But I know a girl who studied at least fifteen hours a day for her entire senior year, and she didn't score high enough to get into a top-tier university," Shaylin said.

Willow thought about Yongmei, a girl at the orphanage who was being tutored to pass the gaokao. She'd always been a pet to the director, a girl who received extra rice in her bowl and got to wear the newest garments that were donated to the orphanage. Willow wondered if she'd taken the test yet and if so, how she'd fared.

"Didn't you participate in mock gaokao exams in high school?" Hanai asked her.

"Yes, I did."

"Then how did you do?" Hanai paused at the board, waiting for Shaylin to answer.

"Sometimes, I did well. Other times, I did horrible."

"Everyone is different, Shaylin. A lot of advanced students fail to do well on the actual test because they can't get their nerves under control. And you don't need to get the highest score possible; you only need to pass to be able to move on to the teacher's exams. That's the deal," Hanai said.

"But there's so much memorization," Shaylin whined. "I don't feel like I'm learning anything new—I'm just trying to freeze facts into my brain."

Willow laughed. She had to interject. "Shaylin. I've heard you teach the kids at school. You know plenty, and you've even helped the older ones work through math problems I couldn't even begin to understand. Have a little faith in yourself."

Shaylin sighed loudly. "Fine. What's next?"

Hanai picked up the textbook and looked through it. "Dynasties.

You'll list every dynasty in order of the year it was created, then the year it was demolished, and then the key events connected to each one."

Willow stood and stretched. "You two are exhausting me. Hanai, I'll go feed your hens, and then I'm going back to Luyan's house so I can be there before she returns from the shop. I'll return this evening if I can get away, or if I can't, I'll see you both tomorrow."

With Sunny padding quietly behind her, she left the house with the sounds of Shaylin rattling off dynasty names trailing in the air.

"I'm going to break up with Shu," Luyan said from her place at the end of the bed. She'd asked—or demanded, really—that Willow join her after supper so they could talk.

"Break up? I didn't know you were exclusive," Willow said.

Luyan shrugged. "He gave me a promise ring a few weeks ago, and I told him I'd wear it for a while, just to see how I felt about things. It made him happy—but it wasn't a big deal to me."

"Where is it?" Willow asked. It was quite a coincidence that she'd lost a ring and Luyan had gained one.

Luyan reached under the mattress and brought out a small box. She flipped the lid, showing Willow a simple ring adorned with one white pearl.

"And what about your rich Taiwanese boyfriend?"

"There's no comparison. My Taiwanese boyfriend is a man—and one with the means to support a woman like me. Shu is barely more than a boy."

Willow gave her a disappointed look. "That's cold, Luyan. Shu has been good to you, and you know it. You should tell him about the Taiwanese guy."

"Well, for one thing, I haven't seen or talked to *the Taiwanese guy* in months. He's probably gone home by now, which means my uncle will more than likely send the driver to pick us up soon, Willow."

Willow hid the sharp intake of breath Luyan's words caused. As much as she missed Rosi and Kai, she couldn't leave just yet. Shaylin needed her right now, and she wanted to see her through at least until the baby was born.

"Have you talked to him?" Willow played it as if it meant nothing to her.

Luyan shook her head, her concentration on her nails. "No, I just have a gut feeling that time here in this backward village is winding up."

"What about your parents? And the shop? I thought you liked working there."

Luyan stood and put her hands on her hips. "Forget about it, Willow. It's my decision and when I'm ready to go, we'll go."

Willow didn't answer. Luyan looked ready to throw one of her famous empress fits, and she didn't want to fuel that fire. But still, she acted as though it was her decision—a confusing statement because Willow thought it was her uncle's decision.

Luyan turned and stomped out of the room. Willow didn't know what was wrong with her, but she aimed to find out. She waited for Luyan to slam out of the front door of the house before she crept down the stairs and headed toward the back door.

"Willow?" Wu Min called out from the living room, just as Willow was about to slip out the back door. She paused, considering whether to stop or to keep going. Sighing, she turned.

"Yes?" She found Wu Min sitting cross-legged on the braided floor, flipping through some new photos she'd just had developed. Willow looked over her shoulder and saw one picture of Luyan behind the counter at the family herb shop, taking care of a customer.

"I just want to thank you again," Wu Min said.

"For?" Willow saw another photo, one she'd taken herself, of the family sitting around the kitchen table playing cards.

"For giving me back my family. She'd have never come home without you beside her."

Willow shrugged. She couldn't say much without getting into the reason Luyan had come home—that she'd been forced to for her indiscretions—and she didn't feel like facing the girl's wrath if that information was leaked to her parents, so she played clueless again. "I don't know what I had to do with it."

Wu Min looked up at her and smiled. "A lot. Whether you acknowledge it or not, her father and I both know it."

"I—I need to go take a walk." Willow turned and made her way back through the kitchen. She took the back door and waited until she saw Luyan head one way down the street, then she took the other. She planned to go by Shu's mother's house to see if he was at home. If he were, she'd have a talk with him.

Halfway through town, she thought she heard footsteps speeding up behind her. Turning, she saw Daming with another rough-looking fellow trying to catch up to her. She hadn't seen him since Shaylin's run for freedom, and the sight of him coming almost made her bolt.

She looked around, trying to find a place to slip into, but as close as they were, she didn't have time. So she stopped and leaned against the wall of the post office, then struggled to appear nonchalant as they bridged the distance between them.

"Willow," Daming said, out of breath as he caught up. "I want to talk to you."

"About what?" Willow said. She noticed his friend looking her up and down, giving her a creepy feeling as he stared.

"Shaylin. I know you have an idea where she is, and I just want five minutes with her. I have a solution to our problem."

Willow ignored the blatant stare of his friend and instead focused on Daming, trying to look deep enough to see the good in him that

Shaylin claimed was there. But all she saw was a desperate man. "You mean the problem *you* have—not her. We're talking about the age-old problem of discrimination against girls that you and your family support. The problem that would mean a mother has to walk away from her child. You mean that problem?"

His friend laughed, a sound as unpleasant as his features barely visible under the hat he'd pulled low over his face.

Daming's eyes glittered dangerously, reminding Willow of the first night she'd met him. She looked around and saw a few people strolling by—a grandmother with a toddler, a couple walking with their arms linked. She felt suddenly glad she wasn't alone, even if she were among strangers. But she wouldn't let Daming know she was intimidated. She stood taller. Daming finally stopped glaring at her long enough to speak.

"I'm not going to lie and say I'd be fine with a girl. I won't. That would mean our next chance to have a boy would be the last chance. We can't afford to have more than our quota. The children wouldn't have a hukou or even be able to go to school. We can't afford a girl. We need a son. Can't you see that?" Daming said, his voice now almost pleading.

Willow thought of Shaylin working hard to study for exams, all in the hope of gaining the teacher's job to help support her family. But Daming didn't deserve to even know of it.

"You might have a boy, Daming! Why couldn't you just wait and see before you tried to force her into an abortion? You're the one who made her run." Willow lowered her voice, brave but not so crazy to broadcast the word into public.

"Because she's lying, that's why. She must know what she's carrying or why not just go through with the ultrasound?"

"She doesn't know, Daming. But she was afraid the nurse would tell her it was a girl. She was afraid of what you'd make her do," Willow said.

Daming let out a frustrated sigh and used his hand to wipe his brow. He'd broken out in a sweat. "Do you know where she is or not?"

"Not," Willow said, her voice sure and adamant.

Daming groaned and ran his hands through his hair. "Damn it, Willow. I know you do. Just listen—tell her I won't make her have an abortion."

Willow tilted her head. "Well, that's so chivalrous of you."

He rolled his eyes at her sarcasm, and his friend let out another guffaw at her sassiness. Daming shot him an expression Willow could tell meant for him to shut up. He turned back to her. "Tell her I found out about this thing they have in Beijing. The locals call it a baby safety island. If we have a girl, we can take her there and she'll be safe. And we can do it anonymously with no chance of being arrested."

"How is that safe—abandoning your own child?" Willow asked.

"It's a small building with a cradle and even an incubator in case the baby's born too early. It'll keep 'em warm. It gives the parents a chance to walk away before an alarm brings someone there to pick up the child and take it to an orphanage. That would be the fairest way to do this."

Willow felt her temper rise at the mention of an orphanage. Just like Daming, most people had no idea how truly terrible an orphanage could be—they simply went with the age-old fairytale of children being tended to by sweet old women. Sure, there were a few Mama Joss' in the system, but nowhere near enough to cancel out the hardship and neglect being an orphan entailed. The description of fair never even came into play in that world.

"An orphanage? That's what you call fair for your child?" she asked, keeping her real anger hidden.

"Maybe fair isn't the right word. But she could be adopted by a family that could afford to take in a girl. It's the best option."

Willow leaned forward until she was close to Daming. His friend took a step back, leaving the two of them in a circle of intimidation.

But Willow was determined to have the last say. "No, the best option would be for your child to be raised by its mother, the woman who already has a deep attachment and love for it. Now I'm done talking to you, Daming. I haven't seen Shaylin, and I don't know where she is."

She walked away, her back stiff and unyielding, contradicting the shaking going on inside her. She wouldn't turn around to see if Daming was coming after her. She wouldn't show any fear. But once again, she said a prayer that if Shaylin was determined to save her marriage, the gods would send her a little baby boy. For a girl born to a father such as Daming wouldn't stand a chance.

Willow

WILLOW WAS GETTING IRRITATED. IT was Saturday afternoon and Luyan had gotten off early. She had asked to come with her on her walk, so that meant she couldn't sneak off to Hanai's house. She'd wanted to see how Shaylin was doing on her studies, as the date of the gaokao was getting closer, but now here she was, rambling through town with Luyan at her side, asking her a million questions.

"I saw Daming with some guy, hanging outside the herb shop. I think he thought you'd be there."

Willow shrugged. Daming was getting close to falling into the stalker category. She'd have to be careful about who was following her from now on. She sure didn't want to accidentally lead him or anyone to Shaylin.

"So where do you suppose she is?" Luyan asked. "Come on, let's get some noodles. My treat."

They turned toward the noodle shop, with Luyan now taking the lead. Willow thought about her last question. *She* was evidently Shaylin—that much was clear. Luyan had danced around the question all morning. Willow wasn't sure what had set her off, but now she was insistent Willow knew where Shaylin was.

"If I knew where Shaylin was—and I don't—I sure wouldn't tell anyone. Daming is the last person who deserves to know after what he and his mother tried to pull," Willow said, feeling a touch of guilt for blatantly lying to Luyan.

"Willow, you just don't understand small-town life. His mother is no different from any other mother here. They all think like it's still old China. Why do you think I always wanted out?"

"You seem to be okay here lately," Willow said. It was true. Since Luyan had come out of hiding in the house all the time and began interacting with the family, and even working in the store, she'd flourished. Not only did she look healthier and happier, her empress persona was coming out less and less often. It was hard to imagine, but some days, she was even a pleasure to be around. Kai would've never believed it could be true, but Luyan could act human after all.

"I'm still going back to Beijing as soon as I can," Luyan said.

"What about Shu?"

Now it was Luyan's turn to shrug indifferently. "He'll find someone else to latch on to."

Willow didn't think that was true. After Luyan had broken up with him, he'd not stopped trying until he'd gotten her back by bringing flowers and chocolate, laying it at the door with a long letter full of flattery. Their relationship amused Willow, but the drama of it obviously appealed to Luyan as she'd accepted his apology. The crazy part of all of it was that no one—not even Shu—knew what he was apologizing for. But he'd been forgiven and they'd taken back up where they'd left off. Willow had to admit, it was amusing to watch the small-town boy in his efforts to win over the worldly girl. Shu refused to be intimidated by Luyan. Instead, he seemed to revel in her condescending ways.

Luyan's grandmother had joked about the relationship, telling them it had grown like 'bamboo shoots after the rain,' which she'd finally gathered meant something like *much too quickly*. Willow had to agree, at least on Shu's part. He was falling fast for Luyan, and she feared he'd be hurt.

They approached the noodle shop. Willow saw a girl squatting beside the door, a cup on the ground in front of her as she bowed her head repeatedly in the gesture for begging.

"That's a first," Luyan said.

"What?"

"I've never seen children begging in Lingshui."

As Willow thought about it, she realized she hadn't seen any begging in the village either. The family-oriented streets of the village were such a difference than the constant flood of poor children who roamed the streets of Beijing.

They stood in front of the shop, literally inches from the begging girl, and Luyan pulled open the door and held it for Willow. As she started to go through, the little girl looked up at her, and Willow felt her heart lurch.

It was Pride.

The shock was mutual. While Willow caught her breath in her throat, Pride eyes filled with shame and she jumped up, knocking over the cup that held a few coins, before she ran around the building into the alley.

"What was that all about?" Luyan asked, and then her attention was on the door again. "Are you coming in or not?"

Willow shook her head, trying to get her tongue to move. "I know that girl from the school. She's not a beggar."

"She is today."

"I'm going to find her," Willow said, leaving Luyan holding the door behind her.

Starting out in a fast walk, she then jogged the rest of the way around the building into the alley. She stood there looking, her eyes roaming around the trash bins and empty boxes piled outside the back doors of the street shops, but Pride had disappeared.

She'd have to ask Shaylin where the girl lived. She felt a wave of guilt that she hadn't done it when Shaylin had mentioned it before, but she'd been so busy every day that it had slipped her mind. Now it was obvious that the girl was in trouble.

She turned to go back around the building to find Luyan when she thought she heard something. Pausing, she listened intently.

There it was again. Someone was crying.

She crept to the large bin where the noise seemed to be coming from. Slowly, she opened the lid and almost gagged from the smell that assaulted her senses. Looking down into the dark, she found a set of tear-filled eyes looking up at her.

"I'm sorry," Pride whispered.

A half hour later, Willow stared at Pride from across the table at Luyan's grandmother's house. After she'd gotten the little girl out of the trash bin and picked all the litter out of her hair and off her clothes, she'd talked her into joining her and Luyan for a hot lunch of savory broth noodles. But Luyan had taken one look at the little girl and practically pushed them out the door, leading them to her grandparent's home.

"Would you like something to drink?" Willow asked her. The smell of the concoction Luyan's grandmother was cooking up for them almost made her dizzy with hunger, and she couldn't even imagine what it was doing to Pride. In the small, outdoor kitchen, the sounds of chopping had faded out and were replaced with the sizzle of cold vegetables hitting hot oil.

Pride looked up and nodded. Luyan went to the small refrigerator and pulled out a carton of milk, and then made eye contact with Willow over Pride's head. Her eyes asked the question of what was going on even as her hands found a glass and poured a small amount of milk into it.

Willow shrugged.

The girl looked thinner than the last time Willow had seen her at school. And the difference in her appearance was immense. How a grandmother could let someone in her care get into that shape, Willow didn't know.

"Fiddleheads," Luyan said.

Pride looked at Willow, her eyes showing her confusion.

"What are you talking about?" Willow asked Luyan.

"My grandmother's cooking up Fiddlehead ferns. She used to make them for me all the time when I was your age, Pride. It was my favorite dish and was how she got me to start coming here to get to know her."

Pride peered hesitantly at Luyan. So far, she'd seemed intimidated by her and had stayed close to Willow. "What are they?" she asked softly.

"They're the fronds from a fern plant that's grown on the mountainside. After Nainai blanched them, she cut them into matchstick-sized pieces and now she's stir-frying them with garlic and ginger."

"And pickled hot pepper and Shaoxing wine," Nainai said as she carried in the first batch, setting it in front of the girl. Pride's eyes glittered in anticipation at the round dish of deep green, curly vegetables. She closed her eyes and inhaled the fragrant and spicy scent, then looked at Willow as if asking for permission.

"Start eating, child. You're way too thin," Nainai said, giving the girl a series of hefty pats on the back. "If you come back tomorrow, I'll make you some smoked tofu stir-fried with celery."

Pride giggled when Luyan rolled her eyes at her nainai's gesture, then she picked up her chopsticks and began eating with gusto. Willow thought it was sweet the way the woman showed her affection with the heavy pats and her willingness to cook up a quick meal. And Willow hoped she'd get to sample some of the tofu as well, as just the mention of it had her stomach growling.

Nainai went back to the kitchen to make up more of the vegetable plate for them, while she and Luyan watched Pride dig in as if the greens were her first meal in a long time. When she took a break to drink a sip of milk, Willow spoke up.

"Pride? How is your grandmother? Does she know you were hungry and looking for food?" Willow watched as Pride refused to look up. She continued eating, but a lone tear made its way down the girl's cheek and plopped right into the plate of food.

"Pride? Is there something you want to tell us?" Willow asked.

The girl slowly chewed the food in her mouth, and then swallowed hard. Willow could see she was having a difficult time making it go down. Finally, she did and then looked up, her eyes full of anguish.

"My nainai's dead."

Kai

KAI STARED STRAIGHT AHEAD AS Ning talked, droning on endlessly about her hometown and the new opportunity there. He'd never seen her so excited. Since the moment they'd left the hotel on his bike, she'd babbled in his ear about her brothers and the family venture they'd invited her to join, all the way until they'd gotten to the park and even now, as they'd stopped at a bench—she just talked on and on. His head felt like it would explode from the high pitch of her voice.

"The best part is... Kai, are you ready for this?" She paused, letting the drama build.

He shrugged. His mind was on Rosi and the news they'd gotten. Her adoption would be final in a week. Mama Su was having a banquet, and Kai wanted to be able to contribute something. He added numbers in his head, trying to figure out what he had available.

"I've told them all about you and how hard you work. They've offered to give you a job. A good paying job—much more than you make at the hotel."

That got his attention.

"How can they give me a job all the way from Maoming?" he asked.

She smiled at him as if he were a child. "You'd have to go to Maoming. With me."

Leave? Could he leave Beijing? Leave Rosi? He refused to think of Willow and what boiled down to the longest wait of his life, yearning for her to return. What good had that done him? There was not a single word from her. Not a letter. Not a phone call. She didn't care anything about him. And Rosi had Mama Su. He had no one.

He *should* leave.

The thought surprised him. Ning watched him carefully, waiting for him to say something. Anything to show an interest in what she was offering. He turned to her.

"What kind of job? And how would we get there? Maoming is a long way off—the train fare alone is more than I can swing."

A huge smile crossed Ning's face. "It's all simple, Kai. My brothers will take care of everything. They want me to come home and be married. All I need is a groom. And I choose you."

Two hours later, after the shock had worn off, Kai pushed down his suspicious thoughts and tried to focus on the parts of her offer that sounded pleasing. They'd left the park and were at Ning's favorite noodle shop, eating dinner.

"The family home will be mine, but my brothers will have to live with us for a while. It's not a big place, but we'll have our own bedroom," Ning said, lowering her eyes in what Kai thought was her attempt to be modest.

She was a little too late for that, he thought. She'd just proposed marriage to him and was now talking about their future sleeping arrangements. Modesty had been thrown out the door as far as he was concerned.

"But I don't have a hukou," he said. "How can we legally be married? How can I even work there?" Usually without a hukou, people coming in from another city or village were only allowed laborers jobs, usually at a ridiculous rate, too. Kai could stay in Beijing and find another position like that; he needn't travel all the way to Maoming.

"My eldest brother has connections. He can get your file pulled from the welfare institute and arrange for a marriage permit. It'll take him longer to be able to work up a hukou, but we can get married without that. And they won't require it for you to work for them. Believe me."

He thought about the conversation with Mama Su and her warning about Ning's family. "What exactly do they do? Or what will I do?" Kai asked.

Ning looked away, and then back to him again. "They sell things. You'd be a salesperson. Real white-collar work, no more kitchen duties."

"What kind of things? I'm not the sales type, Ning. I'd rather be behind the scenes, not up front talking to customers. Is it a store?" More doubt crept in. If he were going to be hired as a salesperson, he'd fail miserably. He'd hoped maybe they were running a restaurant and he could get back into the kitchen, even possibly running it. If he couldn't get into photography, at least he knew his way around a cookstove.

"It's a phone store."

"A phone store?" Kai repeated her.

"Yes, they sell smartphones. It only takes them about two thousand renminbi to make one, and they sell them for twice that."

"But—" Kai started to ask her how they were licensed to sell smartphones but she stood, cutting him off.

"Kai, you either want to go or you don't. I can't see what the big deal is. You're getting a house, a job, and most of all, you're getting me." She put her hands on her hips and smiled at him, her attempt to look seductive coming off as girlish and petulant.

She was right on one thing. He'd never had such an offer before. If he went, he could stop sleeping on Lao Qu's floor and he'd never have to carry a piece of luggage for another stingy businessman again.

Maybe it was time for him to move on and move up in life. Still, he hesitated. Something about the venture Ning talked about raised a red flag within him. He'd heard of the fake smartphone shops popping up all over China, catering to the people's obsession to keep up with the rest of the world. Maybe they were legit, but if they weren't, could Kai stomach doing something illegal and chance landing in prison?

He thought back over his days on the streets. Sure, he'd stolen from food vendors before, but only when his hunger demanded it. And he'd never taken to pickpocketing for extra money like other kids he'd lived with did. Overall, he and Willow had tried to live a clean life in the orphanage, insisting they were different and wouldn't be labeled as degenerates just because they had no family to save face for. But hadn't Willow given up her convictions, leaving him and Rosi behind in the chase for fame and fortune? Why should he alone remain honorable?

"If you're going, we leave in a week," Ning said.

Kai stood up and put his arm through hers. Maybe this was the chance he needed—just a hand up to change the direction of fate in his life, to find some place that would benefit him. And he had always wanted to move somewhere warmer, and from what he knew, Maoming fit that description too.

"Just think, Kai. No more frigid Beijing winters trying to keep warm," Ning said, shifting from foot to foot as she waited for him to say something.

What did he have to lose?

"Give me a few days to talk to Rosi, but I think you might just have you a groom." He spoke softly, hoping she wouldn't hear the hesitance in his voice.

She must not have because she jumped up and clapped her hands, shrieking with joy before she threw her arms around his neck and planted a big kiss on his face. Kai tried to act as enthused as she did, smiling through the heat that flooded his cheeks. He looked around. Others in the small restaurant were grinning with approval, excited to be a part of a special moment.

He just wished he felt the same.

Willow

WILLOW SAT CROSS-LEGGED AT THE head of the bed, doodling on her notebook and contemplating writing Kai another letter as she listened to the exchange between Pride and Luyan. The girl sat on the end of the bed and Luyan sat on the floor in front of her. With nimble little fingers, Pride braided Luyan's wet hair into one long, graceful braid. Nothing could've shocked Willow more than the way Luyan had taken a shine to the little girl. It had been a week since the afternoon of the announcement about her grandmother's passing, and Luyan had refused to allow anyone to call the social welfare department. Instead, Pride had come home with them and settled comfortably into their lives as if she'd always been there.

Since then, the village had come together to combine resources to properly bury the old woman, but no one knew yet what would become of Pride. Willow remembered how Shaylin had said it was rumored the girl was marked by bad luck. Now with the death of her grandmother, Pride's reputation was cemented even more in the minds of the town's people. Still yet, she had to give Wu Min and Yilin credit. Though there were a lot of hushed conversations going on, so far, they had not caved to the neighbors' recommendations to ship Pride off to an orphanage until her father returned.

If only they could find him. He should be the one to take the girl in, as well as be responsible for his own mother's burial. However, the man had yet to show his face. But he would. Of that, Willow was sure. As soon as word about his mother's death made it to wherever he was, he'd be coming around like a vulture to claim his inheritance, even if it was only a dilapidated old farm. Property was precious, especially in a place such as Lingshui where the foreigners flocked every weekend.

Something Luyan said made Pride giggle. Willow thought of the moment they'd walked into the small, brick farmhouse to confirm that yes, the grandmother had died. Pride had been too fearful to tell anyone. The stench had greeted them long before they'd actually stepped in and seen the woman lying in the bed, dead from what appeared to be just plain old age. How Pride had stayed there for the few weeks with her grandmother's body, Willow couldn't fathom.

"Can I go with you to the shop again tomorrow, Luyan?" Pride asked. Willow hoped Luyan would say yes, as she needed to get back out and check on how Shaylin was doing. Her gaokao test was only days away and if she knew Shaylin, the girl was probably a nervous wreck.

"Of course you can. You can show me again how to use that abacus," Luyan said, making Willow wonder where all the sympathy and kindness she was showing now was when they were in Beijing and Rosi was in the picture. What was it about Pride that had brought out another side of Luyan? It was puzzling.

"Can I watch Shu kiss you again?" Pride asked, her voice hushed but not enough that Willow couldn't hear.

She dropped the pencil she was twirling between her fingers and sat straight up. "What? You saw Shu and Luyan kissing?"

Luyan shushed Pride, but it was too late. Willow was still laughing when she hopped off the bed and bent down to retrieve her pencil.

Under the small, metal frame that held the thin mattress, she reached as far back as she could, trying to find the pencil using only her touch. Instead, her fingers found something else. Paper. Or several papers. She got on her knees and looked, seeing what appeared to be a magazine in a pile of dust. She pulled it out and climbed back on the bed, ignoring the chatter between Luyan and Pride.

The magazine was turned over, the back page covered with advertisements of a new line of clothing modeled by the famously popular Liu Wen. Willow studied the fine lines of the black-and-white outfit she wore, imagining herself in it, if only for a night.

Some envelopes poked out of the magazine, and Willow pulled them out. When she saw what they were, her mouth instantly went dry and she felt sick at her stomach.

Her letters.

They were the letters to Kai that Luyan had supposedly sent with the driver to drop off at the hotel. She fumbled through them, counting as she noted each one was torn open, obviously having been read, and then stuffed back into the torn envelope. Looking up at the back of Luyan's head, she felt a red fury overtake her at the lack of respect and privacy the evidence showed. After everything she'd done for her, Luyan had repaid her with this?

Her breathing grew heavier as she thought of the many nights she'd lain sleepless, wondering why Kai was ignoring her, refusing to write her back. Now she knew! She'd trusted Luyan to pass the letters along, but Kai had never received them. Not a single one!

Then she thought of something else.

If Luyan had been devious enough to keep the letters to herself, then what if the letter Willow had left Kai in the hotel room the day she'd left had somehow been confiscated by Luyan? What if he didn't even know she'd said goodbye?

She tried to remain calm. She didn't want to scare Pride. And she didn't want to scare herself if her temper got out of control. Calmly, she called out to Luyan. She carefully held the magazine and letters as if they were a snake that would strike if she shook them up.

"Luyan, I need to talk to you. Pride, please go downstairs for a few minutes."

Pride turned to look at her, her fingers still moving to put the elastic on at the end of Luyan's braid.

"You can talk to me in front of her," Luyan said.

Willow willed her to turn around, to see what she held in her hands. She waited, knowing Luyan eventually would.

Pride finished with the braid. Luyan stood, and then turned. "What do you want to—" She stopped talking when she saw what Willow held.

"Would you like to explain these?" Willow asked, shaking the stack of letters in the air with one hand and the magazine in the other.

Luyan went from looking completely taken aback to suddenly defensive. She pointed at the magazine that Willow held. "Why don't you explain something, too, Willow? So okay, I didn't hand over the letters. But it's not as if you are pure as snow. You were supposed to be my assistant, yet you were taking modeling jobs behind my back. That place on the cover should've been mine, not yours."

Willow was completely confused. "What are you talking about? Do you know how crazy you sound?"

Luyan snatched the magazine from Willow's hand and slapped it down on the bed. "This is what I'm talking about. You. Front page. You and your melancholy gazing into the night stole my limelight." Luyan's voice was icy, dripping with jealousy that Willow didn't understand until her eyes fell onto the magazine again, this time on the front cover.

The letters in her hand fluttered to the floor as Willow stared in shock at her own face splashed across the entire front of *Bliss Magazine*, one of the most famous publications in China.

"I want to know how this happened," Willow said as she paced around the kitchen. She was still dazed and confused. And angry. Both at

Luyan for the letters she'd lied about delivering and at Johnny, who was credited for the photograph of her on the magazine. "And what the hell is this? Face of the Forgotten? Now I'm supposed to represent every abandoned child in China? What kind of sick joke is this?"

She'd read the short article inside, the words describing children who, by the hands of fate, landed to live their lives in the orphanages around China. Thankfully, they hadn't used her name.

The article wove a tale of abuse and neglect, and her flight to find something better. What made it so bad was that most of it was true, but it was her truth and it wasn't anyone else's right to lay it all out there for everyone to know. That burned her up inside, made her feel a shiver of rage she was frightened might escape and prove to everyone she'd deserved that life she'd been given—that maybe she was some kind of degenerate who was rightfully robbed of the family she'd always dreamed of.

"I don't understand how this came to be. Talk to me, Luyan." She was surprised her voice came out quiet and calm when inside, her emotions rolled like the waves of an upset ocean.

"I think you know," Luyan said, her voice now haughty as she refused to make eye contact. They were alone; Wu Min had taken Pride for a walk when she saw the battle brewing in her kitchen. Her excuse was the girl didn't need to be a part of any arguing, but Willow also knew Wu Min couldn't stand controversy or the wrath of her daughter.

Willow looked at the magazine again, and her face flushed with embarrassment. "No, I don't know. I have no idea how Johnny got this photo. I can promise you this, though—I never posed for it. And you still have to answer for my letters. How could you do that, Luyan? How?"

Luyan shook her head. "Why should I be honest with you when you can't grant me the same courtesy? If you wanted to model, you could've told me. How many times did I offer to get you set up with my uncle? All it would've taken was a few words and he'd have gotten you some offers. Instead, you do this—you go sneaking around behind my back with my own photographer! And for all that, who cares about your stupid lovesick letters to Kai? Anyway, he's moved on without you."

For a moment, Willow had thought perhaps she was wrong, that maybe Luyan wasn't involved. But then she remembered back in the hotel, all the hushed phone calls to Johnny. And he was the one who had negotiated with the orphanage director about Rosi. He knew their circumstances. So did Luyan.

They'd done this together—she was sure of it. No one else had all the facts.

She looked down at the photo again. In it, she was staring out into the night. At something—but really at nothing. Where was this taken? Something niggled at her memory.

The scarf.

She was wearing that red scarf, and the last time she'd worn it was the night she'd shared her first kiss with Kai. Suddenly, she felt mortified. She remembered. Not only had Luyan read her private letters to Kai, but she and Johnny had also conspired together to steal her most private moments. The photo was taken when Willow had walked outside of one of Luyan's photo shoots and had been thinking of her birth mother, looking out over the city, wondering who and where the woman might be. Only moments later, Kai had joined her and she'd decided to share her first kiss with him. Somewhere, somehow, Johnny had been there too, watching. And Luyan had probably put him up to the invasion of her privacy.

Her privacy. The one thing she treasured. They'd stolen it.

She picked up the magazine and threw it in the trash bin, then made her way out of the kitchen and into their room.

"Where are you going?" Luyan called out from behind her, sounding nervous.

"Anywhere you aren't." Willow answered. She was done with

Luyan. Done treating her like an empress, done being her slave, and done being blackmailed. Luyan had overstepped her boundaries this time, and Willow would never forgive her.

"Willow, please. Don't go. I'm sorry. I'll make this up to you," Luyan begged, her voice pleading and desperate. "I'm sorry, but I didn't have anything to do with the photo!"

Willow ignored her and let the door slam behind her. It was over. She was going back to Beijing.

"Can you tell us what made you angrier? The letters or the photo?" Hanai asked, putting Willow on the spot.

Both Hanai and Shaylin waited patiently.

"I think I'm most hurt about Luyan. I trusted her—even though Kai always told me not to, I gave her a chance. I thought beneath all the bravado and condescending ways, she had a heart. But look what she did!"

"You feel that she betrayed you," Hanai said, nodding.

Willow felt her face flush with heat. "She knew—that's the worst part—that she knew how much Kai means to me. And she made me leave without telling him first of all, but she promised those letters would be delivered. Now he must hate me."

"Luyan's father has a phone. Why didn't you try to call the hotel? Try to get in touch with that woman you call Mama Joss?" Hanai asked softly. "Willow, I'm just trying to make you understand that you have options. Maybe Luyan shouldn't shoulder all the blame."

"She made me swear not to call the hotel!" Willow said, her indignation making her face flush hot. "She said if I contacted anyone, other than with letters, the deal was off. I was trying to protect Rosi and keep a roof over Kai's head."

"Do you think if you explain to him, he'll understand?" Shaylin said.

"I don't know. Maybe. But knowing Kai as I do, since he probably thinks I disappeared without any contact, he might just refuse to see me or hear me out. I need to get back there."

"You can call him now," Shaylin said.

Willow shook her head. "No way am I going to try to explain all this over the phone. Not now, when I've waited so long. It has to be face to face for me to have even a sliver of a chance that he'll forgive me. I just have to find a way to get back there."

"Please don't go yet, Willow," Hanai said. "You can stay here with me until you decide what to do. Don't make any rash decisions."

Willow didn't answer. She stared down at Sunny, who lay at her feet sleeping after their fast run through the woods. She couldn't imagine saying goodbye to the dog, but she knew it was inevitable.

When she'd left Luyan's house, there was no question about where to go. Hanai's home had come to feel like a refuge for her as well. It was the first place she'd thought of when she'd found herself on the street with Sunny at her side, looking up at her with that silly, tilted ear as if asking her what was wrong.

But now she was here and she felt so conflicted. She didn't know what to do. On one hand, she was done with Luyan and needed to find a way back to Beijing. Even if only to give Kai an explanation. But she loved the village and the humble life she'd carved out. Torn—that was what she was. She looked at Shaylin and her swollen belly, knowing the baby was coming any day. She didn't want to miss that either. And she wanted to be there to celebrate when Shaylin aced her tests and finally got to be a real teacher.

"Yes, Willow, please," Shaylin said, making Willow think she must have read her mind. "I need you. If you aren't here to encourage me, I know I won't pass the exams. Then I'll never be able to get a good job or support this baby."

"You don't have room here for another person," Willow said. She bit at her nails. She'd noticed Shaylin had stopped calling her baby a *he.* She wondered if that meant she was coming to terms with the fact that she might not have a boy.

"Yes, I do. I've cleaned out the extra room for Shaylin, and you can stay with her," Hanai said. "Please, I'm asking you to take your time before you make a decision. It's crowded, but we'd love to have you here with us. And maybe then, Sunny would stay at home."

"Yilin will be looking for me if I don't come back before dark," Willow said. Over the last few months, Luyan's father had started being more protective of her, almost treating her like a daughter. Willow figured he probably wouldn't accept her disappearance unless he knew she was safe. And what if he brought Luyan with him when he came looking? And Willow didn't want to be the cause of unwanted visitors trespassing on Hanai's sanctuary.

"I'll go talk to him," Hanai said, standing quickly. "Right now."

Willow looked up, surprised. Yilin always came to her about the ginseng—she didn't go into the village. "You'd do that for me? Go into town?"

She watched uncertainty flash across Hanai's face, and then determination. "If it will keep you from making any rash decisions, then yes, I will."

Willow thought of Pride. She knew the girl would be fine with Wu Min and Yilin. When Luyan wasn't busy doing it, they smothered Pride with attention. Maybe she should stay a day or two, at least let her anger simmer down enough to help her think more clearly. And anyway, she didn't even have the funds to get back to Beijing. She was going to have to ask someone for a loan. She looked at Hanai, always so kind to accept her as a friend and now into her home. She couldn't ask her. She just couldn't.

She'd wait a day or so and go to Luyan. She'd ask her for the money she so obviously owed her anyway. After all, she was the one who'd been calling Willow her assistant all this time. It was time for her to pay up so Willow could get out.

"*Hao le*, I'll stay for a day or two while I sort through some things."
Hanai and Shaylin looked relieved.

"Good," Hanai said. "I'll make a call and see if I can get them to move the test up for Shaylin. If you can, I'd like you to stay here with the dogs while we're gone. At least if someone comes on the property, they can alert you and you can let them out."

Willow nodded. She could do that. She thought of calling Mama Su to ask her about Rosi. At least now, she no longer owed Luyan to keep her promise of not telling where they were. But something else still stopped her.

Kai.

Now that she knew he hadn't received her letters, he must think her a selfish and cold person. She didn't want to try to explain anything over the phone. She also didn't want him to receive news of her from anyone else. He deserved an apology, and as soon as she could get back to Beijing, she'd give it to him and hope he'd forgive her.

Willow

WILLOW SAT AT ONE END of the couch, snuggled into a nest of pillows as she watched Hanai talk. The emotions played across the woman's face as her quiet words emerged, telling a sad tale of a family in crisis.

"It is true. I haven't seen or spoken to my own mother in many, many years."

Shaylin had taken the other side of the couch and listened while reading through her study notes. She'd admitted that she missed her own mother. Willow could only imagine the subject they'd slipped into made her even more homesick for her family, even though they'd basically turned their back on her when she'd left Daming.

"But I've met your mother, and to me, she seems like a nice old lady. A bit sassy, but that's what makes her interesting," Willow said. "And she just can't get enough of Luyan. She asks us to come over all the time, always wanting to cook and fawn over her granddaughter."

Hanai looked so sad that it made Willow sad too.

"Sure, now she's that way. But for many years, she told my sister and me that if we gave birth to girl babies, she wouldn't accept them," Hanai said. "And believe me, she meant it."

Willow remembered the conversation between Luyan and her parents about her nainai's reluctance to accept her the first few years of her life. It was hard to imagine such petty traditional beliefs causing so much family conflict.

"Is that why you don't speak to your own mother?" Willow asked, hoping she wasn't overstepping any boundaries. Hanai was being open with them, sharing more of her private life than she ever had, but Willow didn't want to push her away by prying too much.

Hanai closed her eyes for a moment, and when she opened them, Willow could see a shine to them, as if a few tears had been blinked back.

"That's a long story. But don't get me wrong, girls. Despite what is between us, I love my mother—and my father. If I didn't, I wouldn't have helped them keep their shop open for so many years until it gained traction again. But though I help them from afar, they know not to intrude on my privacy here. Yilin is the only one I meet with because he's not related by blood."

"That seems so sad," Willow said. From all she'd come to know about Hanai, she would've never guessed the woman to be one to hold a grudge. Especially against her own relatives. It was hard to fathom, and she couldn't help herself. The words came out before she could stop them. "I've always wanted a family, and yours is just minutes away, yet you might as well be a million miles from them. Don't you miss them?"

Hanai stared straight ahead, seeing something they didn't. Willow wished she could pull the words from the air and stuff them back into her mouth, unsaid.

Shaylin stopped reading. "Wait a minute, Hanai. Do your parents realize you've stepped into the role of the coveted son they never had? Assisting them in their old age? Or is that lost on them too?"

Hanai stood and stretched. "That's enough of this deep conversation. I didn't mean for it to go on so long. I'm going to go on to bed now, girls. Shaylin, you should too. Tomorrow is a big day for you, and I'm sure your baby is tired."

She left the room, leaving a heavy silence behind her as she ignored the last few questions. Shaylin's face told of her emotion. Willow tried to determine if the girl was sad for Hanai, or if the story had re-ignited thoughts of her own family troubles.

"You okay, Shay?"

Shaylin shook her head. "I'm afraid I won't pass the tests. Then what will I do, Willow? I have no way to support this child without Daming."

"Don't even think like that, Shaylin. You'll pass, I promise."

Shaylin didn't answer, but her face told Willow of her doubt. It would be hard; that much was true. Because of the new circumstances of her soon departure back to Beijing, as well as the pains Shaylin had started having that pointed to a possible early delivery, Hanai had arranged for both tests to be taken back to back. They'd stay overnight in the city and if Shaylin passed the gaokao, she'd take the teacher's exam the next day.

Shaylin set her notebook aside and held her arms up overhead, grasping one and stretching one way, then grabbing the other and stretching to the other side. "I'm so tired."

"I'm sure you are," Willow said. "Between studying and working with the roots, you've put in a lot of long hours over the last week."

They'd spent days in the work shed and in the woods, separating out the ginseng that would go to market, then pruning and replanting those that needed more time in the ground. Each root had to be carefully washed and examined, then sorted by Hanai before the next stage. They'd all worked well together, and Hanai had seemed pleased with all they'd accomplished. Even though Willow's back was a bit sore from the standing and squatting so often, she'd enjoyed getting her hands dirty and working with the plants. It was hard to believe she was as old as she was and had never felt the pleasurable sensation of the cool grains of the earth running through her fingers, pulsing with an energy that held centuries of history. It was a new experience, and one she knew she couldn't wait to have again.

"Are you sure you'll be okay here alone? All night?" Shaylin asked. She looked doubtful. "Hanai said this is her biggest crop ever, and it's valuable. That can be dangerous information in the hands of the wrong person."

"No one knows but us, so I'll be fine," she said as she looked down at Sunny. The dog lay at her feet, tired from a day of following Willow as if she were her shadow. "Don't worry. Sunny won't let anyone around me. And if they do somehow get past her, they'd have to deal with Moon."

Moon looked up, his deep black eyes droopy with fatigue. He wasn't asleep, proving he was still in charge of the night shift, but he looked as if he couldn't wait for morning to come so he could nap. Willow had developed a healthy respect for Moon, but one made up of caution, as the male dog was much more businesslike in his duties than the affectionate Sunny.

"Willow, what do you make of those cats and their little house?" Shaylin asked, abruptly changing the atmosphere of the room with one question.

Willow laughed. "I think it's smart for Hanai to keep them as little guards against the forest rodents. She's smart, isn't she?"

Shaylin nodded in agreement. "And that tiny cat house. Who do you think made it?"

"I don't know, but getting that thing out of the tree wasn't easy." Looking back now, it was comical, but earlier that day, Willow and Hanai had struggled with the project. Getting the house down from the tree and moving it to overlook a new crop location in the forest had required them both, plus a lot of tools Willow had never seen before. But now she was proud to say she could hammer a nail, among other new skills.

"You think getting the house situated was hard? You should've been the one to do the cat herding," Shaylin said.

Willow had to agree. They'd all laughed at Shaylin when she'd taken on the responsibility of getting the cats to follow her to their new home. Watching her waddle along, her belly low and heavy, as she called out the cats, had given them a hysterical moment that broke up their days' work, filling it with laughter and fun that had energized them to keep going until dark.

It had been a hard but a good day. Willow thought of Luyan and felt sorry for her. She would've liked for Luyan to be able to join them, to let loose and enjoy herself in nature for once. But she'd figured it out. Luyan had betrayed her, using her to help Johnny get higher in the world of photography, most likely so that his new success would filter down to her.

She hoped it had been worth it. For a while there, she'd started thinking of Luyan as family. In the last few weeks or so, her responsibility to the girl had felt like less of a sentence and more of a friendship, but now—they could never work together or even be together again. That relationship was over.

"Willow?" Shaylin called out, bringing her out of her thoughts.

"Yes?"

"I know you're tired, but can you help me study for at least another hour?"

Willow held out her hands. "Of course. Give me that notebook. Let's prepare for the English section, and if you can't name the last dozen American presidents, we'll study for two more hours. Maybe three. Who needs sleep? You can sleep when this is over."

Shaylin smiled and handed over the papers. "Okay, let's do this. I'm going to pass that test, and then I'll mail Daming and his family my acceptance letter. They'll see I can pull my share of responsibilities, and I can support my own child if need be."

Willow agreed. Shaylin needed this success too much to even

consider anything less than a total victory. They'd study until their eyes fell out if need be. This wasn't just an exam or two—this was something that could pave the road to her future. It was too important not to do everything they possibly could to prepare. Tomorrow, Shaylin would spend nine hours just on the gaokao exam itself. The least she could do was help her study up until the last minute.

Willow mentally prepared herself for a long night.

Kai

KAI WAITED, PREPARING HIMSELF FOR another round of Typhoon Rosi. He'd never seen her so angry before. Actually, he hadn't even thought she had it in her to ever be upset at anyone, but boy— was he wrong. When he'd told her and Mama Su that he would soon be leaving with Ning to join her family back in their hometown, and then marry her, Rosi had thrown a tantrum like he'd never seen from her before. She'd expended a lot of energy in her protests until she'd worn herself out.

Now she sat on the steps, her arms wrapped around her legs as she laid her head dejectedly on her knees, refusing to look at Kai. His eyes were drawn to the bright socks that peeked out from her jeans, cartoons of ladybugs crawling up them. He wondered who had brought them to her. Now everyone knew of her fascination with collecting brightly colored socks, so there was no telling who they'd come from.

"Rosi, I'll be back. I promise," he said, though he honestly didn't know when and if they'd be able to afford to come back any time soon.

"No, you won't. Ning won't let you come all the way back here." Her words were barely more than a muffled mumble, but Kai knew what she said. "She'll be glad to get you away from us."

"Ning is not my boss. If I want to come back, I will. Nothing has changed. We're still family, right?" He sat close to her but not too close. She'd grown up a lot in the last few months. Especially due to the fact that her job taught her she had something to offer—that she wasn't just dead weight in an institution as she'd been led to believe for so long. Kai wanted to respect her new persona, even if she was reverting back to little girl status in her anguish at his news. "What about if you come visit when winter comes back around? Wouldn't you like to get out of a cold Beijing winter for once?"

Rosi shook her head. "I'm not leaving Mama Su."

He turned to look at the door, making sure the old woman hadn't snuck out to listen. She'd shot him a look of disapproval before leaving them to be alone. She needn't say anything—just the one condemning glance from her had made him feel lower than pond scum.

"Well, maybe Mama Su would like to come too," he said.

Rosi lifted her head and looked at him, pursing her lips in a scolding expression. Tears still swam in her eyes. Seeing them made Kai cringe. He hated for Rosi to cry. It was like a dagger to his heart for her to shed even one tear.

"Mama Su and I have responsibilities, Kai. We have jobs and can't just leave when there are people depending on us. We aren't like you," she said, then lowered her voice to a whisper, "and Willow."

Kai couldn't reply. That was what it all boiled down to, he supposed. She'd been hiding her feelings about Willow for months, pretending like it was okay, that Willow would be back. But now that Kai was about to do the same thing—about to leave her—it was just too much to bear. No wonder she'd acted so dramatically at his news. Still, he had to live for himself. Rosi was fine now, and if he were being honest, all he had been doing was waiting for Willow too.

It was time for both of them to move on to a new stage of life.

Rosi needed to be cut free from him and Willow—free to completely be Mama Su's daughter. And Kai needed to shake the hold and hopes he'd held onto that required Willow to return because, obviously, she wasn't coming back. He wished he knew what to say, but he had no words to make Rosi or himself feel better. Change was always hard, but in this case, it was going to be brutal. For them both. He looked at her sitting there and realized how big a place in his heart she had claimed. He was going to miss her, at least as much as she thought she'd miss him, but probably a whole lot more.

"How about a hug, Rosi?" Kai held his arms out and Rosi hesitated, but then slid over until she was within reach. He met her halfway and enveloped her, letting her lay her head on his shoulder as she cried. "I won't forget you, I promise."

He felt horrible about everything, but he was determined. The next evening, he and Ning would be leaving on the first train out of Beijing. It was time for him to grow up. But he'd be back, and when he did return, he'd come straight to Rosi and show her he'd kept his word—that he hadn't forgotten her.

Kai felt rather than heard Lao Qu come up behind him. He'd finally extracted himself from Rosi, and now he had a lot of packing to do. He hadn't spent much money on items in the last few months, but he'd still somehow acquired more than he'd brought to the old man's house. He thought about leaving some of it behind, but he didn't know what awaited him in the next place, so he decided to take everything he owned in case it was needed.

Looking at the book laying on the floor beside his bag, he picked it up. He felt rebellious moisture threaten to appear in his eyes. Rosi had insisted he take their book, *Journey to the West*, with him to Maoming. It was their second copy as the first one had been borrowed. When Kai had made some money, he'd bought Rosi her own version. But together, they had read the story of the crazy monkey that ventured across China, and they'd bonded over that book. When Rosi had handed it to him and told him to him to keep it as a reminder of her, she couldn't have known how much it meant to him. He sighed as he tucked the book safely into his bag.

"And you're sure this is what you want to do?" Lao Qu asked from the doorway.

Kai didn't turn around. He didn't want Qu to see his emotion, and he was getting tired of confirming that yes, this was what he wanted to do. It wasn't as if he had any other options. Didn't everyone see that? Did they expect him to keep working at dead-end jobs, barely making enough to pay his rent? All he wanted now was to get packed and get some sleep. The next day would be exhausting, as he'd be responsible for helping Ning take all her things to the station to be tagged and logged into the special cargo hold. Her brothers had sent the tickets on ahead—seemingly happy all the plans were falling into place and their sister would soon be on her way home with her new fiancé.

Fiancé.

The word made Kai feel a bit queasy, but it was what it was. A part of him felt like he was an actor in a play, pretending to care for someone he didn't, but that was the way the world worked. If it were back in the old days, their marriage might have been arranged anyway. He could grow to love Ning, he told himself firmly.

"Yes, this is what I want to do." Kai continued to roll his clothes up, stuffing them in the large duffle bag he'd picked up for a few yuan.

"Lao Tzu says 'If you do not change direction, you may end up where you are heading.'" Lao Qu spoke the words softly before leaving the room.

"That's uh—sort of the plan, Lao Qu," he mumbled to the man's retreating back. It disturbed him that no one, not even the man who had no investment in his future, thought he was doing the right thing. But for so many years, others held his fate in their hands, and at least now, Kai was doing something completely of his own making.

Or was he? Ning's faceless brothers who held the keys to his future came to mind. Kai hoped Mama Su would make Rosi understand. He needed her to know he was making this sacrifice—leaving her and everything he'd ever known—to make a better life for himself.

Willow

WILLOW LOOKED AT THE CLOCK on the wall. It was well past dinnertime and her stomach growled with irritation. She paced the room, wishing she had a way to contact Hanai and Shaylin to ask how the test went. She'd kept herself busy all day, managing to finish many of the tasks Hanai had laid out for her—tasks Willow knew were concocted to keep her mind off the fact that Shaylin was sitting in a room with thousands of other desperate students taking a test that had long been compared to 'a stampede of thousands of soldiers and horses across a single log bridge'. The meaning was clear; only a select few of China's most astute students were ever successful in passing the notorious gaokao. Could Shaylin possibly be as sharp as Willow thought her? She thought of the breakfast Hanai had prepared for Shaylin for good luck. A breadstick next to two eggs—meant to be a visual prediction of the results being one hundred percent in Shaylin's favor.

Hanai had used every minute to quiz Shaylin, even going over some possible essay questions that might come up. She'd said that her prompt so many years ago was something like 'looking at the stars with your feet on the ground'. Then she'd explained to Shaylin that she was supposed to dig deep and find the meaning that would be most accepted by party officials—in her case, the star prompt was something about idealism versus practicality.

Now that Shaylin was gone, Willow could admit it all sounded much too complicated for the average brain. She feared Shaylin would fold under all the pressure.

She paused at the window, and Sunny came to stand by her side. Looking out over Hanai's gated property, she agonized over her decision. But it was made now. When they returned, once she helped to get the ginseng crop loaded to Yilin's truck, she would go to Luyan and get the funds to return to Beijing. She would ask Mama Su if she could stay there long enough to find a job. If she were lucky, she could find and share an apartment with several girls, reducing living costs to something she could possibly afford.

She hated to leave Lingshui. She'd miss Hanai and Shaylin the most, but it was time for her to find her own way. Even if she wanted to stay, there wasn't any work available in the village. And she couldn't remain in Luyan's family home, as she hoped to never see her again. And that meant she'd have to say goodbye to Wu Min and Yilin too. And Sunny.

She looked at the dog sleeping, curled up on the rug like a big puppy, and a lump came to her throat. She couldn't imagine leaving her. What would Sunny think about her sudden disappearance? She'd be devastated—all because of Luyan's selfishness.

She slapped angrily at the window. Sunny jumped up from her place on the floor, whining her displeasure at being awoken.

Willow went to the couch and patted the cushion beside her. Sunny wasn't supposed to be on the furniture, but she needed the dog close. She'd told Hanai and Shaylin she'd be fine, but now that the sun was going down, she felt alone. The house was quiet and though she usually enjoyed the peace it brought her, she suddenly wished Hanai owned a television. At least that would make the time go by faster.

She stood and went to the kitchen. Hanai had left rice in the cooker, water already measured into it and ready to go. Willow hit the button, leaning against the counter. What could she do to take her mind off Shaylin and the impending long night ahead?

She thought of music and looked about her, searching for a radio. Surely if Hanai didn't have a television, she at least owned a radio? That would be something to fill the day with noise when she felt lonely for human voices, wouldn't it?

She didn't see a radio on the small refrigerator or any of the countertops. She wondered if maybe it was in Hanai's room. She went to the closed door, but there she hesitated. Would Hanai be angry if she simply went in to find a radio? Surely not…

She put her hand on the doorknob and began to turn it.

Moon's deadly bark startled her, and she dropped her hand as if the knob was red hot. She turned and went to the front room, quickly taking in the scene of the dark dog barking and pawing at the door, insisting to be let out.

Sunny stood at the front window, looking out and adding her own growl to the chaos. Willow looked but didn't see anyone.

"Moon, hush!"

She went to the side window. Standing behind the curtain, she carefully looked out over the side yard. She squinted her eyes, thinking she might have seen something—or someone. She ducked back behind the curtain, suddenly afraid.

"Willow…" She heard, and then strained to listen closer. It was a male voice, and Yilin wasn't due for the crop until the next morning. Why would he come early?

She heard someone call out to her again and instantly recognized who it was. Shu. What was he doing coming here and how did he even know she was there? She felt a burst of irritation.

"Moon, down. Sunny, down." She was pleased when her commands immediately silenced the dogs. She'd been working with them but wasn't sure if they'd listen to her when or if they were ever in a heightened state of agitation. But thankfully, they did. She went to the door and cautiously unlocked it, then opened it just enough to poke her head through.

Shu had come around to the front gate and stood leaning over it.

"What are you doing here?" she called out. She looked around him, her eyes scanning the yard to see if he was alone. "How did you find me?"

"I need to talk to you about some stuff," Shu answered. "First, d-d-did you know Luyan left?"

An hour later, Willow unplugged the cooker and opened the latches, pausing for the steam to release slowly before taking the lid completely off. She felt guilty she'd let Shu in to Hanai's house, but it was only after she'd seen what a state of distress he was in. Now his arrival had sent her into her own new level of distress, and she'd quizzed him on how he'd known she was there and more importantly, how he'd found Hanai's house.

"Luyan," he'd said.

"So Luyan knows I've been coming here all along?" Willow wasn't surprised Luyan knew where her own aunt lived, but they'd never talked about it.

Shu nodded. "Yeah, she w-wanted to know where you kept disappearing to, so one afternoon, she and I followed you through the woods. She'd already suspected you were coming here, but she wanted to make sure you weren't doing anything you shouldn't."

"Anything I shouldn't? Like what?"

Shu shrugged. "I don't know, Willow. But we saw her aunt w-welcome you and we figured that meant you were friends. We came back around, and you all were working out in the shed together, so Luyan left it alone. She was just happy to know something you didn't think she knew."

Now that sounded more like Luyan. Willow figured the information was being held close to the girl's cold heart, just waiting on the right moment to use it. The thought of someone following her when she'd thought her excursions were private infuriated her, making her even angrier with Luyan.

"Can we get back to talking about Luyan and if you think she'll come back? I mean, who does she have in the city? Who'll protect her?" Shu said.

In the last hour, as the sun had finally disappeared and dark had surrounded them, he'd let loose a string of uncharacteristic swear words, describing the moment he'd seen Luyan leaving with her driver but being seconds too late to stop her as they'd driven away. Willow's first thoughts had been for her parents, and she knew that Luyan leaving would be harder for Wu Min than anyone. She'd worked so hard to try to win back Luyan's affections.

"I'm sure she'll be fine. She knows that town like the back of her hand."

Shu shook his head, letting out a frustrated sigh. "That's just it, Willow. She told me she hated her life there. Why would she want to go back to it?"

Willow turned and couldn't keep the sarcasm from her voice. "Shu, I don't know what kind of crazy talk she's fed you, but she absolutely adored the life of being in the limelight. She's been waiting for her uncle to forgive her so that she can go back."

Shu looked so distraught that Willow felt sorry for him. He rubbed at his eyes, looking for a moment like a little boy who'd failed to get his way. It was also a startling sight to see a man in Hanai's house, a sanctuary that so far had only housed women. She would have to get rid of Shu as soon as they ate, just in case Hanai and Shaylin came home early. But she hoped they didn't—as that would mean the gaokao hadn't gone well.

Shu held his hands up, gesturing as he started to talk. Moon jumped to attention, and Willow told him to stay. "Shu, don't make any sudden movements. The dogs are only allowing you in because

I've told them you're okay, but they're watching you carefully. Just remember, dogs are unpredictable."

Shu froze, looking at each dog before he visibly calmed down and took a deep breath. "No—that's just a story she made up. Her uncle has sent his driver here to get her several times, and she's refused to go back. She told me, and I saw it with my own eyes once. I was with her when the driver said her uncle was getting tired of waiting for her to finish her holiday away."

"Holiday? Oh Shu, she reeled you in good, didn't she?" Willow returned to the task at hand. Scooping rice into two bowls, she then lifted the small bowl of warm broth from the stovetop. She poured it over the rice, making sure some of the scallions fell on top, and then she took the bowls to the table. She'd give Shu a hot meal and send him on his way. Even though what he thought of Luyan was far from the truth, she had to admit that she appreciated his company. It was dark out there, and his unexpected arrival had scared her more than she'd admit. "Her uncle sent her away, Shu. She wasn't here on some sort of holiday or vacation."

She picked up her chopsticks and ate a bite. When she looked up, Shu had pushed his bowl away and sat with his head in his hands.

She put her chopsticks down. "Shu, if your relationship with her was meant to be, she'll come back to you. You have to accept Luyan is a different kind of girl than others. She's independent."

"I th-think that's going around," Shu said.

"What do you mean?"

Shu looked around the room as if someone stood behind him. "I'm talking about the women in this village getting more independent."

"Who are you looking for?" Willow asked, feeling nervous. She'd already told him Hanai was gone. But no one was supposed to know about Shaylin.

Shu gave her a sympathetic look. "You've never lived in a small town, have you? Word gets around, and Daming thinks Shaylin is staying here. His friend was also talking about a big crop of ginseng growing somewhere out here. I don't know who that roughneck is, but he thinks the ginseng out here should belong to the village as a whole, not just one family."

Willow felt a shiver of apprehension. Something didn't feel right—Shu was holding something back. "What are you saying, Shu? Do they know where this house is?"

Shu looked guilty. "That's what I mostly came for. Daming knows. He's planning on coming here, and he told me he's not leaving without Shaylin."

Willow's thoughts jumped around, first worry, and then huge relief Shaylin and Hanai were staying in Beijing. But how would she convince Daming that his wife wasn't staying with them? Her eyes took in the room—Shaylin's sweater draped over the chair, the blackboard filled with her handwriting, her slippers at the door. Willow stood, leaving her bowl half full on the table. She didn't plan on letting Daming into Hanai's house, but just in case, she had a lot to do.

"When? Tell me when he said he was coming here," she asked.

Shu took a deep breath. "Tonight. And he won't be alone."

Willow

WILLOW WAS SO ANGRY WITH Shu that she could strangle him. After she'd threatened to do just that, he'd finally admitted he'd also been on the path earlier in the day, but had turned back when he'd noticed Daming and his cousin following him.

"If you turned back, how does he know where we are?"

Shu looked scared out of his mind, more so from Willow stalking him around the room than from the thought of Daming.

"Be-because he cornered me and told me he thought I was coming to see Luyan out here, and th-that all the girls must be here. You, Luyan, and Shaylin. He told me to lead him the rest of the way and when I re-refused, he said he'd find it himself."

"So let him try. I won't open the door," Willow said, showing more bravado than she felt. She looked down at the dogs. "And if I do, he'll lose an appendage."

"Zi Tao, h-his cousin egged him on, telling him they could leave with more than Daming's wife and be rich by the end of the week."

"Wait, what does the cousin look like?" Willow asked.

Shu talked, and the dark and cagey person that he described told Willow she'd already met Daming's cousin, the day they'd cornered her in town. She prayed he and Daming wouldn't come snooping around.

Shu continued to tell her of how Zi Tao had spoken of riches to be found from the woods around Lingshui.

Willow narrowed her eyes as she stared at Shu. The ginseng—Daming's weird cousin was after it. Willow prayed they wouldn't come out here. A majority of the profits from Hanai's crops was already promised to line the pockets of the officials who'd allowed Shaylin to take the exams, and if she passed, to the ones who would give Shaylin the teacher's job when the old woman retired. Without the ginseng, Shaylin would forever be at the mercy of Daming and his family.

"They'll be arrested if they try to steal from here, don't they know that?" Willow said. She'd stopped pacing for a moment and Sunny paused as well, looking up and whining at her. "Hush, Sunny. I'm okay."

Shu picked at a stray thread on his sleeve. "Daming doesn't care if he gets into trouble. He's been there before. His family has the village officials in their back pockets. There might be a little show of reprimanding, but I doubt they'll arrest him for coming after his own wife. Hopefully, he's not stupid enough to bring his cousin. Zi Tao is a total degenerate—always has been."

So corruption wasn't just in the big cities. Willow wasn't surprised. She looked at the clock on the wall. "If he decides to come, what time do you think it'll be?"

Shu shrugged. "He could be out there now, for all I know."

Willow stood, looking around the room as though someone waited in the shadows. She wondered if she had time to run through the woods and get Yilin. He could come help guard the shed to keep the ginseng safe. He needn't know what this specific crop was earmarked for—as Hanai had already said there'd be enough profit to continue her allowance to her family as well as take care of Shaylin. But since the crop was important to keeping the store afloat, as well as Yilin's family, she felt he should step up and help protect it.

She didn't want to leave Hanai's house or the dogs. But if she stayed holed up, then that left the crops in the trees unprotected too. From what she'd learned over the last week, what was in the ground out there needed a few more years to mature, but would net another huge crop one day. And the only reason the plants were there and doing so well was because Hanai had nurtured each sprout with all she had. It was unfair to think that in one night, it could all disappear. And it was Willow's fault. If she hadn't come to Hanai's house in the first place, Luyan wouldn't have found it and showed it to Shu. But now it was up to her to do something—anything—to make sure Hanai didn't come back to total devastation. And with that, she needed help.

"Shu, I need you to go and get Luyan's father, Yilin. Tell him it's an emergency and he needs to come here."

Shu shook his head. "No way, Willow. I'm not leaving you out here alone."

Willow thought hard. What if they brought the wooden crates of ginseng into the house and hid them? Sunny—and definitely Moon—wouldn't let anyone through the door that didn't belong. That wouldn't keep Daming from digging in the woods, but at least some of the ginseng would be safe.

She felt a little better. At least she had somewhat of a plan. And if all went well, Daming and his creepy cousin wouldn't find the wild crops or even make it as far as the house. And if they did—Shaylin wouldn't return until sometime the next afternoon. Daming should be long gone by then.

Three hours later, Shu had fallen asleep on the couch and Willow was fighting to keep her eyes open when first Moon sat up and growled, then Sunny joined him. They sat alert, ears up like radar and hair standing tall on their necks as they listened.

Willow pulled the crocheted blanket closer and stayed curled in Hanai's chair. It was well after midnight, and she hoped with all she had that the dogs had simply heard a passing rodent. Maybe a possum, or even a raccoon—anything but what her gut told her it was.

Daming. And maybe Zi Tao.

When Moon heard something else, he bolted up and trotted to the window, suddenly wide awake and all business. Sunny left her place at Willow's feet and joined him. When Moon barked, Shu sat up, jerking his head around the room to see what was going on.

"Wh-what is it?" His jet-black hair stuck up all over his head as he tried to get his bearings.

"Moon, *anjing*, be quiet! Someone's out there," she answered, suddenly glad they'd worked to bring the heavy crates inside. Willow had pushed them under Hanai's kitchen table, using a large blanket as a tablecloth. It didn't completely camouflage the boxes, but it was the best they could do.

"H-how do you know?" Shu looked even more frightened than Willow felt.

She gestured to the dogs and gave him sarcastic look. He would've had to be blind not to see how they were suddenly on guard.

"Oh," he said, rising to his socked feet. Going to the door, he slipped his feet into his shoes. He turned back to Willow, fear showing in his bloodshot eyes. "What should we do?"

Willow's neck hurt. Every muscle in her body was so tight she felt ready to spring. How was she supposed to know what to do? Should she let Moon out? She was wracked with indecision. She didn't want anything to happen to the dogs, yet she also wanted any possible intruder to know they faced danger if they came any closer to the house.

"Just let Moon out," Shu said. "He can't get out of the fence, right?"

"Yes, he can! I don't know how she does it, but Sunny always finds a way to get out, so I'm sure Moon can too."

Moon barked again, and Sunny joined him. Both of them pawed at the door, their obvious distress making Willow even more frightened. Willow peeked around the curtain again, but she saw nothing.

"I can't see anything from these windows. I'm just going to look out the door." She went to the door and put her hand on the knob.

"I wouldn't do that if I were you," Shu said.

Willow couldn't just stay in there like a cornered rat. She had to see if they really had anything to worry about. She pointed at the dogs. "Stay." Slowly, she opened the door, just a little. Before she could react or even poke her head out, Moon bolted, shoving his big head around her legs and through the crack, then wiggling out. Willow tried to grab his collar, but she only felt his fur skim beneath her hand as he managed to free himself. Shu jumped up and ran toward the door to help her, but in the ruckus, Sunny also slipped out. Both dogs disappeared into the dark night, barking and snarling as though they were on the trail of something.

"Shu, go after them!" Willow yelled.

"I'm n-not going out there," Shu said, backing away from the door. "They'll be okay. They're dogs. They have teeth and well... teeth."

"What if something happens to them?" Willow strained to see into the dark, looking for any trace of Sunny's light coat to show her the dog was still safe.

She turned and saw Shu shrug. He was scared out of his mind, making Willow wonder just how dangerous he thought Daming was. Surely, he wouldn't go so far as to hurt the dogs, would he?

She hesitated only a second more. Sliding her feet into her shoes, she grabbed the key to the padlock from the nail on the wall, and then slipped out the door. No one was going to hurt those dogs—not on her watch.

"Wait, Willow," Shu called out, but Willow wasn't waiting for him.

She heard a yelp, and it sounded like Sunny. She had to go find her. Then more barking broke out. "Shu, stay there! You need to guard the ginseng we brought in," Willow hissed through the dark, turning back toward the gate.

She hesitated, waiting on her eyes to adjust to the dark. Hanai didn't have any lighting in the yard, but thankfully, the night wasn't completely black. Willow jumped when the long, hanging branches of the Willow tree moved, creating a shadow that danced in the moonlight. She heard the door open again and in the midst of the barking that sounded like it was getting further away, an awkward shuffle and stumble told her Shu was coming anyway. She was irritated at him for not listening, but at least he'd finally remembered he was supposed to be a man.

She started to call out to Sunny but stopped herself. If Daming was out there, she didn't want to alert him to where she was. Quickly, she moved across the yard toward the gate. She heard the dogs running through the woods, as if they chased someone, then she hurried to the gate. She fumbled to get the key into the padlock in the dim light, but she finally did. Clicking the lock, she pulled the chain off and ran through the gate.

"Willow, wait." Shu was behind her, but Willow kept going. She was going after Sunny and didn't have time to wait. He was slow, falling even further behind as she went.

She moved faster while also trying to take care where she stepped. Up ahead, she heard voices—and barking. It sounded like Moon or maybe even Sunny was getting aggressive. She took off running, using her hands to protect herself from the myriad of branches that slapped at her. She heard Shu call out to her again, his voice fainter, but ahead, she caught a glimpse of a shadow being circled by both dogs.

"Sunny! Come," she called. *Please don't hurt my dog. Please don't hurt my dog,* she chanted under her breath.

"Call them off. Call them off!" a voice shrieked through the night.

She stumbled and almost fell, but then caught herself and kept going. It was Daming; she could tell by his tall, lanky form silhouetted

in the moonlight. And he held a thick tree limb, gripping it like a bat
as he threatened the dogs with it.

"Sunny, come!"

The dog looked back and saw Willow, then turned her attention to
something behind her, her growl vicious and unrecognizable.

"That's it, Sunny, come," Willow called out, still running. She
was only twenty feet or so away. Stopping, she held her arms out,
beckoning Sunny.

Daming yelled out. Willow thought Moon must have finally
lunged, but when she looked, he was pointing behind her.

"No, Zi Tao, don't!" Daming screamed.

Willow turned just as Sunny ran right past her, in attack mode for
someone who had crept up behind her. Suddenly, the night went from
dangerous to total chaos.

"No, Sunny, it's Shu!" Willow called out, not sure it really was but
knowing he had been trailing her. She sprinted, trying to grab Sunny's
collar, but missed. Then, in just a flash of a half a second, she caught
a glimpse as a man moved out of the shadow of a tree, and she saw
Zi Tao's hands coming down with a shovel in them. She was close to
both him and Sunny, and as if in slow motion, Willow watched the arc
of the shovel, the tool looming down and about to make impact with
something or someone. She wasn't sure what or who, but in the second
before it all went black, her concern was not for herself, but rather the
dog—her first real friend in the village.

Willow

THE FIRST THING WILLOW REALIZED when her eyes fought to open was that it wasn't night any longer. The second thing she knew was she was lying on a bed, in a room she didn't recognize.

She heard voices, but they sounded far away.

Her head.

It throbbed.

She tried to open her eyes wider, but the light shining in from a window felt like a dagger through her brain. She stopped trying and instead looked through the filter of her eyelashes.

She moved her hand and felt something soft beneath it.

Warm and soft.

She heard a heavy sigh. Her senses instantly recognized the sound and feel of Sunny. With that, everything came rushing back and she remembered the woods, the dogs, Daming, and then Zi Tao with the shovel. She'd been sure he was about to kill Sunny and with the knowledge her dog was safe, a tear of relief slid from underneath her lashes and made a wet trail down the side of her face, dropping into her ear.

The sensation of it dribbling into her ear canal made Willow jerk her head, which caused another agonizing streak of pain to cross her temple. She knew then the shovel had indeed made impact—but it was on her head and not Sunny's.

"Willow, you're awake," a soft, husky voice said from beside her.

Now she knew she had a head injury because she was hallucinating voices. She could've sworn she'd heard Kai.

She turned over, ignoring the pain to put her arm around Sunny, pulling the dog to her as she buried her face in the sweet, soft fur. She'd been so scared that something would happen to Sunny that she couldn't contain her relief. She needed to get up and see about Shu, find out if they'd been robbed, but first—first, she needed comfort.

"Willow," she heard again. She sat up abruptly, turning toward the voice.

Sunny also rolled over and sat up, her attention turning to the person who sat beside them. She whined.

Even as Willow blinked rapidly to focus her eyes, her hand reached out, trembling in the hope that he was real. She felt the warmth and comforting familiarity of him surging through her as his fingers wrapped around hers.

Suddenly, her world was right and no longer tilting precariously on its axis.

"Kai, you're here."

"Yes, I'm here. So this is where you've been hiding," he said, his voice soft and teasing, so familiar to Willow, like a warm blanket falling around her.

It was almost too much to fathom, but there he sat on a chair beside the bed. He looked the same, but different. His face looked more defined, more mature. He appeared older by several years, even though it was only six months since she'd last seen him. Her eyes filled with tears again, this time from what emotion, she wasn't sure. Relief? Shame? Hope?

"But how? How are you here?"

"Luyan brought me," he said. "She arrived at Mama Su's only an hour before I was about to leave town. She told me where you were and insisted I come. She said it was the only way for her to redeem herself with you."

Willow sat up. She looked around and realized she must be in Hanai's bedroom. The voices outside the door told her that the house was full. Had Shaylin returned? Had she passed her exams? Did Daming rob them?

She shook her head. She was so confused. But one thing was clear. The sight of Kai sitting beside her filled her with such complete joy that she felt she would burst. Maybe everything else had fallen apart, but he had come.

"We have a lot to talk about, Willow—as soon as you're feeling better, I mean. Things aren't the same as they were when you left Beijing."

He looked like he was about to give her some bad news. Willow's first thought was of Rosi, but a knock on the door interrupted the question on her lips. She looked up to see Shaylin poking her head in the room.

"Willow?"

"Shaylin," Willow answered, trying to swing her legs over the side.

Kai stopped her, his hand pushing her back to keep her on the bed. "No, be still. You can't get up yet."

His touch sent bolts of sensation up her leg and all the way to her brain, emphasizing how much she'd missed him. She looked from Shaylin to Kai—wishing suddenly Shaylin would leave for a moment and that Kai would envelope her in one of his warm hugs. He was so close. It made her realize just how much she missed him and how much she'd pushed away thoughts of him for the last few months. She swallowed past a lump in her throat. When she spoke, her voice was weak, but persistent.

"Shaylin, what's going on? Please tell me. Did you pass the exams? Did Daming's cousin hit me? Is the baby okay?"

As soon as his name was spoken, Daming stepped forward, filling the door with his tall frame as he stood so close to Shaylin that they looked like one. Willow shrank back. Sunny sensed her distress and began a low growl in her throat.

"Call that dog off," Daming said, his voice low and pleading.

"It's okay, Sunny," Shaylin said soothingly.

Willow couldn't believe her eyes. "No, it's not, Shaylin. Why is he here?"

Before anyone could say another word, Hanai pushed through Shaylin and Daming and crossed the room, hurrying to the bed and sitting beside Willow. She leaned forward. The warm hug she'd been thinking of getting from Kai suddenly came from Hanai as she wrapped her arms around Willow and cradled her close.

"You scared ten years from my life," she whispered, rocking her back and forth. "You are a foolish, foolish girl. But a brave one, I'll admit."

Willow was tense only for a moment, but then she let herself go, relaxing into Hanai's arms as a feeling of comfort she'd never known filled her body and entered her soul.

"I'm not brave," she whispered back. "But I wasn't going to let anyone hurt Sunny."

Hanai continued to hold her, and Willow felt a memory come over her. She was around eight, maybe nine, when she stood at the window of the orphanage and looked down into the courtyard as a girl met her new parents for the first time. The woman, petite with long, dark, and glossy hair, bent down to the ground and opened her arms wide. The girl—someone from the room beside Willow's—was shy for a moment, but then she gave in, letting herself be embraced and rocked back and forth, just as Hanai had just done with her. Back then, witnessing such raw emotion had struck Willow all the way to her soul, reminding her she might never experience that kind of love, or that gesture of total acceptance, from within a mother's arms.

But she was feeling it now. She was feeling it and she was taking it in like it was her last breath, relishing the warmth and what actually felt like love, if only for a moment.

Finally, Hanai released her and scooted back enough to look at her. Willow saw Shaylin and Daming had retreated and shut the door behind them. Kai remained, but that was a relief. She didn't want him out of her sight—not for a while anyway.

"Hanai, what's happened? Please, tell me what's going on. Shaylin? The exams? Your ginseng? Is everything okay?"

Hanai took a deep breath. "All that can wait, Willow. Before another second goes by, I have to tell you something much more important, and I have to beg your forgiveness."

"Is this really the time?" Kai said, confusing Willow even more. Only when she'd talked about her past had Willow seen Hanai look so serious. Now she felt almost paralyzed with anticipation of what she'd say. She looked down at Sunny and thought of Moon. That dog was Hanai's shadow—her everything. Hanai felt about Moon the way Willow felt about Sunny. She looked at Kai and his face told her nothing. She turned back to Hanai.

"What? Was Moon hurt? Hanai, tell me—where's Moon?"

Hanai took a long, deep breath, but she didn't take her eyes off Willow. "Yes, Kai, this is the time. Willow, don't worry, Moon is in the other room and he's fine. What I want to tell you—is that I'm sorry. I knew I was leaving you in a dangerous position, but I had no idea just how dangerous. I can't believe I did something so stupid and almost lost you."

Willow strained to remember, but it made her head hurt worse. Her next thought was that she'd been hit harder than she thought. Not only was she hallucinating Kai showing up in the room, but she was also now hearing things she'd always wanted to hear.

Hanai waited, searching her eyes, looking for what, Willow wasn't sure, but she didn't answer. She didn't know what to say. Lying back on the pillows again, she turned and faced the wall.

She needed sleep. Sleep would make everything normal when she woke again. Thankfully, she drifted off easily.

301

Kai

H E WOULDN'T LET THEM LEAD him out of the room, so he sat watching her sleep for first one hour, then two, and now going on four. He felt as if he and the yellow dog were having a standoff— and neither of them would be the one to walk away before she awoke. As for him, he didn't care how much his body ached; he just wanted to be near her. He thought of Luyan and for the first time since the day he'd met her, he felt he owed her a huge debt of gratitude.

She'd saved him. Simple as that.

He couldn't believe what he'd almost done. Only an hour later and Luyan would've found him gone, and his life would've been changed forever—a rash decision made with no regard to the strain it would cause to the bond he and Willow had spent years building.

His conscience pricked at him, accusing him of carelessly trying to fill the emptiness Willow had left and using Ning to do it. She'd been devastated when she'd given him the ultimatum, and he'd turned to leave with Luyan. Ning wasn't a bad girl. She was innocent, as far as he knew, and Kai had never wanted to hurt her—she didn't deserve his deceit. But the truth was that he never would've been happy with Ning. Despite his oath, he knew he would not have grown to love her because his heart belonged to someone else.

The someone else who lay directly in front of him, curled up like a cat, looking cozy and warm. And inviting.

He studied the curve of her face and the way her eyelashes lay across her brown skin. Her nose, the feature she'd always complained about, teased at him and reminded him of their long talks. Her long hair begged him to put his hands into it and bundle it up in handfuls—just to be sure it still held the same softness that haunted him in his sleep. The sound of her slow breath brought him back to the night she lay entwined in his arms, a feeling foreign but somehow familiar to him.

His thoughts were interrupted when the door opened and an old woman appeared with a bowl of steaming noodles in her hand. She bustled over and handed it to him, along with a pair of chopsticks.

"You've been sitting there all day; you must be starving," she said.

"*Xie xie.*" Kai thanked her, grateful for anything to curb his hunger. He hadn't thought of it before, but now with the spicy aroma of the bowl she held reaching him, his stomach growled loudly, reminding him he hadn't eaten anything since the day before.

The old woman nodded, and then went to stand beside the bed. Willow still slept, and the doctor who had come from the village said to allow it, that her body needed to replenish itself from all the shock she'd been through.

"She's beautiful, isn't she?" The old woman gazed at Willow, and then turned to him.

He still hadn't taken a bite of the noodles. He felt uneasy whenever someone came in to look at Willow. He wanted to protect her. Something he should've been there to do before she'd gotten hurt. That was all he'd ever wanted—was to protect her. "Yes, she is. She always has been."

The woman nodded. "She is everything I would've wanted in a second granddaughter. Everything I could've had if I had just opened my heart. *Aiya*, I was stubborn back then. I wanted my daughters to have sons—something I never had. I wanted it to be an easier life for them—wanted the village elders to respect them—not feel sorry for them because the gods gave them daughters. Just like they gave me."

"Do you know how wrong that sounds?" Kai asked.

"I do. I've known it since the day Hanai came here with her little daughter many years ago, but still, I turned her away. I'd done the same with Luyan before her. I caused a division in our family that spread like ripples in a pond. But know this, young man..." She shook her finger at him. "I've had to live with the repercussions of my actions my entire life. Because of my foolishness, I've been a lonely old woman, distanced from my own daughters and never knowing my granddaughters. I've wasted so much time. And it is your Willow who brought that knowledge to me."

He felt sorry for her then. Just like so many who were born in times of chaos through China, the woman had been inoculated with old superstitions and beliefs. And really, was it completely her fault? Or more so the problem of a country that, by implementing a one-child policy, had staged war on infant girls and added fire to the nationwide obsession to have a boy to carry on the family name?

"It has to stop here," he said.

The woman nodded, lowering her voice even more. "It has stopped here. Hanai tried to keep her baby. She wanted so badly to be a mother, and if I hadn't turned her away, they would have never been separated. But I've been given another chance, and it is all turning around. Because of Willow, our Luyan has decided to come home to stay—and get to know her parents. This time, without any spite. And today, my daughter has forgiven me and invited me back into her life."

Kai remembered something else Lao Qu had whispered to him before he'd left, another mysterious utterance that hadn't made sense at the time, but now did. He'd reiterated the Chinese proverb when he'd said, 'remember, son, one happiness scatters a thousand sorrows'.

It seemed to him the old man had made a prediction that could apply to both him and the grandmother. With Willow's appearance into Luyan's life, and therefore everyone else's, it sounded like many sorrows were being buried. And for him, before she'd fallen back asleep, with only one look into her deep, dark eyes, he'd forgotten all the reasons he'd been so angry with her.

He turned to her again and saw her eyelashes flutter.

Wake up, Willow, he said silently to himself. *Wake up and talk to me.*

Willow

WILLOW COULDN'T KEEP PRETENDING SHE was asleep. She could barely keep her eyes from fluttering as she listened to Nainai talking. She finally gave up and opened them, glad to see the first face that met hers was Kai.

So she hadn't dreamed him, after all.

And she'd heard him call her beautiful.

That either meant he'd forgiven her for her running away, or maybe even Luyan had explained to him about the letters she'd failed to hand over. Whichever it was, he didn't sound mad at her, and that almost made her smile. She still couldn't believe he was really there. Or figure out how.

"What day is it?" she asked, surprised when her voice came out sounding like a toad's croak.

"You've been sleeping for two days, off and on," Kai said. He picked up a glass of water from the side table and held it for her, letting her sip it. The water was cool and delicious, probably the best she'd ever tasted in her life.

Nainai got up and went to the door. Opening it, she poked her head out, calling out to someone. Hanai came and slipped in, shutting the door behind her as the voices that had been loud out there suddenly hushed.

"Luyan is about to beat me up to get in here, but I told her she'd have to wait a few minutes. I want to talk to you again," Hanai said, coming to the bed. She sat on the edge but this time, it felt awkward.

Willow was no longer foggy or disoriented. This time, she remembered everything that had been said and for the first time, she embraced her suspicion and thought perhaps Hanai really was her mother. She knew the first thing they should talk about was why had she lived in an orphanage if that were true, but still, somehow, Willow found herself dancing around the question.

"Are Shaylin and the baby doing okay?" she asked instead. "What about the exams?"

Hanai patted her hand. "They're fine. The little one is ready to come, but I think it will stay put another few days. And we'll talk about the exams later."

That didn't sound good. It worried her, but she didn't want to discuss it in front of Luyan's grandmother. "What happened in the woods?" she asked Hanai.

"According to Daming, he was only coming to beg Shaylin for forgiveness. He brought Zi Tao because the boy knows these woods and claimed to know where my house was, but when they got close, Zi Tao took off and left him behind. When you came out and caught Daming on the path, Zi Tao had gone to my shed to look for the ginseng. When he didn't find it, he grabbed a shovel and doubled back, planning to find the crops and dig them up."

Willow reached up and felt the top of her head, remembering. "He hit me." She looked at Kai and saw anger flash in his eyes, catching the tic in his cheek he always got when he was furious.

Nainai tsked, shaking her head. "He's from a bad family, that one."

Hanai nodded. "Daming tried to stop him, but yes, he hit you. Moon cornered him. Shu stepped up and tackled him to the ground."

"Shu?" Willow couldn't imagine meek Shu being the aggressor.

"Yes, Shu. But he had to let him go because Daming needed his

307

help dealing with you. Zi Tao kicked Moon away, then took off and ran back to the house while Shu and Daming tended to your head. By the time they got you back here, Zi Tao had come and gone, and he took the ginseng with him."

Willow gasped. "But I hid it—how—oh, Hanai, I'm so sorry."

Hanai shook her head. "No, Willow. Don't even say that. I'm just relieved you're okay. The ginseng can eventually be replaced. You can't."

"Just point me toward this Zi Tao's house, and I'll make sure you get your ginseng back," Kai said, and Willow knew he meant it too. She also noticed he looked a lot taller and stronger than before, more than able to back up his threats.

Hanai released a long sigh before she spoke again. "Let's just get past one dilemma at a time, can we? I appreciate your intentions, Kai, but this village runs much like the orphanage Willow told me about. Justice is filtered through who you know, and unfortunately, I may have a hard time convincing the authorities the ginseng was mine, even if they do find it in his possession. I might get some of it back, but only after a long line of officials takes their cut."

"What about Shu? Was he hurt?" Willow suddenly remembered her friend and hoped he'd made it out unscathed.

"Only his pride," Hanai said. "While he wasn't able to prevent the assault against you, he thinks he got a few good licks in on Zi Tao. Then it was he who bravely streaked through the dark woods to get Yilin. His cry for help got everyone stirred up. When I arrived yesterday, my mother, sister, and everyone were all here, waiting for the doctor to declare you'd live. The histrionics going on would've given a Chinese opera a bit of competition."

Willow gave a small laugh. It did all sound a bit overdramatic, even if she had been sleeping for two days straight. Underneath the humor, though, she wondered how Hanai had taken it that her entire family had come to the home that before had been off-limits.

Nainai chuckled too. "*Aiya*, we were nothing compared to Luyan when she got here and came stomping in looking for you." She looked at Kai. "And with that handsome boy right behind her. When she saw you lying in that bed, I had to drag her out of here before her wailing scared you out of your unconscious state and gave you a heart attack."

"Wait—Luyan was crying? About me?" Willow couldn't believe Luyan would feel anything for anyone other than herself.

Hanai nodded. "Yes, she was. And Kai, I don't think we'll need you to go after Zi Tao for when Luyan finds him, he'll probably need a set of dentures to replace the teeth she's pledged to knock out."

That made a real smile cross Willow's face. Zi Tao had better watch his back if he knew what was good for him.

"That boy is clear out of this province by now," Nainai said. "If he got all the ginseng you said he did, he'll never come round these parts again. He'll be living it up in a big city somewhere, blending in with the crowds."

Hanai and Nainai continued talking, filling in the missing pieces as she and Kai listened intently. But even though some things finally started to make sense, Willow was still confused. Hanai must have seen her eyes cloud over with doubt because she stopped talking, then stood and went to the small table beside the bed.

"What are you doing?" Willow asked.

Hanai pulled a box from the drawer. "I'm returning something to you." She handed Willow the box before sitting back down on the bed.

"Open it," Nainai urged.

Willow opened the lid and felt her eyes widen with shock when she saw a ring—her ring—nestled in a small pad of velvet. "My ring. You found it."

"I did. And I wanted to return it to you right away, but first, I wanted to get to know you. I thought once you found it, you might not come back."

Willow plucked the ring out and slid it back on her finger, where it felt so natural. This was the moment. It was time to just come out and ask her. There had been so many signs. But the ring—she felt sure it was proof. She looked up at Hanai. "You recognize this ring. *Dui*?"

Hanai shook her head slowly. "Should I? I mean, I knew it was yours but other than that, I've never seen it before."

Willow's eyes filled with tears. In her heart, she had to admit she'd started to believe fate had led the way to her birth mother. She wanted to believe it was true—oh, how she wanted to, but the truth was, it just wasn't so. Now she realized many of the details she'd thought pointed that way were probably formed simply by coincidence, and mingled with a lot of wishful thinking.

"I thought maybe you were my birth mother," she finally whispered. "That I'd been led here by fate."

Hanai smiled gently. "With all the time we've spent together lately, I was afraid that was what you had on your mind. Oh, how I wish it were true. But I do feel you were led to me because we share something in common. You lost your birth mother, and I lost a child. You aren't her, but you're right about one thing—fate did lead you here, and if you'll let me—let us—" She gestured around the room. "We'll be your family."

Willow took her time to answer. She searched Hanai's eyes and found yearning. The woman was special, that much was obvious, and if Willow could've built her mother from her own list of wanted qualities, the woman who gave her birth would be just like Hanai.

Nainai grumbled under her breath, pointing a finger at Willow. "You know, I saw all this in your tea leaves. It sure took you long enough to figure out the strongest families aren't built on blood. They're relationships, nurtured and strengthened by the gifts of love and acceptance. When you can get the right combination of all that, that's when you see what family is all about."

"So what do you think, Willow?" Hanai asked again, her voice soft. "We want you to belong to us. Officially. Now it's up to you."

Willow looked at those surrounding her, noting the care and

concern etched on each face. She wanted to be on her feet and feeling strong when she gave her answer, but in her heart, she already knew what it was, and it wasn't fair to make them wait any longer. She knew her next words would be the conclusion of the drawn-out drama her life had become in the need to find out who she was and where she came from. It had taken her this long, but she now realized that she'd let the mystery of her birth define her very being.

Sunny's tail wagged, thumping against the bed in a happy rhythm, breaking the solemn moment as they waited for her reply. This was it. Could she let the unknown go and accept the gift right in front of her?

She took a deep breath and held her hands out. Hanai took one, and Kai the other. And it felt so right.

"I accept your offer, and I want you all to be my family," Willow said, smiling at each of them before continuing. "It's taken me some wrong turns and longer than I would've wished, but now I finally know this is right where I belong."

Epilogue

Leaning back, Willow felt so full and at peace that she contemplated a long, relaxing nap. Kai sat in the chair next to her, but he still ate heartily from a plate heaped high, from his third—and Willow hoped final—trip to the long table laden with so many different foods. In the two weeks since he'd come to Lingshui, she would swear he'd eaten like a bear, yet he still didn't show an extra ounce on his muscular frame.

"And you never kissed him?" Kai asked, his voice barely above a whisper and his question so random yet clear who and what he was talking about.

"No, I never kissed him. But I figured out how he knows about my birthmark," Willow said. She and Kai had talked nonstop over the last week about everything that had happened. After it was all said and done, she understood that he was still unable to let go of the fact that Johnny had implied he'd had the opportunity to see Willow unclothed.

"So tell me."

She took a deep breath and told Kai all about her one and only modeling session, set up by Luyan and embarrassingly orchestrated in one of Beijing's malls. She remembered that day as she tried not to see the people peering at her through the small cutouts of the box, that someone with familiar eyes had watched her for an unusually long time. Even though she wore a bikini top and bottoms, his intent gaze had made her feel completely bare. Now she knew it had to have been Johnny.

"So that's how he knew," she finished, her voice low and sad. To think that with only a few well-placed words, Johnny had made Kai think she had been intimate with him. A person only had one reputation, and it could be ruined by interacting with just one unsavory character. She vowed to be careful with it from that moment on.

"You want cake?" he asked her, mumbling with his mouth full. His redirection of the conversation told her he believed her, and he could now stop obsessing over it.

If he could move on, she could too. She changed her tone. "No, I don't want anything else, except maybe a walk. You up for a hike? I can show you what a woodpecker looks like. Do you know why they tap on trees?" She picked a piece of pork off Kai's plate and dropped it under the table, right into the waiting mouth of Sunny.

Kai turned to look at her, the corner of his mouth lifted in amusement. Willow felt something brush her leg and looked under the table to find the chickens Hanai called her triplets. Flora, Dora, and Nora. They strutted around underfoot, pecking the ground for any wayward crumbs. The sight of them made her laugh.

They had all gathered in Hanai's courtyard for a day of celebrations. The entire family was there, even Luyan's grandfather. It was still hard for her to get used to the fact that they were now her family, too. Hanai had again assured Willow she was willing and ready to formally adopt her. Just knowing someone wanted her was already soothing the longing in her soul.

She and Kai had talked about it later, and he'd made a good point. To embrace Hanai, Luyan, and the rest of them was a big deal in the plans for their future together, so Kai had to accept them too.

He had because they'd sworn something else to each other too.

They'd never again be apart.

313

Hanai had invited them to stay on to help with the next crop of ginseng, and they'd agreed. In the meantime, as an additional peace offering, Luyan promised to connect Kai with some important Beijing investors. He had high hopes that one of them would want to invest in his future photography company, but it would be a hard year of laying groundwork. Hanai's offer of a place to stay and a job amounted to giving them time—time to take it all in and plan their future together instead of lunging into one as they'd done before when they'd left the orphanage with no place to go.

After all, when Willow searched her own mind, she realized it would be hard to leave Lingshui. In the short time she'd been there, the small village and its people had burrowed itself in her heart.

She looked at the far end of the table and smiled at Shaylin, a picture of motherhood as she sat with her rosy-cheeked baby in her arms. As if there hadn't been enough miracles to go around, Daming sat looking over Shaylin's shoulder at his daughter, a proud smile across his lips as he talked softly to her. He reached down and played with the tiny tiger slippers encasing her feet.

It made sense to Willow after Wu Min explained that her sister—Hanai—couldn't bear to have the items too close to her and had asked Wu Min to keep them safe. The secret of the baby girl Hanai had given away was one her entire family had worked to keep. But now that it was out in the open, they were all hopeful that Hanai had finally come to terms with it and could stop hiding.

Speaking of Hanai, Willow noticed she also watched Daming and Shaylin. She was probably just as amazed as Willow that Shaylin had been able to salvage and pull her little family together after all. It made her think of Rosi and Mama Joss, and the surprise visit she and Kai were planning for the next week. She couldn't wait to tell them she was an engaged woman. Rosi probably wouldn't be surprised. She'd predicted long ago that Kai belonged to Willow and vice versa. Willow just wished she had listened, as it would've saved everyone a lot of heartache.

The baby let out a sound that sounded like a kitten. Daming and Shaylin looked around, seeing if anyone else heard it. Daming swore she was trying to say baba, though she was only a week old.

"They're enthralled with her," Willow said. "Both of them."

Kai looked up at them for a moment, and then went back to eating. "And well they should be. She's quite the little beauty."

"They chose the perfect name, too." Willow still couldn't believe Daming had ended up doing everything he promised to do in order for Shaylin to give him another shot. With all he'd done lately, he was showing them he wasn't such a bad guy after all.

He'd turned the table on his family and told them they had to accept his daughter or he'd disown them. And he'd even chosen the child's name himself—right away instead of waiting until the one-hundred-day event and allowing the grandparents to choose it. He'd named his daughter Huan Yue—a name meaning delighted and joyful—to prove to the entire village he was happy to bring a girl into the world.

Willow thought he still had a lot of making up to do to Shaylin for all he'd put her through, but now that he'd broken free from his family's demands, he was making a good start of it. He'd also pledged to make Zi Tao pay for his actions, just as soon as he could find him.

Across from her, Luyan picked at her food. She'd been quiet all morning, making Willow nervous with her uncharacteristic behavior.

"Do you want me to bring you some dessert? Or some tea?" Shu asked Luyan, as usual acting the part of devoted boyfriend. He was so thrilled that Luyan hadn't meant to leave for good that he'd stayed as close to her as possible for the last week. Willow didn't think Luyan would ever shake him now, so as farfetched as it seemed, she still hoped the two of them could make it work.

"No, I don't want anything," Luyan said. She looked up. Willow could see her scan the yard, looking for Pride. When her eyes found the girl playing with Sunny and Moon, she sighed and went back to picking at her plate.

"Is there something wrong, Luyan?" Willow finally asked. She thought they'd worked everything out. Once the dust had settled, Luyan—with Kai's help—had explained to her how the photo of her had been taken and published in the magazine. Luyan hadn't been involved. But still, she was guilty of keeping the letters meant for Kai and guilty of having him removed from the hotel. She'd cried when she told Willow she hadn't wanted to lose her, that Willow was the first person who'd ever understood her. She admitted she'd acted out of jealousy over Willow's relationship with Kai, but now she understood there could be room in Willow's life for more than just one person.

The biggest shocker was that Luyan's uncle hadn't sent her away because she had a Taiwanese boyfriend. Despite all her boasting, there never were any boyfriends. Luyan had taken all her money, as well as some of her uncle's, in order to pay all the expenses related to Rosi. Beneath her cold empress exterior, there was a compassionate heart after all. But her uncle considered it a crime—and when he found out what she'd done, Luyan was told she could either go home to the village or have theft charges filed against her.

Willow had cried when she'd found out all that Luyan had done for her, and for Rosi. Now, after all they'd been through together, they felt like sisters—bound by acts of compassion and loyalty. But that didn't mean Luyan could get away with acting like an empress forever.

She nudged her under the table with her foot.

Luyan shrugged. "I don't know. It just burns me that Zi Tao got away with the ginseng and now we all have to suffer for it. If I had it to give you, Shaylin, I'd make sure you had the funds you need. You earned that certificate, and you deserve that job."

Nainai held her hand up to stop Luyan from saying more. "What's done is done, girl. We'll all pull together to make everything work, and we'll be okay as a family. Shaylin and Daming will just have to make new plans for their future. We've already decided that, along with Willow, Pride will be a part of this family. All isn't lost, child. We still have each other, and that's more than we had at this time last year."

Willow looked at Shaylin, catching her eye, speaking to each other without words. The saddest part of all that had happened was that Shaylin had passed the exams. She'd actually done so well she had to do some of it over again to prove she wasn't cheating, which was why she and Hanai had arrived home later than expected. But now there was no money to pay all the *negotiated fees* that Hanai had worked so hard to coordinate. The officials had given her an extra month to figure it out and if nothing were resolved, another teacher who was already approved would take Laoshi Lufei's teaching position at the beginning of the next school term. Shaylin would not be able to teach.

"No, it's not done. I've been thinking," Luyan said, looking across the table where Wu Min and Yilin sat drinking tea. "Over the years, I've sent a lot of money home to you two. If you'd saved even a portion of it, we'd have more than enough to keep us all afloat and pay for Shaylin's certificate to be approved."

"Luyan, it's fine," Shaylin said, her cheeks turning red.

"We can make do," Daming mumbled, but Willow knew at the rate they were going, they'd never be out of his mother's house. She wished there were some other way for Shaylin to get the job, just so they could finally get ahead.

Yilin sighed, and Willow wished she could dissolve right there and not have to witness his embarrassment again. She'd heard the same veiled accusations from Luyan countless times before, but she'd thought those days were over. Obviously, Luyan couldn't get past it.

Wu Min started to speak, but Yilin held his hand up, stopping her.

"It's time to settle this once and for all," he said. He waited. When Wu Min finally nodded, he stood. "Hanai, is it all where I left it?"

"It's there," Hanai said. "Be careful."

Yilin left the table and walked around to the back of the house.

"What's he doing?" Luyan asked.

Nainai grunted sarcastically. "Who knows, but I've told Wu Min for years she needed to bring you home—that we didn't need anything from that man you call your *uncle*. He was bad news when he was married to Hanai, and he's bad news now. He caused the division in our family, and just like I said, because of him, you came to love that sordid life and you turned your back on everything you should've stood for. You turned your back on us. I'll admit I'm no angel in all that has happened, but you should've stayed at home, girl."

"I didn't do anything sordid, Nainai," Luyan said.

Willow suddenly felt sorry for her. But Luyan wasn't going to take Nainai's criticism lightly. She leaned forward in her seat and pointed at her grandmother.

"And for the record, someone should've asked me to stay on those visits, instead of sending me away each time—selling me into servitude for a sum. Did you know I hated staying with Uncle so much that he gave me a room at his hotel? I lived among strangers—surrounded but alone."

No one said anything. The atmosphere that only minutes before was jovial and carefree had now turned dark. Luyan waited for a response and when she didn't get one, she continued.

"I always wanted to come home and the few times I did, I was treated so differently. It felt like I didn't fit in, so I pretended I didn't want to." Luyan paused again. She looked around the table, giving everyone in her family a stern look. "I took care of all of you. My money—my hard work—it supported you all. Especially you, Mama. And what do you have to show for it? Nothing. And now I have nothing too."

Wu Min went to Luyan and put her arms around her. "That's not true, Luyan. We never wanted you to go, but we thought it was what you wanted. Your uncle assured us you were happy, and you never gave us reason to think it wasn't true."

Luyan looked up, her face wet with tears but now angry. "It wasn't true, Mama. You know it. What about the money?"

Willow could see all her hard work going down the drain. All the nights of getting them together to play games, the mornings of encouraging Luyan to go to work in the family shop. All of it, ruined. Just when she thought everything could end with a happily ever after, Luyan just couldn't let it happen.

Silence fell around the table, and no one looked up. They sat that way for another few minutes until a clattering caught their attention.

They turned to see Yilin coming from around the house, pushing Hanai's wheelbarrow. In it were several rows of glass jars, jumbling together to make a cacophony of noise.

"What does he have?" Willow whispered to Kai.

He shrugged.

Yilin brought the wheelbarrow to the edge of the table and began unloading the jars, sitting each on the table in front of Luyan. Willow's eyes opened wider when she realized the jars were filled with colorful bills of renminbi.

Money! It was jars of money.

"What is this?" Luyan asked, her voice barely heard over the sounds of jars hitting the wooden table.

"It's your money," Yilin said softly. "We put up every yuan you ever sent us and hid it here at Hanai's house where we knew it would be safe."

"Little did we know that one day, she'd have a thief at her door, so we were lucky he didn't figure out the fake wall panel in the work shed," Wu Min said.

"My money?" Luyan's voice gave away her disbelief.

Yilin pushed one of the jars closer to Luyan. "Yes, it's yours. We only wanted what was best for you, and we never sold you away to your uncle. He promised us you'd live a life we could only dream of for you. But just in case he was wrong, we wanted to make sure you came away with something. It's not as much as you think, but it's all here."

319

Willow saw Luyan's eyes fill with tears. She reached over and handed her the napkin she still held on her lap. Luyan's face showed it all. She was realizing in that moment just how much her parents loved her—for herself, and not for any amount of money.

Looking at the ring on her own finger, Willow wondered if somewhere, somehow, there were parents out there who'd also made some sort of sacrifice for her. But she knew that now, even if she did continue to keep her eyes and ears open for any clues, the mystery of who they were would no longer define her. With her new revelation, she felt lighter. She wanted Luyan to have her burdens removed too. Willow waited, and when Luyan didn't move, she kicked her under the table. "Luyan, your father's giving it back to you. Say something."

Luyan looked up at Yilin. "And what do you want for it in return?"

Wu Min got up and walked around the table to stand beside Yilin. He knelt beside Luyan's chair and took her hand. "Daughter, all we ever wanted was you. But if you'd like to exchange these jars for your forgiveness for any transgression you feel we committed against you, then that would be all we could ever have hoped to gain from saving this for you for all these years."

Luyan slowly rose out of her chair and pulled her parents into an embrace. She didn't have to say a word. With that one affectionate gesture so unusual to see coming from Luyan, Willow knew forgiveness had been granted.

When she finally pulled away, they all watched as she lifted two of the jars and took them to where Shaylin sat before setting them gently down in front of her.

"Shaylin, I want you to have this," she said, gesturing at the two jars in front of the girl, and then at the others further down the table. "All of it. Use what you need to get that teacher's job and put the rest up to help send your beautiful daughter to school one day."

"I can't do that, Willow. It's yours." Shaylin looked from Luyan up to Daming, and then back to Luyan.

"No, it's not mine anymore. I said if I had it to give to you, I would, and I'm standing by that. This village needs someone like you to lead their children. You care about each and every child that walks these streets, and I know that you—along with some other good examples in the community—" Luyan paused, looking at her parents for a moment before turning back to Shaylin, "—will teach them to be selfless. And that's the kind of teacher that Lingshui needs."

Shaylin reached up and brushed a tear off before it had the chance to fall on her baby's face. "I don't know what to say."

Daming put his hand on her shoulder. Leaning down to her, he whispered, "Say thank you."

Shaylin stood and handed the baby to Daming, then threw her arms around Luyan, embracing her tightly.

Willow chuckled at Luyan's suddenly stiff body language, but it made her happy to know Luyan was trying harder at accepting the affection—and at being more human.

Kai actually did let out a laugh, and Willow turned to him. "Come on, let's go take that walk. You've got a lot of catching up to do in the nature department, city boy."

"Nature department?" he said, raising his eyebrows at her.

"*Dui*. I'm going to show you what a Shantung Maple tree looks like and teach you a bit about the language of trees."

He stood and reached for her, pulling her out of her chair. With his arm wound tightly around her, and the always-loyal Sunny following behind them, he led her away from the table and all the eyes upon them. "That's fine with me, Willow. I'll speak any language you want me to, as long as you never leave me again."

Willow smiled. Kai needn't worry about that ever happening again. From now on, she was going to hold on tightly to those she loved. Her *family*—a word that used to bring her such sadness, but that now filled her with a tremendous amount of love.

Want the inside scoop on new releases, story
conceptions, and giveaways?

Join the
Kay Bratt Newsletter here at my **mailing list**.

Glossary

Aiya (pronounced I-yah)	Expresses surprise or other sudden emotion
Bai jiu (Bye jee-oh)	Chinese liquor
Bang wo (Bong whoa)	Help me
Baozi (Boww-zuh)	Steamed buns, usually with filling
Bu ku le (Boo koo luh)	Don't cry
Bushi (Boo-sher)	No/not
Chi le ma? (Chrr luh ma?)	Have you eaten?
Chengguan (Chung-gwon)	Local Chinese urban-management officers
Da bizi (Da bee-zuh)	Big nose
Deng yi xia (Dung ee sha)	Wait a minute
Dui (Dway)	Correct
Dui bu qi (Dway boo chee)	An apology
Gei wo qian (gay whoa chee an)	Give me money
Guo lai (Gwoh lie)	Come here

Hao le (How luh)	Okay
Hukou (Who-ko)	Chinese identification
Hutong (Who-tong)	Lane or residential area (neighborhood)
Jiǎozǐ (Joww-zuh)	Dumplings
Jie jie (Jay jay)	Big sister
Laoban (Loww-bon)	Boss
Laoren (Loww-run)	Form of title used for senior citizen
Ni hao (Knee how)	Hello
Ni shuo shenme (knee shun muh)	What did you say?
Nuer (New-are)	Daughter
Peng you (pung yoh)	Friend
Pingguo zi (Ping-gwoh zzz)	Apple seed
Shenme (Shun muh)	What
Shi de (Sher-duh)	Yes
Ta bing le (Ta bing luh)	He/she is sick
Ting le (Ting luh)	Stop
Tudou (Two dough)	otatoes
Waiguorens (Why gwoh runs)	Foreigners
Wo gei ta qian (Whoa gay ta chee an)	I gave her/him money
Xiao (Sh-oww)	Title for a young girl or woman
Xiao liwu (Sh-oww lee woo)	*Small gift*
Xie xie (shay-shay)	Thank you
Youtiao (Yo-tee-oww)	Deep fried dough sticks

Zaijian (Zie-jee-ann)	Goodbye
Zao, peng you (Zow pung yoh)	Morning, friend
Zǎo shàng hǎo (Zow shong how)	Good morning
Zaofan (Zow-fon)	Breakfast
Zuo xia (Zwoh sha)	Sit down
Zhi dao (Jer dow)	Know

From the Author

It is my hope that in *Where I Belong*, readers will join me in realizing what my connections to the adoption community have taught me—that families are built in a variety of ways, and it only takes love and acceptance to begin a foundation that can result in a lifelong bond between individuals, whether they share the same blood or not. And for those adoptees who are still searching for answers, I wish them a measure of peace and a reminder that the struggle is part of your story, though it does not have to be the ending. Every person is in charge of their own happily ever after.

Many people believe that modern day China no longer follows old superstitions and bigotry when it comes to having daughters. I wish that could be true, but unfortunately, the elders still have a lot of influence on the younger generations when it comes to coveting the birth of a boy to continue their legacies. While writing this book, the one-child policy changed drastically, and now all couples are allowed two children. Many believe this new relaxation in the policy will mean less infant girls being relinquished. However, the change will still not solve the issue of children with life-threatening illnesses or disabilities who are relinquished.

Around the world, China is judged because of the numbers of children in orphanages, but I'd like for everyone to show mercy and acknowledge that sometimes—*many times*—giving up a child is the only gift a birthparent can give, in the hopes their son or daughter will receive the help and care they cannot afford to offer, and that they will survive and go on to live a full life. There is love and sacrifice even in the hardest choices.

Please consider supporting one of the many non-profit organizations that rescue, support, and help to heal orphans in China.

Thank you to G.M. Barlean and Victorine Lieske for your help in polishing Willow's story in this book. You both write amazing stories of your own; therefore, you make great critique partners. Cynthia Shepp, thank you again for leading me down the grammatically correct, error-free path to publication.

To my readers, thank you for continuing to inspire me to write about the people of China. I also want to thank you for posting such favorable reviews for my work on Amazon and GoodReads. With your help, we are getting diverse books in front of more readers. I do hope if you enjoyed this book, the second in the *Life of Willow,* you will post an honest review or recommend it to a friend or family member.

About the Author

Kay Bratt is a child advocate and author, residing on the banks of Lake Hartwell in South Carolina with her husband, daughter, dog, and cat. Kay lived in China for over four years and because of her experiences working with orphans, she strives to be the voice for children who cannot speak for themselves. Over the years, she has volunteered for numerous non-profit organizations, including Court Appointed Special Advocates (CASA), An Orphans Wish (AOW), and Pearl River Outreach. If you would like to read more about what started her career as an author, and also meet the children she knew and loved in China, read her poignant memoir titled *Silent Tears; A Journey of Hope in a Chinese Orphanage.*